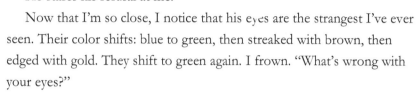

ജ ര

"Drifter." His voice is deep and ri~ known."

I won't rise to that bait. Everyone ~   ~y kind. I demand, "What are you doing here?"

He stares his refusal at me.

Now that I'm so close, I notice that his eyes are the strangest I've ever seen. Their color shifts: blue to green, then streaked with brown, then edged with gold. They shift to green again. I frown. "What's wrong with your eyes?"

His jaw clenches, and his eyes turn blue, as an Earthmaker's should be. He stills as though he's under control now, but the pulse beating hard under my knife and the tension of his lean, muscled body tells me his control is thin.

He says steadily, "What do you want with Martel?"

I press the blade harder and feel a wash of satisfaction when he winces. "I'm asking the questions."

THE GRIEVER'S MARK

KATHERINE BUEL

THE GRIEVER'S MARK SERIES

The Griever's Mark
Chains of Water and Stone
Unbound

The Griever's Mark

Copyright © Katherine Buel, 2014, 2020

All rights reserved. No part of this publication may be reproduced, distributed, or transmitted in any form or by any means, including photocopying, recording, or other electronic or mechanical methods, without the prior written permission of the publisher, except in the case of brief quotations for review purposes.

This is a work of fiction. Any resemblance to actual persons, places, or events is purely coincidental.

Cover Illustration and Design Copyright © Apple Qingyang Zhang, 2014

ISBN-10: 8558493474
ISBN-13: 979-8558493474

BOOKS BY KATHERINE BUEL

The Griever's Mark series
The Griever's Mark
Chains of Water and Stone
Unbound

Standalone novels
Heart of Snow

CHAPTER 1

My eyes slip to the Shackle, and I shudder. It rests like a coiled snake on the stone table, its links of pale bone like a kinked spine. The two cuffs touch each other, which I find somehow grotesque. I rub my wrist. Only once did I wear the Shackle, when I was seven, on the first day I entered the Drift. I am told it was originally a teaching tool; now it is used only for Leashing.

I hold my breath while Belos paces the study. His footsteps stir dust, which whirls yellow-gray behind him. The rug under his feet was probably once red, but the dust of the Dry Land and this crumbling fortress has dulled it to a sickly orange. Belos stops at the crudely cut window, where the harsh light makes his black vest gleam white and flashes on the silver studs along his shoulders. It makes him look like he's bristling.

"Come here."

His voice is deep and commanding. I obey it now, as I always do.

I stand right behind him because I don't want to be told, "Closer." Belos's blond hair bleaches in the light. Over his spiked shoulder I see the spires of broken stone on the horizon, reaching out from the wasted earth like fingers. I have never seen them closer—Belos doesn't allow it—so I don't know if it's true that they are the remains of an ancient city.

"You understand why I hesitate to give you such an important assignment?"

I nod before I realize he can't see me, that he is refusing to look at me. "Yes."

"And you will redeem yourself with your success, correct?"

I'm not fooled. The question is a threat. I speak the words of commitment, as I have so many times: "To serve is to live."

I am relieved that my voice is strong, that it doesn't creak from lack of use. I've been in the dungeon for two weeks.

Belos turns to me. Technically, he is handsome. But to me, with his eyes like blue lights in a face too deeply tanned by the harsh sun, he looks severe. His cheeks are hollowed out, the bones too prominent. I wonder: is it the power he's taken from others that has worn him down to such sharp edges? Or has anger carved him into these lines? Sometimes, it's hard for me to understand why people call him the Seducer. Who would want what he offers? Some of the other names people give him ring truer to me. The Deceiver. The Liar.

Ironically, he throws this last name at me, though I suppose it's true.

"You are a liar, Astarti, and you have been all seventeen years of your life. How can I bind you to me"—I hear the word *Leash*—"more than I already have? Did I not raise you? Give you power, a place? You would be dead if not for me, washed away by the ocean before you had learned to crawl."

He is using my mother's abandonment as a weapon against me, but I am untouched by it. It hasn't hurt me for years.

When I don't react, he digs harder.

"Do you forget that you bear the Griever's Mark? That you have only me?"

The back of my neck prickles at the mention of my tattoo, as though the tattoo itself, roughly shaped like a Y with an extra fork up the middle, crawls on my skin. The Mark tells me two things: that I have Runish blood, for only Runians bear the blue tattoos, and that my mother tried to kill me. It's called the Griever's Mark because they bleed it into the flesh of those about to die: the old, the sick. And unwanted children.

I resist the urge to rub at the tattoo. It won't come off. I've tried. The old crisscross of scars is evidence enough of that.

Belos is waiting for some answer from me, but I won't speak about my mother, or my tattoo. I keep it simple. "You are right, as always. I serve your will."

The last words snap with anger, and I curse myself for carelessness as Belos eyes me over his shoulder. I try to look meek and contrite.

"You could serve my will. Directly."

Another threat, and a reminder. I may be Leashed, but my mind is my own—for now. Through my Leash, Belos can take even that, and he did once. My first great transgression, my first great punishment. He made me a body only, a tool, not a person at all. At the memory, something dims inside me.

Belos leans against the windowsill, his leather pants scraping noisily on rough stone. "What is it you want, Astarti? I can still hardly believe the report. You stood against one of my Seven, which is to stand against me, and let that Earthmaker Warden escape."

He's asking me for justification, but I won't walk into that trap again. I tried to explain myself two weeks ago, and the tug of healing flesh from the lash marks across my back reminds me of my foolishness. Only to myself can I say it: the Earthmaker was a child, younger than I am. I could not let Straton kill her. I just could not.

A rap at the door puts a scowl on Belos's face, so I assume there was more he wanted to say, but he barks, "Enter."

Straton sweeps into the study, closely followed by Theron. Both wear the silver shoulder guards of the Seven, though there is little need for protection here. Who would come to this dead place? The dark blond of Straton's hair shows how much time he spends inside the fortress, and the shocking white of his tunic seems impossible in all this dust. Theron wears green, as usual, and I am struck by a pang of longing for the Green Lands. I wonder how he bears the reminder of all he gave up to follow Belos.

I try not to shrink at their approach, but I am conscious of my greasy dark hair in its ratty braid, of the sharp stink of clothes I have been wearing for two weeks. Dust, pasted to my skin with sweat, cakes my neck and chafes the corners of my eyes. I close filthy fingernails within my fists. Theron glances at me, and I think I see a flash of sympathy, but then his face is stone again. He might be my friend on occasion, but not right now.

"Well?" Belos demands.

Straton's eyes slide to me. "Is it wise for me to speak in front of her?"

"Do the wise ask questions to which the answer is obvious? I know she's here."

An ugly flush bleeds through Straton's pale skin. He hates when Belos mocks him.

Straton says stiffly, "Martel is in Tornelaine. For the past three nights, he's been seen at a brothel called the Trader's Choice. He's asked each night for a whore by the name of Imelda. Where his men are, we have not yet been able to determine."

A cold smile tugs at the corner of Belos's mouth. "Perfect."

"My Lord, shall we approach him?"

I wonder if Belos hears the way Straton sneers when he says, "My Lord," but nothing in Belos's casual demeanor suggests it. Belos pushes away from the window. He ambles past the stone table holding the Shackle, runs his finger along a stone bookcase by the wall, stirring dust. The battered volumes hint at their former colors, but this land is determined to bury us all under its yellow-gray skin. He brushes dust from a map of the Green Lands, scrubbing methodically at Kelda and the king's city of Tornelaine. He leaves the northern and eastern countries hidden in dust; they don't concern him. The Floating Lands of the Earthmakers, who were once Belos's people, are marked only by a burn hole in the Southern Ocean.

When Belos turns and stares at me, I cringe inwardly at the satisfied look in his eye.

"Astarti will approach Martel. She will have to clean up considerably, but I know she can look…attractive if she puts in a bit of effort."

My heart sinks. I will approach Martel at the brothel. I will pose as a woman for hire, a whore. Belos smiles at the understanding in my eyes.

"But you don't expect me to—"

"I expect you to do whatever is necessary. And to do it with gratitude, considering where I could have left you."

I swallow my anger and bow my head. I will myself to think only of my return to the Green Lands. "I will prepare."

When Belos says nothing to stop me, I stride for the door, my shoulders forced back. I will not give him the satisfaction of my dread. Theron shifts out of my way, but I have to brush past Straton, who refuses to move for me. I catch the cloying scent of clove oil when I edge around him. It should be a relief from the flat smell of dust and my own stink, but it makes my stomach turn.

The hallway is dim, lit only by what light cuts through the high window slits. Dust hangs in the wedges of light, and it feels like I'm breaking through physical barriers. The heavy tread of my boots is muffled by dense stone; this place refuses to give me even so small a thing as my own sound.

I follow one hallway to another until I reach the winding stair that rises to my chamber. The stairs are crumbling, like so much of the fortress, and when my foot slips, I break another fragment from a step. Belos shaped the fortress sixty years ago, when he lost his war with the Earthmakers and had to flee to this desolate place. No one here would dare say it, but Belos is weak in earthmagic, and that is why the fortress crumbles. I have often suspected that his weakness in earthmagic is why he turned to the power of the Drift. No one can accuse him of being weak in that.

I shoulder open the heavy door, its wood salvaged from human lands because no tree can grow here. It always sticks because the fortress shifts, and I have not opened it for two weeks.

My chamber is plain and bare, like the rest of the fortress. I open the door of the dresser, which screeches on dry hinges, and dig through my clothes. I choose a pair of brown leather breeches and a loose shirt of undyed linen. I throw them on the bed, causing fine dust to whip into the air before settling over them again.

At the rickety bedside table, I pour tepid, stale water from a tin pitcher into a chipped earthenware bowl. I'm tempted to go to the pump room for fresh water, but I don't want to see anyone and don't want to delay. I just want to get out of here.

I strip off my soiled shirt, wincing as it catches on the scabbed stripes across my back. I dip a coarse washrag into the grayish water and begin to scrub.

છ ભ

Twenty minutes later I'm standing in the courtyard, blinking in the blinding light, gasping in a heat that makes the fortress seem cool. The courtyard is bare and dusty, like the roughhewn fortress behind it. The only feature of the broad space is a dead and twisted tree. Belos brought the tree from human lands decades ago. It didn't last long in the harsh climate of the Dry Land. Belos left it there, Theron once confided in me, to remind himself not to cling to things long gone.

The fortress sits on a high mound of jagged rock. The dull plain below is as empty as the sky. The only water here lies deep beneath the surface, pumped into the fortress by a feat of earthmagic that makes Straton far too proud of himself. That water is certainly too deeply buried to nourish anything green, and the wind has long since blown the surface of this place flat. The fingers of stone puncturing the horizon in the distance offer the only relief to the flatness.

I have to descend the fortress mound to pass the barrier. Belos's twisting of the Drift makes it impossible to travel straight to the fortress. To my mind, there is little need for this precaution. Only Drifters can enter the energy world of the Drift, and there are few of us left. Besides, who would challenge Belos?

I am told there were once many Drifters, but no longer. Too many have been killed or driven into hiding because "normal" humans distrust us, and the Earthmakers hate us. Sorcerers, some call us. I wonder, briefly, if that is why my mother left me to die. Did she know what I would be? Did I horrify her?

I trudge to the long slope, which winds around the base of the mound. The hidden stair is faster, but I'm not supposed to know of the stair. One thing Belos has taught me is that you collect information where you can and you don't let anyone know that you know it.

When I reach the flat plain, my knees ache from the descent. Sweat is trickling into the scabbed cuts on my back, and I shift my pack to lessen the sting. I breathe deeply, as Belos taught me to do. I draw my thoughts into myself and ease along my mooring, the glowing thread of energy that connects my physical body to the energy world of the Drift. Though every living thing has a mooring, and every living thing is part of the Drift, only Drifters can travel along their mooring to actually enter the Drift, or to draw power from it.

As I squeeze through my mooring, pressed and swallowed briefly by its darkness, I am collecting myself, pulling myself fully into the Drift. Sudden weightlessness marks my entry. Around me the Dry Land resolves itself into its dull energies. Everything is dim, like dusk. The fortress is a dark hump, but faint threads of light twist and tangle around it. Belos's barrier. The threads seem alive, like the other energies of the Drift. They strain and wind, a confusion of light. But barriers are one of those things that Belos refuses to explain.

Beyond the twisting of the barrier, I see the points of light that identify the Seven. I myself am also a lighted echo of my physical body, silvery-white edged with gold, with hints of blue and pink. Here, at least, I am beautiful. Belos, though I can't see him clearly, is still in his study. I know that because my Leash, which glows whitish-blue, flows straight from my heart to him. Beautiful except for that.

I feel for any disturbance that would mark the approach of the Hounding. No one knows what the Hounding is really, but it has always been the greatest danger of the Drift. It comes usually as a fierce wind, angry and deadly. Once, though Belos tells me I imagined it, I felt a hand reach from the wind and touch my back.

The faint blur of light that marks the Green Lands is far away. I don't know how far. I don't know where, exactly, the Dry Land is in relation to other places. I would estimate south and east of the Green Lands, but I can't be more specific. Belos will certainly not tell me, if he even knows. It's been many years since I have bothered asking such questions.

I focus all my energy on the distant glow until a faint, wavering thread develops, connecting me. I have heard it explained many ways, but the simplest explanation is often truest: all living things are connected by currents—or threads—of energy. That is why some describe the Drift as a web. The threads shift and thin, depending on distance, depending on how strongly one person is focused on another. Most people are unaware of these threads because only in the Drift can you see them. Only in the Drift can you use them.

I blend myself with the faint thread and drift along it. It strengthens as the glow in the distance builds to a flood of light, as the flood separates into thousands—millions?— of individual lights. As always, I am overwhelmed by my immersion into the roiling energy of the Green Lands, and I have to pause for a moment to orient myself within the chaos of shifting points and lines.

I am uncertain of my exact location until I see a familiar pulsing energy. Now I know I've reached Tornelaine because I'm sensing the presence of King Heborian and his fellow Drifters. Drifters are brighter, stronger, easily identifiable from within the Drift.

King Heborian has ruled Kelda for twenty years, but it's not only because he is a foreign conqueror—a Runian, from the far north—that so many Keldans resent him. Many will never accept a Drifter on the throne.

As for Martel, he is the hidden remainder of the royal line that Heborian destroyed. It's no surprise that Martel wants Tornelaine back, but he lacks the resources to take it.

That's why Belos has sent me to strike a deal.

Chapter 2

Stepping from the Drift into the physical world is bound to draw unwanted attention, so I make my shift outside of Tornelaine. I'm told that this southern part of Kelda is fairly arid, but coming from the Dry Land, I feel a rush of moisture to my parched skin. I'm in a vineyard a little northeast of the city. It's already spring here in the south, and the dark vines are covered in tender, folded leaves. Rocky hills block most of my view of the southern ocean, but I spot a wedge of blue in a notch between hills. Within that notch lies Tornelaine. From here, it looks like a splotch of rusty orange from all the tile roofs.

I brace one hand on a sturdy old vine, breathing deeply until I stop shaking from the energy lost by traveling so far through the Drift.

It's a long walk to Tornelaine from here, but that's what I want. Despite my weariness, it feels good to move after two weeks in a cramped cell. An image of the pitted stone walls and the overhead iron grate flashes in my mind, but I force it away.

11

At least Belos let me out. He's right, I suppose, that I should be grateful. There were dark moments when I thought he would just leave me there.

I wander between rows of vines, breathing the scents of green things and soil. In the distance, a man moves along another row, tying the new vines to the training wires. As usual when I have first come from the Dry Land, I am dazzled, shocked by so much life.

The walk to the city takes me through hilly farms. I startle a flock of sheep grazing a steep hillside. The freshly shorn ewes call, "Baa," in their deep voices as the lambs dart about with frantic, "Maa's!" The lambs are cute, but the mothers have coarse, heavy heads.

It's nearly an hour before I reach the high stone wall surrounding Tornelaine. I avoid the main gate with its twin guard towers and make instead for the smaller gate that leads to the port and the brothels.

It's midafternoon, and the guard on the high platform is obviously bored, his glazed eyes roaming with disinterest over carts and people. To my right, the buildings mount higher and higher up the hills toward the king's castle, where pale towers and battlements pierce the blue sky. To my left lies the port. Small fishing vessels skim between the slow-moving trade ships. On the deck of a broad, heavy ship loaded with timber, burly men from the bordering country of Valdar shout to one another, their harsh consonants connected by rolling vowels. The ships from Ibris, loaded with huge earthenware jars that probably contain spices and oils and with wooden chests no doubt full of silks, are quieter. The Ibrisians are a dark, suspicious people who tend to quietly watch the western countries with disdain.

Straight ahead lies the stone-paved port road, which is lined with brothels and inns. I am elbowed by Valdarans in their leather jerkins and skirted by Ibrisians in silk shirts heavily stained by salt-water. A cart mounded with silvery fish trundles noisily along the road beside me, bringing me a strong wave of the sea's salty tang. I step out of the way of a wet-shirted fisherman with a soggy pipe clenched between his teeth. He grumbles in a heavy, south-Keldan accent about "idlers." After the isolation of the Dry Land, all this commotion puts my teeth on edge, and I'm starting to get jumpy.

I scan the wooden signs that hang from the eaves of squat buildings, looking for the Trader's Choice. Finally, I ask a sun-weathered, squinting fisherman for directions.

The man adjusts his salt-stained cap as he stares me up and down. He smirks. In his mind, I am either trying to track down an errant husband or am looking for work. Apparently, he finds either possibility worthy of his contempt. I breathe calmness into my belly. He is not worth the fight.

"Take the last right before the end of the port road, second...establishment...on the left."

I nod my thanks, unwilling to give him any more than that. When I've taken three steps, he chuckles.

Heat flares in my chest. My fingers edge to the knife strapped to my forearm. I will just scare him.

No.

Just a little. Because he deserves it. Because he will scorn the next woman also.

No.

I walk on.

The Trader's Choice looks like all the stone buildings surrounding it, but when I push through the heavy wooden door, I cough from the thick, oily smell of burning incense. Linen, painted to look like silk, hangs in swags over the windows, making the place dim. I blink until my eyes adjust.

Serving girls in colorful, low-cut dresses, their waists jingling with fake gold chains, move among the tables where a scattering of men watch them over the rims of beer mugs.

"Madame!" calls one of the girls. "A new one!"

With a start, I realize she's referring to me. My eyes narrow at the insult until I remember this is why I'm here: to be one of them, at least for tonight. Besides, I should not look down on her, as the fisherman looked down on me. Desperation drives women here.

I try to look appropriately desperate as "Madame," a heavyset woman in coarse silks with her hair piled in a messy bun, swaggers from the back. The girl who called out jerks her chin in my direction, and Madame narrows her eyes at me.

"Yes?" she demands in a harsh Valdaran accent that is at odds with her Keldan title and the bright red Ibrisian lipstick. "What do you want, little bird?"

I try to look flustered. "I, I'm—"

Her lips purse. "I see."

She motions me forward, and I step further into the room, my cheeks flaming as she walks a circle around me, as the men at the tables look on. She tells me to drop my pack. When it hits the floor with a thud, she tsks disapprovingly at my rear. She pinches my arm, which makes me jerk, and shakes her head when she squeezes one of my breasts. I am breathing furiously through my nose by the time she stands before me, arms crossed.

"Too wiry," she pronounces. "Men do not like this. Breasts too small. How will you impress them, with a footrace?"

One of the men chuckles.

I color and have to stop myself from clenching my fists. I am a desperate young woman. This is my last resort. I say, putting a quiver into my voice, "Please, Madame."

Madame sighs, and a thoughtful look comes into her eyes as she gazes at me, a finger now on her lips. "Some will like these pale blue eyes. Hair is good. So dark is unusual. From Rune? Doesn't matter." She waves it away as I open my mouth on a made-up story. "Skin very nice, if dry. Face pretty. Any experience?" I color further, and she says, "You will learn. Imelda! Take—name?"

"Amara," I lie.

"Take Amara upstairs and get her changed."

A slight young woman with rich brown hair and slanted eyes glides toward us from one of the tables. Ibrisian, very pretty. The one Martel has been seeing.

Imelda gives me a small smile of sympathy, a rare thing from an Ibrisian, and says, "Come."

I grab my pack and am about to sling it over my shoulder. Instead I hold it to my chest, like I am frightened. I hate that deception comes so easily to me, even though it's useful. I follow Imelda past the bar, where stout mugs hang in neat rows on the wall and jugs of wine stand on a shelf above kegs of beer. We enter a wide stairway lit by a gaudy, gold-painted sconce.

The stair leads to a hallway lined with doors. Most are closed, but a few stand open to reveal beds draped in fake Ibrisian silks and walls painted to look like tiled frescoes. The scenes they depict make me blush. I spot a simpler room marked only by a thick sheepskin rug and an iron brazier glowing with coals. A blonde Valdaran woman in a short leather skirt and a leather top that reveals more than it conceals scowls at me and shuts the door.

Imelda leads me into a room at the end of the hall. Silk hangs around the bed and over the window, some of it real. A small fireplace graces one wall, and an intricate rug in a dizzying Ibrisian pattern stretches before it.

Imelda notices me looking. "It takes many years to earn a room like this one, but if you are good with the clients and do what Madame Adessa says, you can hope to have such as this one day."

I smile weakly. I am sad to think of these women aspiring to no more than a nice room in a brothel, as though this is the best life can offer them. But I remind myself that these women are, in truth, freer than I am. They may have chosen this life out of desperation, but they still *chose* it. No one forces them to stay. No one has Leashed them.

"It will be an adjustment, I know," says Imelda, and I am startled by her gentle tone. I can see why a man would like her, especially compared to someone coarse like me. She's soft and makes you feel like she really *sees* you. Suddenly, I am uncomfortable.

She moves silkily to the door. "Wait here."

I am standing in the same place when she returns a moment later, a green dress in her arms. She lays it on the bed, smoothing its coarse linen against the dark red coverlet. It looks far too small. She lays a corset beside it and steps back.

"Madame does not ask new girls to attend gentlemen"—I almost snort at the word—"on their first night. Unless, of course, there is an insistent request from a well-paying customer. But this is rare. You will serve tables tonight. If you hope not to be requested, be quiet and avoid notice." She pauses. "This is not so bad, you know. This is how women gain power over men, the only way for us to do so. You will win back something of what you've lost, even if you don't see it at first. You will have a new kind of pride." She smiles, adds teasingly, "Even a king may be brought low by a whore. Now. Do you need help with the dress?"

"No," I say, a little too quickly. I don't want her to see the lash marks on my back. Or my tattoo.

Imelda seems to think nothing of my sharpness. Perhaps she thinks I am nervous. Well, I am.

"Unbraid your hair. Men prefer it loose." When I finger my braid unhappily, she gives me an encouraging look. "Everything will be all right, Amara."

But she's wrong. Tonight I will persuade Martel to Leash himself to Belos, as I myself am Leashed. Or I will fail and face Belos's wrath. Nothing is "all right" at all.

80 Q3

I wait tables for the rest of the afternoon, carrying trays laden with beer to men who watch me openly because that is why they are here. And why I am. The corset digs into my ribcage and chafes my sore back. The dress hangs too low in front and Madame slaps my hand away when I try to hitch it higher. After the second time, she snaps, "You can't afford to hide any of that."

I scowl at her back as she walks away.

Ten minutes later, when a man pinches my rear, she bustles over furiously, one of the burly men who helps her ensure order hard on her heels.

She demands, "Does this look like a common pub? You pay for that here."

I unclench my fist. Look, don't touch, I guess. Unless you pay. At least she has rules. And the manpower to enforce them.

By early evening, the kitchen is torturing me with the rich scents of baking bread, roasted lamb, potatoes, and caramelized onions. The windows darken, and the fake silks begin to look less garish. I am having trouble remembering all the food and drink orders and have just taken a cup of wine to the wrong table again when Martel walks in.

I know it's him by the scar across his left eye where a sword cut him from forehead to jaw. With that conspicuous face, it's little wonder he's staying so far from the king's castle. No one at this poor end of the city would have seen Count Martel up close twenty years ago when he was cousin to King Barreston, before Heborian killed him. Besides, he wasn't scarred then.

The years have been hard on Martel. He has the look of a big man who has spent too many years hungry, his body worn down to thin, tight muscle. His clothes mark him a merchant, and I wonder what act he is putting on here, and what he's doing in the city in the first place.

The man at the table before me snaps his fingers. "You there, girl. I don't drink Keldan piss. Bring me a beer."

I mutter an apology and hurry to the bar. While I'm filling a mug, I watch Martel. He sits comfortably at a table with a few other men, talking about nothing: when the spring wind will come, what the winter was like.

Then I see him.

A Warden.

He must have slipped in while I was watching Martel.

He looks fairly young, though he's older than I am. It's hard to guess the age of Earthmakers because they live long and age slowly.

Like so many Earthmakers, he is handsome. No. More than that. He's gorgeous, the kind of gorgeous you can see from across the room. His jaw is strong and clean. His dark blond hair, thick and wavy, is raked back haphazardly from his face, as though he has a habit of running his hands through it. Most of his body is hidden by the table where he sits, but he is obviously tall and fit, broad-shouldered. Where his dark blue linen shirt hangs open at the neck I see hard lines of muscle. His elbows lean on the table. The fingers of one hand drum into the palm of the other, as though he is trying to contain his energy. He has such an air of impatience that I half expect him to get up and pace the room.

"Hop to, girl!" chides Madame Adessa, and I hurriedly fill the mug in my hand, grimacing at the extra foam that results from my haste. No doubt there will be more comments.

℘ ℆

Martel sits with his companions for most of the evening, and nothing looks conspiratorial. I'm not surprised. He would hardly be discussing his plans to overthrow King Heborian in such a public place. Imelda serves his table, but his eyes never show her favor. Perhaps she is just a whore to him. The thought makes my stomach clench around the greasy meal I ate earlier. The new girl only gets the oily scrapings from the bottom of the pan, and it's not agreeing with a stomach grown used to the dry bread of imprisonment. Perhaps I should have remained hungry.

I feel eyes on me, and I look up to see the Warden staring. A chill flashes over my skin. Earthmagic might not be as quick as drifting, but it's more powerful, in its way. A Warden strong in the element of earth could rip the ground out from under my feet. If he handles fire, he could burn this place around me. Wardens are also trained hard in the sword. But what worries me is their determination; they will do anything to capture or kill a servant of Belos.

I look away, hoping I have only caught his attention because of my low-cut dress.

I wait impatiently for Imelda to go upstairs. When she does, I will follow. I'll restrain her—hopefully I won't have to hurt her—and meet Martel in her stead. It will happen any moment.

The Warden gets up, a hand resting on the pommel of his sword. His eyes find mine, and I look away. He wends his way over to Madame Adessa, where she is scolding one of the girls. Madame sends the girl away quickly and fawns over the Warden. Her smile is flirtatious, her body language too familiar. The Warden takes a small step back, which pleases me for some reason. He says something to her, and she frowns. Then I see the glint of silver as their hands meet briefly. He returns to his table, and Madame bustles over to me, still slipping the coins into a hidden pouch at her waist.

"Well, little bird, you've had a request."

My throat constricts.

"Now, if you're a good girl and make the gentleman happy, I'll give you three coppers on top of your wage."

It's a fraction of the money he gave her. I want to say something snide, but of course I can't. Desperate Amara wouldn't dream of it.

"But, Madame—"

"Upstairs with you. Unless you prefer to leave?" She nudges me toward the stairs. "Fourth door on the right. There's a good girl."

If I run, or refuse, Madame will throw me out and I'll lose my chance at Martel. There is only one thing to do. I must kill this Warden quickly and get to Imelda's room.

Chapter 3

As I pace the room, averting my eyes from the lurid painting over the bed, I decide to get information from the Warden before I kill him. Belos will want to know why he's following Martel. Information is everything. It changes plans, changes people. Because the Warden is bigger and stronger than I am, I'll have to surprise him. I breathe deep and squeeze through my mooring into the Drift.

As the world resolves itself into its bare energies, with the dark spans of dead wood and heavy stone marking the buildings and the faint but rhythmic draw of the tide marking the ocean beyond, the Warden enters the room. The energy of normal, non-Drifter humans is a steady pulse and flow contained within a sharply defined form. It varies, of course, as emotions or injuries alter the flow, but it's generally predictable. Earthmakers look similar to humans but are typically dimmer, more subdued.

The Warden's energy rages.

It floods through his body in streams of gold and silver, flashes of green and blue, beating against the barriers of his form. It doesn't look like anger, exactly; it just looks wild. I've never seen anything like it.

He scans the room, the energy of his face shaping his suspicion. As I thought, he is not just looking for a whore with dark hair. I gave something away. I'm not sure how, but I did.

I gather energy from within myself, teasing it into a bright thread, easing it along my mooring. I'll have to be quick.

When the Warden moves to the window, I race along my mooring and burst into the physical world. My sudden appearance creates a whoosh of air. I loop the threads of energy around the Warden and bind him tight. He gives a startled yelp as his arms slap to his sides and a grunt of pain as I slam him face-first into the wall. He starts to yell, but I clamp a hand over his mouth. With my free hand, I grab the knife strapped to my thigh. The linen dress makes a ripping sound as I tear the knife free. I hate dresses because of this. How are you expected to move?

I press the knife point to his throat. "Make a sound and I'll kill you."

I am leaning against his back, pinning him to the wall, though he's much taller than I am. Even through the tight binding, I feel him shivering with rage, struggling against my control. His back is ridged with tense muscle. At odds with his anger, a clean scent, like ocean breeze, wafts from his clothes and skin.

I unclamp my hand from his mouth and tug at the binding to turn him. I keep my knife at his throat, but the position keeps me pressed against him, and I am uncomfortable with the intimacy. Generally, I fight with the spear, keeping my distance from larger opponents. Knives, I prefer to throw; at close range, they are too personal. I set my jaw, closing my mind to the fact that my thigh is pressed against his, that I can feel the heat of his body through the worn leather of his pants, that my knife arm rests against the dense muscles of his chest.

"Drifter." His voice is deep and rich beneath the scorn. "I should have known."

I won't rise to that bait. Everyone knows Earthmakers hate my kind. I demand, "What are you doing here?"

He stares his refusal at me.

Now that I'm so close, I notice that his eyes are the strangest I've ever seen. Their color shifts: blue to green, then streaked with brown, then edged with gold. They shift to green again. I frown. "What's wrong with your eyes?"

His jaw clenches, and his eyes turn blue, as an Earthmaker's should be. He stills as though he's under control now, but the pulse beating hard under my knife and the tension of his lean, muscled body tells me his control is thin.

He says steadily, "What do you want with Martel?"

I press the blade harder into the tender skin of his throat until a thin line of blood appears. "I'm asking the questions. What do *you* want with Martel? What does a Warden care about a washed up old noble who's been in hiding near twenty years?"

The twitch of his dark gold brows tells me I just answered one of his questions. "So you are after him."

I grit my teeth. Maybe Straton is right: I am stupid.

"I knew you weren't one of Madame Adessa's girls."

That piques my curiosity. "How? What gave me away?"

His expression lightens, and I think I see humor in his eyes, which are holding a steady blue. "Your movements are careful, deliberate, like those of an assassin. Oh, you're good with your act, don't get me wrong, and I can appreciate a low-cut dress like the next man, but I know a fighter when I see one." He pauses, enjoying my blush, no doubt. His voice drops. "And you, apparently, know a Warden. No one else has recognized me. So my question is this: what kind of young woman, and one who knows her way around weapons"—the line of blood has slipped down his throat and under the collar of his dark shirt—"knows a Warden the moment she sees one?"

"Wouldn't you like to know?" I tease, though my heart skips. He's smart. He's putting it together.

His voice drops to a growl, like it's crouching in his throat. "You serve the Unnamed, don't you?"

That's what the Earthmakers call Belos, as though when he turned against them, they took his name away. Fools. Do they really think such a small thing could diminish the likes of Belos?

I remind him of my knife and demand again, "What do you want with Martel?"

His mouth twists. "How can you serve him? What makes you people sell yourselves?"

His question reaches into my gut and twists. I want to snap, "I didn't!" but it doesn't matter what this Warden thinks of me. I press the blade harder and feel a wash of satisfaction as he winces.

With pain tightening the skin around his eyes, he presses into my blade, making me cut him deeper. "I'm not going to tell you anything, so you might as well get on with it and kill me."

This makes me shift. I've never actually killed anyone in cold blood. "Just like that? Aren't you going to rumble the earth beneath my feet? Or blow me over with a gust of wind?"

His eyes darken, like a sky ready to storm. A muscle bulges in his jaw. So hot-tempered. Most Earthmakers are annoyingly calm and difficult to ruffle.

I prod him again. "It's nice to see not all of your kind are devoid of emotion."

His face goes still as he pulls that mask of control over himself again. He says woodenly, "Are you going to kill me or not?"

I flush. All right, yes, I've been stalling. Then I flush deeper as I realize how much this man has made me blush in less than five minutes.

"You're not, are you? I didn't think so. You've never killed anyone like this before, have you?"

I try to smile wickedly. "You can be my first."

"Just press it in here." He lifts his chin, forcing my eyes to the clean lines of his jaw and throat. "I might cry out a little, but no one will think anything of it in a place like this. You'll hear me choke. Blood will gurgle in my throat. My eyes will bulge. But it won't take long. I'll gasp and slide down the wall, and you can watch the life drain from my eyes."

"Why don't you just fight already?"

"And make it easy for you? Help you justify your murder?"

I bare my teeth at him.

His eyes soften. "You're not one of them, not really. What are you doing, girl?"

My knuckles whiten on the knife handle. Then I hear her voice.

Imelda is in the hall, no doubt heading to her room to prepare for Martel.

I turn the knife around. The Warden's eyes register understanding in the brief moment before I clunk him in the head with the handle.

He slumps against the bonds, and I release him to fall to the floor. His scabbarded sword scrapes against the wall.

I should run for the door, but I linger a moment. Unconscious, he looks so young, his face relaxed and peaceful. I check the cut at his neck. He's fine. But my fingers tremble when I touch his warm skin, when I accidently brush a lock of dark gold hair curling from behind his ear. I see a shiny scar peeking from under the open, unlaced neck of his shirt. I shift the fabric. His chest is hard planes of muscle, and the ridged line of the scar starts high on his chest and disappears somewhere around his ribs. A bad injury. I snatch my hand back, feeling like I've done something wrong to touch him when he's unconscious.

Briefly, halfheartedly, I argue with myself. He is my enemy. I should kill him, before it's too late.

But I get up.

I jog to the door.

CHAPTER 4

After a second's thought, I use my knife to cut strips from my already tattered dress. Hiding the cloth and knife behind my back, I crack open the door and lean into the hall. Imelda is about to walk into her room.

"Imelda," I call, not needing to fake my frantic tone.

She looks back. "Amara? What is it?"

"I need your help."

She frowns. "I'm expecting a gentleman any moment."

"Please, Imelda! Just for a second."

Her petite shoulders fall with her sigh, then she walks briskly back to me, her perfectly shaped brows pinched together with irritation. I withdraw into the room so she will be forced to enter before she speaks with me.

She steps inside. "What is it?" Then her eyes fall on the Warden slumped against the wall. "Divine light, what happened?"

When she starts toward the Warden, I grab her from behind, clamping a hand over her mouth. She is small and weak, and I easily wrestle her to the ground. I shove a wad of cloth in her mouth and gag her. I wrench her thin arms behind her back and bind them, then drag her to the foot of the bed, where I tie her up. Her legs flail, and I grunt as a kick lands in my gut. I force her feet together and tie her ankles.

Air whistles angrily through her flared nostrils, and I have to look away from the hurt and fury in her eyes. She was kind to me, even when she didn't know me, and I have betrayed that.

Then I tell myself: she was only kind *because* she didn't know me. If she knew I was a Drifter, she would look at me with disgust. Ibrisians hate us almost as much as Earthmakers do. I leave the room without looking back, ignoring Imelda's muffled shout.

₧ ℂ

A fire crackles in Imelda's fireplace, washing my legs with heat as I pace the rug before it. I go over what I'll say to Martel, the lines I worked on this afternoon as I waited tables. I halt midstride. When Martel walks in, I must look calm, collected, confident. I am a representative of Belos, making an offer to a man who needs it. He is the desperate one, not I. This is a business deal, not a fight.

When Martel eases the door open, I am sitting in Imelda's plush chair by the fire, my elbows resting casually on the dark wood arms, my back pressed to the deep orange cushion.

His eyebrows snap together, puckering the scar that runs through the left one. "Who are you? Where's Imelda?"

I smile invitingly. "Please come in, Count Martel."

He jerks a little at the address. "How do you know my name?"

"I know a lot of things about you."

He edges back.

"It would be ill-advised for you to leave this room before talking to me. King Heborian, no doubt, would be very interested to know of your presence here."

His nostrils flare, but he closes the door firmly behind him. "Who are you? What do you want?"

"Have a seat." I indicate the chair across from me. I stare pointedly into the fire, refusing to speak until I hear him drop impatiently into the chair. His boots clunk awkwardly against the chair legs. He's uncomfortable. Good.

"So. Twenty years is a long time to wait, isn't it?"

At first he says nothing, then he grinds out, "Eighteen."

"I'm afraid it could be eighteen more before you can take back what is rightfully yours."

He huffs, "I don't think so."

I give him a patronizing look. "Count Martel, Heborian is a Drifter—"

"A sorcerer."

I wave that away. "I don't care what you call him. And he has at least *five* other Drifters in his service, and that's not including his son."

"A child," scoffs Martel, the scar tugging down the left side of his face when he frowns.

"Perhaps." In truth, Prince Rood is fifteen, only two years younger than I am. "But you know the castle as well as I do." I have never actually been inside it, but Martel doesn't need to know that. "Come now. You know you'll never breach it."

"I don't have to breach it if Heborian comes out."

"And why would he do that?"

Martel smiles, refusing to give anything more away, but it's clear he has a plan. And he thinks it's a good one.

I remind him, "Heborian has never been seen outside the castle walls without a heavy guard and at least two of his fellow Drifters. Do you think yourself so lucky?"

His lip curls, giving him an ugly expression that has nothing to do with his scar. "Luck is for cowards and women. Men make plans."

I ignore his jab. "My employer would probably agree with you. He, too, makes plans. But he has something you don't."

"And what is that?"

I let part of my mind travel along my mooring and into the Drift. I tug at a thread of my energy and pull it through myself. I cast it around him, binding him as I bound the Warden. He gasps. I draw more of my energy and shape it into something familiar, something that fits perfectly and comfortably into my hand. The steel-encased butt of my spear rests on the floor near my foot. The smooth shaft stretches high above my head, where the notched blade gleams orange with firelight.

Martel's eyes bulge. "You're a Drifter." His voice is faint. Then fear flashes in his eyes. "One of Heborian's?"

I give him a moment to fear that possibility before I smile. "I work for someone much more powerful than Heborian."

His mind is clanking through possibilities, but he's not getting there.

"Someone who'd like to offer you a deal." I let the last word fall like a stone.

Everyone knows Belos's most common title: the Dealmaker.

Martel freezes, his eyes wide with fear. This doesn't surprise me, and he's wise to be frightened. He would be wise, in fact, to refuse. To accept a deal with Belos is to Leash oneself to him. Belos would have control of Martel, be able to take his mind and use his body, be able to kill him by absorbing his lifeforce through the Leash, thus adding to Belos's own power. Martel would be as I am, a slave.

But.

Power can travel both ways along a Leash. I have seen Belos give a man enough strength to tear off another's head with bare hands. I have seen him give a man the power of voice and will to raise an army. I have seen him give a man the power to drift. For the desperate or greedy, it's tempting. The question, then, is whether Martel is desperate and greedy enough.

"I will never give him my soul."

This is a common belief among humans, that the lifeforce Leashed to Belos is actually something more nebulous and precious, something no one has ever been able to define to my satisfaction: the soul. The word, as always, makes me uncomfortable.

"Belos can make you invincible. And he can join himself and all his...resources...to your cause. Think about that, Martel. You'll have everything you want."

Of course, there can be no actual guarantee of success. But Belos's deals tend to work out well for people. At first.

Martel is shaking his head. His voice is weak and frightened when he says, "Please let me go."

I suspect he fears that Belos will Leash him against his will. It's true that he could, that he's done it before, but Belos prefers to make deals. Oh, it's not out of any sense of decency, of course. It's simply easier to have willing subjects. To constantly control the mind of another is, as Belos once said, "Too much bother, unless it's necessary."

I load my voice with warning: "Be wise, Martel."

He's breathing hard, his broad, thin chest heaving. Sweat plasters a lock of brown hair to his forehead. With enough time, he might crack. But I don't have that much time. Eventually someone will discover Imelda. Or the Warden will wake up.

I lean forward impatiently, my hand tightening on my spear. "This is your one and only chance to negotiate. This is when you have choices. Later, when you have failed and you come begging to Belos, you will take what he offers. And it will be less."

I have to scare him, make him want this. But he's still shaking his head, and his breathing has calmed. I have to give him credit: he does have a spine.

Even as he's giving me another refusal, I hear raised voices downstairs. Boots thump along the hallway.

I leap from the chair, relaxing my grip on the spear, automatically preparing to fight.

The last of the fear leaves Martel's face, and his mouth sets with satisfaction. I'll get nothing more from him now.

The door bursts open, and two of the Madame Adessa's burly men charge through, clubs in their hands and snarls on their faces.

One of them says in a coarse Valdaran accent, "Put the stick down, little girl, and we won't hurt you."

I don't waste time on banter. Two running steps bring me to Martel, still bound in the chair. I use him as a stepping stool and hear a grunt of pain when I plant a sandaled foot on his leg. I spring up, leaping over his head, spinning my spear like a staff. I strike one of the men on the side of the head, and he falls back through the open doorway, unconscious. I land before the other man and bring up the steel spear butt to crack him under the jaw. His head snaps back and he falls against the wall, the club clattering from his hand. Martel's yell for help twists into a grunt of disgust.

Another set of boots pound down the hall. I shift away from the door as the Warden, sword in hand and one eye squinted in pain, charges into the room. His eyes skim over the fallen men and Martel, giving me a second to ready my spear before he spins toward me.

I can't afford mercy with someone this dangerous. I lunge, corset digging into my ribs, spear point flashing toward his belly. He knocks my spear aside with a hasty block. I leap back for space, already bringing the spear around in a slash.

His sword whips out and takes the blow hard, making the spear vibrate in my hands.

He leaps at me. I catch the downward blow on the spear and force it to slide away. I will not win this hand-to-hand. He is too strong, too fast, and I will trip over these damn skirts at any moment.

I reach into the Drift, drawing energy into my fist. Hand glowing with power, I throw myself to my knees, sliding under his sword. I punch hard into his muscled stomach. He grunts as the blow lifts him from his feet and flings him against the wall.

Amazingly, he holds onto his sword. Using the wall for support, he pushes himself to his feet.

"Just stay down." I draw more Drift-energy into my body. "Don't make me kill you."

He wheezes, hunched over what will no doubt be some horribly bruised ribs. When he straightens, his face goes still, masking his pain as he masked his anger earlier.

"You're the one who must die, Drifter."

"Astarti." The name is out of my mouth before I can stop it. Stupid, of course. I have no excuse, except that I don't like being called "Drifter."

His eyebrows rise a little, but he gives back what I've given to him. "Logan."

I wish he hadn't done that. It will hurt more, now, to kill him. Perhaps that was his point.

I motion with my spear. "Come on then."

He shifts his grip on the sword and pushes away from the wall.

More boots thump down the hall. I step further from the door to make space for my spear. Five men, all bearing pikes, which means they are probably part of the dock watch, file into the room.

I knock the first pike thrust aside, twist away from another. I can't fight this many in this small space. I slip along my mooring and into the Drift.

The five men freeze when I disappear, their energies swirling in a confusion that shifts quickly to fear.

Yeah, that's right, I'm one of those.

Martel is gone. I lost my hold on him sometime during my fight with the Warden—Logan—and he slipped away.

Logan is leaning against the wall, the wild energy of his body a bright swirl and rush behind the ordinary forms of the other men.

There's nothing more I can do here right now. I won't kill the Warden. I should—but I won't. As for Martel, I'll need something more to hold over him before he's willing to make a deal.

I am still considering my options, thinking about where to drift to, when the Warden's wild energy moves toward my location in the Drift. Coincidence? Or can he sense me?

I know it's not possible. Earthmakers don't use the Drift. They can't. Even if they could, no one should be able to sense the Drift from outside it.

He is so close. Impulsively, I reach out and run a finger through his energy. I feel the spark of him, the inexplicable power; it runs through me like a current.

He freezes. He shouldn't have been able to feel that.

He stares right at me.

My energy surges with fear. Not possible.

I flee.

CHAPTER 5

I step from the Drift at the edge of Belos's barrier, where the lighted threads twist and confuse. It's night, and the Dry Land, so hot during the day, is freezing. I shiver in the skimpy, tattered dress and hug myself for warmth. I'm shaking hard, but it's not just from the sudden cold. My mind roils with what happened. The Warden sensed me inside the Drift. He felt me touch him. How is that possible?

I shake it away. It's not the Warden that matters. My assignment was Martel, and I failed.

I shouldn't have come all the way back here. I panicked when the Warden sensed me in the Drift, and I took the most familiar path, running home like a fool. I have to leave before Belos realizes I'm here. I must get back to Kelda and figure out another plan.

Before I can ease into the Drift again, Belos's voice drops from the courtyard above: "Astarti?"

Fear spikes through me. What is he doing up there?

"What are you doing down there? Come up." His voice snaps with anger. Not good.

I take a steadying breath and make my way toward the sloped path. You don't say no to Belos. And you never, ever run from him. I learned that the hard way.

As I trudge up the dark slope, making my way by memory and feel, my teeth chatter with cold and my mind clicks through excuses and lies. When I reach the top, the scattered stars, devoid of any pattern here in the Dry Land, lay faint lines of light over the jagged fortress. Starlight also paints the pale branches of the dead tree in the courtyard's center. Belos, all but hidden in his black clothes, stands under the twisted branches. Only his pale hair catches the light.

"What happened?" Anger radiates from him. This isn't just me. He's mad about something else.

"I had some trouble."

"I gathered." His voice oozes with scorn.

I clear my throat. "Martel seems to be planning to draw Heborian out of the castle. I don't know how he imagines he'll get Heborian out and unprotected, but that is clearly his intent—"

Even though Belos's pale eyebrows have risen with surprise, he cuts me off impatiently. "I asked you what happened. Why are you back here?"

"I thought I should pass along my information—"

"You lie."

My heart thumps into my throat. "There was a fight. I was outnumbered—"

"You're a Drifter, Astarti."

I know what he's saying. There's no excuse for me to lose a fight unless there are other Drifters involved. Or Earthmakers. But I don't tell him about the Warden. If I do, the Seven will kill him, and I don't want that. I want to know why he could sense me in the Drift. I want to know who—or what—he is.

I insist, "I wanted to pass on my information and make a new plan. I was getting nowhere with Martel. He believes that making a deal means giving up his soul."

Belos's mouth twitches at the word, and I wonder suddenly what he thinks about the idea of the soul. "But you ran, Astarti. Perhaps Straton is right that you're a coward."

He's digging at me on purpose, looking for a fight. Unfortunately, he knows me too well, knows just what to say. Heat flares in my chest. I don't know what angers me more: the word, or the fact that it comes from Straton.

"That's right," I snarl, even though I read my danger in Belos's shadowed eyes. "Listen to Straton. And when that bastard turns on you, as you must know he will do—"

Belos moves so fast I have time only to register the faint blue outline of power around his fist before the blow to my chest sends me flying back. I skid across rough stone, which abrades my already torn back. I gasp, shocked lungs refusing to draw air. Panic floods me as Belos tromps near, a faint heat emanating from his lean body, telling me he is drawing heavily on his Drift-energies. Heat and light only bleed through like that when a Drifter is pulling hard through his mooring—and Belos has a lot of power to draw. That is why he Leashes, why he makes deals. Any energy, any lifeforce he absorbs, adds to his own.

Instinctively, I reach along my mooring, drawing out a thread of power and shaping it into my spear.

Belos stomps on my wrist, and the spear vanishes with a hiss. He crouches over me, teeth gritted, blond hair falling forward. I force myself to face the shadow that hides his eyes.

He will kill me. I saw him once, in a rage, drive his sword through the heart of one of the Seven—back when they were the Eight. He wept afterwards, but it was too late for the man dead at his feet. My anger cools. I have to stop him, and if I have to beg forgiveness to do it, I will. "Belos, I'm—"

He hauls me up by the hair, fingers twisting through the loose tangle. I pull away instinctively, wincing at the flash of pain across my scalp. He wrenches me closer, his body pulsing with heat.

I hear the rushing air of his Drift-sword forming. Panic leaps into my throat.

I shape my own sword, though it's not my favored weapon. The tip aims at Belos's belly. He releases my hair. As he swings, I duck, spinning to slice at his knee. I feel the light pressure of my blade's contact. It can't have given him more than a scratch, but Belos screams, rage flooding his voice.

He hacks at me wildly. In an ordinary man, such loss of control might be a weakness. In Belos, it is a force of nature unleashed. His sword glows bright, snapping heat across my face as I desperately block each blow.

He drives me backward, and I trip over the raised roots of the tree. As I fall, I reach along my mooring. Perhaps the Drift will buy me a moment. I can hide in it briefly, even if I can't cross the barrier. When my back hits the gnarled roots, I feel a pull. It tugs right under my heart. Even though it doesn't feel quite right for the Drift, I follow the pull, desperate for escape.

₨ ⌒

It's dark, though something faint and gold, nebulous as smoke, flows around my lighted form. Is this some part of the Drift I've never seen?

I steady my mind, feeling for other energies, but there is only the strange golden flow, almost like a current. It runs around me, runs *through* me, and I realize I have been instinctively bracing against it. I discern a low hum. I follow it, letting it sweep me along.

The golden glow intensifies. When, the flow branches, I brace against it, panic threatening. This is not the Drift. I don't know where I am or what to do. I don't know how to get out. I can't feel my mooring.

When I see a light, far ahead, along one of the branches, I flow toward it. At least it's something. As I draw near, the light takes on the shape of a familiar male body. The energy pulses and whirls wildly.

The Warden.

I push within the flow, and I feel like I'm swimming. He senses my approach and spins to face me. I see shock—and a little fear—in the lighted planes of his face.

I'm trying to say a word when he grabs me. He pulls me, and it feels like I'm being dragged from water.

℘ ℭ

Stunned, I kneel on the damp earth, the Warden's arms around me, his heart pounding against my back. Then he lets go and falls away from me. I hear him scramble back a pace, hear his ragged breathing.

"What—how—" He swallows. "How were you in the Current?"

We're in a forest. Moonlight, filtering through the budding branches overhead, paints his face with lacy patterns. His eyes, though their color is hidden, are wide. He's sitting, leaning away from me, hands planted on the ground behind him. His chest heaves. Why has this unsettled him more than anything, more even than the fact that I work for Belos?

"Where are we?" I ask, my voice shaking. My hands are shaking also, and I'm cold. I rub my arms. "What happened?"

"You were in the Current." His voice is shaking as much as mine.

"The Current?"

He says nothing. Then he pulls himself together, as I have seen him do before. He sits straighter, hands on his knees, ready. "It's how Earthmakers travel. How did you get into it?"

I think back. I was fighting Belos in the courtyard. I fell into the tree. It pulled me down and I used it to escape Belos. But there is no escape from Belos. He will find me, right at the end of my Leash, where I always am.

I shoot to my feet.

The Warden scrambles up beside me. "What?"

"You have to get out of here."

"But—"

"Listen, Warden—"

"Logan."

"Fine." My heart hammers. I don't have time to explain things to him. I stiffen my voice, "You have to get out of here."

"Astarti." I jump when he says my name. I forgot I gave it to him. "Slow down. Maybe I can help you."

The way he says it makes me pause. The way his body is so close to mine makes me want him to. He is warm, strong, certain. Something about him makes me trust him. I know what deception and manipulation feel like, and I feel none of it in him.

But it doesn't matter how strong Logan might be, or how much I might want to say, "Yes!" No one is as strong as Belos. No one can help me. But I can help Logan, if I can get him away. Belos will kill him on sight.

"Listen to me, Logan. Belos"—Logan stiffens at the name— "yes, *Belos* is on his way. He will find me. And if you're here, you will die. Don't shake your head. He will torture you, he will learn everything you know, then he will kill you. That's how it is."

Logan's jaw hardens, and the moonlight lying over his handsome features looks suddenly cold. Then it passes, and his voice is gentle and curious when he asks, "Why would you protect me?"

I am silent, uncertain. Then, "Why did you pull me from the Current?" I know if he hadn't I would not have found my way free of it.

Now it's his turn to be silent.

"You won't go, will you?"

"No."

"Even though Belos will kill you?"

"Why do you serve him?"

I snap, not looking at him, "What choice do you think I have?"

He closes the distance between us. He grips my arm in a strong hand. His other hand lifts my chin, forcing me to look up into his moonlit face. "Everyone chooses."

"Not me." I am trembling, terrified. I have never talked about this to anyone.

"How can that be?" He's not skeptical, exactly, but he wants an answer. I can't give it to him. I can't say the word. He says it for me, slowly, "Leashed."

It sounds as dirty out loud as it does in my mind.

He stiffens and lets go of my arm. "But you must have chosen—"

I step back angrily, making space. "You don't know anything about me!"

"That's why I'm asking! And not fighting you!"

That shuts me up.

We stare at each other.

I say, "Yes, I am Leashed"—the word is filth in my mouth—"but I didn't choose it, whatever you might think. I have to go. If you won't save yourself."

"Astarti, please—"

That's the last thing I hear from him, and the last image is his hand reaching for mine as I enter the Drift.

I haven't gone far when I feel a pull on the white thread of my Leash. The pull is nothing like I felt when I entered the Current. This slides into me, violates the boundaries of my very self. Even within the Drift, distanced from my body, I feel sick.

Two forms approach.

Belos I recognize at once. Even if I couldn't feel him at the end of my Leash, I would know his energy anywhere. He is like dozens of people blended into one. Logan's energy is wild, but it's a wildness that moves together, with its own strange rhythm. Belos has no rhythm, no flow. He has absorbed the energies of so many, and they fight within him. It's unnatural, nauseating.

As the two draw near, I recognize Theron. Theron's energy, as usual, is controlled. Tidy.

Belos stops before me, and the white Leash pulses between us. I feel his anger through the Leash, and I try to step back. Belos squeezes, and a shock of pain surges through me.

"You know better." His voice is strained within the Drift. It's not easy to make sound here.

I am silent. There is nothing I can do or say. Leashed, I'm at his mercy, which is not something he generally shows.

But when I hear a scream of wind, a mad lash of sound, I realize that Belos is not the most immediate threat.

"The Hounding," says Theron, and I can hear his fear despite the strain of speaking here.

Wind, sharp and furious, slices through me, disrupting my energies, disorienting me. Theron screams and disappears along his mooring. Belos snarls as the wind plucks at his chaotic form.

He vanishes. For one moment, I think I will get to choose between Belos and the Hounding, but then, with the wind shrieking around me, my Leash is tugged, crippling me with a wave of nausea.

I am ripped along my mooring.

Chapter 6

I fall to my knees in a field, freezing from the fierce wind of the Hounding, wracked by nausea from the pull on my Leash. The corset digs into my ribs as I hunch around my rebelling stomach. The patter of fleeing hooves and frantic bleats of sheep tell me I am far from the eyes of people. Of course. Belos would want it this way. He bends over me, harsh breaths ruffling my hair.

"How did you do it?"

"Do what?" I force out through chattering teeth.

"Don't play with me. You traveled from the courtyard. How?"

I climb to my feet, making Belos take a step back. If he wants me on my knees, he'll have to force me.

He doesn't. His arms are crossed, his neck too tense, his footsteps a little too quick. He's shaken. Why?

Behind him, Theron shifts uncomfortably, his eyes darting to me then away.

"I don't know. I don't understand."

"You fell," Belos prompts. "And then?"

I hitch the front of my tattered dress a little higher. I don't like feeling this exposed in front of Belos. What I wouldn't give to trade this dress for pants and tunic, these sandals for a pair of stout boots.

"Yes, I tripped over the tree roots. I fell...*into* the tree." I shake my head in frustration. "I don't understand what happened." I watch Belos warily, waiting for his anger, but his crossed arms only tighten.

He asks testily, "But what did it look like?"

"Kind of...gold. And it was strange. I was swept along, like there was some kind of...stream?" I avoid the name Logan called it, not wanting to open the door for other questions.

Belos and Theron exchange a look.

"How did you get out?"

My heart thumps with the memory of Logan, but I say, "I don't know."

Belos's arms uncross. "Describe it."

I try to remember the sensations, to imagine how I might have done it alone. "I dragged myself from it. It was like...getting out of water. I ended up in a forest. Then I stepped into the Drift. To come back." Before Belos has a chance to call me a liar or ask further questions, I launch into questions of my own. "What was that place? What happened?"

Again Belos and Theron exchange a look. What do they know that I don't?

Belos says, "It's part of the Drift, difficult to access."

He's lying—I know his tricks, and he just lifted his chin in that confident way that screams, "liar"—but of course I can't say that.

Theron's eyes dart to mine, then he squares up to Belos. "My Lord? The plan?"

I know Theron's tricks, too, and he is redirecting, helping Belos cover something up. Belos, never one to be grateful, glares at him.

I interrupt, "I already have one." I have to assert myself if I hope not to be thrown out of this and back into a cell. "I'll go to Heborian. I'll tell him Martel is in Tornelaine. Martel has a plan of his own, and we need to destroy it before he can make good on it. If we put him on the run, with Heborian at his heels, he'll be desperate. Desperate enough, perhaps, to accept a deal."

A smile tugs Belos's mouth, which looks eerie in the moonlight. He lays cool hands on either side of my face, like he used to when I was a child. I am reminded that he wasn't always so angry with me. When I was young, he would smile at me and call me "Little Drifter." When did that change? When did he start to hate me? But I know the answer. I know exactly when things changed. When I refused his command. When he took my mind. We will never forgive each other.

The thought seems to occur to him also because he drops his hands and steps away.

He says stiffly, "Theron will accompany you."

Theron dips his head. "To serve is to live."

Belos accepts this coolly, then throws at me, "Don't disappoint me this time, Astarti."

A glow forms around him, lighting him to brief, harsh beauty, then he's gone.

I rub my arms for warmth and try to still my shivering. I'm not sure what chills me most: the cold night air slipping through my tattered dress, or the warning in Belos's tone.

Theron unbuckles his cloak, shakes it out, swings it around me. He fastens it at my shoulder, and his fingers linger there. Has he forgiven me for my failures? His breathing is a little too shallow, his leaning toward me a little too purposeful. He's looking at me as he does sometimes when we are alone.

I shift uncomfortably. "Theron—"

He drops his hands and turns away, nodding south. Theron would never go against Belos, would never presume to take what belongs to his master. "Tornelaine is that way. Do you want to drift?"

I let it go. I don't know what I would have said anyway, had he done more than let his hand linger on my shoulder. It can never be, and I don't know that I even want it. True, I am lonely sometimes, but Theron is one of the Seven. He has no regard for the lives of others. He kills easily, sometimes cruelly.

I dismiss these pointless questions and focus instead on the present. I say, thinking of the Hounding, "Don't you think we should wait?"

Theron shrugs carelessly, as though he did not scream in fear only minutes ago. He turns south.

I catch up, trudging through the grasses, the hem of my skirt and Theron's too-long cloak bunched in my hands to free my sandaled feet. There is no elegance in me. I just want my boots.

We crest a hill. To the right, the ocean spreads below us, moonlight washing its surface. Far off, the dark hump of an island tells me the Floating Lands of the Earthmakers have drifted near. Earlier today, that was empty water. I wonder if Theron misses it. If any of the Seven do, it would be him. Cruel, yes, but gentle sometimes. I wonder suddenly why he joined Belos. As I grew up, that fact was simply part of my world, as the Dry Land was. It didn't occur to me to wonder.

"Theron—"

"You make things hard for yourself, you know that, right?" His voice is more frustrated than angry. He hates to see me in disgrace, though he would never speak or act for me, not against Belos.

"Yes. I know that."

"Why do you do it?"

I shrug, but he only looks at me, waiting. I say, feeling how stupid my words are but unable to think of better, "Things bother me. I can't just…do them."

Even in the faint, uncertain light of the moon, I see puzzlement in his eyes.

I insist, "I can't, Theron. It would go against—" I almost say "my soul." What does this mean? Why did this word come to me so easily when I don't understand it?

Theron reminds me, "But you always have to in the end anyway. You must do what he says, as we all must. Why not save yourself the pain?"

I tug his cloak around myself, losing track of my skirt, letting it drag and catch on the grass. I don't have an answer for him. I don't have one for myself.

ဆ posterior

Tornelaine comes into sight when we reach the top of a rocky, scrubby bluff. We know we'll have to drift into the city because the gates are closed for the night. Luckily, when we enter the Drift, the Hounding is gone.

We step from the Drift just beyond the bridge to Heborian's gates, where Heborian's barrier falls. It's much like Belos's barrier, a twisting of lighted threads, a straining of energy. Someday, someone will explain these to me.

Theron insists on waiting for me at the foot of the bridge, and he won't tell me why. When I push him, all I can learn is that he doesn't want to see Heborian. I don't see the problem; there's no reason that Heborian would recognize one of the Seven. Theron gives some vague answer about how it wouldn't look right. I shrug. I know a lie when I hear it, but I'm used to being kept ignorant.

The plan is simple: when I get to the castle, I'll tell them I'm a whore from the Trader's Choice. I am, after all, dressed the part. I'll say that I saw Martel there. I recognized him by his scar because my father, who had served in the war, told stories of Count Martel's slashing. The story is simple, clean, with an edge of truth. The perfect lie.

The castle sits high on the bluff, connected to the city by the wide stone bridge. I will be seen long before I reach the gates, which offer the only entrance to the stone-walled courtyard. As the bridge curves high, I catch a glimpse of the moonlit ocean beyond. The Floating Lands are hidden behind one of Heborian's towers. I crane my neck to see them but snap back to attention when a guard yells from the platform over the gate.

"Halt! Show your hands!"

I raise them. I am lit by the moon. My shape and the pale expanse of chest above my low neckline reveal that I am a woman.

"I have information for the king."

"Come back tomorrow and request an audience. No admittance after dark."

"This can't wait until tomorrow."

I continue my approach, ignoring the shouted warnings. When I am ten paces from the gate, I stop. Torchlight shines on the guards' crossbows.

"I have urgent information for the king." That alone will not get me through the gates, so I add, "Count Martel is in the city."

The crossbows don't move, but the guards whisper to one another. One shouts, "Where?"

"Let me speak to the king."

"You will speak to me!"

"And let you take credit and cheat me of my reward? Not a chance." I am fully in character now. I'm a woman who knows what it means to buy and sell; I'm a woman who gives nothing away for free.

More whispering. A groan of metal and a clatter of chain. The heavy gate creaks open.

One of the guards meets me at the bottom. He pats me down, searching for weapons. Good thing I thought to pass my knife to Theron. Good thing, too, I suppose, that he stayed behind. My story is more believable like this. Maybe he wasn't lying. Maybe my instinct was wrong. The guard is thorough in his search, and I have to grit my teeth as he runs his hands under my breasts and down my hips and thighs. I want to punch him in the face when I see his grin.

Instead I comment, "You're lucky Madame isn't here. That would have cost you a copper."

His grin widens, and he says, friendly now, "Come on, lass. Let's get you your reward. But mind you, if you're lying, thinking to get a silver for false information, Heborian will have you whipped and locked in the stocks, pretty face or none. You're sure you want to disturb him?"

I give the guard a cool look. "I'm not lying."

"All right, then."

He leads me across a cobbled courtyard lined with trees. The king's castle, unlike Belos's rough fortress, has perfectly rounded walls, smooth sided towers, ornate doors, and stained-glass windows. The moonlight doesn't reveal everything, but it shows enough.

As the door guards, smartly dressed in black and silver and holding sharp-edged pikes, push open the thick, finely carved doors of the castle, I feel an edge of nervousness. I'm about to meet the king of Kelda. Another Drifter, and a Runish one at that. I know it's silly to be impressed. I'm here for Belos, and no king's power, no Drifter's power, can compare to his. Besides, though I don't know all of Belos's plans, I do know that if he succeeds, Heborian won't be king much longer.

I wonder, though, as I have before, why Belos doesn't try to make a deal with Heborian. Surely Heborian would be the stronger ally? Then it occurs to me: could Heborian have already refused him? Is this revenge? As I follow the guard into the foyer, I drive these questions away. As Belos so often reminds me, it's not my place to wonder, only to serve.

The ceiling sweeps high, but the vast overhead space is nearly filled by a massive crystal chandelier. The chandelier's candles are unlit, but silver sconces lining the stone walls blaze with light, picking out a few sparkles in the glass faces above.

I wonder if the guard will lead me to a huge audience chamber, where the king will look down on me from a raised dais, his hands draped casually over the gilded arms of a throne. To my relief, he takes me instead to what looks like a sitting room. Chairs with short, curved backs are clustered before a huge, empty fireplace. Paintings line the walls, but none of them are portraits. They are horses, dogs, battle scenes. The room is so casual that I am uncomfortable, and when the guard tells me to wait and his footsteps fade down the hall, I pace.

I pass a painting of a huge black horse with a high, proud head and streaming tail. Another horse. A battle scene. Another battle scene. I stop at the third one. It features all the typical elements: horses rearing, men trampled under them, spears, swords, armor. But in the background, almost hidden behind the fight, is a pale glow surrounding a dark figure. Some might take it for a mistake in the work, but I don't. It's a Drifter. One standing back, watching.

"I see you admire LeCarte's work."

I spin at the low, gravelly voice. Heborian stands in the doorway. It can only be him. Tall and broad, handsome, just like people say. His hair, as dark as mine, is braided down one side of his face in the Runish style but otherwise makes a dark mane around his shoulders. His beard is neatly trimmed. A blue tattoo curves along the outside of his right eye and spikes down his cheek. I am suddenly conscious of my own tattoo, glad it's hidden under loose hair. Most people don't know what it means, but a Runian like Heborian would see it for what it is: a symbol of my mother's rejection, a failed attempt to kill me.

I don't know the meaning of any of Heborian's tattoos. Another peeks above the fur edging of his tunic. A third curls around his right wrist, twisting down his hand and around his fingers. Those fingers are relaxed, his body language easy and confident. All of it gives him a predator's grace. And his dark eyes, narrowed at me with hidden study, tell me why they call him the Wolf.

He paces into the room with that animal grace and nods at the painting. "You like it?"

I want to say, "Yes," because it's an eerie, powerful image, but Amara the whore would not think like that. I want to ask about the Drifter in the background, but Amara would never notice it. So Amara mutters, "I don't like the fighting."

He halts, disappointment washing the curiosity from his face. "I hear you have information regarding Count Martel."

He is formal now, a king, and I feel an unexpected loss as the chance to speak casually with him slips away.

I grasp at my story. "I work at the Trader's Choice, a brothel—"

"I know it," he cuts me off irritably.

That surprises me. There must be fifty brothels in the city. Why would he know of a little place like that?

"Tonight," I go on, "Count Martel came in. He may be gone by now, but he was there when I left to come here. I thought you'd want to know."

"How did you recognize him?"

"His scar."

Dark eyebrows come down. "Many are scarred."

"My father fought in the wars. He told stories. He says the king"—I let my eyes dart to Heborian—"you—cut him, but he escaped."

"Who is your father?"

"He's dead, my lord, but his name was Jean Adarre. You wouldn't have had cause to know him."

Heborian studies me. "That's a Keldan name. You're Runish."

I shift uncomfortably. I didn't expect him to ask so many questions. "My mother," I mumble, feeling exposed by the information, by this thread of truth.

His eyes narrow, and he starts to walk a circle around me, as Madame Adessa did. I can't help but tense. I don't like to be the center of attention; I've learned it's a dangerous place. When he comes again to the front, a crease wedges between his brows, and his mouth is drawn low in a frown. There's something in his eyes I don't like and for a second I think it's recognition. But I know he's never seen me. He can't know I work for Belos.

He's about to say something when a man, dressed in the black and silver of the house guards, bursts into the room.

"My lord! Prince Rood! Gone!"

Heborian wheels on the guard. "What?"

"You told us to tell you at once if he—"

"I know what I told you. I also know that I ordered discretion." Heborian grounds out the last word.

The guard's eyes dart to me, and he swallows hard.

Heborian says nothing more, but his face warns of punishment. He glances back at me, eyes narrow with suspicion, then stalks from the room.

Heborian's footsteps beat down the hall, and I am seemingly forgotten. My mind races. Prince Rood missing. Is it just coincidence? The prince could be out doing whatever it is fifteen-year-old boys do, even royal ones. He is, I've heard, a little wild. But. I came here tonight because I was expecting Martel to move quickly. Could this be his move? But how could he have gotten Rood out of this castle? Impossible. The prince must have left. But why? More importantly, could Martel have intercepted him? But how would Martel have known where the prince was going?

The questions roll through my mind, disconnected. But then I remember something Imelda said when she took me to her room, something that has been in my mind like an itch all evening: *Even a king may be brought low by a whore.*

Heborian knew of the Trader's Choice, and he was irritated by it. Perhaps Prince Rood has been there, against his wishes.

I jog for the door, glad to have been forgotten. I have to get to the Trader's Choice. I have to find Imelda.

CHAPTER 7

Theron and I navigate the Drift—blessedly free of the Hounding—to the Trader's Choice, where I recognize Imelda's lighted form by her quiet beauty. But energy shivers through her. She's nervous.

I step from the Drift into her room, where a broken chair has been pushed into the corner. Imelda halts her pacing when I appear. When Theron appears beside me, she stumbles back, her heel clanking the folding fireplace screen, which screeches against the brick hearth. To her credit, she doesn't scream.

I pin her with a glare. "What do you know of Prince Rood?"

She swallows nervously. Good. She won't be much of a liar.

I shape my Drift-spear to speed things up. "Where is he? Does Martel have him?"

Her eyes fix on the spear and her mouth works, but no sound comes out. Theron stalks toward her and grabs her throat. I wince as he slams her into the fireplace mantel. "Speak!"

Imelda whimpers. When Theron growls, she stammers, "He-he was here. He comes here often! The Count took him, yes! Please!"

I lay a hand on Theron's arm, and he lets go. Imelda sags, coughing, and rubs her throat. She flinches when I touch her shoulder. "Where did they go?"

"Who are you?" she whispers without looking at me.

"Imelda," I warn.

"I don't know where they went! Do you think Martel would tell me?"

"Land or sea?"

She thinks. "They had horses."

"When did they leave?"

"Twenty minutes ago?" she guesses.

At least that gives us a radius. It would have taken them half that time to get out of the city. They can't have gone more than a few miles.

I'm turning to Theron to suggest we search through the Drift—Rood is a Drifter, so we should be able to identify him—when Heborian bursts through the door. Imelda screams. I jump. Heborian stares at me. He shouts something I don't understand because Theron and I are already stepping into the Drift.

♒ ♑

By the time we locate Martel and his band of sixty men, they are about five miles from Tornelaine, cutting through a forest that spreads wide from the Kiss River. Another four or five miles away, a much larger group of perhaps two hundred is waiting. We have to slow Martel down so that Heborian can catch up before Martel reaches his other men. Two things have to happen: Heborian has to rescue Rood, and Martel has to escape. We need Martel alive and desperate to wrest Tornelaine from Heborian. We also need Martel to believe we had nothing to do with his failed plan.

While I am still in the Drift, following an unconscious Prince Rood held in the saddle by one of Martel's men, I notice two disturbing things. First, my Leash is glowing too brightly, which means Belos did not go back to the Dry Land—he's nearby. Second, so is the Warden. I sense his wild energy not far behind. I only hope Theron didn't notice and that Logan has the sense to stay away.

I position myself ahead of the horse carrying Rood and his captor, who is thankfully not Martel himself. I have to time this right.

I step from the Drift as the horse bears down on me. The animal spooks, wheeling away, and Prince Rood and his captor are thrown from the saddle. The man rolls and skids. Rood tumbles like a rag doll. Theron appears and grabs the man. They both vanish, and I swallow a brief queasiness. I know the man had to die, to prevent him from informing Martel that he saw me, but Theron's method, however expedient, is cruel. To take a non-Drifter into the Drift without proper preparation is to do more than kill him. The unprepared human mind cannot comprehend the Drift and will be severed from its body. The man's body will dissolve into the energy of the Drift. But his mind? His soul, if such a thing exists? No one really knows. It seems to vanish. Not a thing to do lightly. But I have no more control over Theron than I have over Belos.

Sliding over deadfall, I rush to Prince Rood, hoping the fall didn't break his neck. Martel's company surges forward, not realizing they've lost their prize. By the time they are straggling to a stop and turning back, I've reached Heborian's son.

He looks like his father, broad for his age and handsome, though his face is soft with youth. Unlike his father, he has no tattoos that I can see. A gash crosses his forehead, but he is breathing. Nothing appears broken. I grab him and step into the Drift. Because he too is a Drifter, it will do him no harm.

From within the Drift, I watch Martel's men mill about in confusion as they search, arguing, gesturing. I glance at Theron, who hovers nearby, his energy form bright with power. There is no sign of the man.

I wait.

Soon enough, the blazing energy of several Drifters streaks toward us. I pull Rood from the Drift, not wanting to be caught there. Fighting within the Drift is dangerous.

Heborian appears moments after I step from the Drift. His eyes are wild with fury, his mouth curled in a snarl. The tattoo around his right eye seems to sharpen.

He says nothing but grabs his son from my hands. They vanish into the Drift. My heart hammers in my throat.

I turn to the fight, where Heborian's Drifters are tearing through Martel's company. Even though it's a fight of five to sixty, Martel's men hardly stand a chance.

I see Theron guarding Martel, and I travel through the Drift to them. Unfortunately, Martel is not a Drifter, so we can't simply take him into the Drift and away to safety. We'll have to fight.

One of Heborian's Drifters appears before us, a blaze of light and heat around his fists. He channels this at Theron, and the burst of energy strikes Theron in the chest before he can dodge or block. As Theron falls back and Martel shouts in surprise, I shape my spear and lunge for the Drifter. He vanishes.

He appears behind me but doesn't strike; he's not after me. Martel blocks the Drifter's first blow with his own sword, giving me time to spin. I catch the Drifter across the shoulder with my spear, though his shoulder guard takes most of the damage.

The earth rumbles. It shakes me and the Drifter both to our knees. Horses bolt. Men shout. Stony spikes burst from the earth, spearing men and spreading chaos.

Theron's signature earthmaking.

My opponent is scrambling away from blades of stone when Theron leaps for him. I don't see what happens because pain, white-hot and blinding, splits my side.

I scream and swing my spear blindly to drive off the attacker. My spear connects with a sword, and the blow shivers up my arm. The moonlight filtering through overhead branches and the faint glow of my opponent's Drift-sword reveal the towering figure of a man. His sword whips and darts. He is fast and strong. I block clumsily, hampered by the wound in my side and the too-close engagement. When I manage to hit him in the gut with my spear butt, he makes a grunt of surprised pain. I seize the chance to step back, to make room for my spear and whip its deadly, notched blade into position.

I don't get the chance to use it. Pain bursts across the back of my head.

I fall to my knees as the world darkens and recedes. A dim part of my mind knows that I should get up, but I can't. I wait for the next blow, the last one.

As though they are far away, I hear the ring of swords, the shouts of men. The earth rumbles again, shaking me flat onto my stomach. I smell leaf mold, damp earth, and blood. Then a hand clamps on my shoulder, pulling me up, drawing my cheek away from the cool, moist ground.

As I flop onto my back, the Warden's face, a blend of shadow and moonlit beauty, comes into view. He pulls me up, and I am caught in his strength. He is otherworldly, powerful, and for a moment I believe the stories of the Lost Gods, who the Runians claim shaped this world. The Lost Gods, they say, were chaos and danger and heartbreaking beauty. My fingers stretch toward him, drawn, as they were when I studied his wild energy from within the Drift.

He is shouting something, and I recognize the shape of fear in his face. At last his words pierce the haze of my mind: "Get up!"

When he shouts it again, I will strength into my legs and stand on my own, though his hands don't leave me. They are on my wound, like he's holding me together. Then he cries out in pain. His hands slide away as he drops to one knee. I dimly register the fading glow of a Drift-arrow in his leg. My mind sharpens at once.

"No!" I shout thickly, surprised to find my voice. Theron shapes another arrow and sets it to his faintly glowing bow.

Logan staggers to his feet. He shoves me behind him, and I brush against his hip and back. He is shaking, with pain perhaps, or anger.

Then nausea wracks me, and I clutch at Logan's shirt. My blood runs cold with the familiar violation.

Belos.

CHAPTER 8

Belos steps from the Drift, light and heat washing from him like water. As it fades, moonlight glints on his shoulder studs, gleams in his pale hair, flashes along the edge of his sword. He stares at Logan, at me. His lip curls.

"Earthmaker scum," he snarls. "Another blind fool, about to die."

A growl thrums through Logan's body. I can't hear it, but I feel it in the hand I have pressed to his back.

Belos and Logan charge at the same time. I am alone, my hand still raised, my thoughts lagging from the blow to my head. Their swords ring against each other twice before I stumble forward, my right arm pressed to my side to protect the wound.

Logan makes a downward cut that sweeps inches from Belos's face, but that is the last strike Belos allows. The glow starts in his fist and travels down his sword. When he swings and Logan blocks, Logan's blade shatters like glass.

Logan staggers back.

Belos draws back his sword with a cruel grin.

Heart leaping, I do the stupidest thing I've ever done, the thing that guarantees Belos will take my mind, that he will make me no more than a body, a vessel for his will. I shape my spear—and I throw it.

It flies through moonlight and shadow, arcing silently toward its mark. Belos looks up as the point flashes toward his face.

A Drift-sword, flung from somewhere to the right, spins end over end. It catches my spear, and the two weapons tangle and clatter into the underbrush.

I barely register Theron straightening from his throw before Belos lets out a scream of rage. He vanishes.

My heart gives one hard thump before Belos appears before me. So fast. His teeth are bared, his eyes wide with madness. He grabs my throat, his fingers cold and tight. I can't breathe, can't think. My eyes play tricks with light and dark. I scrabble uselessly at his hands.

The surge of panic fades. Belos's face darkens and recedes. I start to float. Thank the Lost Gods, or the Divine Light of the Ibrisians, or luck—I hardly care which. He will kill me. I will die with my mind my own.

When the earth cracks and shakes, I don't feel it until I'm falling. Belos staggers back, bracing. Air rushes into my lungs.

Earth breaks and rises. It rolls like a wave on the sea, shaking the fighting men to their knees. Wind begins to shriek. For one disoriented moment, I think it's the Hounding. Then I see Logan, face wild with power, standing in the wind's heart. Air whips and streaks around him, tearing through the trees, ripping leaves, cracking branches, throwing stones.

Two paces from me, Belos staggers to his feet. He yells something furious and inarticulate. The earth rumbles away from him.

Logan stumbles, catches himself. He drops to a knee, one fist coming down like a hammer. When he strikes the earth, it ripples and buckles, catching men in its heaving.

Belos vanishes.

I cry out as the earth jerks beneath me. I tumble and roll, banging over roots and stones. I catch myself against a tree and cling to its rough bark. Wind and earth roar. This is not Belos. Or Theron. Neither have such wild earthmagic. Primal fear spikes through me. This power is uncontrolled. It's chaos. It will destroy everything.

I strain against the screaming torrent of wind and earth, nails bending against the tree's bark, muscles burning. I cry out when a loose branch streaks by, scraping down my injured side. I manage to work an eye around my tree and try to blink Logan into focus, but he is a shape only, a wavering one within the furious heart of the wind. Something glows beside him. I recognize Belos's dark figure within the glow, like the painting in Heborian's castle.

What happens next is unclear. My eyes must lie to me because Logan does something impossible. He vanishes into a wild rush of wind.

The wind streaks toward me. It tears at my face and chest, ripping my dress, scouring my skin. I scream.

Suddenly, it calms. In what seems a dream, the wind slips around me, envelops me.

But what holds me becomes real, solid, a strength already familiar. I smell ocean breeze, clean linen.

Logan presses me to his chest.

The world disappears. I am gone.

₲ ℛ

I wake at some point to find myself in the golden flow of the Current. It moves in many directions, like a network, like the Drift. But it lies deeper, moves more slowly. Though it flows, its points don't shift.

I am pressed against Logan's lighted form, enveloped by his wild energy. It is primal, and something in me answers to it, and our edges blur, blending us. I feel him, I know him. I know that rage and pain lie deep within, that it wears him down to control them, to keep them hidden. I have never known such intimacy. Some distant part of my mind is shocked, frightened of what he might sense of me, but I don't draw away. His face angles down, and his eyes look pained. I have no strength to ask him why, so I let myself float, losing myself in his wild, beautiful pattern.

℘ ℭ

The Current changes. What had been a flow strengthens to a torrent. I am suddenly alone, with the Current alive around me. It is aware of itself, and of me. It doesn't like me. I struggle as it pulls at me, twists and bends me. I will drown. I will die.

Then I feel Logan tugging, dragging. The Current clings, not wanting to let me go. Logan's form flares silver-gold. At last I tumble from the Current and into the cold, dark night.

℘ ℭ

Moonlight lays silver stripes between dark tree trunks. Earthy scents of clean soil, fresh leaves, and blossoms fill my nostrils. The cool air plays over my exposed face and hands. I sigh, letting exhaustion pull me down into this dream.

Someone shakes me, calls my name. I know that deep, rhythmic voice. Logan.

His arms wrap around me, and the warmth of his body lulls me. I will sleep.

He lifts me. For some reason, his heart is pounding. Suddenly, I am being jostled and shaken. He is running. I feel an edge of annoyance. I just want to rest, to sleep, to go down into this darkness.

I dimly register sounds: the trickle of a fountain, the far off flow of a waterfall, the distant wash of tide. So much water. Where am I?

Logan's feet pound across stone, his moving body jarring mine.

I hear a voice ahead, light and musical. A female voice.

Light blooms over my face. I feel it against my closed eyelids, which are too heavy to open.

The light voice grows high, alarmed. It bars our way. Logan shouts. I can't focus on any of the words until I hear the female say, surprised, "Primo Loganos? Is that you?"

CHAPTER 9

My mind cycles through those words: Primo, Loganos, Primo, Loganos. My thoughts refuse to coalesce, to bring understanding.

Logan shouts again, something about a Healer.

More voices, bare feet slapping across stone.

Logan lowers me to a cool stone floor. Finally, I force my eyes to slit open. Firelight flickers somewhere, dancing against the white and gray pattern of a high ceiling. Bodies move at the periphery of my vision. Logan's worried face, eyes swirling blue and green, appears in my line of sight. That word echoes again: Primo. I know that word. What does it mean?

Cool, smooth hands cradle my head. They are too delicate to be Logan's. They weave through my hair, and a low female voice eases me, lulling me nearly to sleep. I wonder if this is what a mother is like. I wonder if this is *my* mother, come to take me into death, as she always meant to do.

When I feel a tug deep within me, at the core of my being, I gasp. My Leash! Belos! But the tug vanishes, and instead of being sickened, I feel the strangest sense of completion, of immersion. I feel the immense weight of earth, the living breath of wind, the rhythmic lull of water, the fierce lick of fire. I am surrounded and filled. Whole.

More voices. Deep and angry this time, male.

The sense of wholeness vanishes, and I am shivering with cold. There is no water, no wind, no earth, no fire. I feel loss. Emptiness. And pain. My side is on fire, and my hand finds it instinctively. It's wet and sticky, still oozing blood. Reality plucks at me. I am in a building. People are arguing. I open my eyes.

At first, nothing makes sense. I'm in a long, wide hallway. On one side, the moon shines through a balustrade, washing the pale stone floor with cool light. On the other, a sweeping white wall hung with tapestries gives way at intervals to dark, arched passages. Bronze braziers, some glowing dimly with coals, others burning bright, cast uneven light up the walls and onto the high ceiling. The stone floor is patterned like the ceiling, but I can't quite make out the design.

I sit up, and my head is almost clear, the pain at the back of it a dull ache. Logan stands in front of me, his left leg bearing most of his weight. The worn leather of his right pant leg is dark with blood. His whole body is tense, furious. But the sharp, clipped voice isn't his. I peer around him.

Facing Logan is a shorter, broader man wearing traditional Earthmaker robes, belted at the waist. A gold lantern with glass faces swings in his hand, flashing its light over the man's broad face and flaring in his short-cropped red-gold hair, which sticks up in places, probably from interrupted sleep.

The man barks, "Who is this? This is a human. Why have you brought her here? Where have you been? Explain yourself!"

"Aron," Logan warns. "Let Feluvas finish Healing her, then I will explain. Not before. Feluvas?"

Logan glances over his shoulder, and I turn to follow his eyes. A stern-faced woman kneels behind me, giving me a look of suspicion. She wears loose blue Earthmaker robes gathered at the shoulders. Her arms are bare and slender.

I am in the Floating Lands. In Avydos.

My blood chills.

The woman, Feluvas, explains calmly, "I'm sorry Logan. The word of the Arcon overrules."

Arcon. Essentially, the Earthmaker king. I struggle to my feet. I have to get out of here. They will kill me.

Logan turns to me, grips my arm. "Sit down."

I pull free of him and edge around Feluvas, who is rising to her feet. I back away, one step, two. I don't know where I'll go, but I know this is a bad place for me. There are too many of them.

"Stop her!" shouts the Arcon.

My heart leaps at the words, and I spin to run. A sword lowers in front of me. Gripping it is a young girl, perhaps fifteen. She wears a leather vest and gauntlets. She is small with a long blonde braid and a pretty face. She's familiar somehow. Her eyes widen like she recognizes me then her mouth gapes.

She cries out, "She's the one I told you about! The one who let me get away!"

Understanding hits. This is the young Warden that got me in so much trouble two weeks ago when I let her escape. And now she has just revealed who—or rather *what*—I am. What is it the Keldans say? No good deed goes unpunished.

The Arcon shouts, "Then she is a servant of the Unnamed! A Drifter!" He looks accusingly at Logan, and I use the moment to feel for my mooring.

Something is wrong. I can sense my mooring, but I can't access it. I fight down panic and try again. My mooring feels dim and far away. Fear surges. This has never happened before.

I back away, looking for space. I don't like to be trapped. The young Warden shifts toward me but keeps her sword neutral. She is conflicted. Maybe I can use that.

The Arcon tries to step around Logan, but Logan blocks him. Shouting, Aron tries to shoulder past. Logan grabs him, and the lantern swings wildly.

Other Earthmakers, perhaps a dozen of them standing back from the conflict, stir uncertainly.

I take a shuddering breath. I cannot run from here. There is only one escape. I breathe deeply, feel for my mooring, feel for the Drift. There! It feels wrong—sluggish, far away—but it's there. I try to slide into it, to will myself deep into its far off energies, but nothing happens. I am frozen, shocked.

A blast of air knocks me loose. The Drift vanishes. I slam into a body behind me and hear a surprised cry. A sharp pain slices my back. My knee bangs painfully against stone. My elbow lands on something soft.

The young Warden and I disentangle ourselves. Her sword, which slid across my back, scrapes against the stone floor as she scrambles away from me. I stagger to my feet and look to the real threat.

The Arcon's lantern is rolling across the floor, its light extinguished, its glass broken. The Arcon, face red with anger, grabs the front of Logan's shirt.

"Stop!" commands a smooth, melodious voice.

A woman flows into the hall, her light ivory robes tied with a silken coral sash. Her neck is long and slender, and blonde hair curls down her back.

"Mother!" Logan and the Arcon shout simultaneously.

Understanding clicks. They are brothers. Primo Loganos. Brother to the Arcon.

Their mother glides over to them, moving quickly without seeming to hurry. Like water.

KATHERINE BUEL

She lays a light hand on the Arcon's arm, and he lets go of Logan's shirt.

She looks from one son to the other. "What is going on?" When Logan, favoring his right leg, steps back from his brother, she cries, "Loganos! What happened to you? Aronos?" Her voice is a warning—no, it's an accusation.

"I didn't do that!" Aronos exclaims. "He came in that way. With her!" He points at me. "She's a Drifter, Mother, and a servant of the *Unnamed!*"

Along the wall, the hovering Earthmakers mutter. One steps forward, a man in loose night clothes.

"Prima Gaiana?" he directs at Logan's mother.

Prima. Logan's mother.

Primo Loganos.

"Polemarc Clitus, please help Korinna."

Polemarc Clitus. I know that name—and that title. He's the commander of the Wardens.

No.

Oh no.

"Mother!" Logan exclaims, but I don't hear the ensuing argument. I have more immediate problems.

Polemarc Clitus, who is short and thick for an Earthmaker, strides toward me. He is frowning, determined. Even in night clothes, with loose pants and his tunic hanging halfway to his knees, he looks dangerous. I edge away.

"Be easy, Drifter."

I step back again. I know I can't escape, but I can't just let him take me. Better to die fighting than to sit in a cell and wait for a headman's axe.

"Clitus! Clitus!"

Logan jogs—limps—toward us.

Clitus pauses. "The Prima has spoken, Loganos."

"I know. Just—wait. Let me help." Logan's eyes, swirling with color, are pleading.

Clitus's jaw tightens, but when no counter-command comes from the Arcon, he nods, and Logan brushes past him. As he approaches me, I back away again. He's helping them. He's turning on me. *Of course he is*, sneers a voice within. *What did you expect?*

Logan raises a hand as though to calm a frightened animal. "Astarti. Let them take you. You cannot fight them. We will figure this out."

"You're the Arcon's brother," I accuse him. I know he had no reason to tell me, that his part was well-played, but I still feel tricked, a little betrayed. He is a prince of Avydos. He will never help me. He probably never intended to. I've played right into their hands, have given myself to them.

"You must let Clitus take you."

I edge back again, feeling hopelessly for the Drift.

"You cannot drift from here. You cannot fight."

I reach half-heartedly for the Drift once more. Nothing. I can't escape. Even if I could, I have nowhere to go. I can't go back to Belos. His name brings a wave of fear. My Leash! He will find me, he—

He can't enter the Floating Lands.

This is the one place he can't get me.

Despite my situation, I feel a sudden sense of safety, of immunity. The Earthmakers may take my life, but they cannot take my mind.

Clitus shifts impatiently. I have to decide: would I rather die fighting or let them take me?

Logan's eyes plead; his hand reaches for me. He has not asked me to trust him, has not promised to protect me. Why would he? Of course his loyalty is to his people, to his family. But I remember his panic as he carried me. He was worried. He didn't want me to die. Could it be that he only wanted me to live so he could get information from me? They don't know how little Belos tells me; I must look like quite a prize. I don't know, I just don't know.

Suddenly, I am worn out, too tired to think. If only they would attack, I might find the strength and will to fight. But they don't. They wait.

Wearily, I incline my head. Polemarc Clitus stalks over and grips my arm.

Chapter 10

We pass from the main hall into one of the arched passageways. We're swallowed briefly by darkness, but I don't have to see; Clitus never eases his grip on my arm, and he clearly knows where we're going. Logan, the Arcon, the young Warden whose name I've already forgotten, and Prima Gaiana are behind us. The uneven footsteps are Logan's. I know I shouldn't care, but I'm worried about him. He should get off that leg.

We turn a corner to find an arched doorway filled with moonlight and pass through it into a large square courtyard. The courtyard is lined on all four sides with covered walkways, and we are moving through one of those, passing by sturdy columns. I hear wind rising beyond the building, but it doesn't reach us here. The dark shapes of the courtyard's trees are still. In the courtyard's center stands a pale stone fountain. Water trickles from the mouth of some sea creature that forms the central figure, the cheery bubble incongruous alongside our silent, tense passing. Around the sea creature are carved even stranger shapes, half human, half fish. I can't make out the details, and we are soon at the end of our walkway, moving again into darkness.

I try to memorize the turns, knowing I should collect information, but my mind won't focus well enough. My side hurts. I know it was partially Healed, or else I would probably be dead, but it bites at me, drains me. And I'm tired, so tired. I've used the Drift heavily today and been in several fights. I haven't eaten since I wolfed down the plateful of greasy meat at the Trader's Choice.

At some point, Clitus stops me. My eyes have adjusted to the dark, and I see him taking something from the wall. He goes silent and still, then fire blooms by his face, engulfing the head of a torch. I'm used to earthmagic, but I still jerk back at the gleam of his Earthmaker eyes. He looks euphoric, like Theron or any of the Seven when they use earthmagic. I wonder, do I look like that when I use the Drift? Somehow, I doubt it. Then again, I rarely enjoy those things I use the Drift to do.

The Polemarc turns and tugs me forward.

We pass into an older part of the building. I can smell its age. The airy entryway where all this started smelled clean and fresh, a mix of ocean breeze and healthy plants. Here the smell is musty and damp. In the flare of Clitus's torch, the stone is revealed to be darker and rougher, the ceilings lower. When we reach an opening, cool air seeps from it.

Clitus dips the torch toward a sconce secured to the old stone wall. The sconce flares to life, doubling the light, revealing a winding stair that can only lead to the cells. I try to breathe deeply, to calm myself; I knew this was where they would take me.

Each step down pulls at my side and the slice across my back. I'm starting to get dizzy again. When I waver, Logan's hand finds my shoulder blade. He steadies me, but he is trembling himself. With each step, he makes a low, restrained sound of pain. He's trying to be quiet, but in our silent procession even that small sound can't be hidden.

Clitus looks over his shoulder. "Loganos, you don't need to come down."

"Yes," Logan grits out. "I do."

By the time we reach the bottom of the stairs, Logan's hand is shaking so hard he takes it away. But he stands straight, and his face betrays little.

I can't quite match his control. My side flares with pain, spiking through my whole body. I hunch around the wound, and my back screams in protest as the movement opens the cut from the young Warden's sword and tugs at the scabbed lash marks that Belos left two weeks ago.

Logan's brow furrows. "Mother, can't you—"

I give a strangled cry when the Arcon shoves me in the back. I don't see it, but of course it's him.

Logan spins, and I hear the start of a fight. Prima Gaiana shouts, and they both go still, though I can hear heavy, furious breathing. Clitus leads me forward.

The torch reveals that we are in a fairly small underground room. There is a weapons rack, a table, and two chairs, which are no doubt for the guards they will position here. The air is cold and damp, like a tomb. I shudder and think: all that beauty above ground, but beneath it, the Earthmakers are just like the rest of us.

Beyond lies the cell door, heavy, with bars across its small window. Of course I'm not surprised, but my heart still thuds to see it. It seems impossible that only this morning I was released from a cell not unlike this one.

Clitus opens the door and leads me inside. There's a cot and chamber pot along one wall. Shackles are nailed to another wall, the cuffs lying on the ground. It reminds me of the Shackle, and my breath catches.

The Arcon commands, "Chain her."

Logan responds, the danger in his tone unmistakable, "No."

Relief teases at me. Will he protect me after all?

Gaiana says the Arcon's name chidingly, and he grumbles, "On your heads be it."

Clitus leads me to the cot and releases my arm. The prickling rush of blood to my hand tells me how hard he was gripping. I fall onto the cot and dust billows up from its thin cushion. No one has been in this cell for a long time.

Clitus moves away to stand at the door with the Prima and the young Warden.

The Arcon stalks near. "So," he says, crossing his arms. "Let's hear it. Who are you?"

I don't answer. I will him to go away.

He grabs my shoulder and slams me against the wall. I can't stop the cry of pain. Logan jerks his brother's hand away. More shouting.

I am dizzy, sick. The voices recede. The movement looks far away. I start to float.

The Prima crouches in front of me. Her light fingers tug at the slice in my dress, and I wince as fabric pulls away from the wound.

"It needs to be cleaned at least, but it should be Healed."

"You know the law, Mother. We don't Heal Drifters. And she's a servant of the enemy. It shouldn't even be a question."

Logan mumbles something.

The Arcon's voice sharpens, "It's absurd for me to be treated as cruel because I say so. I don't care if she's a girl. I don't care if she's young. I don't care if Logan's *fondness* for humans has blinded him—and neither should anyone else. She is our enemy, and she will be treated as such. If I didn't have questions for her, she would be dead already."

Gaiana's light gown rustles. "If you want her alive to answer your questions, then get me water and bandages. Better yet, bring Feluvas down to help."

The conversation continues, but I lose track of it, and of time. I float again.

I wake later to feel hands on me. I try to pull away, but they hold me still.

Someone unlaces my tattered dress, and I hear a gasp. I try again to draw away, knowing they are staring at me, at my lash marks. I feel fingers, sense a gathering around me. I start to struggle. The hands become soothing, the voices low.

I float again.

I open my eyes to see the Prima, golden hair lit by torchlight, fair skin seeming to glow. She looks at me from deep blue eyes, which are filled with curiosity. But no anger, no malice. Her face is smooth and lovely, and I can see that she is, indeed, Logan's mother.

I hear his voice but can't make out the words. I am too tired.

I float.

Chapter 11

I am running.

The barren Dry Land stretches before me with its yellow-gray dust. The sky is empty and blue.

I'm pushing as hard as I can, but my steps are slow, as though I am moving through water, even though the air is dry and hot.

Something is behind me.

I don't look back. I just run, fighting panic. I can feel the thing catching up.

A bony hand grabs my shoulder, digging into muscle and bone. As I fall, dumb with horror, Belos engulfs me in arms that are thin and hard as iron bars. His face is skeletal, eyes and cheeks sunken, skin tight like it's too small. His mouth, though, is huge and lined with sharp teeth. He dives at my neck, teeth gnawing, tearing.

ℝ ℞

I wake in darkness, gasping. I am frozen, too frightened to move or even scream.

Light falls through iron bars, lying in stripes over my chest. I'm in a cell. In Avydos.

§୦ ଓଃ

I am walking along a beach, looking for something. The waves crash toward me and draw away again. Sand washes from under my feet.

I hear a woman's voice in the distance. I run toward it, straining and desperate, but it drifts away.

§୦ ଓଃ

I am in the courtyard of the Dry Land, under the dead tree. Someone is fitting a pale, lightweight cuff to my small wrist. No words are spoken, but I hear them in my mind, *This will help you learn, Little Drifter.*

§୦ ଓଃ

I am in the Drift.

Energies flow around me: white, gold, silver, edges of blue. I am elated, overwhelmed by beauty.

Something tugs at me, below my heart. I look down into my own humming energies. A white cord flows from me and away, into the dark.

Something pulls the cord. I resist. It pulls harder. I plant myself against it, but it pulls harder still. I am dragged through the Drift, powerless, picking up speed. I thrash wildly but can't get free. I try to scream, but no sound comes.

CHAPTER 12

I wake shivering. I rub my arms for warmth and feel sleeves of soft linen. My head feels stuffed with wool, and I open bleary eyes. I'm still in the cell. Of course I am. Light falls in stripes through the barred window, crossing my chest. The light is not like the sun, which moves and changes. Time seems to have stopped for me.

I'm wearing strappy Earthmaker sandals, a loose linen shirt, and close-fitting wool pants. In the striped light, the pants look brown, the shirt blue. My side and back ache. When I put a hand to my torso, I feel layers of soft bandage.

I swing stiff legs over the side of the cot. Clutching my side to keep the wounds from pulling, I push myself up and shuffle groggily to the door.

I peer through the barred window. The young female Warden and another, a young male, sit at the table. They're playing a game of stones. The male studies the checkered board, a finger curled above his lip. The girl watches him, trying to hide her impatience. The male picks up a dark stone, holds it hovering over the board, then places it. The girl grins, and her hand darts toward one of the white stones. When she sets it down, the young man's face falls. Her grin widens.

The boy says, "I hate playing with you, Korinna."

"Come on, Nicanor," she teases. "It's good for you. Keeps that swollen head down to size."

I'm glad I let her escape, even if it meant trouble with Belos. I like her.

Korinna freezes then looks over to my window. "Nicanor, go tell Aron she's awake."

He protests, "Why don't—"

"You lost the game. Shut up and do it."

Nicanor pushes back from the table without further complaint and disappears up the stairs.

Korinna listens for his receding steps then rises from her chair. She crosses the small space to my cell. Her blonde hair is bound in a tight, intricate braid. She wears a leather vest, laced down the side. The front bears the print of a branching tree. Her eyes are deep and blue, like most Earthmakers'. Her cheekbones are high and, though her face is still soft with youth, she is already elegant.

As I study her, I decide that she does, indeed, look about fifteen. Earthmakers age at a normal rate until they are around twenty-five, so that is probably her true age. So young. Why on earth did they send such a young girl into danger? Of course, it was only by chance that Straton and I encountered her. She was spying on Martel much as we were. What, I wonder as I have so often over the last few weeks, is the Earthmakers' interest in Martel?

She says abruptly, "Thank you."

"For what?"

She rolls her eyes. "For letting me go that day. I know what you did."

"Oh. Yeah. Well."

She persists, "You saved my life."

It's true. I grabbed Straton's arm when the glow of Drift-energy formed around it. It was automatic, because all I saw was a young girl who would die a horrible death if Straton took her to Belos. What else could I have done?

She is staring me down, her earlier grin having vanished within a stern, earnest face. She wants an answer, but I'm not sure what kind.

I try to explain why I did it. "I know what Belos would have done to you."

She flinches a little at the name, and her expression grows troubled. She wants something more from me. I have made it worse, not better.

I change the subject. "What time is it?"

"Afternoon."

"I slept that long?"

"Longer than you think. Two nights."

I draw back, shocked. No wonder I'm so stiff.

I want to ask her what they will do to me, but I don't. I'm not naïve. They will question me, then kill me.

That knowledge seems to hang between us, silencing us both.

Korinna's eyes pinch briefly, like she's upset. "I tried to speak for you."

I nod. I suppose I should thank her, but the words won't come. Instead I say, "You shouldn't have bothered. It won't change anything."

"It might help."

"The Arcon will see me dead. I know enough of men to know that."

Korinna frowns. "He's not as bad as he seemed the other night. He gets angry with Logan. But he's calming down.

Earthmakers always do. He will make a good decision. Well, I mean he will argue for one."

A good decision for whom? And what does that mean, argue for one? I voice only the second question.

Korinna looks surprised, as though I should know. "He will present his argument to the Council."

Council? My heart sinks. Why did Belos not educate me better? "What does that mean? Doesn't the Arcon make all decisions?"

"Of course not. He must listen to the voice of the Council. Sometimes he may overrule them, but an Arcon can be removed from power if he does not work within the will of the Council, and of the people. Of course, no such thing has happened for generations."

"What about Prima Gaiana? She's his mother."

"She has a voice. Sometimes she speaks her will. But Aron has served as Arcon since his father, Arcon Arathos, was killed by the Unnamed. Five years ago."

That stirs a memory. I picture Belos and the Seven in the feasting hall. I had never eaten such a meal. Figs and dates, olives, candied almonds. Then my mind flicks to an image of what was impaled on a spear in the hall's center. Blood stained the haft of the spear. The face—gray with death, mouth gaping, eyes wide and dull—flashes into my mind. Arcon Arathos. Aron's father. And Logan's. I swallow hard and will the image to recede into the dark confines of my memory, where so many other things are hidden.

"I see. I understand why Aron hates me so much. You're a fool if you think he'll spare me."

"But you didn't kill Arcon Arathos. Logan was there, and he says it was the Unnamed. Logan never mentioned a girl."

I shake my head. "It won't matter. Don't you know anything about revenge?"

Her eyebrows draw down in confusion, and I realize that, though she may be only a few years younger than I am, she has lived much less. I turn away from the window and walk to my cot. I sit down, lean my head back against the rough wall. Korinna watches me, her expression frustrated.

"Korinna!" barks the Arcon's voice from behind her, and she jumps. "I told you no one was to speak to the prisoner before I did."

Korinna disappears from the window. "I will accept my punishment. What do you command?"

"Just go," he says irritably, and I hear the quick patter of her feet ascending the stairs.

Two sets of feet, one with the slap of sandals, the other booted and uneven, cross the stone floor to my cell. A key turns in the lock. The door creaks open.

The Arcon, dressed in a dark red tunic with broad short sleeves and geometric designs along its hem, sets a torch into an iron bracket by the door. His tunic, belted at the waist, falls to just above his knees, leaving his muscular lower legs bare except for the sandal straps that crisscross up his ankles.

I expect to find Logan in similar garb now that he's among his own people, so I'm surprised to see his leather pants and plain wool shirt as he comes in behind Aron, a head taller. He's still dressed like a Warden. His hair is clean and combed, but the tidiness and order are surface deep. His eyes are upset, shifting in the torchlight, and dark circles hang under them. He looks like he hasn't slept since the last time I saw him, which was, apparently, almost two days ago. He limps into the room. I frown. Why hasn't his leg been Healed?

The Arcon drags two stools from outside the cell into the center of it. He takes a seat, then stares at Logan until Logan does the same. Logan's movement is slow and awkward, and he leaves his right leg jutting out straight. The corner of his right eye tics.

The Arcon doesn't waste any breath. "Tell me what you were doing with Count Martel. What does your master want with him?"

"Why should I tell you anything?"

The Arcon looks smugly at Logan. "My brother here tried to give me the impression that you had turned against your master. Perhaps he misread your actions."

Logan ignores his brother's stare. "Astarti, you protected me from the Unnamed, as you protected Korinna, by her own account." This last he says loudly, directing it at his brother. "Why?"

"I don't know."

"You must have had a reason," challenges the Arcon.

"I didn't have a reason. I don't know why I did it. I just—I don't know. Don't you think Belos asked me the same thing?" The Arcon's eyes narrow when I say Belos's name, so I say it again. "Belos was…very angry."

Logan looks at me thoughtfully, frowning slightly. I can't see his eyes well with the torchlight behind him, but I imagine them swirling with color. "She did what she felt was right."

The Arcon snarls, "Don't feed her words to justify herself."

"Then how do you explain it?"

"If she's so full of conscience, why does she serve him?"

We are all silent a moment. I, for one, am happy to stay out of this conversation. Then Logan says slowly, making my guts twist, "She is Leashed, Aron."

The Arcon's glare jumps from Logan to me and back again. "Why didn't you tell me that before?"

Logan shrugs, and I almost smile. He seems to enjoy riling his brother. Logan takes a steadying breath before his next question, as though he's afraid of the answer. "Astarti, why did you let him Leash you?"

A chill runs through me. I shiver. I shake my head. I see myself curled up in the dusty courtyard, vomiting until my stomach is empty, Belos looming over me. Even here in Avydos, I feel the ghost of that violation, stirring up nausea. I feel my shame, my weakness. No. I won't tell them. I don't want to talk about it, don't want to even think about it.

"Well?" insists the Arcon.

I shake my head.

Logan leans close, lowers his voice. "Did he force you?"

The Arcon snaps, "Stop making guesses. You're leading her. You're determined to be on her side. Leashing is almost never forced. Besides, what use would he have for her?"

"Don't be stupid, Aron. She's a Drifter. What use do you think?"

"A simple Drifter? When he has the Seven to serve him?"

"Who's making guesses now? Do you know his mind so well?"

Aron's face purples, but he doesn't rise to Logan's bait. Instead he sneers, "So you're suggesting that she's a *captive* of the Unnamed?"

"Astarti." Logan's voice is gentle. "You said, that night that I pulled you from the Current, you said you didn't choose it. What did you mean?"

I am shaking, freezing. I cross my arms in front of my chest, holding tight.

"How old were you when he Leashed you?"

I can't breathe. I will be sick. Why would he ask that question?

"Please tell me." His eyes are intent but gentle, as though only he and I are in the room.

I look down but give him the word, because I can't seem to refuse him. "Seven."

I hear Logan's sharply indrawn breath, the angry curse. The Arcon is silent, still.

Logan says furiously, "He Leashed a child. I've never even heard of such a thing. Who would—how could he—" He cuts himself off, remembering whom he is talking about.

I stare at my knees. I do not like this attention. I'm exposed now for everyone to see. The legs of Logan's stool scrape across the floor. I feel his nearness. Part of me wants it, but another part of me wants him, both of them, to go away. When he touches my arm, I jerk back. I do not want to be touched.

The Arcon says, though there is no conviction in his voice, "She could be lying."

Logan ignores him. "Who are your parents? Where did he take you from?"

"I don't know."

"You don't remember?"

"I was a baby." My voice is flat, alien. I don't feel like I'm controlling it.

I wish they would just ask me about Martel. I wish they would beat me. I could endure those things. This, I can't stand.

Logan bends down and picks something up off the floor. A blanket. He pulls it around me. His hands linger on my shoulders.

I feel my eyes prickle with shame, so I do the only thing that will save me: I find my anger.

I stand from the cot and throw the blanket down. The wound in my side tears, but the pain is distant. "What do you want from me? Are you going to talk me to death?"

Logan rises, takes my arm. I jerk it free and punch him in the chest. I feel such release in it that I hit him again. He grabs my wrist. I don't look at his eyes; I don't want to see his disgust. I jerk free and march to the corner, as far from him as I can get.

"Leave me alone, both of you! If you want to kill me, fine! If not, get out of here!"

Both of them are still, wary.

I punch the wall, relieved by the flash of pain across my knuckles. "Go!"

The Arcon stands up. He strides from the cell, grabbing the torch from its bracket.

The cell dims as the light recedes. Logan, shadowed, stands within.

"Just go," I whisper, and, at last, he does.

I sink to the floor, cradling my throbbing hand, the fight quickly going out of me. Already, embarrassment is edging in. How stupid I must look to him. How weak. My head falls to my knees as two sets of footsteps recede up the stairs.

CHAPTER 13

I doze on my cot. I'm not sure how much time has passed, but I think it's still the same day. One of my new guards—Korinna seems to have been relieved of her duties—brought me a meal and water a few hours ago. I didn't want to eat it, didn't want to accept anything from my captors, but I was hungry. Lamb roasted in olive oil with rosemary and thyme, fresh white bread, honey—my stomach is growling for more. I guess I'm not very good at pouting or making statements. Or killing myself with starvation.

When footsteps approach my door, they are even, so I know they aren't Logan's. I brace as the key clanks in the lock, as the door swings open.

As a man walks in who is not the Arcon, I blink in surprise. Broad-faced, with red-gold hair, he looks much like Arcon Aronos, though his long hair is gathered at the nape of his neck instead of cut short, and his face is more careworn despite its calm surface. He's taller and leaner than the Arcon, built more like Logan. He wears a white Earthmaker tunic belted at the waist.

"Hello, Astarti."

"Who are you?"

He slides a torch into the bracket and walks over to my cot. I shift to the end when he sits down beside me. I am stiff, wary.

He studies me with his deep blue Earthmaker eyes. "I'm Bran. I came to see how you're doing. Logan is worried about you."

I don't allow myself to react.

"After he and Aron talked to you"—the forced casualness of his voice tells me that Logan reported on my actions. I squirm inwardly—"he came to find me. He wanted to come with me now, but I told him I wanted to meet you alone first."

I shift at that word, alone. A deeply ingrained distrust makes me tense. The guards have left, and an unknown man is in my cell. I have no weapons and can't access the Drift, though I've been trying all day. I feel exposed and vulnerable, and I don't like it.

My wariness must be obvious because he says, "I won't hurt you."

I say acidly, just so he doesn't think me frightened, "I'd like to see you try."

His mouth quirks. "Logan would throw me off Mount Hypatia. He's my brother."

Figured as much. "Any more brothers I should know about?"

He chuckles. "Don't worry. It's just the three of us."

"Your poor mother."

He grins. "Trust me, you don't know the half of it."

His light tone puts me at ease. "Let me guess: Logan was the wild child?"

Bran's red-gold eyebrows lift in mock surprise. "Whatever gave you that impression?"

I laugh, but when I hear myself I grow suddenly wary again. I can't let him trick me into trusting him. Bran is an Earthmaker, and he might be Logan's brother, but he is also the Arcon's brother. "What do you want from me?"

Bran sighs and leans back to study me again. Once I've grown thoroughly uncomfortable, he admits, "Logan wanted to know what I thought of you."

"Why?"

Bran looks briefly troubled. "Logan has been taught not to trust his own instincts, not to trust himself."

That doesn't really answer my question, but Bran's closed expression tells me it's all I'm going to get. "Where is Logan?"

"With our mother."

The Prima.

I still can't believe Logan is a Primo, a noble, which Bran, of course, must also be.

"Is he the youngest?"

Bran pretends to be offended. "Do I look so old?"

"You look older than he does."

"All right, fine. Yes, he's the youngest. By about thirty years."

I swallow my surprise and assure him, "You don't look *that* old."

His mouth quirks again. He's handsome, like Logan and, if I'm honest, like Aronos. He says offhandedly, "One advantage of being an Earthmaker, I guess."

That might be true, but I know they can still die young, and be hurt. I think of Logan limping, of the tic in the corner of his eye, telling me of pain and fatigue. "Is Logan all right? Why hasn't his leg been Healed?"

Lines set around Bran's mouth, and suddenly I believe that he is much older than he looks. "Logan is refusing to be Healed until you are."

That makes me sit back. "Why would he do that?"

"Because he wants you to be Healed, of course. He is trying to use it as leverage. Foolish. Aron won't cave to that."

"I thought the Arcon didn't have absolute power," I say bitterly. "What about your Council?"

Bran hesitates. "They agree with Aron."

"I bet they do."

"But he's not a bad man, Astarti, though that may be hard for you to believe right now. He is angry, yes. But he tries to do what's right. To live up to our father."

The image of Arcon Arathos's severed head leaps into my mind again. Before I can stop them, the words escape me: "I'm sorry. About your father."

I could never have said that to Aronos, but it feels right to say it to Bran.

Bran only looks at me. "How old are you, Astarti?"

"Seventeen. Why?"

"My father died five years ago. You were twelve. I hardly think you bear any responsibility for it."

"Aron thinks I do."

"Aron was very close to our father." His voice grows bitter when he adds, "Don't feel singled out. He blames himself, too. And Logan."

"Why would he blame Logan?"

"Logan was there. He was badly hurt, but he survived. Our father did not."

I remember the terrible scar on Logan's chest. I wonder who did it. Straton? Ludos? Theron? Belos himself?

I say, "That hardly seems like Logan's fault."

"It's not. But Aron has convinced him that it was. Not that Logan needed much convincing. He already felt responsible."

I hear the subtle anger in Bran's voice, and I realize that he truly cares for Logan. Not just with a sense of familial duty. They are friends. This makes me like him. I hesitate, then prompt, "Logan seems...different...from other Earthmakers."

The torchlight plays over Bran's face as he studies me. "You're very interested in him."

I feel myself blush. I hope Bran can't see it in the wavering light.

He says gently, "He's curious about you also."

My jaw hardens. I'm letting myself grow soft, exposing myself again. I tighten things up by saying, "He just wants to know whether to agree with the Arcon or not."

"I don't think so." There's a question in his eyes that makes me uncomfortable. How did this become about me again?

"Can I ask you a question, Astarti?"

I stay silent, wary, not committing.

"Why do you think Belos took you as a baby?"

The question surprises me. "I don't know. Because I'm a Drifter? I never really thought about it."

Bran looks thoughtful, troubled. "You know nothing of your parents?"

"No."

"You have no mementos from them?"

I think of the Griever's Mark, the one thing my mother left me. "No."

"Hmm."

Bran falls silent. He leans back against the wall, hands on his knees, fingers drumming slowly. The torchlight wavers in a breeze I can't feel.

Finally, I demand, "What?"

"Belos is smart."

"Yes."

"He does things for reasons. He plans."

I frown. "How do you know so much about him?"

"He was once one of us, remember? I was very young, but I remember him, in the beginning."

I'm surprised to hear an Earthmaker acknowledge Belos as one of their own. I also find it strange to think of Belos before he became what I know him to be. I'm about to ask Bran about the younger Belos when footsteps sound on the stairs. One set is heavy, uneven, and I'm surprised by how relieved I am to hear Logan. The other set is light, almost silent. Not the Arcon, then.

When Logan and Prima Gaiana enter the cell, Bran quips, "Couldn't stand it, could you?"

Logan grunts and limps over to us.

I snap at him, "Let them Heal you, for pity's sake. What's wrong with you? Do you want to ruin your leg?"

Gaiana comes to his shoulder in a flow of pale green robes. They are gathered at the shoulders in the Earthmaker style. "See, Logan? Astarti agrees with me."

Logan crosses his arms stubbornly. "Like I said, her first."

Gaiana mutters, "Aron is going to be furious," but she floats over to me and motions Bran off the cot.

He practically leaps out of her way, and she settles beside me. I smell jasmine and eye the elegant fall of her wavy blonde hair. I am suddenly self-conscious of my own, unwashed appearance. My hair feels greasy, and I know I must smell bad.

Gaiana reaches for me then pauses, waiting for my permission. I hesitate before nodding. She shifts closer and lifts the hem of my shirt.

"Hold this," she commands gently, and I take the lifted edge.

Her fingers work the bandage loose and unwrap it. Logan and Bran both shift uncomfortably, looking away, looking back, looking away, and I stifle a snicker at their discomfort.

As the facts start to click, I ask in surprise, "You're a Healer?"

"Yes. Feluvas and I are the only ones in Avydos. It's a rare gift."

I am awed by this, that the Prima is about to Heal me.

As Gaiana drops the bandage, which is stained with dried blood, I hear Logan's sharply drawn breath. I study the wound myself. It looks several weeks old, partially Healed already, but it's still ugly. A round hole, raw, ringed with bruising. Gaiana looks at my back, and I feel her fingers tremble slightly.

I tense, thinking she is looking at the Griever's Mark, but she asks breathlessly, "Did *he* do this to you?"

Ah. The lash marks. I know "he" means Belos, but I don't know why it should be a question, why it should surprise her.

"Yes."

Her fingers curl against my back. "Why?"

The question almost sounds rhetorical, as though she is not expecting an answer, but I say, "For letting a Warden get away."

"Korinna."

"Yes."

"You saved her life. Thank you."

I shift uncomfortably and clear my throat. Why do these people have to make everything so awkward?

She persists, "You saved my son as well."

I say roughly, wishing she would dispense with the thanks, "He was only in danger because he was saving me."

Gaiana studies me from deep blue eyes, looking suddenly like Bran. "Why do you diminish everything you do?"

When I start to pull away, Gaiana's hands grow firm, and she places them over my wounds. I freeze when I feel again that sense of immersion: water, earth, air, fire. I am swimming, enveloped, floating, burning. The elements move around and through me; I am part of them. My heart seems to lift from my body.

Then it's gone, and I gasp. I'm cold, in a dank cell. I ache with loss, wondering if that is what it feels like to command earthmagic.

Gaiana sits back. She is studying me once more, but there is something different in her expression this time. Is it suspicion? Fear? What did she feel in me? My Leash, perhaps? Can an Earthmaker feel that? She opens her mouth as though to say something but closes it again, and her expression returns to smoothness.

I look away, certain she was only sensing my dirtiness. I prod my stomach where a faint scar marks my flesh. I am whole. I've never known such power, not in Belos, not in the Drift.

I swallow hard. "Thank you, Lady."

Gaiana smiles at the Keldan word, and I color. Again she looks about to say something, but it vanishes once more.

I clear my throat and look to Logan, whose expression betrays his relief. His whole body sags, as though tension has drained from him and left him exhausted. I was right: he was worried. No one has ever worried about me before. I can't help it; it makes me feel warm. "Now you."

"Later. I want to talk to you now."

Everyone, it seems, has questions for me.

Gaiana saves me. "You are not walking up those stairs again on that leg. Sit down. Right now."

I pop up from the cot without being told, marveling at the easy, pain-free movement. I slip over to Bran as Logan limps to the cot.

Gaiana says, "I need to be able to touch it.

Logan looks flustered. "I'm not taking down my pants."

"Then cut a hole in them. I don't care. But I need access to the injury. Right now." She snaps her fingers, and I smile privately to see the Prima vanish within the mother.

Logan sighs. He unbuckles his belt and unlaces his pants. Now it's my turn to shift uncomfortably. I look away, staring at Bran's shoulder, at the torch, at the door.

When I hear Logan sit with a thump, I glance back. Black undershorts show below the hem of his tunic. His legs are long and muscled, well-shaped. My heart skitters. I have never stared at a man's body before, but I know I'm staring now. He unwinds a white bandage from his right leg, and I draw a sharp breath at the sight of the bruising and swelling. The ragged puncture seeps blood. I am suddenly furious with him for not letting it be tended.

So is Gaiana. She's shaking her head, muttering, and I'm sure I hear the word "idiot" in there somewhere.

She falls silent when she puts her hands on the wound. Logan grunts in pain at the touch, then sighs as the wound Heals. When he sags against the wall, I realize how much it has been hurting him, and I'm furious all over again.

When he stands to pull up his pants, I look away. Only when I hear the slide of his belt do I dare turn my face back.

When I see Bran's face relax, I realize how tense he was also. Relieved silence fills the cell.

Logan breaks it with, "Give us a moment."

Bran and Gaiana's hesitation tells me that Aron has likely forbidden this, but I'm glad to see them incline their heads. Even if I don't want to answer more questions, I want a moment with Logan when others aren't looming. I want to judge his loyalties and his intentions. I tell myself there is nothing more to it, that it has nothing to do with simple *wanting*. Deep down, I know myself a liar.

Gaiana lingers in the doorway a moment. She studies me, and I sense once more that trace of suspicion, of an unasked question. None of the others have hesitated with their questions. Why does she?

Finally, she takes Bran's offered arm. Logan and I are frozen, waiting for privacy. Overlaying Bran and Gaiana's footsteps are their voices, but they are too low for me to make out the words.

When we're alone, with the torchlight flickering over Logan's shoulder and playing along his jawline, he says, "I need to know something, Astarti."

My name in his mouth is a wave, with crests and troughs of sound, drawn out and lovely. Usually, people pronounce it harshly.

I train my own voice to steadiness. "What?"

He takes a step closer. "Why did you not kill me when you first had the chance? Why did you not let Belos do it later?"

"You Earthmakers dig and dig until you get the answers you want. I already told you I didn't know."

"I believe you. Partially. I want more."

I am keenly aware of the small space between us, the way we are both torn between closing it and distancing ourselves.

He asks, "Have you ever killed anyone?"

"Yes. Have you?"

"Yes."

Silence.

Then he asks, "Are you ashamed of any of your kills?"

An image flashes. A young man with a cleft lip crouching in a horse stall. Belos, eyes livid, snarling at him, "Deal breaker." Belos staring at me. "Kill him." Belos's fingers clenching on my throat. Blood spraying across the straw and wood paneling of the stall, dripping into the feed trough.

I close my eyes, willing darkness to fill me and take away this memory.

I feel Logan draw near. He lifts my chin, lets go when I open my eyes. There's too much shadow for me to read his eyes. He asks again, gentle but insistent, "Why did you not kill me?"

"Belos may own me. But he does not *own* me." I shake my head, frustrated. I cannot explain this; I can only feel it. I try again, "I will not just be his creature. I am, I know. But I will not."

I turn away, grind my palms against my eyes in aggravation. Why must he drag up such things?

Logan's fingers touch my shoulder. "He doesn't own you."

Even though I just said that, I cannot agree with him. "I am *Leashed*, Logan."

"He doesn't own you. You will break free."

I laugh hollowly. "A Leash cannot be broken."

"Not unless he dies."

The laugh, bitter and ugly, shakes through my whole body. "Right," I say sarcastically. "Unless he dies."

Logan's fingers tighten, digging painfully into my shoulder. "Don't lose hope."

"Don't you see, Logan? I haven't lost it. I never had any to begin with." The words burn like acid in my mouth, in my chest.

"Yes, you did. And you do. Or you wouldn't have saved me. Or Korinna. You have not given yourself fully to him, even though he's all you've ever known. I don't pity you, Astarti. I am angry on your behalf, but I don't pity you because you are strong and don't need it. You need faith in yourself. That's all."

I swallow a lump in my throat. No one has ever spoken to me like this. It feels good, but it hurts, too. It daunts me. He's suggesting that I challenge Belos, defy him. I know I did that already when I protected Logan, but I wasn't really thinking then, and it was a small act anyway. Do I have anything more in me?

I don't know when Logan leaves. I am deep within myself, thinking.

෪ ෬

I am sitting on my cot, running my fingers through the stripes of light that fall over my knees, when someone tromps angrily down the stairs. I've been trying to access the Drift, getting a little closer. Once, I summoned a light into my palm, though I let it go quickly in case the guards outside noticed.

I hear sharp words, the Arcon telling the guards to go.

Then Polemarc Clitus's voice calls after them, "If one of you tells Loganos, you will both answer to me."

That makes my heart skip.

I am standing, fists clenched, when the key rattles in the lock. The Arcon wrenches the door open, and it bangs against the wall.

"You," he says, "will give me some answers."

CHAPTER 14

The Arcon's voice cracks like a whip, and I wonder what set him off.

He doesn't leave me in suspense.

"First, you beguile my brother; now you have my mother convinced of the most absurd nonsense. What is this? Some Drift-work? Some manipulation your master has taught you?"

"What are you talking about?"

"Don't play with me."

My heart pounds in warning, but thankfully my voice holds steady. "I really don't know what you're talking about. I don't know what you mean about Logan. Or the Prima."

He sneers, "Of course you don't."

Clitus says, "Aron, focus."

The Arcon grits his teeth. I'm shocked by how much he hates me. Even Straton, with his sly condescension, doesn't show it like this.

Aron takes a shuddering breath, and that Earthmaker control slides over him. His voice is suddenly brusque, even cool when he asks, "What is your master's interest in Martel?"

His abrupt shift takes me aback, but I recover quickly, and I sneer at him as he has done at me. "You need me to answer that? He wants to Leash him, of course."

My sharp answer cracks Aron's calm façade. He glares. "You might pretend to be stupid, but I don't believe you actually are. Why does your master"—he emphasizes the word nastily— "want him Leashed?"

"Beyond the obvious purpose of absorbing Martel's lifeforce and increasing his own power?" I don't know why, but I can't help but needle Aron. He only stares at me. "I'm still not sure why you need me to tell you. Belos"—I love watching him flinch when I say Belos's name—"wants to control the next king of Kelda."

"As simple as that, is it?"

My mouth opens on a snarky reply when Clitus cuts in, "Why Martel? What does he offer? The Unnamed could choose any man."

I have to accord Clitus a grudging respect. At least he asks the right questions. Still, he shouldn't have to ask me. "Don't your Wardens know? Isn't that their job? Do you not realize how many men Martel has gathered?"

Clitus's face is stone. "None have reported a sizable force."

I cross my arms, growing more comfortable. For the moment, I have the power here. "Clearly you haven't been watching Martel long enough. Or closely enough. He got stupid because he panicked"—I don't add that I manipulated him into that—"and he almost ruined everything for himself, but he's been preparing for years."

Clitus demands, "How?"

"Gathering supporters obviously." Unfortunately, I am already reaching the end of my knowledge. I know Martel has men hidden in the mountains east of Tornelaine. I've heard rumors that there are more to the north. Beyond that, I'm as ignorant as Aron and Clitus. Because I'm still annoyed, I poke them again. "Why haven't your Wardens reported this to you?"

Aron and Clitus share a furious look. I've touched a nerve. Then I grimace inwardly; I hope I haven't just gotten Logan in trouble. He is, after all, one of those Wardens.

The Arcon turns a stiff face to me. "Logan reports that you held a private conversation with Martel. You offered him a deal?"

"Yes."

"The terms?"

"Haven't we covered this? Martel will be Leashed. Belos will support him in his war."

"But the Unnamed will control him."

I grin wickedly. I have never enjoyed this part of the deals, but I am enjoying Aron's horror. "That part is always...implied."

Aron's look of disgust gives me a wash of satisfaction.

Clitus flicks a warning glance at Aron before eyeing me. "And what was Martel's response to your offer?"

I hesitate. Nothing I have yet said has given them useful information, but I don't know how they will use this next fact. Do I want to help them? Then I wonder: why am I protecting Belos?

I admit, "He refused."

Aron's shoulders drop in relief.

"Why do you care about Martel?"

Aron snaps, "I'm asking the questions," so quickly that I know my question matters.

I cross my arms confidently. "He will give in to Belos eventually. It's only a matter of time."

Aron shoots me a dirty look.

I ask, not letting go of my suspicions, "Why is he important to you?"

"Do you really think I would give information to a spy of Belos?"

I blink in surprise. It had not occurred to me that they might think me a spy.

The Arcon stalks closer, stopping just beyond arm's reach. "You can play innocent all you want, but you won't fool me. You did a very good job of fooling my brother, but I'm sure that was all part of your master's plan."

I am struck dumb for a moment because I can see the logic behind his suspicion. I can also see that it will be impossible for me to prove him wrong. I say simply, my voice tight because I know he won't believe me, "I'm not a spy."

"Oh, you'll have to do better than that."

I wonder out loud, "Why didn't Belos think of this?"

"Better, but I'm still not convinced."

I look up in surprise. It's dim in here, but everything in the Arcon's body language tells me that his eyes are glowing with satisfaction. With triumph.

"Didn't you think we would suspect you?"

"I didn't think. That's not why I'm here. I never *expected* to be here."

"Your master must value your life very little to have sent you."

"You're right he doesn't value my life, but I'm still not a spy."

Frankly, I'm at a loss. I cannot prove my claim. "Why don't you just kill me then?"

"What's this? Giving up already?"

"I can't prove you wrong, as you well know. You're toying with me. Just get it over with."

Aron frowns, disappointed that I won't argue. His eyes narrow. "Why do you serve him?"

That rouses me, as he meant it to, and I snap, "I already told you that."

"Right. Leashed as a child."

The way he says it—condescending, disbelieving—makes me feel ugly. What a horrible lie that would be. I tell him, "You're as cruel in your own way as he is. Because you understand where to hurt people."

He doesn't like the comparison. He storms toward me, grabs my arm. "I will not be insulted by a servant of the Unnamed."

I jerk my arm free. "Touch me again, and I will break your face."

He grabs me anyway and starts wrestling me toward the wall. "You will learn respect. The shackles, Clitus!"

The familiar word sends a thrill of terror through me. I twist frantically. I'm free only a moment before Aron's hands latch onto me again. I reach for the Drift, hunting it through that strange haze, finding my dim mooring.

I spin toward Aron. Light flashes hotly from my hand. It's not much, but it makes Aron cry out in surprise.

I turn instinctively for the open cell door, but I have taken only two steps when the earth shakes. Soil and stone erupt from the floor. They rise in a barrier around me, closing rapidly.

Reaching for the Drift, I feel it dimly, but my world is stone, stone, stone. Above, around, below. Blackness. The arguing voices are far away. I am buried, my nose filled with the smell of deep earth, my body pressed by its cold, hard bones. I can barely breathe. I search for the Drift, search for the power within myself, but there is only stone.

I will not die like this: buried alive, suffocating.

I pound at my stone prison, my hands bursting with pain. I push with my mind, willing it to give way.

I sense a tingling response, like the Drift but different. I latch onto it, press myself into it. I am filled with the ponderous weight of stone, the deep, sleeping energy. And energy, I understand. I draw on it, make it bend to me. The energies respond, shifting, shifting.

I push harder with my mind—with my will. Finally, it breaks, like a dam bursting as it surrenders to the will and force of water.

Stone crumbles.

I fall through the rubble.

My knees strike stone with sharp pain, but I scramble to my feet. Dust swirls in the rectangle of torchlight made by the open cell door. Stone litters the cell. Aron and Logan—I jerk a little to see him—lower their swords. Polemarc Clitus staggers back.

"That"—Aron swallows—"is impossible."

Chapter 15

"What's impossible?" I say into their silence.

Aron and Logan share a look.

"How did you do that?" Clitus demands, his broad, plain face filled with shock. Or horror? I'm not sure.

"Do what?"

He says weakly, "You broke the stone."

Logan lowers his sword and picks his way through the rubble. He gazes at me wonderingly. "My mother was right."

"About what?"

"It doesn't change anything," Aron argues. "What difference could it make? She's still a spy."

"You don't really believe that, Aron," Logan says with annoyance.

"Why not? It makes more sense than her story."

"There's no evidence."

"She's here. That's evidence enough."

When Aron starts toward us, Logan growls, "Stay back."

"Why do you defend her? What would Father think of you right now?"

A sound rumbles from deep in Logan's throat.

Clitus says, businesslike, "Loganos, what are your intentions?"

"Astarti comes with me."

The Arcon and the Polemarc say at once, "No."

"She's not a spy and she's not a danger. And if you weren't so blinded, you would recognize that she could be a useful ally."

That chills me a little. Is that what Logan wants of me, why he's been defending me? He wants to use me against Belos?

Aron's eyes gleam with anger. "You will never be able to trust her."

Logan darts a look over his shoulder at me. "Get to the door."

Clitus edges forward. "Loganos, you cannot take her. You can't just decide on your own and expect others to accept it."

Logan raises his sword to halt Clitus and his brother. "Now, Astarti," he says, and I move, picking through the rubble.

Clitus says warningly, "Logan, do you realize what you are doing?"

Logan hesitates a moment, regret flashing briefly across his face, then he follows me from the cell.

℘ ℭ

Despite my expectation that we will be swarmed by guards at any moment, no one meets us at the top of the stairs. Logan takes the lead, and we're soon running along one of the covered walkways lining the interior courtyard. I squint in the strong light. After days of shadow and torchlight, I had begun to think of all time as night, and the square of blue above the courtyard looks surreal to me.

We enter another hallway, also empty, and jog to what at first I take for a dark, dead end. Logan feels along the wall while I wait impatiently behind him, looking over my shoulder every two seconds.

A bolt scrapes into its housing, and the hidden door swings open onto an overgrown stone path lined with trees. I follow Logan onto the path, which rises to higher ground. At first, we are so enclosed in green that little else makes an impression on me. Then the trees begin to open.

I stop. Logan calls my name, but I am frozen, stunned.

Through a break in the trees, I look down into a broad horseshoe bay with rocky arms. Sunlight sparkles on the water, rippling over it like a living thing. Pale stone buildings, some round with domed roofs, some square and flat, seem to grow out of the rocky slope. Wide porches and balconies stretch before the buildings, and columns and balustrades stand everywhere. Bridges arch over numerous little waterfalls, and trees and gardens color everything.

Logan appears beside me. He takes my hand, gives it a quick squeeze of understanding, and tugs me onward.

Our path takes us over stone bridges, where the water hurries beneath, and up flights of stairs. The air is cool and moist, and I smell greenery and stone and soil.

Ahead, smooth round columns mark some kind of boundary. Logan doesn't hesitate before he runs between them. I follow and find myself in a wood. Though the trees are beautiful and healthy with little undergrowth or dead wood, there is no question: this wood is wild. I feel it in my bones.

Logan has slowed to a walk and I follow him between thick trunks, some flaky with papery bark, others rough and ridged. The hair rises on my neck and arms. Something is brushing over me, brushing *through* me. I spin, swatting, but nothing is there.

But something, somehow, is touching me. Something conscious, living.

I stop, breathing roughly, fighting panic.

Logan stops, looks back. Surprise wrinkles his forehead. "You feel it?"

"What is it?"

"Don't be afraid."

I repeat, more insistent this time, "What is it?"

He comes back to me. "The Wood. I'm surprised you feel it. Well, I guess, maybe I shouldn't be." He gives me a searching look that I don't understand. "The Wood is one of the best guards we have against the Unnamed."

"What do you mean?"

"It would never let him through."

"How can it…" I gesture, unable to find the words.

"The trees here are awake. Aware of themselves and of us."

I stare at him dumbly.

A look of impatience crosses his face, but he drives it away and explains, "The Current flows between all trees. They're connected in a way that even the Earthmakers don't fully understand. Any Earthmaker—even the Unnamed—can enter the Current. But not here. The Wood is different from other woods. Other trees are idle. Asleep, I guess. They take no notice of who passes by them. But the trees here *do* notice. And they make their own decisions."

My mind races with this disturbing information. A sudden thought occurs to me. "You brought me here through the Current, didn't you?"

"It was that or swim."

"It let me in?"

Logan hesitates before he admits, "It didn't want to, but yes."

I look around at the trees with distrust, expecting them to lash out with limb and branch, to devour me. I shiver at the thought of their consciousness.

From far behind, voices shout.

Logan shifts anxiously. "Astarti, take my hand."

"Why?"

"They're too close. We must use the Current."

"But the trees—"

"Take my hand."

His eyes, which I have actually never seen in daylight before, swirl with bright blue and green. They beg me for trust. They are beautiful.

I put my hand in his.

ℰ ℛ

The Current is a whirlpool of gold, and I feel the truth of Logan's words: the trees are alive, aware. They reach out with ghostly fingers, and their touch is light, chilling. I shiver in fear. They see my heart, my Leash. They know what I am.

Logan's wild energy shifts beside me. He says nothing, but he smiles assurance. I let him pull me into the flow.

Fingers trail over me, tugging now and then, reaching into my energies. It is uncannily like a pull on my Leash, and I don't like it.

Suddenly, Logan is tugging at me, and I feel the suck and draw of the Current, reluctant to let me go. I break free abruptly and tumble into Logan.

Blue sky and trees flash across my vision as I fall, taking Logan with me. He hits the earth with a thump, my shoulder driving into his sternum.

I scramble off him, planting a hand on his hip in my haste. I snatch it back. "Sorry."

He rubs his chest, sitting up. "We made it," he says in relief, and I realize with a chill that he wasn't sure we would.

"What would have happened if the Wood hadn't let us"—I don't say "me"—"pass through?"

Logan drops his eyes and says again, firmly, "We made it."

He stands and offers me his hand. My heart is still pounding with fear of the Wood, but his offered hand makes me smile wryly. I'm not exactly a lady to be helped prettily to her feet. I take his hand anyway. It's warm and dry, calloused along the palms from years of sword practice. The touch is like a shock of energy from the Drift; it shoots from my hand and up my arm, into my breast. I take my hand back quickly. He gives me a puzzled look, and I am suddenly awkward. I clasp my hands together in front of me.

We're at the edge of a wood—is this still part of *the* Wood?—in the foothills of mountains. They rise beyond the trees into rocky, jagged peaks.

"Where are we?"

"The Outer Islands."

Though Avydos is located on the large, central island of the Floating Lands, I know that numerous smaller islands lie scattered around it. Beyond that, I know nothing.

Logan jerks his chin. "Come on."

A faint trail, little more than a goat path, winds through the foothills. It's littered with loose stone, and the smooth soles of my sandals make me slide. What I wouldn't give to have my boots right now. I left them at the Trader's Choice. They're probably already out with the trash.

We're moving down, not up, and the trees soon give way to scrub. Before long I hear sea gulls. After perhaps half an hour, the ocean comes into view. My breath catches. On the horizon, pale blue sky meets dark water. The water lightens as it reaches toward the beach, its deep, rich blue melting into bright turquoise until the white sands emerge.

As we wind down to the beach, coarse rock smoothes into sand beneath my feet. A breeze comes off the water, light and cool, slipping through the weave of my linen shirt and wool pants. I rub my arms for warmth and remember that it's not yet summer.

The beach is small, a slim white crescent between slopes of sharp-bladed sea grass. I want to know where we're going, but the moment is so beautiful that I hesitate to shatter it with questions. Instead, I study Logan as he walks ahead of me. This is the first chance I've had to really look at him without his notice. His white linen shirt slides over the muscles of his shoulders and back, tugging with each step to show the cut of his waist. Dark blonde hair curls along his collar, messy as usual. The sword at his waist hangs comfortably; he is obviously used to moving with a blade and clearly was quick to replace the one that Belos broke. The black leather of his pants is scuffed, and I can't help but think that he dresses nothing like his people and that he looks very rough for a noble, if that's the right word for a Primo. I like it.

As we slog across the beach, sand working its way into my sandals and between my toes, I notice a house tucked into the rolling sand hills. The house is white and has the smooth look of plaster.

"Who lives there?" I ask.

Logan stops in surprise, as though it had not occurred to him that someone might occupy the house. "No one."

"No one?"

"I found this place when I was young. It was abandoned even then. I don't know who lived there. An old hermit, most likely."

"Are there many old Earthmaker hermits?" I ask teasingly.

Logan's mouth quirks. "You'd be surprised."

As we draw near the house, I see that it is, indeed, abandoned. Wind and sand have worn away much of the plaster, leaving patches of exposed beams. Many of the roof tiles are broken or missing. Stone steps, almost entirely covered with sand, lead to the door, which hangs crookedly. The windows are shuttered, though one has fallen off its hinges and into the sand.

Logan opens the door, which scrapes against the stone porch. He motions me inside with a grand gesture.

"Home," he announces.

Chapter 16

Sand has blown through the door and open window and lies in beautiful, whipped patterns over the red tile floor. A table stands along the back wall under a wide shelf that holds bowls and plates, jars, lanterns, tools, and candles. Along another wall is a faded green and blue curtain that probably separates a sleeping area from the main room. In the fireplace, a kettle hangs on a blackened chain and a grate straddles long-dead coals. A thick, dusty sheepskin lies before it.

Logan takes a ratty broom from beside the door. He begins to sweep briskly, and I move out of his way to stand by the fireplace. When the worst of the sand is gone and dust dances in the light, he leans the broom against the wall again.

"I'll fix the door. Will you go get some water? There's a freshwater stream about a hundred yards that way." He points.

I am dumbfounded by these ordinary tasks after all that has happened.

Logan disappears through the door and returns a minute later with a wooden shoulder yoke from which two buckets are suspended by rope.

I stare at him in disbelief. "What are we doing?"

"Are you not thirsty?"

"Logan."

He takes a shuddering breath, and his eyes meet mine with a brief swirl of color. "I don't know, Astarti."

I reproach myself. It's not like any of this was planned. And he has just put himself in great trouble with his brother, the Arcon, and with his Polemarc. For me. Of course he doesn't know what we're doing, not any more than I do. I take the yoke and fit it to my shoulders. I manage a smile, hoping it doesn't look too grim.

I find the stream easily. It's about ten feet wide and three deep. I crouch in the sand beside it and cup water in my hands to drink. The water is cold, no doubt coming from the snowcapped mountains. The taste is clean. I fill the buckets.

When I return to the house—more of a hut, really—Logan is testing the swing of the door. A hammer lies on the ground by his foot.

"Is carpentry part of a Warden's customary training?"

He looks up in surprise, then smiles a little, not answering my question.

I set the water by the empty fireplace and eye the dusty sheepskin. I roll it up and take it outside to shake it. Dust and sand fly from it, making me cough. Even Logan hides behind a sleeve.

He says, eyes watering, "I'll take the boat out."

"Boat?"

"It's behind the house. Hopefully still sound. There aren't food supplies here anymore, so it's fish or nothing."

Again I want to ask him what we are doing, what the *plan* is, but I hold it back. I nod.

From the doorway I watch Logan drag the boat from behind the house and down to the water. Nets and spears litter the hull. Logan's movements are brisk, a little jerky, and I realize how worried he must be.

I go down to the beach to collect driftwood for a fire. The boat is close enough that I can see Logan rowing. I worry briefly. It's a very small boat in a big ocean, and clouds are forming.

Several trips to and from the house builds a substantial pile of driftwood. I find flint on the mantel and am surprised. Wouldn't an Earthmaker just call on fire? Why use these tools?

Soon a fire is crackling, and water heating in the kettle. I find soap and a linen towel on the shelf above the table. I pour hot water into a large earthenware bowl and sit on the sheepskin by the fire. I scrub my face and body with a corner of the towel and wash my hair as best I can. When I am done, I throw the dirty water outside and resettle myself by the fire, drying my hair with the cleaner parts of the towel.

The flames dance and warm my face. I've always loved the play of fire. It fills my eyes and mind until I'm nothing but flame. The rest of the world dies away. Worries fade.

When a spark pops and lands on my exposed arm, I start. I look around, expecting…something. But there is only the quiet room, its simple features lovely in the half light of the fire. Beyond there is sand and ocean. No people. No conflict.

This place is, most definitely, an escape. Logan said he found it when he was young. What was he escaping then?

The rain starts a muted patter on the tile roof. I enjoy it at first, but then I think of Logan out on the water. I go to the door but can see nothing on the dark stretch of water. The rain isn't heavy, but it's cold.

My hair is almost dry when I hear Logan pull the boat around the side of the hut. When he comes in with a bucket, I smell fish and salt water. He lets the bucket drop with a thump and comes straight to the fire. He crouches beside me, chafing his hands together near the flames. His wet shirt clings to his back, and water drips from his hair onto his neck. He's shivering.

"You're freezing. Are there any blankets?"

His teeth clack when he says, "Behind the curtain."

When I pull the curtain aside, I find a narrow sleeping cubby with a bed and a chest at the bed's foot. I open the chest. It's too dark now to see anything much, but I feel wool and sheepskin. I gather an armful and return to Logan. I drop the pile to the ground and dig through it for a heavy blanket.

"Take off your shirt. It's soaked."

He hesitates. Then he pulls the shirt over his head. My breath catches when I see the scars crisscrossing his back. They are deep, puckered, evidence of a much worse lashing than Belos gave me. Probably multiple lashings. He is tense, expecting me to comment, hoping that I don't. When I drape the blanket over his shoulders, the tension goes out of him. He doesn't look at me. I hand him a towel for his hair. He scrubs quickly and starts to get up.

I press fingers to his shoulder. "Stay. Get warm. I'll start the fish."

"There's some olive oil in the stone jar. It might still be usable."

I find the jar on the shelf and pop the cork. I take a wary sniff. It has the usual rich aroma. I dip my finger in and taste. My mouth waters, and my stomach rumbles in expectation. I pour a little oil into a cast iron pan. Selfishly, I'm relieved to see that Logan has already gutted the fish.

I slide the pan onto the grate straddling the fire. When it's hot, I drop in the fish. Oil splatters, making me jerk back.

"Careful," Logan warns, and I smile at the irony. This is certainly among the least dangerous moments of our day.

"I don't suppose there's any salt?"

Logan says excitedly, "I think there is," and pops up from the rug. He must be at least as hungry as I am. He rummages along the shelf and comes back with a little wooden box of salt. He sprinkles the sizzling fish, whose silver and gray striped skin is starting to crisp.

While the fish cooks, I hunt the shelf to find plates, forks, and tin cups for water. I scoop up some water for Logan and he drinks greedily. I offer him more, and he drinks that too. I know it's a very small thing, but it feels good to take care of him. I have never taken care of anyone before.

When the fish is white and flaky, I fill our plates. Logan is spearing fish and shoveling it into his mouth before I'm even settled on the sheepskin. Yes, hungry. I smile to myself, relieved that he doesn't eat with royal manners. That would make me uncomfortable.

"Sea bream," Logan says when I ask him what we're eating.

Delicate and mild. I imagine it with fresh bread and tomatoes, maybe some soft goat cheese.

When we're both full, I take the plates outside and wash them, then return to the fire and sit by Logan. Now that we have nothing with which to busy ourselves, I am keenly aware of the nearness of our bodies and the fact that we are so far away from other people. His knee brushes mine when he shifts position.

Questions churn within me. I want Logan to speak about himself. I want to know why he helped me. I want to know why he comes to this place. I want to know why his back is scarred from a lash. Even Belos never beat me like that, and Logan is a

Primo. Who would have beaten him so brutally? But I can't ask any of these questions. Logan's closed face tells me they are all off limits. So I ask another question, one that has troubled me almost as much.

"What did you mean when you said your mother was right? What was she right about?" My voice breaks awkwardly into the silence.

Logan stares into the fire for so long that I think he'll refuse to answer even this. Then, "Do you know what you did in the cell today?"

My heart leaps. I have been trying not to think about that. "When I broke the stone?"

"Yes." His words are slow and careful. "When you broke the stone."

I give him the only answer that makes sense to me, the only one possible. "I finally got to the Drift. How is it that the Drift is so…buried here? It's like searching through the dark. No. More like trying to find something in a dream, but you can't. When your movements are slow and what you want eludes you. Do you know what I mean?"

He studies me with his strange Earthmaker eyes until I grow uncomfortable. What is he seeing? "It's always been that way."

"Always?"

"Always."

His answer doesn't satisfy me, and I'm about to push for more when he asks, "How did you enter the Current that day when I pulled you out?"

I shrug. "It was an accident. I fell into it."

"How?"

His tone makes me feel like I've done something wrong. "I don't know."

"Describe it."

I consider refusing, because this makes me uncomfortable, because *he* is making me uncomfortable, but he just waits. "Belos and I were fighting. He was very angry, and I thought he would kill me. I fell against the tree, and I was...willing myself to escape. I thought I would go into the Drift, but I fell into the Current. Belos told me it's part of the Drift but difficult to access."

"It's not part of the Drift," Logan says firmly. "Only *Earthmakers* can use it."

I stare at him blankly.

"Do you understand?"

I try not to agree with Straton on questions of my intelligence, but something about what he's saying refuses to penetrate.

Gold flickers through his irises. He asks again, "How did you break the stone?"

I cannot allow myself to take him seriously. I force a laugh. "I'm a Drifter. You can't possibly think I used—"

"My mother is a Healer. When a Healer Heals, she is in close communion with the...inner self...of her patient—I can't explain it; I'm not a Healer. But she says that you have earthmagic. She could feel it in you."

My blood goes cold, but I force another laugh. "That's absurd."

"Aron thought so too—until you broke the stone. Even Bran was skeptical." A shadow seems to pass over his face. Some thought about Bran? Does he worry what Bran will think of him for helping me? "But I would imagine that Bran will be convinced by now."

"And you?"

"I found you in the Current remember? Either the Unnamed took you into it or you got there yourself. Initially, I chose to believe the former because it made more sense to me, but given the other evidence…well. I believe my mother is right: you are part Earthmaker. Why don't you believe that?"

"I'm a Drifter. That's all. What you're saying, it just can't be." I brighten as I think of another reason to disbelieve him. "That's not even possible. Earthmakers don't—you know—with humans. Isn't that against your law or something?"

Logan looks away from me, into the fire. A muscle bunches in his jaw. "Yes. That is our law. Earthmakers cannot be with humans, especially Drifters."

I feel the sudden distance between us, and my chest hollows out. His knee may be inches from mine, but there is a divide between us greater than the distance between Avydos and the Dry Land. I am a Drifter, dirty in his eyes. I tell myself not to shift away, not to acknowledge this Earthmaker prejudice, but my knee, with a mind of its own, edges away from his. I have heard what Earthmakers call my kind: the Unclean.

He says emphatically, "It's not impossible."

For a brief, euphoric moment I think he means it's not impossible for us, and then I realize he means it's not impossible that I am of mixed blood. My cheeks flame. What "us"? I speak the Earthmaker word to myself, imagining it in Logan's mind: Unclean, Unclean, Unclean.

Logan's fingers play with the whorls of fleece, winding and unwinding it from his finger. "There are old stories of those with mixed blood. The names are lost, blacked out. But the stories remain as cautionary tales." He shakes his head. "I don't remember the stories, but I do remember the lesson, that the mixing of blood is forbidden."

"What makes it so bad?" I hate the whine that slides along the edge of my voice. Why do I care what they think?

"They say it's dangerous."

That catches my interest. "How so?"

"No one says exactly; no one seems to know. Or maybe I just can't remember. But you can use the Drift, and, it seems, you can use earthmagic."

"I can't use earthmagic." Maybe if I keep saying that, fear will stop twisting my stomach.

"You used the Current. Alone."

I say nothing. I don't even allow myself to think.

"You really know nothing of your parents?"

I say hotly, "I told you—"

"I know. I'm sorry."

"This theory is ridiculous."

"It's not ridiculous, Astarti, and it would go a long way to explain why Belos wanted you."

"He didn't *want* me. He found me. My mother left me at the water's edge"—I don't say *to die*—"and he picked me up."

"Oh, and he's in the habit of adopting orphans, is he? I suppose he takes in lost puppies as well."

Heat washes through me. I lurch to my feet and stride for the door, swinging it open. The rain is gone. I breathe deep in the fresh, moist air, calming myself. Logan is suggesting that Belos sought me out specifically, that he knew what I was. Can that be? Does Belos, perhaps, know who my parents were? Did my parents know that Belos—

I cut off the question because even the first edge of it fills me with black despair. I sit on the wet stones of the porch, ignoring the seep of moisture through the seat of my wool pants. I force my mind to empty. I'm practiced in that; it's one of the first things a Drifter learns to do. I feel for my mooring, for the Drift. As in Avydos, it's dim, far away. I pull on the faint, sluggish thread of my mooring anyway. No real power comes to me, only the light and heat of wasted energy. I let it roll from one hand to the other, calming me with its familiarity while I stare out to the moonlit bay. My light is the same color as the moon: pure and lovely. How can the Earthmakers find this dirty?

I don't hear Logan's approach, but I feel it. I let the light vanish.

He crouches beside me. He left the blanket behind, and the moonlight glows on his bare, scarred chest, his arms and shoulders. "I'm sorry, Astarti. I didn't mean to be flippant."

"If I'm part Earthmaker, why have I never used earthmagic before?"

"Are you sure you haven't? You didn't seem to realize you were using it today."

I ignore that. "But when I used the Current, Belos was surprised. I know him, Logan, and I've never seen a look like that on his face. He was surprised. So he must not think I'm part...whatever."

Why I am saying that like I believe it?

Logan stares at his hands, thinking.

"Wouldn't Belos have wanted me to use both? I mean, of course, if I could. It would be to his benefit for me to use it. If he knew or suspected, wouldn't he try to teach me?"

But when I say that, memories coalesce. Belos asking me to feel the air, feel the earth. Belos gritting his teeth in frustration. Straton raising a smug eyebrow.

"What have you just remembered?"

Logan's question makes me jump, but I shake my head, not ready to explain. I force the memory to recede.

"Your father must have been an Earthmaker who lay with a Drifter woman and told no one. A woman, of course, couldn't have hidden the deed. But a man? He must never have told anyone. He would have known that he would be Stricken for it."

"Stricken?"

"Cast out."

I stare at his moonlit face until he explains. "Some crimes are considered unforgivable, but Earthmakers don't execute their own. Instead, they cast them out, and their names are taken away, *stricken*, as…Belos's was. That is why they call him the Unnamed. He is Stricken, as though he was never one of us. They are meant to be forgotten, but the Unnamed, of course, won't quietly accept that censure. The Stricken can never return to Avydos. No one may speak with them. We're not supposed to even speak *about* them. They usually die within a year."

Gooseflesh rises along my arms. "That's awful."

From the corner of my eye, I see Logan's elbows wrapped around his knees. His head is bowed. I remember, with a wash of horror, what Clitus said to him before we fled the cell. *Logan, do you realize what you are doing?*

"Please tell me you're not going to be Stricken for helping me."

He shudders at the word, as I do at the word Leashed. I am struck by the irony of these opposites: one is a binding, the other a loosing, but each is terrible. Each takes the person's self away.

Logan admits, "It's possible."

"Why did you do it?" I'm angry now. If I were not already Leashed but knew that Leashing might be my punishment for helping someone, would I do it? I shudder, as Logan did. "You should not have done it."

He shrugs. "I doubt it surprised anyone. They all think I'm reckless."

"Don't shrug it off like that. This is serious."

He gives me a hard look. "I did what I felt was right, as you did. For Korinna. And me."

"But what I did wasn't even close—"

"They'll probably be lenient because I'm the Arcon's brother. It's not fair, but there it is."

"And if they're not?"

He shrugs again, as though it doesn't matter.

I stand up, looming over him. "You have to take me back. Right now. Maybe if you turn me in, they'll pardon you."

He doesn't look up. "No."

"They might. You don't know that."

"I will not take you back."

I stare down at his moonlit hair. "Why not?"

"What if they killed you? Do you think I want that on my conscience?"

His words are sharp and angry, but so are mine. "Do you think I want it on my conscience if you're Stricken?"

He looks up now and grins. "It seems we're at a standstill."

"Don't smile. It's not funny."

"What should I do then?"

"Take me back, like I said."

He gives me a measuring look. "How is it that the Unnamed did not corrupt your heart?"

That sparks my anger again. "Don't say that. You have no idea what's in my heart. You have no idea what kind of person you are taking such an absurd risk for."

"Tell me then: what is in your heart, Astarti?"

A word explodes within me. I want to scream it, to get it out, but it will do no good. The word will still be there, poisoning me.

Logan's voice softens. "What's in your heart?"

I shake my head. I won't say it. I won't tell him. He already thinks me dirty; I won't make it worse.

"Come here, Astarti."

I edge back.

He holds out his arm. "Please come."

I swallow hard. I wait for his arm to drop, for him to shrug indifferently, but he doesn't. He waits, bare arm catching the moonlight.

When I sit stiffly beside him, he puts his arm around me. Through my linen shirt, I feel muscle and bone and cool skin. I don't know when the stiffness leaves me, but I find myself relaxing against him, my cheek pressing to the warm muscle of his chest, his fingers playing through my hair.

Chapter 17

I wake by the fire, which has burned down to coals. My head is on a feather pillow, and a heavy blanket covers me. I don't remember leaving the porch. Did Logan carry me here? Sunlight floods through the open windows. The little house is so rustic and peaceful with its wind-weathered shutters and stone fireplace, its simple brass candlesticks and cast-iron cooking tools. I even like this sheepskin that is always filled with sand no matter how many times I take it to the door and shake it. For one moment I let myself think, *I could live here.* Part of me wants to crush the thought with harsh reality, but I can't quite make myself. I let it float away instead, a thought for another life.

I stretch and go to the door. I see Logan at the edge of the water, digging with a spade. He bends to pull something from the sand, washes it in the water, then tosses it into a nearby basket.

I smooth my rumpled shirt, wishing I had a change of clothes. I ignore my sandals on the porch and walk barefoot down to meet him.

"Breakfast," he announces, showing me a gray-brown clam.

"It seems you are a man of many talents."

He grins. It makes him look so young, and I realize how grim he usually is. Here, in this place, he seems at ease.

I sit in the sand, working my feet into the cool depths, while he continues to dig. More than once, he gets down on hands and knees to paw through the wet sand, his face and body relaxed. I watch him unabashedly: the sure, strong motions, the flex of muscles, the perfect grace.

When the basket is full, Logan shows it to me and jogs his eyebrows. "Yum."

His eyes are blue. I have never seen them hold a single color for so long.

I smile. Then I eye his soggy, sand-covered clothes with suspicion. Only the back of his shirt remains white, and his pants look like he's been dragged across the beach. His bare feet are caked. "You're not coming in the house like that."

He rolls his eyes.

He drops the basket and strips off his shirt. The ridged scar arcs across the left side of his chest, fading into his ribs. Sand clings to the notched muscles of his belly. I tear my eyes away because I'm staring. I hope he didn't notice. He wades into the knee-deep water and bends over to swirl and scrub the shirt. When he wades back to the beach, I force my eyes beyond him, to focus on the horizon instead of his body. Eyes thus averted, I am unprepared for the wet shirt he tosses at me. A dripping sleeve smacks me coldly across the face. I squeal.

He laughs.

"You think that's funny?"

He is grinning like a boy.

I give him my most wicked smile to tell him how he will pay for that trick.

His face falls comically. In a burst of motion, he takes off down the beach.

I leap up and after him.

His legs may be longer than mine, but I've always been fast. His legs pump; his elbows fly in smooth counterbalance, but it's not enough to beat me.

I am reaching for him, about to grab his belt, about to show him who is the best, when he veers off into the surf, splashing through the waves. I leap the waves behind him, laughing at the splash and tug of cold water. I can barely breathe I'm laughing so hard, and I finally stop, bracing palms on thighs, tears in my eyes and my chest aching. Three paces ahead, Logan makes an ill-timed leap. He goes down with a surprised cry.

He doesn't come back up. I search the spot with my eyes. I wade closer, starting to worry. When something grabs my ankle, I scream.

Logan bursts from the water to grab my waist. I thrash, half in surprised terror, half in fun. Water drags at my legs when he pulls me from it, slinging me over his shoulder. He starts tromping toward the beach, his shoulder bumping hard into my stomach.

"Put me down!"

"Not until you agree to play nice."

I laugh. "Are you serious?"

He shifts me, and I am shocked by how strong he is, how my weight is nothing to him. "I can't have you running all over the place attacking people."

I point out, "You're the only other one here."

"Exactly. Now. Will you be nice?"

I know there's a big, stupid grin on my face, but I let it stay. "I can't promise that. How about I agree to make breakfast instead?"

We are at the water's edge. He stops, pretending to think. "That might be an acceptable compromise."

"If you do the laundry."

"What?!"

"You heard me."

He sets me down, grumbling.

Briefly I think, *I just asked a Primo to do my laundry.* But Logan only mutters with good humor, and I allow myself to forget what he is and what I am. Maybe, for just one day, we can be Astarti and Logan and nothing more.

℘ ℃

The day passes in small, ordinary tasks. I steam the clams over the fire. Logan disappears during this time but comes back when the clams are almost done. My mouth waters when he shows me a handful of jewel-like strawberries.

I spend the morning sweeping the floor, beating the sheepskin for the ninety-fourth time, shaking out all the blankets, hauling water, and collecting more driftwood for the fire. Logan takes the boat out again to fish and brings back enough for lunch and supper. As I eye the bucket of fish, I consider that I could soon tire of the stuff.

In the afternoon, Logan drags a wooden washtub from the shed around back. Neither of us has a change of clothes and when Logan asks for mine to wash, I shift uncomfortably. He disappears behind the curtain of the sleeping cubby and returns with a linen sheet.

While he withdraws to the porch, I slip out of my clothes and wrap the sheet around myself. I tie it as best I can. When I take my clothes out to the porch, Logan is already scrubbing his shirt in the tub. He looks up, and I see a smile threatening the corner of his mouth.

"Oh, shut up."

He catches my clothes when I throw them at him.

I wander the sand hills behind the house while Logan washes the clothes. Even with my sandals on, the sharp grasses slice at my feet. Soon enough the sand turns to rock and the grass to scrub. I see a rocky ledge in the distance and decide to climb up there before I go back. Hopefully by then my clothes will be reasonably dry.

When I reach the ledge, with the sheet dirty and torn in places and my feet sore, the view is not what I expect. The house is still visible, its tiled roof a dark spot against the white sand. But to the north I see another island beyond the edge of ours, one much bigger, its mountain peak jutting high.

The main island. Avydos.

Somehow, hidden in our little bay, I had forgotten how close it was; I had let myself grow comfortable. I do not stay to enjoy the view.

I am silent and brooding when I return. Logan doesn't ask what's wrong, but I know he feels my mood. I see the moment it happens: his smile fades, his eyes darken, his movements grow careful and controlled. Until now, I did not realize how much he had relaxed. I am angry with myself for doing this to him, for ruining his ease—and my own—but I can't get it back. We are in the shadow of Avydos. Nothing has changed just because we're hiding. The world is still what it is.

When Logan starts on dinner, I don't offer to help. I tell myself that the meal is simple, that it's a one-person job, but I just can't make my arms move. I stare into the fire.

After putting the fish in to sizzle, Logan walks out the door. My mood drops lower; I should at least *try*.

He comes back with a pottery jug bound in coils of rope meant to protect it from shattering. He raises the jug. "Wine."

"Been hiding that?"

His mouth quirks. "I forgot about it."

He walks to the table and rummages along the shelf. The wax seal makes a pleasing crack when he breaks it.

When he hands me a tin cup brimming with bright red wine, I say, "I'm not much of a wine drinker."

"Just try it."

I take a cautious sip. It's sweet and tart all at once, and I blink in surprise. "It tastes like raspberries."

Logan's mouth quirks again, and I realize how rarely he actually smiles. "It is."

"Raspberry wine?"

"Bran makes it. He found some old manuscript talking about a land to the east that makes plum wine. He started experimenting. Believe me, the first few batches did *not* taste this good."

"Somehow I can picture Bran surrounded by a stack of old manuscripts."

"He probably is at this very moment."

"Not a Warden, then?"

Logan's face darkens. "No."

I curse myself for stumbling onto a bad subject. For a moment, everything was right and easy again, and I ruined it.

Logan uses a long fork to spear the fish from the pan. He slides a few onto my plate. I blow on them, and the steam curls in the firelight. The salty fish and the sweet wine make a nice contrast of flavors.

Logan sips his wine and picks at his food. How can he not be hungry? I search for some conversation to distract him from whatever he's thinking about.

"Does anyone live on this island? On the other side maybe?"

"Not that I know of." Logan frowns thoughtfully. "But I haven't been here for several years. Someone could be somewhere."

"Do Earthmakers live on many of the Outer Islands?" I had always imagined them empty and wild.

Logan takes a bite. "Actually, yes. Many seek solitude, especially the old. They want to be close to their element— whether it's earth, water, air—and nothing else."

"What about fire?"

"Most of those die young."

I know that Earthmakers tend to favor one element or another, typically to the point that they have very limited control over the other three. Those who can master two or three often become Wardens. I don't know of any who control all four, not even any of the Seven.

I study Logan in the firelight, watching him eat. Green moves along the edges of his irises. I want to ask him about his eyes. I know they are not normal, not even for an Earthmaker. But I asked him that when I first bound him at the Trader's Choice, and he went very still, which, I've learned, is what he does when he's most upset. But I still want to learn *something* about him. I know he's a Primo and a Warden; I know he can fix a door, manage a boat, wash clothes, cook dinner. But that's all I know. He's told me nothing about himself that really, deeply matters.

I ask, thinking it will be a safe starting place, "So what are your elements?"

Logan's face stiffens, and his fork freezes over a piece of flaky fish.

Why did that upset him?

He says carefully, "I can control no element better than another."

I rock back. "You control all four?"

He sets down his plate. "That's not what I said."

"I don't understand."

He is silent for so long I think he won't answer, then he says softly, "I can't *control* earthmagic."

"But you used it that night, when Belos came. I saw you."

His body is perfectly still, but his eyes swirl with color. "And did you see what happened?"

I try to remember, but the events are a blur. I remember roiling earth. I remember tumbling away, falling. Violent wind. Were there screams?

Logan climbs carefully to his feet. "I'm tired. Do you want the bed?"

"It's warmer here," I say, silently begging him to stay with me.

He nods. He walks to the curtain, pulls it aside. It falls shut behind him.

My heart is skipping with uncertainty. What did I say?

ဢ ௸

I sleep lightly, tossing and turning on the sheepskin. I cannot get comfortable. When I hear murmurs and low moans coming from behind the curtain, I recognize the sounds of nightmare. I lie still, waiting, hoping they will subside, hoping I don't have to intrude on something so private. But they go on, rising now and then to nearly a shout. I creep to the curtain and pull it aside.

The bed is washed in moonlight. Logan shifts restlessly in a twisted mess of blankets. He grunts, mumbles something. I hesitate again, unsure whether to wake him. Surely this is none of my business? But when a low whine sounds in his throat, I make my way along the small gap between the bed and wall. I touch his shoulder.

He explodes awake, shouting. I jerk back and collide with the wall. I say his name—once, twice—and he realizes it's me, that he's safe. The animal energy leaves him, and he rubs his face with both hands, scraping them through his hair. Harsh, ragged breaths tear through his throat. In the pale light of the moon, I see that he's shaking. His pain unfreezes me, and I sit on the bed and reach for him.

He is stiff and unyielding at first, trying to control and harden himself. I know I have exposed him, caught him when he is vulnerable. Maybe I should leave, let him pull himself back together in private, but instead I tug at his shoulder, my fingers insistent. At last he lies down on his back, rigid, eyes staring into the darkness above. I lie against his side, hoping he doesn't pull away or tell me to leave. His chest and torso are slick with sweat; his heart hammers. I feel him trying to control his trembling: the effort at repression, the failure, the effort.

Slowly, slowly, the tension drains away.

"Are you all right?"

He answers roughly, "Just a dream."

We lie together for a long time, he on his back, with me curled against him. I grow aware that nothing but thin cloth separates us. He is wearing only his undershorts and I my shirt. His body is warm and solid, a man's body. I have never lain so close to a man. His fingers trail through my hair, and the touch sends shivers through me.

His hand leaves my hair and brushes from my shoulder down my side, leaving a trail of heat behind it. His fingers come to rest lightly on my hip. My own fingers, as though with a will of their own, trace the curve of his chest. They glide down his muscled belly. His breathing quickens, and his fingers tighten on my hip. Then he takes a shuddering breath and moves his fingers back to my hair.

I snatch my own hand back, tucking it safely between my breasts, which I realize suddenly are pressed to his side. I am burning with conflicting needs: the need to escape and the need to touch him again. I have never felt this before.

But neither of us moves, and eventually, I doze.

I wake later when the moon has set. The curtain glows dimly with the light of the dying fire, but otherwise the room is dark. Logan stirs beside me.

My fingers curl against his sternum. "Are you all right?"

No answer.

"Will you tell me?"

Silence. Then, "You know how I said I couldn't control earthmagic?"

I don't answer. Of course I remember.

"I—" He cuts himself off.

"You don't have to tell me. Not if you don't want to."

His lips press to the top of my head. He takes a shuddering breath.

I splay my hand against his chest, trying to will peace and comfort through my skin into his.

He begins abruptly, "When I was young—five, six, I'm not sure—they tried to teach me to control the elements. It's the standard age for introduction, though most children can do very little at this time. I—"

Silence.

I wait, not willing to push him.

His heart thumps under my hand. He swallows hard. "I destroyed four buildings. Killed two people."

I freeze at his words. He misreads my shock, taking it, perhaps, for revulsion. He starts to draw away, and I pull him back. I press my cheek against his chest, wrap my arm around his torso.

He asks harshly, mockingly, "Aren't you going to say, 'You were a child. It was an accident'?"

I crane my neck to look at him, but it's too dark. I run my fingers along his jaw, feel it unclench at my touch. I smooth my fingers to his hairline and down the side of his neck. They linger at his throat.

"You already know those things." I don't need to add that they haven't helped.

He looses a shaky breath. "They tried…everything to get me to control it. Nothing worked."

I trace the hollow of his throat, mulling over his words. Something troubles me about the way he said that, about the word he stumbled over. "What do you mean 'everything'?"

He doesn't answer, and I know with instinctive certainty that he won't. But I think of the scars on his back, and I shudder. Could his own people have done that to him? I thought only terrible people, like Belos, did such things.

I chew at my lip, unsure what to say. At a loss, I let my hands speak, smoothing over his chest to try to still his renewed trembling. I slide my hand around his ribcage, gripping him. I turn and press my lips to his temple, then his throat.

His breathing quickens, and so does mine. Our bodies start to shift against one another. Heat spreads from low in my belly. My skin tingles, sensitive to every brush of his flesh—his hand gliding down my back, his hip shifting against my belly as I ease a leg over his. I want to let go, to let this happen. It feels so right.

But he will be Stricken.

Cast out.

Condemned to a fate as bad, in its way, as Leashing.

I freeze.

No. I cannot do that to him. Not even when this feels right and that stubborn Earthmaker law feels wrong. I tell myself that he is upset now, perhaps not thinking clearly. What if he regretted this in the morning? How could I bear the reproach in his eyes?

He goes still when I do, breathing hard against my neck. He swallows, gets control of himself.

I know how vulnerable he must feel right now, having exposed such a dark secret, and I feel I must say something, give him something for what he's given me. I wedge my face into his shoulder. "You know when you asked me what was in my heart? Yesterday?"

I feel him shift, as though he is trying to look at me. "Yes."

"It's—" Can I say this ugly word?

He waits, fingers resting on my shoulder.

I whisper it, as though that will make it less black. "Hate."

He takes the word in, but he doesn't draw away from me. His fingers trace my spine. "For whom?"

"Belos. Myself."

He is silent, thinking. Then, "Him, I understand. But why for yourself?"

I swallow hard, already regretting my decision to speak. I try to finish. "For—"

"For what?"

I whisper it, trying to diminish it again, knowing I cannot, "For what he's made me. For what I am." Shame blooms hot in my chest; I have never allowed myself to acknowledge this before, and it hurts every bit as much as I thought it would. Yes, I hate myself.

I tense when Logan's fingers glide up my spine to my neck, unknowingly brushing the Griever's Mark. What might I be, if not for that?

It doesn't matter. I am what I am. Nothing will change it.

He grips my neck, gently but firmly. Does he know the Mark is there? Did he see it?

"You will remake yourself, Astarti."

I let his words linger in the silence. My eyes prickle. Could I? Is that possible?

We lay there, holding each other until, as the sky begins to lighten, we sleep.

CHAPTER 18

I wake to the sound of someone knocking on the door. I bolt upright, fear clenching my throat. I am disoriented, blinded by the sunlight flooding the room. Belos!

No. Not here.

Logan draws his leg from under mine and rises calmly from the bed. I take a breath. Despite the unknown threat outside, I can't stop myself from watching him as he slides along the wall to the bed's foot. It's not that I have never seen men unclothed before. But this is different. Logan's muscles slide smoothly under his skin, and even in the cramped space, his motions are graceful, powerful, controlled. Even the terrible curving scar on his chest seems a natural part of him. My eyes drift to the band of his undershorts, but there I stop myself, self-conscious.

Logan finds his black leather pants on the chest at the bed's foot and tugs them on. When he turns to pull the curtain aside, the silvery lash scars on his back catch the sunlight.

Another knock sounds on the door as Logan disappears through the curtain. I scramble to follow.

Logan peeks through one of the shutters while I paw through the blanket by the cold hearth, looking for my pants.

"Bran."

I sag with relief. "Alone?"

"He wouldn't bring anyone here." He calls through the window, "Just a second!"

Even though I know it's Bran, I still jam my feet through my pant legs, hopping clumsily. I feel like I've been caught doing something wrong.

"Breathe, Astarti. It's all right."

I slow down, finish more calmly. It's not like me to get this frazzled. I tuck part of the billowy shirt into my waistband and comb my hair back with my fingers. I take a deep breath and nod to Logan, who opens the door.

Bran, dressed in a white Earthmaker tunic belted at the waist, stands on the porch with a leather sack. He is looking out at the ocean, waiting patiently. When he turns to us, his face is composed, unreadable, but he looks from Logan to me and back to Logan. Logan's jaw clenches, and I blush. I want to shout, "Nothing happened!" but I know it's better to read the situation first, to react only when I know where others stand. I wait for Bran or Logan to take the lead.

Bran jostles the sack. "Tired of fish yet? I have bread, honeycomb, and fruit."

My mouth waters instantly, and I glance hopefully at Logan. He won't refuse, will he?

Logan's nostrils flare, but Bran only waits. Bran, I realize as I watch them, is the peacekeeper in this family. Logan, most certainly, is not.

"Bread," I say to Logan with an edge of desperation.

He sighs.

Bran, smiling slightly, goes to sit on the porch.

Logan sits beside him on the sand covered stones. As I approach, I study the brothers. Bran, with his tidy red-gold hair pulled into a queue at the nape of his neck and his fine white tunic, sits cross-legged, at ease. He looks like a Primo, even here on the porch of a dilapidated hut. Logan, with his shorter blond hair a wavy mess, his scarred back tense, crouches with one leg tucked under himself and the other bent, his foot planted. He looks ready to push to his feet. How can these two even be brothers?

Logan looks over his shoulder at me. Caught staring, I jerk into motion and sit beside him as Bran pulls a round loaf from the sack. I jump back up and dart inside for a cutting board and plates, wincing when my impatience sends a knife clattering to the stone floor. What is wrong with me?

When I clumsily pass off the cutting board to Bran, he gives me a brief smile. I tear my eyes away from him, feeling more reproach from his kindness than I would from a glare. Accusation would make me defiant; kindness makes me guilty. I have gotten his brother in trouble—why be nice? Logan, I decide, is right: having a pleasant little meal won't change things.

Such thoughts fade when Logan passes me a plate with three thick slices of bread, a section of golden, oozing honey comb, and a little mountain of strawberries. I take the plate greedily, tearing into the food with manners that must surely remind these Primos that I am no lady. I can't even stop the moan of pleasure when I bite into a strawberry coated with honey.

Bran chuckles. "Thought so."

I color with embarrassment, but Logan is giving me that half-smile of his, and I grin back sheepishly.

Logan's plate rests on his knee, the food untouched. "Well? How bad is it?"

"Eat, Logan," Bran and I say at once. We stare at each other in surprise.

Bran recovers first. "You heard her."

Logan takes a heavy, noisy breath to communicate his annoyance, but he does turn to his plate with a business-like attitude. Though he manages to avoid any indecent sounds like the ones I made, he does eat more like a soldier than a royal. I am oddly relieved.

When Logan's plate is empty, which doesn't take long, he gives Bran a pointed look.

Bran fingers a bit of honeycomb onto his bread. "It could be worse."

Logan waits for more, and so do I.

Bran raises the dripping bread to his lips. "The Council is demanding your return."

Logan shrugs. "That's to be expected."

I interrupt, "How does the Council work?"

Bran's eyebrows twitch, and he lowers the bread. His body language tells me I should know this. I hate feeling ignorant and stupid.

"Surely Belos"—Logan glares at him, but Bran is unrepentant about the use of the name—"has taught you of the Council? His father, after all, was once a member."

I blink. Somehow it feels like Belos should have sprung into being, fully formed. It's strange to think of him having a father at all, of being a child like any other.

Bran explains, "Essentially, the Council debates issues and speaks with the voice of the people, but the Arcon puts words into action. It's more complicated than that, and there are certain duties and decisions that fall straight to the Arcon, some straight to the Council. But basically, they work together."

I am about to ask about Belos and his father, but Logan has other questions. "The Council's terms?"

"You must hand over"—Bran's eyes dart to me and away— "You must hand her over. They plan an inquiry, of course."

"But they wouldn't—I mean, Logan won't be—"

I can't say the word. I won't. Even so, it hangs in the air.

Bran's eyebrows are low and thoughtful. "Surely not." But it sounds less like belief and more like hope—or denial.

"And Astarti?" Logan asks darkly. "What do they intend to do to her?"

"I don't know."

"Then why even bother coming here? You know me better than that."

I frown to myself. What does that mean? And what, exactly, do *I* mean to him? Is it principle only? That he won't undo what he did? Is it—could he possibly care for me? *Me?* I shut that down. Of course not. He knows what I am. But his words from last night echo through me: *you will remake yourself.* He was challenging me to do it, telling me that he believed it possible.

"There's more," Bran says, and I don't miss the edge in his voice. "The Council is pushing for our involvement in the inevitable war between Martel and Heborian. It's all but settled. The Wardens are being gathered. They will fight for Martel."

"Why?" I demand. "What do the Earthmakers care about this?"

Bran hesitates, and I realize from his discomfort that he doesn't really trust me. He thinks it possible that Aron is right, that I am spying for Belos. Though I know it's unfair of me, that his suspicions are natural, I resent this.

Bran tenses further when Logan answers, "Heborian is a Drifter. The Council has always hated that he's king. We fought for King Barreston, when Heborian invaded. That defeat stung the Earthmaker pride as much as the Keldan pride. But, unlike the Keldans, who mostly just want to live their lives, we don't forgive easily."

Bran is stiff and unhappy with Logan's depiction of their people, but he doesn't contradict it. Does he agree with Logan? Or is silence just part of his peacekeeping?

Logan rises suddenly, a smooth unfolding of his body. I scramble to my feet beside him.

He stares down at Bran. "Anything else important?"

Bran shakes his head.

"I need to think. I'm going to walk."

I nod understanding, and he tromps down the sandy steps, his back flexing with the descent, the silvery scars sliding over muscle. The scars bother me. Because I have my own. Because I know what they mean. Someone hurt him. Someone wanted him to feel that he was wrong, unacceptable.

Logan has almost reached the water by the time I realize Bran is standing beside me.

Before I can lose my courage, I ask angrily, "Who whipped him?"

Bran doesn't answer, and I look up to see him studying me.

"What did he tell you?"

"Practically nothing. I mean, well, he did tell me he has trouble with his earthmagic. He said that he destroyed some buildings when he was first learning." I shrug it off as though it's not as horrible as it is.

Bran says slowly, "And he told you what happened when those buildings came down?"

I don't answer, but Bran can see it in my face. I can't shrug that away.

Bran takes a deep breath. "I'm shocked he told you that much. He never speaks of it."

"I am…assuming that—"

"Yes. They tried to teach him control. Focus. I'm sure you think it cruel, and it was. But it did help a little."

"How? By teaching him not to use his power? By teaching him shame?" I am breathing hard. Anger pulses through me.

Bran rubs a hand across his face. "There's much you don't understand about our people. And about Logan. Don't be so quick to judge."

"So tell me then what it is that I don't understand."

"Why don't you tell me something first." Bran's voice is light, as though the matter is closed.

I stare at him.

"Why do you care so much about my brother?"

A flush creeps up my neck.

"You know our law?"

I feel like he just slapped me, like he just accused me of throwing myself at Logan like a whore. I am indignant. Then I recall the way I have watched him, how I've studied the shape and movement of his body, the structure of his face. I remember how my body shifted against his last night, how I wanted him. My flush deepens. Am I so obvious?

"Yes. I know your law."

"It's been less than twenty years since someone was last Stricken. The Council would hate to do it again so soon, but I think they would."

I look away from Bran, to the beach and the water. Logan is gone. "And what was that man's crime?"

"It was a woman."

I glance at him. "A woman?"

"Her name was Sibyl."

His face is solemn, his eyes unseeing, and I know he is picturing this woman, whoever she was. I say softly, "I thought being Stricken meant your name was forgotten."

He turns deep blue eyes on me. "Officially, yes."

"And what was Sibyl's crime?"

He hesitates. "Dissent."

"Dissent?"

Bran takes a deep breath, looks out to the ocean. "Sibyl had…ideas. Theories." He shakes his head a little and ends harshly, "They were unacceptable to the Council."

Bran's face is closed now, and I can tell he will say nothing more specific about her "crime," so instead I ask, fearing the answer, needing to know, "And what happened to her?"

"She disappeared. No one knows. I'm sure she died. No Earthmaker can live long away from her own kind. Or *his*."

I swallow hard. "I don't want that for Logan."

Bran gives me a searching look, and I meet his eyes, even though they invade my space. "I believe you."

I release a breath I didn't realize I was holding. "And do you have a law against being friends?"

Bran's mouth quirks. "Nothing official. But don't expect anyone to like it. And don't expect them to be without suspicions."

"Nothing happened."

Brans nods slowly. "I see the way he looks at you. The way he…is different around you. It can't be good."

I am torn between wild hope—how *does* Logan look at me?—and black despair. What a fool I am. Did I really think, even for a second, that I could have him?

ᔈ ᔆ

Bran doesn't try to stop me when I walk down the sandy steps, doesn't follow when I start across the beach. Logan is nowhere to be seen, but that's all right. I need time to think also. Or perhaps to not think. To let my thoughts settle.

At the end of the beach, where the sand hills rise to scrub and rock, I find the outlet of the freshwater river that winds from the mountains to the sea. It spreads flat and wide here at the end, and I wade through it easily to reach the rocky slope beyond.

The rough stone abrades my bare feet, but I don't mind. The pain helps clear my mind.

About twenty feet up, I find a cozy niche and sit down. The high sun—it must be early afternoon—beats down on me. I listen to the waves crash against the rock below, imagine them carving away at the stony face. A seagull screams overhead. Far out in the water, a dark shape appears briefly and vanishes.

I must doze off because I jerk to awareness in the cool shadows, the afternoon sun having disappeared behind the western ridge. A question grips me like a vice, making my heart pound: what does Belos want with Martel?

Before, this was an idle question, the answer seemingly simple and obvious. But now I realize there might be more to it. No, not "might."

I think about what Bran said, about the Earthmakers joining Martel for no reason other than that they want Heborian out of power. Predictable, really. I'm sure it will not surprise Belos.

In fact, I bet he's counting on it.

I think of the map in Belos's study. A dusty stretch of vellum with Kelda scrubbed clean and the Floating Lands nothing more than a burn hole in the Southern Ocean. Burned out, vanished. Like they do not exist. Like they are Stricken.

℘ ℭ

When I burst through the door of the hut, Bran and Logan leap up from the sheepskin. The iron tongs clatter to the hearth, and the fire winks out.

Logan strides toward me. "What is it?"

I say breathlessly, "We have to go back to Avydos."

"No. I just explained this to Bran. We will not go."

I grip his sleeves, which are rolled to his elbows. "You don't understand. Belos—"

"Astarti," Logan warns.

Bran takes a step toward us. "Let her finish."

I loosen my grip on Logan's sleeves, step back so I can see them both. I direct a question at Bran. "You really think the Wardens will join Martel?"

"Yes. I'm sure of it."

"They can't. It will be a disaster."

"What do you mean? Why?"

"Don't you see? That's exactly what Belos wants."

CHAPTER 19

I have no trouble convincing Bran to return to Avydos, but convincing Logan is another matter. After the second time he asks, "You understand that I might not be able to stop them from seizing you?" I grip his hand and say, "Stop."

His eyes swirl with color.

"You said I could remake myself. How should I do that, Logan? By hiding here?"

His jaw clenches, and his eyes search mine frantically. What is he thinking?

From the corner of my eye, I watch Bran tense. But he isn't looking at me. He's looking at Logan.

We trek along the path that brought us from the edge of the wood to the house. The sun is just low enough that we move from shadow to light, depending on the position of the peaks and troughs of stone. Logan wears his sword belted at his waist. The weapon has stood in the corner, by the broom, for the past few days. I had almost forgotten it. But it's back in its place now, with Logan's hand resting on the pommel.

When we reach the trees, mostly pine, I watch Logan and Bran's faces. They each take a breath, relax. Logan puts out his hand and I take it. He leads me to a pine tree with bark that looks like huge, uneven scales.

"Touch it. Feel the tree's energy. Pay attention to the way it responds, the way the Current sweeps around and through it."

I press my palm to the tree, which oozes sap between its scales of bark. I empty my mind, as I would when entering the Drift. As Logan takes me into the Current, I feel something of what he says: the way the Current licks out at me from the tree as it flows, the way the tree is a gateway.

I know the moment we reach the Wood itself. The Current intensifies, whirling around and through me. The golden fingers of the trees grab and tug at me. Fear clenches me. They see me! They *know* me.

Logan, in his beautiful golden form, shifts beside me, and I feel the energy of his touch.

As he pulls me from the Current, I try to feel the gateway. I sense a gap, but that's all. I know I could not have found it, could not have escaped on my own.

I shiver as the physical Wood resolves itself around me. High above, the tops of the trees rustle in a breeze that doesn't reach into these depths. I will my heart to settle.

Bran is looking accusingly at Logan. He says nothing, but I can guess his thoughts: Logan should not try to teach me earthmagic. I am a Drifter, unclean. I might be a spy.

As we emerge from the Wood, no one marks our presence. We take a stone path different from the one down which Logan and I escaped two days ago. We wind along the slope and emerge onto a paved road. Men and women, all dressed in the Earthmaker style, go about their business. In many ways, Avydos looks like any human city. There are sailors in broad hats, tailors with yards of cloth in their arms, bakers with fresh bread. I hear the ring of a blacksmith's hammer, the screeching of seagulls. The main difference, other than clothing, is that the people here are quieter, more reserved, and the buildings are grander. Everything is beautiful, but I'm not sure I like it.

We take a side path to the royal house, the building with smooth columns and wide porches. The place is less square than I first thought. Wings and additions have complicated what was perhaps originally a more basic shape.

We climb the stone steps to the huge porch and arched front doors, which stand open in the cool spring air. They must really trust the Wood to protect them. I can't imagine Heborian ever leaving his gates and doors open like this.

We pass through the doors into the open, airy hall that I remember from the first horrible night here, when Logan brought me to be Healed. My heart starts to pound. I did not escape then; I will not now.

The hall is crowded, or at least it feels that way after the open, empty beach. Men, some wearing knee-length, broad-sleeved tunics like Bran's, some wearing longer tunics and swathed in soft robes that wrap from right hip up to left shoulder, stare at us with hard eyes, their mouths grim. Women, who wear light, filmy dresses gathered at the shoulders, glance over us with disdain. One woman actually glares, and among the reserve of Earthmakers, it's like a shout. One or two men, whose purposeful strides make me suspect they are Wardens, shoot Logan questioning looks, which he ignores.

I notice golden bracelets on the wrists of those more simply dressed. Are these the servants? Should I interpret their bracelets as marks of prestige or marks of ownership? Earthmakers don't enslave, but something about the bracelets makes me think of the Shackle, and I shudder inwardly.

An older boy that I recognize as one of my former guards stops dead when he sees us.

"Nicanor," Logan calls. "Where is Prima Gaiana?"

The boy's face twitches nervously. "With Arcon Aronos and Counselor Demos. On the Prima's balcony."

Logan grimaces. "Just as well."

"Arcon Aronos said to—that is, if you were seen we were to—"

Logan's mouth quirks. "By all means. Lead the way."

Nicanor straightens his lanky frame with sudden dignity. Bran glances at me with a half-smile. I hide my own. Nicanor is probably about fifteen, but he seems so much younger to me. When I was his age, I was already—well, I had done a lot of things by then. This boy looks like he's hardly been out of the city.

At the end of the spacious entry hall, we turn into a narrower passageway. Even preoccupied with worry, I cannot help noticing how beautiful it is. Like the entry hall, the sea-side wall is partially open. The stone columns here are smaller and more ornate, carved with climbing vines of grape and clematis. Amazing—almost creepy—that stone can look so alive.

The solid wall opposite the sea is cut with arching niches that hold fine porcelain vases and lifelike statues. Some are lost in shadow, but those at just the right angle catch the orange-gold glow of sunset. The glow reveals the statues to be strong, stoic figures, their faces beautiful but severe. Even those gripping spears or swords show no emotion. Most are nude, or close to it. Bygone Arcons? Earthmaker heroes? I know so few stories of the Earthmakers that I could not begin to guess, and I am reminded of how ignorant Belos has kept me.

We soon come to a winding stair that, similar to the hall, is cut with arching windows. At the top, another short hallway brings us to a wide, vaulted doorway, which leads to a covered balcony.

I peer around Logan. The balcony's smooth floor stretches to a finely cut stone railing, which looks out over the bay. We are higher now, and the view reaches beyond the rocky arms of the bay to the dark expanse of the ocean, which gleams sunset orange in the west.

Prima Gaiana sits within the graceful curves of a wooden chair softened by a tasseled velvet cushion. Her light gown of pale green is gathered at the shoulders and cinched at the waist in that elegant Earthmaker style, and a shawl has slipped down her arms to leave her slender shoulders bare. Delicate gold earrings dangle from her ears, and a gold bracelet shaped like a snake winds around one wrist.

At the Prima's elbow is a round table with clawed feet, which bears a porcelain tea set so fine that the light from a nearby brass brazier shines through it. The pot is set in a silver stand with a short beeswax candle burning beneath to keep the tea warm. But her cup rests on the table, full of tea, untouched, no longer even steaming. Whatever has been under discussion has been going on for some time. Gaiana appears calm and composed. Were I not learning to read subtle signs of Earthmaker emotion, I would not even realize she is upset. It shows only in the slight crease between her pale brows. In a human, that would mean nothing.

An Earthmaker I have never seen, dressed in a tunic and cross-body robe, perches at the foot of a wide divan. This must be Counselor Demos. He is one of the oldest-looking Earthmakers I have yet seen, which is to say he looks about fifty. His body is clearly fit, his bare legs muscled, skin toned. Most human politicians are pale and fat by the time they reach thirty. Is it fitness that makes the Earthmakers attractive? It's not that they are all beautiful, but they all have a certain *something* that makes you believe them so. Is it their confidence? The sense of power? The simple absence of defect?

Demos and Gaiana's backs are to the door because they are listening to Aron, who stands at the stone railing, flanked on either side by terracotta pots, which contain rose bushes not yet in bloom and ivy that twines through the railing. I'm saddened a little; this seems too lovely a space for the conflict that I know is coming.

Aron sees us in the doorway and pushes away from the railing. Gaiana and Demos twist to look. They both rise to their feet, a slight parting of their lips the only sign of surprise.

Gaiana glides over to Logan and takes his face in her hands. Her deep blue eyes search his face, and worry, impossible for even an Earthmaker mother to fully conceal, etches into the faint lines around her eyes. "Loganos, what have you done?"

I squirm guiltily. Any moment she will notice me, accuse me. I have done this to her son. What mother would not blame me?

Aron's sandals slap across the stone floor. Though his face is still, his hands are clenched into fists. Despite the loose robes meant for the indoors, there is nothing casual in his demeanor. He's ready for a fight.

"You've come to hand her over?" Aron's voice is half question, half command.

A muscle bulges in Logan's gold-stubbled jaw. Gaiana steps back, but I see her fingers lingering on Logan's wrist. To reassure him? Or to hold him back?

"We've come to talk," Logan says shortly. "Astarti insisted."

Surprise flits across Aron's face in the slight lift of his eyebrows. This is the prime moment, and I grab it. I edge past Logan to face Aron. He is only three paces away, close enough to charge me. But I won't back down now. I came here for this.

"Where is Polemarc Clitus? I would address him also."

Aron's eyes narrow with suspicion. "He is away."

Bran's voice comes over my shoulder. "Let's not stand in the doorway. There is much to discuss."

The tension breaks a little as we move into the room. Nicanor, after a curt dismissal from Aron, hurries away. Aron tries to linger in the doorway, no doubt thinking to block any escape, but Logan glowers at him. Aron moves stiffly to the railing and stands before it, arms crossed. Gaiana and Demos sit, as does Bran. Logan and I stand in the open space between the chairs and the railing.

"Well?" prompts Demos. "What do you have to say?"

Logan glances from him to me. "Astarti, this is Counselor Demos."

Even though I've gathered that, I appreciate the introduction. I nod thanks to Logan, even as Aron gives him a dirty look. Apparently, everyone but Logan would prefer to keep me as ignorant as possible. I grit my teeth.

Aron looks at me expectantly.

I force my hands to unclench and, even though they are sweaty, I refuse to reveal my discomfort by wiping them on my pants. "I understand your people intend to join Martel."

Aron shoots Bran a withering look, which Bran receives calmly. Perhaps I misjudged Bran. Apparently, he wasn't supposed to tell me even that. Could it be that he does trust me, at least a little?

"Aron," Bran says patiently. "If she is a spy, wouldn't she have tried to get away by now? To tell the Unnamed of this plan?"

"A *good* spy would wait to learn the location of our force." Aron looks at me pointedly, then back to Bran. "I trust you did not reveal *that* to her?"

"No."

Aron turns to me again. "I won't tell you. And I won't tell Logan. Because I don't trust him right now either."

"Aronos!" chides Gaiana. "Logan would never betray us. Mind yourself."

"I'm sure he wouldn't intend to, Mother, but you have to admit that his judgment right now is...compromised."

Logan says in a low, dangerous voice, "I would say the same of you. You have a source of information here, and she has come willingly, in order to spare us disaster. At great risk to herself. And yet, your anger is so strong that you cannot even let her speak." What Logan says next he says in the tone of lecture, as though the words have been drilled into his head, "Anger is unseemly in an Earthmaker."

Everyone goes still. What does this mean to them? Logan's eyes are a swirl of color, all but flashing as they reflect the light of the brazier. The swirl I have come to expect; what troubles me is the Earthmaker stillness of his face. His expression is almost dead, and it doesn't look right on him. Though he is a Primo, a noble, he is not quite one of them. Why? And what is he thinking? There is so much I wish I could ask him. But this is not the time or place.

I clear my throat and turn to Aron, whose face has paled. "You cannot send your people to Martel. It is surely a trap."

Aron's eyes focus on me as though he has been somewhere else. "What do you mean?"

"Belos"—everyone tenses at the name, and I almost roll my eyes—"*Belos* will expect that."

"Why would he expect that?" This comes from Counselor Demos. At least *someone* is paying attention.

"Belos was once one of you, his father a Council Member. Who knows the Earthmaker mind better than he?"

Aron's lip curls. "One such as he never understood what it means to be an Earthmaker."

"Don't underestimate him. You would pay for it dearly."

Aron breathes control into himself and nods acknowledgment. "Go on."

"I believe Belos's main goal in this coming war is not to take Kelda, not at all. I think he means to destroy you, your people, Avydos itself if he can."

Counselor Demos leans forward on the divan. "You think he doesn't care about Kelda, that it's a ruse?"

"Oh, I'm sure he'll try to take Kelda. But it's not his primary goal. I think he is waiting for you to join Martel, then he will destroy you. You will be gathered together, away from Avydos, unsuspecting. Do you have any idea what he could do to you?"

Aron turns away, braces himself against the stone railing. "You keep saying 'I think,' 'I believe.' You are not sure of any of this. Even if you are not trying to manipulate us, you could be wrong."

"Belos does not tell me his plans. He has not trusted me since—" I cut that off and start again, "He does not trust me with valuable information. But I know him, Arcon, as you, perhaps, do not. I have seen him burn men to ash for imagined slights. I watched him kill one of his most loyal men for telling him an ugly truth. Any who stand against him, any who tell him he is wrong—"

Understanding fills me so suddenly I am dizzy. I know why he hates me. He sees that I don't agree with him, even when I say I do, and he can't stand it. How could I not have seen this before? And why, I wonder suddenly, has he been so lenient with me? Others have died for less.

I finish, "Any who question him or act against him or try to make him see he might be wrong are destroyed. And who has told him more loudly or more often that he is wrong? You. Your people. He will strike you out, as you have Stricken him."

Never in my life have I spoken so much at once, demanded so much attention. It has never been my place to pose an argument, to persuade. I am meant only to serve. And so I feel awkward and self-conscious as they stare at me, as they absorb my words like they might be important. But beneath this self-consciousness stirs another feeling: pride. This is a new kind of power.

"Even if this is so," says Aron, and I hear in his voice an edge of fear, "the Unnamed cannot destroy us if he cannot find us. And we will be an army. Two armies."

"But he can find Martel," I argue. "And that second army, you will quickly discover, is *not* your ally."

Demos stirs on the divan. "It's not so easy to find one man."

I spin to catch a view of everyone. "Are you all mad? Martel is Leashed by now!"

Aron turns to stare out over the bay. "You don't know that."

I stride toward him. "You're right, I don't *know* that. But I do know that Belos always gets what he wants, and he wanted Martel *very* badly. Belos will take him against his will, if need be."

Aron turns to me. He searches my face. "How can I trust you? How could I ever trust you? You're asking me to withdraw support from Martel. You're asking me to let Heborian stay in power. A Drifter. How do I know what *you* want?"

I shake that away. "Belos will see Heborian destroyed. He hates him, too."

I pause to wonder once more: why *does* Belos hate Heborian? He hates those who defy him. How could Heborian have done that? Is there some history between them?

"Belos is smart," I remind Aron, and saying that brings more into focus. I gasp with realization. "He will let you and Martel kill Heborian, and then he will destroy you. He will have everything he wants, with half the effort."

Aron's Earthmaker control slips. He throws up his hands. "This is all guessing!"

I turn at the sound of footsteps and find Demos at my shoulder. His face may be fairly young, but his eyes are old, settled, wise. "Aron, you were young when the Unnamed was Stricken. But I was not. His father was my friend. And I remember him in those early days. I think what the Drifter says could be true." He ends sternly, "We will have to verify it, of course."

"But, Counselor Demos," interjects Bran, "how could we possibly verify any of this?"

"By knowing if Martel is indeed Leashed."

"But we can't see that," Gaiana reminds him gently.

"No," Demos admits, "but *she* can."

"*No.*" Logan's voice.

He strides toward me and Demos.

"That is *far* too dangerous. Have you forgotten that Astarti is also Leashed?"

I flinch like he's struck me. It always sounds so dirty.

"The Unnamed could find her and take her. He will kill her. She cannot leave Avydos."

Annoyance flares within me. Does he think to command me, as Belos does? "I cannot hide here forever, Logan. I will not."

He grabs my arm, and his fingers dig painfully. "He could take you."

There is such pain and fear in his eyes that I soften. He cares for me. He truly does. I have denied it to protect myself from hope, but I see it in his eyes. It makes me want to give in, to do what he says, but I cannot. This is too important. "Belos can only sense me if he's near."

"And what if he's near?"

"He rarely travels the Drift. The Hounding is drawn to him. I don't know why, but it is. He will let the Seven do everything until the final stages."

"And they cannot sense your Leash?"

"No."

Not from outside the Drift, anyway. And from within it, they won't need my Leash to sense me. As a Drifter, I'll stand out like a candle in the dark anyway. I don't mention any of this, but then, that's not what he asked. Is that a lie?

"But how can we trust her report?"

Aron's voice makes me jump. For a moment, I had forgotten that any were in the room but Logan and me.

Aron stares around. "I see you are all eager to throw away your suspicions, but I am not. Have you forgotten that the Unnamed is known also as the Deceiver? Do you not think that one of his own is trained in deception?"

I wince inwardly. I *am* trained in deception, and I *did* just deceive Logan. Even if it wasn't technically a lie, I deceived him.

Demos rubs at his clean-shaven jaw. "Someone will have to go with her." He looks to me. "Isn't that possible? Can't you take another into the Drift?"

Aron looks appalled. "Counselor Demos, are you really suggesting—"

I square my shoulders. Now we're getting somewhere. "Yes, it's possible but very dangerous. And the person has to be willing—that is extremely important. Any non-Drifter taken against his will dies instantly. The shock of the Drift is too much."

This sobering statement hangs in the air.

Demos nods. "Aron? What do you say?"

Aron is shaking his head, but it's more denial than refusal. "This is madness. She's a Drifter. A servant of our enemy. Why are we even listening to her?"

Logan's hand clenches on the pommel of his sword. "Because she's the only one making any sense!"

"Logan," Gaiana warns, and I realize that Bran is not the only peacekeeper in this family. "Aron's concerns are natural and legitimate. But you are right that Astarti's claims ring true.

And Counselor Demos is also right that we need verification. There is no need for hostility among us. Let us move forward on an agreed upon course."

Logan's shoulders drop, and all the heat is gone from him. I wish I had Gaiana's ability to cut through his anger. "You're right, Mother. Aron? Is the course agreed upon?"

"We have nothing better," he grits out, refusing to give a more direct sign of acceptance. "You two must clean up and change. Logan, shave off that awful stubble. Then I'll take you to our Wardens."

My heart skips with apprehension. Aron is coming with us.

Logan's jaw clenches briefly. "Twenty minutes."

Chapter 20

I am taken to a private room by one of Prima Gaiana's maids, a slim young woman in flowing white robes cinched at her tiny waist, golden bracelets on her wrists. Logan has gone to another room to change. I felt nervous when we parted ways; I don't like being in this place without him. But I cannot act uncomfortable. One thing Belos taught me: show your enemies no weakness. I know these people are not exactly my enemies, that I am actually helping them, but I'm still uneasy.

The room is gorgeous, like everything else here. I'm on the seaward side of the building, and the wall is another partial one, open to the bay. A bed with a golden coverlet and four posts carved like twisting shells stands against the far wall. A dark wood dresser, its face carved with wild roses, stands against another wall, and a tilting oval mirror takes up a corner.

With one hand curled around the flame to protect it, the maid takes her candle to the bedside table and uses it to light the wick in a glass-faced lantern. I am behind her and when the light blooms at her front, it shows her willowy shape through the gauzy robes. I lower my eyes. Earthmakers are less modest even than humans. Perhaps for them the body is only one more thing to perfect. They seem to approach it with the same detachment as everything else.

But not all of them are so detached. Logan certainly is not. And I have caught hints of something warmer in a few others, such as the young Warden Korinna. I am left to wonder whether warmth is more common in Wardens, because they spend so much time in human lands, in the young, who have not yet learned to distance themselves, or simply in individuals who are not quite like the rest.

Footsteps at the door make me spin. Another bracelet-marked maid, her arms full of clothes, steps into the room.

"Ligeia is bringing water," she says and walks past me to the bed, where she lays down the stack of clothes. She sets two pairs of boots on the floor. "We did not know what you would prefer. Some of these are more Keldan in style."

I start to dig through the pile, making a mess of it. I find wools and linens, all high-quality, all far too fine for the likes of me. Mostly they are tunics, which I have not seen on the women here, except for Korinna. I wonder if these clothes are meant for young boys. I wonder, too, how many female Wardens there are. I have never met any but Korinna.

Another maid arrives with a bowl of steaming water and a white towel draped over her arm. She sets these on another table, along with a bar of soap from her pocket.

The three gather at the door. One asks, "Do you need anything else?"

"Er, no." I am uncomfortable with this entire situation. I have never been waited on before, and these are the Prima's women. Surely they must resent this duty? If they do, it doesn't show on their faces. But then, it wouldn't.

"Thank you," I remember to say as they turn to go.

"If you need us, tell Nicanor. He is waiting outside."

I frown. Even now I'm guarded. They may pretend it's all courtesy, but that's just on the surface. Even so, it's better than the dungeon, and I turn gratefully to the steaming washbowl as soon as the door clicks shut.

When I'm clean and smelling like rose water instead of saltwater and sweat, I braid my hair. I paw through the clothes and find clean undergarments and a dark blue tunic embroidered with a yellow geometric design along the neck and hem. It's fancier than I usually wear, but it's the simplest thing in the pile. I choose a pair of slim-fitting black breeches and smooth wool socks. I try on both pairs of boots, and one of them fits better than the other. The boots are tall, almost to my knees, and lace up the front. The dark brown leather is soft and comfortable. Lastly, I pull on a padded leather jacket. It is still spring.

Nicanor snaps to attention when I open the door, and I ask, before I can stop myself, "How old are you?"

His pale skin colors. "Fourteen, my lady."

I snort when he calls me "lady," but when his head hangs I realize he thinks I'm laughing at him. Maybe I am, a little. But he's even younger than I thought, so I try to be nice.

"Are you a Warden?"

"Oh, no, my lady. I'm a house-guard."

I can't help but think how that must not be a very serious duty here if fourteen-year-old boys are trusted with it. Once again I am reminded of how removed Avydos is, how protected.

Nicanor offers, "Becoming a Warden takes years of training. I am only three years into mine."

"They don't start you until eleven?" It surprises me because most training programs in human lands start the boys younger.

Nicanor looks shamefaced. "I didn't show my second element until then."

Ah. No doubt this is disgraceful among Earthmakers.

"Besides, I'm from Korith." At my quizzical look he adds, "It's a village on the eastern side of the island. We don't do as much testing there. For potential, I mean."

"Why not?"

"It's just not as common."

Earthmaker society has so many more delineations than I would have guessed. I've always thought they must all be pretty much the same, but I'm beginning to see that's not so. I also begin to understand why Nicanor has less of the Earthmaker reserve than others here. He's a village boy. I would guess that most here consider him a bit of a rustic. No wonder he always looks so self-conscious.

I gesture for him to lead the way. "Tell me about your training."

As Nicanor takes me through several passageways, he leaps into excited explanations. "There's weapons training, of course. That's what I like best, though Master Panteros says I'm awful with the sword. I'm a great shot with the bow, and that, he says, is something at least. We also learn geography, politics, history—"

"History? Of where? Avydos? Kelda?"

"Yes, both of those. And more. All the known histories, particularly the war with the, uh, the Unnamed." His eyes shift to me and away.

Now I'm really curious. "What do they teach you about him?"

Nicanor pulls at the neck of his tunic, and I gather that he's not supposed to talk to me about Belos. Perhaps he's not supposed to talk to me at all. Now that we are in the more heavily-trafficked entry hall, men and women are staring, and his neck is bright red.

I lower my voice and prompt him anyway. "So what's the first thing you learn of him?"

His lip twists, but I give him an encouraging smile. "How, uh, how he went into the land of humans, to the far north, and came back a Drifter." He shudders.

"The far north? Where? Rune?"

"Rune, yes. Where there used to be so many of…that kind."

I frown. I have heard there were once many Drifters in Rune, but then they disappeared. I've heard various rumors: that Belos killed them, that the Earthmakers did, that they killed each other, that they fled to other, unknown lands. I don't know the truth of it, but it happened around sixty years ago, when Belos came into power. I highly doubt the timing is coincidental.

I have so many more questions for Nicanor, but we've reached the open front doors. I see Aron and Logan waiting on the porch. How long have they been there? I'm suddenly self-conscious of how much time I spent washing up.

Logan is clean-shaven once again and dressed much as he was when I first met him at the Trader's Choice: leather pants, leather jacket, long-sleeved dark gray tunic that hangs open at the neck to show hints of muscle and the tail end of that curving scar. A sword is belted at his waist.

Aron's heavy green tunic is finer than Logan's and cut in an Earthmaker style with short, broad sleeves over a tighter long-sleeved shirt of stark white. He wears loose trousers, which I have not seen on him before. Like Logan, he has a sword belted at his waist, though Aron's scabbard is more intricately tooled. I cannot wait to get back to Kelda, where I can shape my Drift-spear at any moment. I hate feeling this defenseless.

Logan gives me a failed attempt at a smile. "Ready?"

Aron makes no note of my presence and turns away before I can answer. He tromps down the steps.

I nod to Logan, and we follow Aron across the stone-paved courtyard to a tiny grove of trees.

"We can enter the Current from here?" I ask, surprised. I expected to walk all the way to the Wood.

"You can enter the Current from a solitary tree," Logan says. "But you should know that. You did it once, remember?"

I think of the dead—well, almost dead—tree in Belos's courtyard. I still don't quite believe that I have Earthmaker blood, so it's hard for me to assimilate these sorts of facts. Part of me knows Logan, and Gaiana, must be right, but it still feels wrong. I'm a Drifter. That is how I know myself.

When I follow Logan into the Current this time, I am less fearful of the touch and tug of the golden Wood. I don't like it, but I can deal with it. It's let me through several times; it must be safe.

We trail Aron through the Current because he still won't tell us exactly where we're going. He's right to be cautious, even though it irks me to admit it. He doesn't know me.

When we step from the Current, the rush of cool night air makes me shiver in spite of my padded jacket. We're in a dark wood, though the paleness of sky through the overhead branches suggests that it's still early. As my eyes adjust, I make out Aron's form. He's staring around, orienting himself.

He jerks his head. "This way."

We follow him up a rocky slope. I hear Logan and Aron stumbling over hidden undergrowth and roots. After the second time I trip, barely catching myself against a tree, I fill my palm with Drift-light. The quick rush of energy along my mooring makes my breath hitch. So fast, so easy. Tension that I didn't know was there drains out of me. I am myself again. Whole.

My pale light reveals Aron three paces ahead, staring back at me with disdain.

I stare back. "Do you want to split your face open?"

His jaw sets. "Walk up here, then."

When we reach a rocky ledge where the trees open, I look out to see moonlit slopes studded with trees. I can't pinpoint our location, but we are definitely in the foothills of a mountain range, and my guess is that it's the low, green mountains of eastern Kelda, which the Keldans call the Green Wall because it separates them from Valdar.

We trek on, climbing again.

Lights bloom ahead in what looks to be broad, flat space.

"Halt."

We all stop at once at the warning tone, which comes from overhead.

Aron tilts his head. "Good work, Galen."

Someone drops to the ground, and my Drift-light reveals a man about Logan's age wearing a light leather breastplate and greaves. Galen inclines his head. "Arcon. I didn't recognize you."

"No matter. Take us to Polemarc Clitus."

We follow Galen past the horse line—how did they bring horses here?—and through the camp, where men and women cluster around cook fires, eating from tin plates. So. There *are* more female Wardens. For some reason, this pleases me. My stomach rumbles at the wafting scent of roasted meat, probably boar at this time of year. I am reminded that Logan and I haven't eaten anything but bread and honey today. He, who is so much bigger than I am, must be starving.

The tents are small and simple, made of waxed canvas stretched between wooden cross poles. Nothing about them screams Earthmaker. In fact, the only thing about this camp that suggests these are not humans is the organization and quietness. The Wardens are dressed in simple, functional clothing, performing the ordinary tasks of soldiers: eating supper, cleaning weapons, checking gear. But then, Wardens have learned to blend in. Experienced ones are often difficult for even me to identify when they are among humans.

Even though I let my Drift-light vanish before we entered the camp, I feel eyes on me. Do they know who I am? Are they staring at me with that Earthmaker contempt? Or it is just curiosity about why their Arcon and his brother are here with some unknown woman?

At one campfire, a young woman stands up, and I recognize Korinna. Her mouth crooks in a half-smile.

Galen takes us to the middle of the camp. We stop at a tent whose large size and scalloped edges distinguish it as the commander's. The tent glows with light from within. One of the guards at the tent front ducks his head through the flap to announce us. After a brief exchange, he holds the flap aside. Aron ducks through first, then I do, then Logan. He has stayed at my back the whole time, tense and untrusting. I can't help but torment myself with the question: Does he distrust me? Or his own people?

With all of us inside, the tent seems smaller than I first thought. A cot takes up one wall and a small table is strewn with papers. A lantern rests on the table, casting light over Polemarc Clitus as he studies a parchment. He is dressed for war in a short-sleeved tunic like Aron's, belted at the waist. His armor hangs on a stand in one corner, but he wears his bronze greaves and wrist guards.

His face betrays no surprise, even when his eyes flick to me. "Aronos, what brings you?"

Aron waits until Galen leaves, then he says, "We have reason to suspect that Martel might be Leashed to the Unnamed.

Which, I don't have to tell you, would make him an unacceptable ally."

I feel like he's also referring to me right now: Leashed, unacceptable.

Clitus sets down the parchment he was studying. "And what leads you to this suspicion?"

Aron looks pointedly to me, and Clitus's eyes narrow. "How did you apprehend her?"

"He didn't," Logan growls. "Astarti came freely."

Clitus's searching eyes shift to Logan. "And you, Logan? In what manner did you return?"

For the first time, Logan looks uncertain, uncomfortable. Because Clitus is his commander? He doesn't seem to have that much respect for authority. But it *is* respect I see in Logan. His head lowers. He doesn't want Clitus to think poorly of him. I am filled with guilt again. I've caused so many rifts for Logan.

"I've done what I must, Polemarc." He picks his head up. "You will see, in the end, that it was right."

Clitus's expression softens fractionally. "I hope so, Logan, I truly do. Now tell me what's going on."

Aron explains my suspicions. I let him. If he'd rather talk for me, that's fine. I do correct him once or twice, which irritates him and gives me little pulses of pleasure.

When Aron finishes telling Clitus the plan, Clitus raises an eyebrow. "And who will go with her?"

"I will," both Logan and Aron say at once.

They glare at each other.

"Clitus," says Aron reasonably, "you must see that there's no question of who should go. Logan is compromised. More than that, with his…limitations, he's all but defenseless if she turns on him."

An ugly red creeps up Logan's neck, and I want to shape a Drift-spear and swing it at Aron's head. He didn't have to say it like that.

"I'm afraid Aron's right." Clitus's tone is businesslike, neither cruel nor kind.

Logan crosses his arms. "Why can we not both go? I don't want Astarti to be—"

"If she's true to her word"—Logan's eyes flash—"Aron will see her safely back."

Clitus looks to Aron for confirmation. After a slight hesitation, Aron nods.

I shrug. I don't need Aron. If the Seven are there and they sense me, there will be nothing he can do. My heart skips at the thought. Should I not do this? Why am I helping them?

I chase that away. I have decided. There is nothing to be gained by waffling. This feels right. The rest doesn't matter.

Logan's nostrils are flared, and his breathing is too fast. I put my fingers on his wrist, as I saw Gaiana do. I don't want him to get into any more trouble. He takes a deep breath, closing his eyes. When he opens them again, they are steady blue. I almost smile. He responded to my touch as to his mother's. I feel light and happy. But then I feel Aron and Clitus's eyes on me, and I take my hand away.

℥ Ω

We learn that Martel is encamped some twenty miles deeper into the mountains. The Wardens have been slowly gathering here. Their current numbers look to be about fifty, but I assume more will come. Of course, no one will tell me how many.

Clitus suggests we wait until morning, arguing that if we are in the Drift, no one will see us. When I insist that we go tonight, they stare at me suspiciously, and I am forced to explain that if any of the Seven are there and accessing the Drift, we could be sensed. Better to go at night when they are more likely to be absent or sleeping. The fact that Aron nods acceptance tells me he's starting to believe me, and the fact that Logan's jaw tightens hard tells me that he's not happy about this possibility.

Eventually, after wolfing down some meat and bread that Logan insists I eat—not that I resist it—I get him and Clitus to leave. Aron will have to concentrate to enter the Drift safely. We can't have any distractions.

When the flap falls shut, I sit cross-legged on the thin mat and point to the floor in front of me. Aron hesitates, looking uncomfortable, then he mirrors me.

I explain, "The Drift is a web of energy. It's not unlike the Current really, but where the Current has fixed points, because trees don't move, the Drift is constantly shifting. As living things move, they change its pattern."

"I don't need to know how the evil thing works. I just need you to take me through it."

"You *do* need to understand the Drift. Those who are unprepared do not live through the shock of entering. All the world is torn away. You are reduced to your bare essence—"

"I understand this. The Current is the same." Aron's hands are clenched on his knees.

"Sort of. But in the Current, you have the flow between trees. *It* moves *you*. You flow with it from one certain point to another. When you first enter the Drift, you will feel…adrift." I shake my head, frustrated. I can't think of a better word.

Aron's forehead crinkles. "Then how do you stay grounded? How do you know where to go?"

I perk up. This I can explain. "You must feel your connection to other living things, using it to orient yourself. It is difficult to travel to a precise location unless you know the place to which you are traveling very well. For example, when I travel to Tornelaine, I recognize it by the shape in which the moving energies are contained, the shape of the city. But I also know that Heborian and his Drifters are there, and Drifters always burn brighter. When I see them clustered, I know I'm near Tornelaine."

"But how will we find Martel within the Drift?"

"It won't be that hard because there are few people here. We'll follow the threads in the basic direction Clitus indicated. We'll be able to see something of the land, just not much. When I feel the nearness of a group of humans, we can assume we are close to Martel's company."

"But how will you know which one he is?"

"By his Leash, of course."

Aron frowns, still wanting to doubt my theory.

I lean forward a little. "Now, listen. This is important. Everyone knows that the Drift is deadly to any but a Drifter, but most don't understand why, and you *must* understand why if you want to live."

Aron's fingers, still clenched on his knees, are white with strain. Behind me, the tiny flame in the lantern blooms brighter, licking at the glass panes that contain it. Aron's tense face glows in the light, and I wonder if his exterior is as fragile as that glass. But no. He is stone. The light dims again as Aron regains control of himself.

I warn him, "If you resist the Drift in any way, you will be unable to enter it fully. Your body will come, because I am pulling it. But I can't control your mind. If you resist, if you don't *will* yourself *fully* into the world of the Drift, your body and mind will be severed. Do you understand?"

"I think so."

"You must be fully honest with yourself. If you tell yourself you are willing, but then you instinctively pull away, or if you panic, I cannot save you."

Aron's nostrils flare, but he gives no other sign of fear.

"This would be easier with the Shackle," I tease, trying to lighten the mood. "It would bind you together, bind you to me. I could hold your mind within mine, and you wouldn't be able to pull away." I crack a smile. "You'd actually be safer."

Aron's eyebrows lower. "I wouldn't be safe at all. You could Leash me."

"It was a joke." Earthmakers. No sense of humor.

"Oh. So. What do I need to do?"

"When I take you into the Drift, you must stay relaxed. Do not panic. You will have to trust me."

The corner of Aron's eye twitches.

"You know I could kill you right now, right?"

"Oh, please."

"I could. You see my hand?" He glances down to where my right hand is curled as though around a spear. A spear that would be pointed at his belly. "Within a heartbeat I could shape my Drift-spear, and it would punch right through your gut. So if I wanted you to die, I could find easier ways to do it than taking you into the Drift."

His jaw sets. He knows I'm right.

"I will do everything I can to get you through the Drift. The rest is up to you. And that means not fighting me. You will have to trust me, let yourself flow with me. If you can't do that, we shouldn't continue."

Aron unclenches his fingers and lets out a breath. His head lowers a little, and I can see him fighting within himself. I wonder if he is thinking about what I told him before Clitus and Logan left, that I've never heard of an Earthmaker, other than the Seven, of course, surviving entry into the Drift. Even if he tries his best, he still might fail. Entering the Drift goes strongly against the nature of an Earthmaker. Can he overcome his nature for a few minutes?

For the first time since I met Aron, he looks vulnerable. I try to tell myself that this is his choice, that if he would simply trust my report, this wouldn't be necessary. But I understand why he doesn't. And I respect his courage. I don't want to respect anything about him, but I do.

He looks up, and I see the resolve in his eyes. "All right. I will try to trust you."

"Not try. You will *have* to trust me."

He nods.

I hold out my hands. "Hold them."

He recoils.

I roll my eyes. "If you can't even touch my hands, you'll never be able to travel the Drift with me."

He sighs and puts his hands in mine, keeping the touch light. I grip him, and he tenses, but I don't let go. When he relaxes, I tell him to breathe deeply. I scoot closer until our knees are touching. One of his feet is pressed against my shin. It's a strange intimacy, holding his hands, feeling his pulse, his breaths, his tiny movements. His hands are strong, the palms callused. Like Logan, he knows the sword.

I make him breathe in time with me. I say, adopting the tone I've heard the Keldan priests use, making up the words as I go, "Flow with me, know that you are safe with me, that if you accept the Drift, it cannot hurt you. You want to be there. You want to travel with me. Say it."

"I want to be there. I want to travel with you."

"You are safe."

"I am safe."

"You want to flow."

"I want to flow."

"You want to drift."

"I want to drift."

I open myself to the pathway of my mooring. I want to rush along it, as I am used to doing. But I ease myself into it, drawing Aron with me through touch. As the world around me dissolves into its bare energies, I flare with joy. I feel Aron hesitate, and I calm myself, trying to send reassurance through our linked hands. He steadies.

Then our hands vanish, and the physical touch is gone.

My own energy is bright, with its whites and golds against the dark, remote background of the trees and tents. My glowing white Leash trails away into the distance. Relief floods me as I realize it flows away from Martel's camp. Belos is not there. The faintness of the Leash suggests he is in the Dry Land, as I suspected. Maybe luck is with me tonight.

Aron's energy, like that of most Earthmakers, is slower and quieter than mine. Dimmer. I look around to see many such forms gathered around us throughout the campsite. It's almost like they are...not as alive? Not as connected? The threads between them are faint. Then I see Logan.

He is pacing at the edge of the camp. His energy roils and burns. He is brighter even than any Drifter I've ever seen. I sense Aron's attention on him. Aron tries to speak, but he doesn't know how to in the Drift.

I notice another form that burns more brightly than the others. Nothing like Logan, certainly, but bright enough to pass for human. It's Korinna. I stare. What does this mean?

Aron shifts uncertainly beside me, and I force myself to focus on him. I strain to speak. "You did well. Stay with me."

He nods.

Faint lines run between the energy forms, showing those who are connected by attention or feeling. A strong line runs between me and Aron because we are willing ourselves together. We must maintain that. But another strong line runs between me and Logan, and I must break it. I turn away, forcing myself not to think about him anymore.

I feel for the energies of others in the basic direction that Clitus indicated. They are faint, far away, but recognizable.

I dredge up sound again. "Stay focused on me. *Will* yourself to follow me."

He nods, and I hope he does understand because I have no more energy to speak. I let myself drift toward the far off energies.

Aron stays with me remarkably well. I continue to think reassurance in his direction, to keep a connection between us. I don't know if it helps, but we reach Martel's camp without incident.

Thousands of lighted forms dot the dark slope of the mountain. I did not expect so many. But they are ordinary, human, and my energies settle with relief. No Drifters. None of the Seven are here.

Aron follows me among the lighted forms. As we find nothing remarkable, I begin to think I was wrong about Martel.

Then I see him.

A lighted shape with a white tail that flows in the same direction as mine.

Aron's energy churns suddenly beside mine. He sees it too.

I want to feel triumphant about my correct guess, but I am saddened. A new Leash is nothing to celebrate.

We saw what we came for, and I am about to turn away when I see—feel—a new, bright energy rushing toward us. A Drifter.

Panic flares within me as I recognize the controlled pattern of fury, the calculated anger.

Straton.

CHAPTER 21

I have no idea how Straton hid himself, but I have only a moment to feel surprise. We have two immediate choices: flee through the Drift or step into the physical world. If we flee, Aron will probably not be able to keep up, and if it comes to a fight, he could panic. If he tries to get out of the Drift on his own, he'll kill himself.

I manage a weak, "Follow me."

Straton is a like a fireball shooting toward us, so I don't wait for Aron to nod. I rush him along my mooring, hoping he can keep up. His energy hand finds mine as I push through my mooring and into the physical world. His sweaty hand slips from mine, and he collapses, heaving. I hope the shock doesn't kill him.

Chaos spreads from our location like we are a stone dropped into a still pond. Men leap up, yelling and grabbing for weapons. Horses whinny in panic.

I draw energy along my mooring and shape my Drift-spear. I step away from Aron, hoping to keep him out of the fight. The men start to charge me, but they stop dead when Straton explodes into the space before me, his Drift-sword already swinging.

I duck under the blade. He is too close for me to use my spear point, so I charge the weapon with energy and slam the haft into his ribs. The blow flings him back. I whip the spear around and leap before he can recover. I stab toward his throat, but the tip scrapes and skitters against a faintly glowing barrier. As my weapon twists out from under me, I fall, rolling over Straton's shoulder and into a campfire.

The fire flares to huge, angry life. It washes around me as I scramble up. Pain burns down my right arm. The flames flash and lick, and my world is fire, nothing but fire. I scream.

Suddenly the flames vanish.

I fall to my knees, the scream dying in my throat. Air heaves through my lungs.

Three paces away, Straton growls. He spins to face Aron, who is swaying on his feet, his face full of the euphoria of earthmagic.

Straton staggers back and mutters weakly, "Impossible." Then he straightens himself, and the condescension comes back into his voice. "Ah. The son. Or one of them."

Aron's face goes deathly still, but his eyes blaze with life. Fires flare all around the camp, flooding the space with light. Wind howls through the trees, which creak and sway. Men run, screaming.

One fire rises from its bed, writhing and swirling, twisting itself into a point.

Straton's eyes widen as the flame shoots toward him.

He vanishes.

The fire explodes into a tent.

Canvas and wood crackle and blacken in the conflagration. Horses scream in fear. Men are shouting. The flames lick toward the branches above.

I force myself to uncurl from my burned arm. My jacket and shirt are partially burned away and red, oozing flesh shows beneath. "Aron!"

He stares at the flames.

I push myself to my feet. "Aron!"

The fire winks out, leaving a smoking ruin of charred canvas and wood.

I jog over to him, wincing as the motion shoots pain through my right arm.

"Are you all right?" I ask him.

"Yes." His voice is cold. "Are you?"

"I'll live."

He looks down at my burns. "You need a Healer."

I want to laugh, after all his rules against Healing Drifters, but there's no time for it. "We have to get back to camp. Now."

"That coward. He hardly even tried."

"Straton may be a coward, but he's a smart coward. He knows we saw Martel's Leash. He knows the Earthmakers will no longer join Martel. Belos will be furious and Straton knows it. The next best thing is to kill the Earthmakers gathered right now. At least he will salvage something and maybe appease Belos."

"Can he find them so easily?"

"Gathered together like that? Away from humans? They're a beacon."

"He'd still be stupid to take on fifty Wardens."

"I doubt it will be just him. He was hidden somehow; I didn't see him. I don't know how he did it. Others could be nearby."

I don't have to say anything more. Aron strides through the camp, where men are starting to move again, though they stand back from us. I see Martel's scarred face in the crowd. One of his men takes a step forward, but Martel puts out a hand to stop him. Martel is studying me, confused. I don't need to study him. I know what he is: a pawn of Belos.

Aren't you the same? demands a voice deep inside me.

Another voice asks whether Martel chose this, but I don't have time to seek answers.

I follow Aron, but my mind is hazy with pain. By the time we reach the trees, I am dizzy. Aron looks at me worriedly when I sway but says nothing. He lays one hand against a tree and stretches out his other. I take it. It will be easier and quicker for him to take me through the Current than for me to take him through the Drift. Fear reaches its fingers around my throat: it will still be too slow.

As the golden Current sweeps us along, I want to scream with impatience. Anything could be happening. Logan could be—

Aron pulls me from the Current. The earth shakes, and I stumble into him. Pain shoots through my arm.

We are just beyond the edge of the Warden camp, and I stare at the chaos, so surreal after the quiet Current. Wind screams through the trees, fires burst, spears of ice fly glittering through the air. Straton and two others of the Seven, Ludos and Koricus, are at opposite ends of the camp, hemming the Wardens in. They protect themselves from the onslaught, sliding away from fissures and flame, but they aren't attacking. They are containing the Wardens, waiting. Fear thuds inside me.

I grab Aron's arm. "Everyone must get back to Avydos. Now."

"But there are only three. If we take that one by the slope and then—"

My hand clenches on his arm. "They are holding everyone for Belos."

I feel him shiver. Is it Belos's name or my tone that silences him?

His eyes dart across the fight, and his mouth sets into a grim line as he sees that the Seven are acting as sheepdogs, holding the Wardens in a tight group. His face goes still, and his eyes fill with that Earthmaker euphoria. Every fire in the camp shoots straight and high into the air and vanishes.

Darkness swallows the camp. I hear the lingering rumbles of earth, the creak of trees. I hear running steps, but I don't understand them. Only when my eyes adjust do I realize that dark shapes flood toward the trees. Some drag the wounded, but many still forms are left behind.

Straton, Ludos, and Koricus attack the fleeing Wardens. Their onslaught of Drift-weapons and energy blasts is met with rumbling, cracking earth. A fissure opens behind the Wardens. Someone screams.

My eyes sweep over the fleeing Wardens. Where is he?

Aron grabs my left sleeve, avoiding my burn. "Come on."

Aron tugs, but I jerk free. I enter the Drift.

The dim forms of Earthmakers flee from three brighter shapes. But there is one brighter yet, a wild flow of energy. He's at the back of the retreat, too close to Ludos.

When I leap out of the Drift, Logan shouts in surprise and jerks his sword in my direction.

"It's me!"

"Astarti!"

A bluish-white spear arcs toward us. I shape a barrier just in time to send the spear clattering aside. Logan grabs my hand, and we run to the nearest tree.

The Current is a golden flood of Earthmakers. When three more shapes enter the Current, the Wardens split to follow multiple branches. They will force their pursuers to choose and divide. I follow Logan through the golden flow from forest to grove, from tree to tree, losing track of our turns and shifts. My energy pulses with fear as I look back again and again, but none of the Seven have followed our group.

When the brilliant gold of the Avydos Wood glitters ahead, my whole being fills with relief and joy. We made it.

We're safe.

I am brushing the edge of the Wood, reaching for the answering touch of the trees, when my Leash burns white-hot.

CHAPTER 22

I scramble for the Wood, begging it to let me through, but the pull on my Leash is inexorable, and I am dragged away. My mouth is open on a scream, but there is no sound here.

Logan sweeps back to me, grabbing for me, but our hands scrabble uselessly. Nothing can break a Leash.

I close my eyes and turn away from Logan to face Belos. I won't let him take me from behind.

Belos braces himself in the golden flow. He is a barely contained battle of energy. All those he has Taken live within him somehow, and they are fighting. One thread of energy below his ribs snakes around another, strangling it. Another fights in his neck. Twist, bend, constrict. Then the threads unwind and slip away, under control again. Belos's golden face is lit with power, and I know those energies—those souls—will never escape.

And I am one of them.

He will Take me.

Despair buries me; I am dead within it. Belos hauls on my Leash, and I let him. The pain of it eases. Should I never have fought him? Would it all have been this easy?

Golden branches snake around me. The Wood is shoving me out, giving me to him.

But instead of glowing with triumph, Belos's face contorts with rage, the power churning madly within him. But it's not just rage. What is that other emotion that makes him draw back instinctively?

Branches whip and lash around me, a grabbing, twisting whirl of gold. They surround me, and I lose sight of Belos. The hold on my Leash falters. Hope spikes through me. I scramble back and stumble into something, some other, wild energy that embraces me. I struggle briefly until I see Logan's beautiful golden face. I grab for him, and he pulls.

My Leash tugs again, and pain shoots through me. Can my Leash be ripped from me? Can I be torn in two?

Suddenly, the tug is gone, and I fall into Logan. Lines of power swirl through his face, and I want to stay here, holding his bare self against mine, but he pulls me along. His pull, though, is nothing like Belos's; there is no pain or fear in it, only strength. I glance back, but I see nothing of my master, only a writhing mass of branches.

Logan drags me from the Current into the cool night air. The shock of pain returning to my arm makes me cry out. I am shaking; nausea wracks me. I sink to the ground and vomit, my nose inches from the dirt. I feel Logan hovering over me, and I want to yell at him, to tell him to go away.

When I struggle to stand, Logan helps me to my feet. I push him off. I don't want him to see me like this. I don't want to be weak in front of him. Worse, Logan saw what I most truly am: a dog on a leash, someone's property. I refuse to meet his eyes. I walk away.

I emerge from the small grove outside the royal house. A few stragglers are crossing the stone-paved courtyard, wearily climbing the steps to the open doors. Open doors. I marvel at it. Belos was a mere breath away, but he might as well have been on the other side of the world. So safe here, guarded by the Wood. In some part of myself, I understand Avydos is a sanctuary. Another part of me, though, feels too dirty to be here among the fine buildings and proud people who cannot imagine being Leashed, and that makes me hate this place.

Logan hovers at my shoulder, moving with me across the moonlit courtyard.

The hall is already settling in to a bustling order, all movement efficient and controlled under the warm light of lanterns and glowing braziers. Those who are uninjured help the wounded over to the stone balustrade. Aron and Clitus are calling the captains together, conferring in a tight circle. When he sees us, Aron's face melts with relief. I don't fool myself that Aron is relieved to see me, but why would he be so relieved to see Logan? They seem to hate each other. I have never seen them do anything but argue and cut at each other. I am reminded that I know nothing of families. I cannot begin to guess how I would feel about a sibling. My curiosity fades, leaving me deeply, completely alone. No, I will never know what it is to have a sibling.

Logan nudges me toward the wall, but I resist. I have enough pride left that I won't wait to be Healed only to have someone throw me out. I won't let them laugh at me. When someone grabs my hand, I jerk away, then see it's Korinna. Her leg is crooked at an unnatural angle, her face horribly white.

"Sit," she says, her voice giving no indication of her pain.

I hover uncertainly, but I really have nowhere to go. What will I do, sit on the porch steps? Korinna's eyes plead. I sigh resignation, promising myself that if any of them laugh, I will kill them.

When I'm crouched beside Korinna, Logan leans against the railing. In one breath I wish he would go away; in the next I fear he will. The toe of his boot edges into the corner of my vision. I shift my eyes away. I know I should thank him for pulling me from the Current, for not fleeing when Belos appeared, but I can't. Maybe tomorrow. Right now, I am too ashamed to speak to him.

Bran, who has been helping with the more seriously wounded, tries to catch my eye from down the hall. I ignore him but see in his face that some silent communication has passed between him and Logan. They know each other well enough to talk without words. Envy gnaws at me, that someone knows Logan so well, that some people have family.

Feluvas and Gaiana move down the row of wounded. There are twelve of us, and both Healers are pale and drawn by the time they are halfway down the line. I didn't realize that Healing drained them.

I feel Earthmaker eyes on me, no doubt wondering why the Drifter is here, wondering what makes me think I deserve Healing. I shift uncomfortably among these people who hate me. I don't belong with Earthmakers. I know I can't go back to Belos, that I will not, but I know I can't stay here either. This may be a sanctuary for them, but it's not for me, even if it is the one place Belos cannot reach me.

I jerk in surprise when Gaiana kneels before me. She studies me. I want to squirm, but I hold myself still. I stare at my knee, though her airy blue gown and shapely hands blur at the edge of my vision.

"I once had a very good friend. You have her eyes. Earthmaker eyes."

That startles me into looking at her. She is swaying a little, tired from Healing so many. Even so, her face is delicate, perfect.

"My friend was beautiful, like you."

I don't respond to that. I know what I am: coarse, clunky, dirty. Gaiana is making up comparisons as though to say I belong here. If I believed her, I might be comforted, but I don't. I know she's being kind, but I wish she wouldn't. It only makes me more uncomfortable. Me, like her friend? Spare me. I grit my teeth.

But I do study Gaiana in turn because I am curious about her. Her eyes are pinched with more than weariness. Is it loss? Regret? I want to ask who this friend was and what happened to her. Maybe because I'm curious, maybe because I want to think about something other than myself. But I can't bring myself to be so intrusive. Instead, I ask a polite, meaningless question, "What was her name?"

Gaiana's lips part, but no sound comes.

Beside me, Korinna stiffens. Gaiana's gaze drifts to her, and sympathy fills her eyes. Gaiana whispers, still looking at Korinna, "Her name was Sibyl."

Sibyl. Bran mentioned her as well, a woman who was Stricken, whose name is not to be spoken. What did Bran say was the cause? Her ideas? I wish now that I had pushed him to explain. I wish I could push Gaiana now, but I let my questions die. It doesn't matter, and it's not my place to interrogate the Prima.

Gaiana helps me remove my jacket, and I try not to wince as the fabric rubs against my oozing, blistered arm. It looks disgusting. Gaiana tears the hole in my sleeve wider and puts her hands to my skin. I grunt at the pain, then gasp as sensations of earth, air, fire, and water flow through me. I seem to disappear within a living, shifting pattern of elements.

Then they are gone, and Gaiana sways before me. Logan jumps down from the railing to catch her, but she brushes him off.

I marvel at the absence of pain, at the way I can move my arm again. I am humbled by what a Prima has lowered herself to do for me, and not for the first time. I mutter, "Thank you."

I suppose I should feel uplifted by her generosity, but I don't. I feel low and undeserving. When the Prima's light fingers touch my knee, I can only stare at them, at the perfect nails, the pale, flawless skin.

Korinna is the only one still waiting to be Healed. Gaiana shifts closer to her, and I breathe relief to be forgotten. Feluvas, who has just finished Healing a man's neck wound, joins her. Together they straighten Korinna's leg. The girl cries out as the broken bones scrape, but she bites the sound back quickly. She is breathing hard, crushing her lip between her teeth. Her face is white and sickly, but she makes no more sound. Brave girl.

The Healing is soon done, and Korinna leans back in relief, muttering her thanks. She does not look ashamed to have been Healed by the Prima. Is it such a natural thing for one of her kind?

Feluvas and Gaiana share a look, then both stare curiously at Korinna. Feluvas's lips thin. Gaiana's eyebrows crook. But whatever troubles them is soon put aside, and they rise, clutching each other for support. Several maids with golden bracelets hurry to them and guide them away.

Korinna's eyes are closed. I could not possibly feel that comfortable. I am edgy, twitchy. Any moment Logan will speak, and I'm not ready for that. I nudge Korinna.

"You know something about this woman the Prima mentioned."

Her eyes pop open.

Somehow, I don't mind pushing Korinna in a way I would never have pushed the Prima. Perhaps because Korinna is young, perhaps because I once spared her life. This gives me some leeway, doesn't it?

When Korinna offers nothing, I prompt, "So who was this Sibyl?"

Korinna eyes me warily. "I'm not supposed to talk about her."

I wait. I feel Logan's attention on us, and so does Korinna. She shoots him a worried look. I don't follow her eyes because I can't yet look at Logan, but she must find permission in his face because she whispers, "She was a Healer, like the Prima."

That makes me sit back. Healers are the most valued of all Earthmakers. And this woman was a friend of the Prima. What could such a woman have done to have been Stricken? What ideas could have been so terrible?

Korinna whispers, so low I barely hear it, "She was my aunt, my mother's only sister." She stops my next question by adding, "I never met her. She was…gone before I was born."

Korinna pushes up from the balustrade. She inclines her head to Logan, and I'm reminded that he is an authority figure to her.

Logan says formally, bowing, "Thank you for your service."

She responds with equal formality, "My service is my life, and I give it freely."

Her words make my chest feel hollow. I wonder how it feels to say such words honestly, to choose to serve, to choose *how* to serve. And to have Logan offer honor in return. Honor. The word weighs like a stone under my heart.

I stand as Korinna crosses the hall to Aron. He says something brief to her. She inclines her head and walks away, disappearing through the arching passageway that has swallowed the other Wardens, no doubt heading for whatever passes for barracks here. They are probably beautiful.

The hall has almost emptied. I shift uncertainly, wondering what they will do with me. Suddenly, I am glad that Logan has not yet left me. He hovers at my shoulder, perhaps as uncertain as I am.

Footsteps ring across the stone as Aron approaches, Bran at his side. I force my shoulders to loosen, my hands to relax. If Aron tries to apprehend me, I will fight him.

He stops several paces away. His mouth works on something he doesn't want to say, then, "You were right. About Martel."

My eyes widen a little, but I make myself shrug. I don't need his admission. We both know I was right. What concerns me is what he will try to do with me.

He looks like he has something else to say, but he swallows it. He gestures to a young woman hovering in the background, a woman wearing gold bracelets. She comes forward.

Aron turns away, already striding off when he says, "Leitha will show you to your room."

I stare at his retreating back. My mouth is hanging open slightly, so I close it. I take a step toward Leitha but stop when Logan's hand comes down on my shoulder.

I see Bran looking at me—no, at Logan—with pain in his eyes. What does he see?

I take a steadying breath and turn to Logan. His eyes swirl green, blue, and gold. A muscle bunches in his jaw.

"I will see to her needs," Leitha assures him.

Logan's jaw loosens and he takes his hand back. He looks…angry? Hurt? I bite my lip. I owe him something. I owe him everything. But all I can say is, "Goodnight."

Logan nods, accepting it, which makes me feel wretched, but I turn away to follow Leitha down the hall.

Leitha takes me to the room where I changed my clothes—could that have been only a few hours ago? A lantern glows beside the bed, where the golden covers have been turned back to reveal white linen sheets. A bowl of water steams on the elegant little table. Fresh towels lie folded beside it. A nightgown hangs fluidly from the face of the dresser.

"This is a lady's room," I say sharply.

"The Prima chose this room for you."

I stare at Leitha, wanting to ask her why, wanting someone to tell me where I stand here, but Leitha's face is cool, composed. I won't make myself look a fool in front of her.

She folds her hands before her, and the gold bracelets gleam in the lantern light.

I narrow my eyes. "Why do you wear those?"

Leitha glances down. "They are a sign of my service."

"They look like shackles."

I don't know why I'm being nasty. Perhaps I just need *someone* to squirm. I hate how calm everyone is here.

Leitha regards me steadily. "Shackles have chains. I am not chained. I have chosen my service, as all must do."

"The Wardens serve, but they don't wear bracelets."

A little color finally creeps into Leitha's neck. "We each serve as we can. Can I get you anything else?"

"No."

She leaves in a flow of light gowns, and I clench my hands. I am a bully. A mean, awful creature. I feel my face twist, and I imagine how ugly I must look, how low and vile. I close my eyes and picture my Leash, how it would look if I could see it now. I work my hand under my tunic and scrape at my sternum, at the edge of my ribcage. Only when I feel pain do I realize I have clawed away a layer of flesh.

I force myself to the washbowl. I strip off my clothes and scrub hard at my face and body, bringing a deep flush to my skin. Watery lines of blood trickle down my belly. When I throw the dirty scrubbing cloth into the water, my hands are shaking. I glance at the nightgown, admiring its filmy ripples, but I won't wear something so fine. I pull my torn tunic back on and pace the room.

A glitter of crystal behind the lantern catches my eye. A decanter, its contents gleaming bloody red in the light.

I pull out the stopper and sniff. I don't like wine, and this stuff smells earthy and strong. I try a sip. The wine seems to dry my tongue, to bite me in the back of the throat. I wonder idly how expensive it is. I raise the decanter again, tipping my head back this time to chug. Better. This, I realize, is the key. Don't let it sit too long in your mouth.

Before long I am weaving through the room, swigging from the decanter. I chuckle as the room sways around me, like I'm on a ship. No wonder people do this.

I trip over the rug and catch myself against one of the bedposts. The decanter slips from my grip and shatters against the stone floor in a bright tinkling of sound. Glittering shards fan out from a red splatter, which swims in and out of focus. I sigh and haul myself onto the bed.

❧ ☙

I am in a stone room with no windows. The walls expand and contract, like lungs. A pulse, a heartbeat resonates through the room, not quite in time with the give and take of the walls. Though there is no source of light, I can see the grime darkening gray stone to scummy brown. Something heavy circles my neck.

A collar.

A chain runs from the collar to the ceiling, like a hangman's rope. Panic rises. I want to tear at the collar, claw it from my throat, but I'm afraid to touch it.

Chapter 23

Lamplight flickers over me, and I stare at the bed's embroidered canopy, a pattern of blue and green waves. My hand drifts to my throat, but I find only skin and the strings of my tunic. I sit up and have to clutch at the bedpost for support as the room lurches and sways. Nausea rolls through me, and I swallow a bad taste. I squint in the direction of the balustrade. Still dark.

I push myself from the bed and gasp as pain slices my foot. I squint the broken glass into focus. I have to rest my hip against the bed as I lift my right foot and pluck a jagged shard from it.

I hobble across the room to where my pants lie in a heap. I shake them out and drag them on. When I pull on my socks, blood seeps through the bottom of my right one. I tug on my boots and lace them up with slow, clumsy fingers. I get one tighter than the other, but I don't bother fixing it. I steady myself against the table, waiting for the room to stop that obnoxious swaying, then head for the door.

A dozing guard whom I've never seen jerks awake when I open the door. Even through my dull and dizzy mind, I feel annoyance.

"Who are you?"

"Varus. Are you going somewhere?"

I lean against the doorframe. I hadn't really thought this far. When he wrinkles his nose, I realize I'm breathing at him.

I scowl. "Oh, shut up."

I feel him looking at me, but I keep my eyes on his chest instead of his face. A silver brooch worked with a branching tree secures his cloak at his left shoulder. His shoulders are broad and strong, like Logan's. I squeeze my eyes shut. No. I won't think about Logan right now. Then my eyes pop open, and I dart a glance around, hoping he's not lurking somewhere, witnessing my disgusting display of myself. I groan as the hallway dips and sways.

Varus studies me. "Why don't I take you to the kitchens?"

My stomach lurches at the thought of food. "Oh, gods, no."

"How much did you drink?"

Is it that obvious?

I shrug.

"And how much did you eat?"

I rub my eyes. "You are making my head hurt."

"Don't you know anything?"

I look at him sharply, then clutch at my head. I must remember not to make fast movements.

I hear him sigh as he pushes away from the wall. "Come on."

Because I have no energy to argue or to make my own decisions, I follow him down the hall. We move from sconce to sconce, passing through overlapping circles of light. His shadow is tall and straight. Mine is hunched ridiculously, limping from a sore foot. I exaggerate the posture, chuckling at the answering shadow. Varus's eyes slide to me.

"What?" I demand, my voice too loud.

"Through here." I follow him along another passageway.

Light fills a doorway ahead, and I smell fresh bread baking. It must be later—or earlier?—than I thought if they're already starting the day's bread.

Varus leads me into a huge kitchen, where a girl no older than fourteen crouches in front of a huge fireplace. She looks up when we enter, stifling a yawn.

In the center of the kitchen, an enormous work table is already set for the morning's work with a bowl of eggs at one end, spring onions and cured ham beside it. Empty mixing bowls, knives, and spoons lie clean and ready. The firelight draws gleams of copper from pots and pans that hang in neat order above the table. Along one brick wall, arching, open-faced bread ovens glow.

An older woman emerges from a far doorway carrying a tray laden with a porcelain tea service. Like the girl, she wears a set of golden bracelets, but she is dressed for work with a red apron over her blue dress. Her hair is pulled up in a graying bun.

"What's this? Can't anyone wait for breakfast?"

She sets the tray on one of the tables and bustles over to the fireplace, shooing the girl away. She uses a fire poker to swing an iron bar away from the flames. The bar holds a heavy black kettle, which she lifts with surprising ease.

Varus clears his throat. "Any bread ready yet, Melora? This one needs something in her stomach. *Other* than wine."

I glare at him, but he ignores me with that irritating Earthmaker imperiousness.

Melora fills the teapot with water. "Rolls in two minutes. Roxana, you may take this to Arcon Aronos." The girl stifles another yawn and lifts the tray, making the porcelain clatter together.

"Careful, girl."

The girl dips her chin and hurries from the room.

So. Aron is awake.

Because everything still sways a little, I stay where I am, surreptitiously leaning against a counter while Varus wanders over to the fireplace to warm his hands. His back is to me, as though he doesn't need to worry that I'll run or attack. I can't help but feel annoyance. Just because I'm a little slow right now doesn't mean I'm not still dangerous.

With a cloth protecting her hand, Melora reaches into one of the bread ovens. She draws out a tray of rolls, and the smell wafts through the kitchen. Though the sweet smell of ham has been making me a little nauseous, the rolls bring a rumble from my belly.

When Melora hands me two steaming rolls wrapped in a cloth, I take them eagerly. Only when she turns away do I remember to say, "Thank you."

She starts taking pans down from their hooks, and the scraping sounds of metal make my head scream. I turn for the door, and Varus follows.

"So," I say around a mouthful of bread. "Where can I find Aron?"

"What do you want with the Arcon?"

His tone chides me for using such a familiar name for Aron, as though I should bow in awe of the mighty Arcon. But I have lost my awe. "Did he say I couldn't see him?"

Varus hesitates. "No."

"Then take me to him."

Varus lets out a noisy breath, but he leads me from one hallway to another.

I try to memorize our route, but my head is too fuzzy to acknowledge more than that we are moving. I finish the second roll and stifle a belch. Varus goes stiff, but he doesn't say anything. By the time we reach a lighted doorway, some of my nausea has subsided, and I send grudging mental thanks in Varus's direction. My head, though, still pounds.

Varus puts up a hand to stop me while he goes through the doorway, but I follow him anyway. He glares, but I do my best to ignore him with an Earthmaker-like imperiousness of my own.

The room is gorgeous, its stone floor softened with thick, colorful rugs, and its dark wood shelves stacked with books in endless shades of dyed leather. A fireplace crackles along the far wall, and a pair of swords is crossed above it. Huge, open windows look out to what I take for a garden, though shadow cloaks it too heavily to be certain.

Aron sits at a wide table in the center, one piece of paper in his hand and a stack in front of him. The teapot leaks steam from its spout, but he hasn't poured any to drink. Light pools on his table from the brazier beside it, highlighting his handsome face. As he squints at me over the top of his paper, his eyes are pinched with fatigue. Strange how he both does and doesn't look like Logan. I shake that away.

"Astarti." Aron lays the paper neatly into the stack.

"You're up late. Or early. Depending on whether you've been to bed."

He says nothing, and I blush. His sleeping habits are none of my business, and it's not like I care anyway.

He looks to Varus. "You may go."

"Yes, sir."

"And, Varus?"

"Sir?"

"Your orders are unchanged."

Varus bows in acknowledgement.

I frown. What orders?

While Varus's footsteps fade down the hall, Aron fingers the stack of papers, and I make my way toward a chair that faces his desk. I accidentally sit on the arm and have to slide awkwardly into the seat. Aron's face swims in front of me. I blink him back into focus.

"Are you drunk?"

"Sort of."

He closes his eyes for patience.

One thing I actually like about Aron: he's not as cool and collected as some of his kind. He's got nothing on Logan, of course—why do I keep thinking about him when I'm determined not to?—but he does have a little fire. I suddenly recall the way he controlled the flames during the fight. Maybe that's his element. What did Logan say about those who align with fire? Ugh, his name *again*.

"What do you want, Astarti?"

Somehow, I had been hoping he would start this conversation. I'm better at reacting than prompting. Since he's staring at me, though, I leap right to the big question.

"What will you do?"

He raises an eyebrow. "If you're trying to get information from me, you're not being very sly."

Between that comment and the presence of Varus outside my door, I think I know approximately where I stand. Not in prison, but just above it. Highly suspect.

I stare at Aron, knowing that if I blink he might go out of focus again. His short, red-gold hair is combed straight back, making his face severe. His jaw is squarer than Logan's, as Bran's is. Gaiana, like Logan, has a more angled jaw, so that squareness must come from their father. An image of Arcon Arothos's severed head threatens to shape in my mind.

"You and Bran look a lot alike."

"Many say so."

"But Logan looks more like your mother."

Aron stills, staring at me, then he leans his elbows on his desk and steeples his fingers. "A little bit of questionable Earthmaker blood doesn't make you acceptable here. Or for him."

That might hurt if I allowed it to. It might even carve a hole in my chest. But I let it roll off me, refusing to feel it. For good measure, I snarl. If I'm a dog here, I'll be a dog.

Aron regards me steadily, unmoved by my curled lip. "If anything, it makes things worse. The mixing of blood is forbidden."

That annoys me. "Well, I didn't mix my own blood. My parents did that for me." Parents. The word feels strange in my mouth.

"True," he admits, "but it doesn't matter. You are what you are."

We stare at each other for too long, neither of us wanting to look away first. But he is more uncomfortable with me than I am with him, and his eyes slide away. My victory, though, is empty because we both know that he actually has the power here.

"So, then. What's to be done with the unacceptable Drifter?" I throw the question off lightly, as though I don't care, as though it doesn't drive a spike of fear through me.

Aron picks up the stack of papers and squares it on the desk, still not looking at me. "The Council will have to debate it. Until decisions are made, you may remain here."

So. I will not be kicked out. Yet.

Relief floods me, but embarrassment comes fast behind it. And that makes me ask myself: can I tolerate the waiting, the uncertainty? Can I stay here like a beggar, a stray dog, hoping they don't throw me back to Belos? Part of me screams desperately, *Yes!* but another part speaks over it with a resolute, *No.*

"Is that *may* remain? Or *must* remain?"

Aron leans back in his chair, raising deep blue eyes to mine, his confidence back. "You cannot enter the Drift from here. How would you leave?"

I don't answer his question, and he doesn't answer mine.

"Why did you help us, Astarti? You took me safely through the Drift, to see Martel's Leash. If you are not just trying to get into our confidence to betray us later, what is your motivation? Drifters and Earthmakers have long been enemies, even without the added complication of you being a servant of…his."

The silence rings in my ears as I study my knee. I've been avoiding this question even in my own mind, and now it hangs in the air. Why did I help them?

Instead of answering, I ask him, "Why did you save me from Straton's fire? You could have let me burn."

No answer.

I look up to see Aron staring blindly at the stack of papers, a finger propped against his temple, thumb curled under his jaw.

I say softly, "We don't always know why we do what we do."

I can't bring myself to thank him for saving me, as he can't bring himself to thank me for showing him Martel's Leash. But I know my debt is the greater one, and I hate that I owe Aron my life. If only I had saved his instead. How nice it would be to hold that over him. But, as usual, it is others who hold power over me.

To get away from this topic, I ask Aron again, "What will you do?"

He picks up a pen, rotating it slowly with the fingers of one hand. "The Council will have to debate it."

"Is that how you do everything? You talk and talk. Meanwhile, Belos gives his orders, and things happen. Kelda burns."

"Why should we care about Kelda?"

"You want Belos to have it?"

Aron's pen stops. "Of course not."

"Then you must warn Heborian. Immediately. Do you have any idea how soon Belos could act? Martel's army is gathered, and they will occupy Heborian's troops while Belos and the Seven go after Heborian and his Drifters. Belos was waiting before, waiting for Martel, waiting for your Wardens. Don't you see that he has nothing else to wait for?"

Aron frowns at the pen in his hand, a line wedging between his brows.

"They could be moving right now."

"Heborian is a Drifter."

"He is. And he's also the only thing that stands between Belos and Kelda."

Aron's thumb presses hard against the pen, and I wait for it to snap. But Aron's grip loosens. He sets the pen down neatly.

I ask impatiently, "Do you think Belos won't use his new center of power to attack you?"

"What do you want, Astarti?"

Each moment of his indifference leeches away at my patience. "I want you to warn Heborian! Why wouldn't you? You have nothing to lose."

"What do you care about him? About Kelda? What has Kelda ever done for you?"

My hands are clenched on the arms of the chair. I loosen my fingers with an effort, but they clench again of their own accord. "Why should Belos have everything he wants so easily? Snap his fingers, tug this Leash or that, speak one order, and we all fall on our knees before him. It's disgusting." I am on my feet now, hands like hammers at my side. I want to use them to break something, to smash Aron's calm face, to punch the brazier and watch the sparks fly, to rip the books from their shelves. "Every single one of us that stays silent, stays hidden, looks to our own selfish interests, is throwing that power at him."

Aron asks softly, almost wonderingly, "How can you still be so proud?"

I grit out, "You will do nothing?"

"The Council will debate it."

I swipe my hand across his desk and send the papers whipping into the air. One spins into the brazier. The fire flares, and the paper curls blackly within it.

Aron's jaw hardens with anger, but he refuses to respond, refuses to act.

I point a shaking finger at him. "When Belos is tearing this house stone from stone, I hope you will remember that you had the chance to fight him, to stop him—at least to try!—and you *debated* it."

"The Wood—"

"Is not the only way to get here! Are you not surrounded by ocean? Can he not sail here with an army of Keldans in his thrall?"

"These are the *Floating* Lands. There is a reason for that."

"So it's impossible for him to sail here? Utterly impossible? Even if he sends out every ship in Kelda? Even if he extends his reach into Valdar and Ibris—which you're an idiot if you think he won't do—he still couldn't get any ship here? None? Ever?"

The corner of Aron's eye twitches. His silence is answer enough.

My anger fades, and I am chilled by the same fear that I just worked so hard to inspire in Aron. Nowhere is safe from Belos, not even Avydos.

I harden myself, and the fear rolls away. Belos gave me many years to practice this: you turn your thoughts in such a way that they don't absorb anything from the outside, distance yourself so that you feel nothing. Like entering the Drift. It is the key, I learned long ago, to conquering fear. You don't allow it to touch you.

"You know we must stop him."

"What could you possibly do? You are Leashed, Astarti. He owns you. You cannot fight him."

There is no malice in his words, only simple fact. He is right, and I am hollowed by the truth of it.

"No. I cannot fight him directly. But others can. If you won't warn Heborian, I will."

"You cannot drift from here. And even if you could, your master would find you."

That glances off me like a pebble. Don't feel. Don't think.

I turn away and shove the chair aside. It screeches against the stone floor.

"Astarti."

I don't pause and don't look back. Perhaps Belos should not have taught me to conquer fear. It is a lesson that I will make him pay for.

ℰ ℛ

The sky is paling toward dawn as I wander the rocky bluff that forms one arm of the bay. Varus has long since given up trying to stay hidden, and he trails about a hundred feet behind me. Clearly, he won't try to stop me from doing anything because he thinks there's nothing I *can* do. He is there only because he—or rather, Aron—wants to know where I am. Though I suppose that suggests some measure of trust, I am beyond caring whether they trust me. I have more important things to think about.

The rocks here are rough, even jagged in places, making a sharp contrast to the smooth curves of the city. I stumble from time to time, but the cool ocean breeze does wonders to clear the lingering fuzziness from my head. By the time I reach the end of the arm, my headache has dulled to simple annoyance.

I stare out at the grayish-black melding of ocean and sky. Dawn is beginning to reveal the horizon, but it's not definite enough to show whether we've floated near to Kelda. It doesn't matter. Distance means little in the Drift.

My heart gives an uncertain thump as I adjust my footing at the edge of the bluff. The sky is light enough to hint at the shapes of rocks below me. I consider going back, finding another route, but this will be quickest, and I can't be certain Varus won't try to stop me once he realizes what I'm doing. I hear him moving closer, and I ready my feet. He shouts my name and starts running as I gather myself.

I leap.

Air rushes past me. I reach along my mooring, searching for the Drift, for the edge of the barrier around Avydos. I feel it dimly, a throb of energy, but interwoven with that are the complex currents of air. I am sensitive to them like a bird, and I think I could catch one and ride it. In some distant part of my mind I am waiting for the cold rush of water, for the blossoming pain as I crack like an egg against rock. But my reality is the swish and swirl of air. I am not even falling anymore.

I reach into the currents, slide myself along one. I imagine myself like smoke, curling in their breezes. I am buffeted by them, spun this way and that. But I begin to unravel their complexity, understanding how one current plays with another. I ride them, change them with my passing. I am one of them.

I feel the rest of the world around me, the roll of water, the heavy, ponderous earth beneath it, the deeply burning fires in the earth's heart. I fly over it all, both part of it and separate.

I feel the ocean floor rise, emerging in the distance to sandy beach, mounding beyond that toward the Green Wall of eastern Kelda. Dimly, at the edges of my awareness, I sense people. The ordinary crowd of the city hums in Tornelaine. Farther off, winding through the foothills of the mountains like a snake, moves an army.

CHAPTER 24

LOGAN

I wake shuddering. The nightmare clings, haunting me with its new images. Belos seizes my father's neck in a hand twice the size it should be. My father's face bulges grotesquely as Belos squeezes, fingers cutting through flesh and bone until my father's head pops off and rolls wetly toward me. But when the head stops, the face, contorted with a silent scream, has changed.

I choke on the image of Astarti's dead face. I lean over the side of the bed and vomit, my stomach jerking with the horror of it. When I am weak and empty, my panting brings the reek of vomit back to me. I roll away and shove myself off the other side of the bed. I stagger to the washbasin and scrub the inside of my mouth with white paste.

I catch sight of myself in the corner mirror and grimace at my wrinkled shirt and the tangled mess of my hair. I know I should wash and change, but I won't take the time. I just need to see her, to make sure. Most likely she's sleeping. It's still early, after all. My chamber, high in the upper floors, looks out to the Wood, and the upper braches are just starting to catch the dawn glow.

As I make my way through the house, all the maids are up and busy, and I spare a guilty thought for the mess I left in my room. It's not the first time. Fortunately, none of the maids talk to me and no one else is around. I'm not yet fit company for anyone.

When I find Astarti's room empty, my heart lurches. The bed covers are still drawn up, the pillows in place. A wrinkled section crosses the bed sideways, as though she slept there. When I see a red stain across the stone floor, my breath stops, but I soon recognize the glittering shards of a wine decanter. I guess we're both messy.

The wine, though, worries me. She doesn't even like wine, so why would she drink the heavy stuff they keep in here? I knew she was upset last night. I didn't know what to do. She wouldn't *let* me do anything, and I let her go. I did it because that's what I would have wanted, to be left alone, but I wish now that I had come after her, checked on her. Did I make her think I don't care? Was she even thinking about me at all? Probably not, but it doesn't matter. I shouldn't have left her alone, not after Belos almost—

I shiver and refuse to finish the thought. If he ever lays a hand on her—

I lean my forehead against the doorframe to calm myself. I breathe, three seconds in, three out, as they taught me.

I wander back toward the entry hall, unsure where to look for her, when I grow suspicious. Would Aron have seized her? Was that broken decanter a sign of struggle? Surely there would have been more damage? Not, perhaps, if they surprised her.

Only too happy to confront Aron, I make my way toward his study. I know he didn't go to bed last night. He never does, not when there's work to do, decisions to make, things to mull over.

I expect to find him at his desk, frowning at maps or reports, but instead he's at the windows, looking out over the little garden beyond his study. His arms are crossed, his head bowed. When he hears me and turns partway toward me, his gaze is far away, then he blinks me into focus and that familiar frown sets into his mouth.

I know how I must look to him, disheveled and filthy. Even though he's been up all night, his tunic is neat, his short-cropped hair smooth. He looks every inch the Arcon. No wonder people mutter that I must be a bastard.

Anger simmers in my belly when I look at him, but I've grown used to it, and I accept it as part of me. For the past five years, since I failed to save our father, we've hated each other.

"Where's Astarti?"

Aron raises an eyebrow at my rudeness, but I just glare at him.

"Taking a walk, last I knew. She needed to cool down a little. Humans are so hotheaded."

"She's not human. Not entirely." When he says nothing, I demand, "What did you do to her?"

Aron gives me that condescending look of his. "What do you think I am, Logan, a Drifter? I don't break my word four hours after giving it."

"Not unless you can find some justification for it."

Aron, arms crossed, is still half turned away from me, as though I'm not worth his full attention, as though this conversation bores him. "She came here, we talked, she left."

I'm losing patience. "What did you talk about?"

"Why don't you ask her?"

"I will."

Aron turns fully toward me, and even though he is all the way across the room, I freeze under his gaze. I hate that he can do this to me, make me feel like a child, as though he's my father. I hate that he's forty years older than I am, even if the difference looks more like five.

His eyes narrow. "Why did you help her, Logan? In the first place, I mean. You knew what she was from the start. She's one of *them*. One of those who killed—"

Aron cuts himself off, jaw clenching. He looks suddenly vulnerable, and I don't like it. Better that he be strong and hateful; *that* I can handle.

I remind him, "He took her as a child."

"That only makes it worse. She's been shaped by him, Logan, as all children are shaped by their parents."

I move deeper into the room and grip the back of a chair to control my hands. "He is *not* her father."

"You know that's not what I meant."

The chair screeches an inch across the floor under the pressure of my hands. "You can see that she hates him."

"And you know that only means so much. She is Leashed, Logan. Don't ever forget that."

I close my eyes. I see her in the golden flow of the Current, the white thread streaming away from her. Belos, pulling. Her mouth open on a silent scream, like the dead face in my dream. I shudder.

Breathe. Three seconds in, three out. "You realize he Leashed her as a *child*, right? She was *seven*. It's awful."

Aron turns away. "It doesn't matter."

Anger snaps. "It does."

He spins back to me. "And you trust her so much? You would gamble your own life on it? How about mine? Bran's? Mother's? You would put all of us in her hands?"

My fingers whiten on the back of the chair. I hate Aron for being right. I hate him for making me silent. I want to trust Astarti. I really want to.

Aron looks at me sadly, like I'm pathetic. "You know it's forbidden." When I don't answer, he goes on, "I'll grant that she's beautiful, but so are our own women. Find one of them, and stop looking at that Drifter like you do."

"And how do I look at her?"

Aron regards me steadily, not answering.

An image of Astarti fills my mind. Rich dark hair, strong body. Fierce pale eyes. A phantom pressure ghosts my side, and I remember her pressed against me that night on the island, when we lay together. By the Old Ones, I wanted her. My body, as usual, was at the edge of restraint. I clench my jaw until my teeth ache. I know that Aron is right, that my tutors were right, that all my people are right: I have no control.

"What's going on?"

I spin at Bran's voice. Like Aron, he is neat and tidy, his knee-length tunic clean and white, his hair combed. Bran is taller and leaner than Aron, built more like me, like our mother. Aron has always hated being the shortest, and Bran has never cared about comparisons.

Aron uncrosses his arms, planting his hands on his hips. "We were just discussing our young Drifter." He shoots me a look. "And all related issues."

"Ah. I wanted to talk to you about one of those. I've been thinking about Heborian—"

Aron leans his head back, staring at the ceiling. "Not you, too."

"We need to consider that Heborian could—oh. Varus. Yes. Come in."

Bran moves aside for Varus, the guard that Aron assigned to Astarti. Varus's face is white, and he swallows hard. He's been running.

My heart pounding with sudden fear, I take a threatening step toward him. "Where is she?"

"Logan!" snaps Aron. "I want you out. And Bran. Both of you."

I growl, "Not a chance."

Aron and I stare at each other. He knows I'll let this come to blows. The question is, will he?

Of course, Bran steps in. Usually in these situations, he tries to calm me down, which is very annoying. But today, surprisingly, he sides with me. "Logan has a right to know."

"Why? Because he brought a stray dog home? Does that make it his property?"

I am around the table and inches from Aron when Bran's hand clamps on my raised arm. I let him stop me, but then I am stuck, undecided.

Aron, it satisfies me to note, has stepped back, his face pale. But then he says, "Someday, Logan, you will kill someone again when you lose control of yourself."

All the energy drains from me, like I'm a water skin that's been punctured. Aron always knows just how to cut me, just how to shame me. Bran's hand reaches up toward my shoulder, as though he would comfort me, but I shake him off roughly. I move away from my brothers and stand by the bookshelves, my arms crossed.

The silence is deafening.

Varus shifts uncomfortably, and Bran says, "Please report, Varus."

Varus waits, and I'm sure he's looking to Aron for confirmation. I'm shaking with impatience.

Finally, Varus clears his throat. "After the Drifter left"—a little spark of anger rekindles in me. She has a *name*—"she walked out to the west arm of the bay. I—well, sir, you said only to watch her, so I was too far behind to do anything—"

My head snaps up. "What happened?"

"She, uh"—Varus tugs at his collar—"she jumped from the cliff and—"

I feel like I've been punched in the stomach. I double over, and the roar of the ocean fills my ears. I fall against the shelf behind me, dimly registering the flutter of pages as books fall to the floor.

My hearing comes back when Varus says, "I've never seen such a thing, vanishing into the wind."

"What?" I mutter.

Varus's brow wrinkles. "Like I said, she jumped and vanished."

"She didn't fall?"

"No, she disappeared. Right in front of my eyes. I'm sorry, Arcon Aronos, I—I really don't know what happened."

"There is no fault here," Aron assures him. "Report to Polemarc Clitus for reassignment. And Varus," Aron calls as the guard turns to leave. "Don't tell anyone about this."

Varus swallows and dips his head, then he hustles from the room, his footsteps a quick staccato.

I am still getting my breath back, and my brothers are staring at me like I've lost my mind. Let them stare. That scared the shit out of me.

"That sounds like what you said happened in the cell, when she went into the stone."

Silence. I'm not sure to whom Bran was speaking.

He goes on, "It must be some blending of earthmagic and drifting. But I've never heard of such a thing. To my knowledge, even the Unnamed and his Seven don't do that. Nothing in the old texts—"

Bran cuts himself off, and I look at him. He has that far-off look of concentration, the one he gets when he's studying some boring, dusty manuscript.

Aron's eyebrows lower. "What is it?"

Bran shakes his head. "I'll have to do some reading. Something about that"—he frowns—"I'm just not sure."

"While this is a wonderful intellectual puzzle," I let the sarcasm drip, "we're ignoring the more important question: where did she go?"

"Tornelaine."

I whip my head in Aron's direction. "How can you be sure?"

"What's this? Are you thinking she might, after all, have gone back to her master?"

I growl.

"I know she went to Tornelaine because the last thing she and I discussed was warning Heborian of Martel's new friends."

Bran says slowly, "And why did she feel it was necessary for her to go do this?"

Aron shrugs. "Because I refused to."

"Why would you—"

"Bran, you know the Council must make a collective decision."

Bran grumbles at the truth of this, but I don't care about politics right now, not that I ever do. There are more important questions. "How could you let her go? If the Unnamed senses her, he will take her! She cannot go to Tornelaine."

"Logan, I hardly expected her to vanish into thin air. I wouldn't have let her out of the house if I'd known she would—"

"You clearly have no idea how powerful she is."

"And did you realize she could do that? Vanish?"

"No," I have to admit.

Bran redirects the discussion. "What do we do?"

I straighten. "I'm going after her. Right now."

Bran puts up a hand. "Logan, wait—"

"I won't wait! Not for one minute."

Aron moves to his desk, already in administrator mode, as though this isn't a crisis. "Bran is going with you."

Bran and I both say, "What?"

"You heard me."

I glare at him. "So now you don't trust *me*?"

"I don't trust you to be sensible, no. But I do want the two of you to find her. Because I certainly don't trust *her*. Bran, I hope, I can trust to make wise decisions. And to remember where his loyalties lie."

I won't waste time arguing with Aron any further. I gesture to Bran. I don't really mind if he comes, as long as he doesn't slow me down or get in my way.

"Let's go."

"I just need a few minutes to—"

"Then you can meet me in Tornelaine. I'm leaving now."

I push away from the bookshelf and make for the door. I hear grumbling, the start of an argument, but I'm soon halfway down the hall. Someone jogs behind me, and I recognize Bran's light steps, but I don't look at him and don't talk to him. Only one thing matters right now, and that's reaching Astarti. Because if Belos finds her, if he takes her—

My throat closes. I break into a run.

CHAPTER 25

I have trouble separating myself from the air, and for a moment as I hover over Heborian's turreted castle, I think I will be stuck here. But I focus on the energies of the people, use that to orient myself, and slide from the air currents much like I slide along my mooring. But I'm too high, and the air currents buffet me and send me swirling around one the thin spires topping a round tower.

My stomach drops when I find myself clinging to the spire, hundreds of feet in the air. I close my eyes until the shivers pass. If I'm going to travel like this again—and what *is* this?—I need to learn how to land better.

I open my eyes to find the sun, rising over the steep hills of eastern Kelda, sparking in my eyes. In the distance, sheep graze the steep slopes. The city and closer hills lie yet in morning shadow.

Within the city walls, the early risers, bakers and stablemen most likely, move along the streets, looking like ants from this height. A few tiny merchants' carts roll through the city gates, and fishing boats skim out of the bay. Such ordinary activity. It won't last. Soon this city will be locked down.

I feel for the Drift along my mooring, but I can't enter. I am still outside Heborian's barrier. I study the steep slope of the tower roof. There's a six-inch wide ledge at the lip of it. Before I can worry about the danger, I make myself let go of the spire and slide down to the ledge. I gasp when my feet hit the ledge, and I hug the roof, clinging to tiles. When my heart stops hammering, I peer down. Walls and towers, courtyards. The castle is a complex weaving of stone, and I have to close my eyes again.

I've had some fortune in this disaster: there is a window a few feet to my right and two feet down the wall. The rolling coo of pigeons tells me I've landed on the pigeon cote, which is lucky because there's probably no one in there. I edge over until I'm right above the window.

Slowly, very slowly, I scrunch down to grip the ledge at my feet. One breath, then I slither off the ledge and arc through the window.

White and gray wings fill the air, beating frantically, brushing my face and body. Startled coos surround me. My elbow and hip smack hard against stone, and I roll to my side, hugging the pain.

I sit up as the birds settle, returning to their perches and stone cubbies. Dust and feathers spin through the air. I cough on the sharp scent of droppings. I push to my feet, and my hands shake as I brush pigeon droppings from my clothes. I grimace when some of it smears in fresh white streaks, but I try to be grateful that nothing worse happened.

The heavy wood door is unlocked. I have to smile to myself. I suppose they don't expect anyone to break in through the pigeon cote.

The door opens on a turning stairway, which is dark and damp. I run my hand along the wall to find my way through the darkness. When my fingers bump a heavy wooden door, I hesitate. What, really, is my plan?

I need to get to Heborian, but if I wander through the castle halls, I'll be apprehended, and the chances of getting to the king after being caught as an intruder are slim. Even if they do let me speak with him, there will be a delay. By then, it could be too late. Better to surprise him. He'll be angry, of course. He may arrest me or try to kill me, but at least I'll have the chance to tell him Martel is coming.

Now that I'm within Heborian's barrier, I can enter the Drift, and I ease along my mooring. My whole being fills with joy and power. There is nothing as immediate, as wonderfully intense, as the Drift. Stone walls become dim and irrelevant.

All around me, the castle is full of energies, and I am shocked by the number of people here. Nobles, servants, guards. There must be hundreds people in this sprawling building. Among the ordinary lighted forms of humans, a number of Drifters burn more brightly. None of them are within the Drift with me, so they can't know I'm here. A few are scattered throughout the castle grounds, but three are clustered together. One of those three burns brightest of all, so I figure it must be Heborian. I had hoped that at this early hour he might be alone, but nothing, it seems, will be easy today.

As I move through the castle, I catch dim impressions of hallways and staircases, one of which sweeps grandly toward the entrance hall. The forms of servants bustle along, burdens in their arms. If I concentrate, I can make out baskets of fresh linens and curved brass hoppers of wood to start the morning fires.

Flickering candles in the wall sconces lick within the Drift. The elements have always felt so removed from the Drift, but

I'm beginning to wonder if they are not so distant after all. At least, not for me. My father, apparently, was an Earthmaker. Is this how I traveled the air? Did I use just the element? Or did I use some part of the Drift as well? When I entered the air and when I entered the stone, I was attempting to reach the Drift. Entry into the elements was accidental.

I pass my hand through one of the candle flames idly, but nothing happens. The fire is empty here, meaningless.

I put my curiosity aside. I have no time, right now, for questions. I can worry about my parentage another time, if I want to, which I probably won't. My mother abandoned me. It doesn't matter what man, Earthmaker or not, passed through her life. I was nothing to either of them.

They are nothing to me.

The deep, regretful clenching in my energy calls me a liar, and, yes, I am a liar, but it's useful sometimes, even with myself.

I move through what I take to be a broad foyer. A fountain trickles in the center, its bubbling water silent and gray in the Drift. A high, domed ceiling arcs overhead, and two guards flank a set of closed double doors. They are oblivious to my passing.

The room is large, with a fire burning in the hearth. One Drifter, slender and young, stands with his back to the fire. Even looking at him through the Drift, I recognize the smooth planes of Prince Rood's face. Heborian is at the window, his energy a pulse of silvery-blue power. Another Drifter stands with his fists planted on a table, staring at something, probably a map.

I don't allow myself to hesitate. I made my decision when I came in here. No, I made it when I left Aron's study. Nothing to be gained by fear. I ease along my mooring.

I brace myself for a fight, but they are so deep in their own thoughts they don't notice me at first. Prince Rood's chin is tucked to his chest, and his dark eyebrows are scrunched in thought. The Drifter at the table is an older man, white-haired, the blue Runish tattoos along his neck and across the backs of his hands blurred with age.

The rosy glow of sunrise highlights Heborian's hunched back as he stands by the lead-paned window. A thick blue robe edged with silver fur hangs from his shoulders. Even with his head bowed, I can make out the blue tattoo that hooks around his right eye and spikes down his cheek almost all the way to his beard. The glossy dark hair braided back from his face catches slivers of orange from the glowing hearth.

When I clear my throat, the reaction is immediate. Heborian's head snaps up, surprise replaced at once by fury, and the blue of Drift-energy. The old man jumps back from the table with a yelp, and a Drift-sword flashes into his hand. Prince Rood whips a knife from his belt and flings it at me. I throw a shield of energy in front of myself, and the knife bounces off, clattering to the floor.

"I want to talk to you!" I shout, but Heborian bellows, "Guards!"

The doors burst open behind me.

"Wait!" I shout, but I have to dart away for space, dodging as one of the guards hurls his pike. It buries its head into a stuffed chair.

I leap aside as the second guard lunges. I shape my spear as I roll. I come up fast, whipping my spear around to slap the guard in the side of the head. He slumps to the ground unconscious. I'm not here to kill guards who are just doing their jobs.

The first guard has drawn his sword. When he charges, I hit him with a blast of energy that knocks him back through the open doors. He doesn't get up.

"Just wait!" I yell, but Prince Rood is running at me with a raised Drift-sword, and I have to spin my spear around to jam the butt into his stomach. He makes a loud woofing noise and staggers away, clutching his belly.

I'm stepping back, making space, my eyes darting around the room for the next danger, when a blast of energy pummels me in the chest. I skid across the floor, scrunching one of the carpets and banging into a side table, which crashes to the ground. Something shatters with the high, light sound of glass.

I try to get to my feet, but I fall, unable to breathe, my chest hollowed by pain. My spear has vanished. I manage to get to my knees as Heborian stalks toward me, the glow of power lingering around his fist. I'm impressed. Only Belos has ever struck me such a blow.

I am scrunched with pain, unable to raise my eyes above his waist, but I put my hands over my head. I gasp, "I just want to talk to you."

Heborian's deep voice rumbles out, "We have an audience chamber for that. People who want to talk to me come on petition day, or they make an appointment if their business is pressing. Sneaking into my private rooms and attacking my guards is something else entirely."

"I was only defending myself. I could have killed them, but I didn't. I could have killed you before you knew I was here, but I didn't."

He grumbles, weighing the truth of that, then snaps, "How did you get in here?"

My breath is back, so I raise my head, craning my neck to look up at Heborian as he towers above me. With his dark eyes narrowed in angry suspicion, the tattoo down his right cheek seems to sharpen.

Suddenly, his breath catches and his eyes widen. He takes an involuntary step back. Does he recognize me from the night I came here from the Trader's Choice?

But there's something more than surprise and recognition in his face, some deeper shock. Is it horror? But he could not possibly know who, or what, I am.

The white-haired Drifter steps forward, Drift-sword still in hand, Runish marks all down the blade. "Why did you sneak in here, except to threaten the king? Why not approach openly and honestly?"

"This was expedient, and I have no time to waste. Nor do you."

The Drifter's hand clenches tighter on his sword hilt. "Speak clearly: are you threatening the king?"

"No. *I* am not. Martel, on the other hand—"

"We know all about Martel."

"Are you sure about that?"

I let them decide whether they want to hear me. If I make them ask for my information, they will be more likely to listen. I look to Heborian, because he's the one who matters. But his dark eyes are far away. What on earth could be occupying his thoughts at a time like this? He refocuses on me, and his eyes soften, then harden, then soften again. I wait for him to speak, but he doesn't.

The white-haired Drifter looks to him, finds nothing, and turns back to me. "Out with it, girl. What can you tell us of Martel?"

I keep my eyes on Heborian, who, surprisingly, looks away in discomfort. "Martel has gathered an army. He's moving from the Green Wall as we speak—"

"We already know that," Prince Rood says sharply. One hand braces on the heavy table littered with maps, the other clutches his stomach. His face looks a shade green. I certainly haven't made any friends here.

"But." I pause for emphasis. "Do you know that he's Leashed to Belos? That Belos and the Seven are coming to tear this city apart?"

The prince's face drains of color, but the old man stalks near. "How do you know that? Who are you?"

I should have anticipated this question and come up with a plausible lie. I certainly can't tell them who I am. They'd never trust me, no more than Aron does.

I decide to say I'm a Drifter-whore who ran away with Martel, just in case Heborian recognizes me from our first encounter, when I hear, "Her name is Astarti."

My eyes snap to Heborian. How on earth does he know my name? His shoulders are sagging, as though under an immerse weight. His eyes are crinkled with pain, but he holds them on me. "She works for Belos. That is how she knows."

From the edges of my vision, I see Rood step back and the white-haired Drifter freeze. But my eyes are really on Heborian, hunched now like an old man.

"How…" I shake my head to clear it. Something in Heborian's tone, his resignation, seems to rob me of focus. "How could you possibly know that?"

He doesn't answer at first, then his shoulders draw back and he takes a deep breath. "Because I sold you to him. Seventeen years ago."

CHAPTER 26

Silence fills the room like water, enveloping us, making everything slow and surreal. Only my pulse marks the time, beating remotely with strange, heavy dullness.

"Father." Rood's voice, which seems to come from far away. "What are you talking about?"

The white-haired Drifter, who's been staring at me like I've grown an extra head, shakes himself and looks to Heborian. "Sire, do you think it wise?"

Heborian ignores him. "You came here, that night Rood was taken. That was you."

When I don't answer, Heborian nods his own confirmation. "I knew it. I didn't believe it, but I knew it. I dreamed that night of Sibyl, and I have every night since."

Sibyl?

Sibyl?

I am trying to assimilate this information, to make some sense of this madness, but my mind churns, and the answers skim by me and away.

The white-haired Drifter shifts uncomfortably. "Sire."

I find my voice, though it stumbles out barely above a whisper, "My mother abandoned me and Belos found me. I wasn't sold."

Heborian snaps, "That's a lie."

His anger wakens me fully, and I am shaken by his certainty, by the way he is trying to shatter everything I know. I fixate instead on what I have come to accept. Even if it hurts, at least it's familiar. "She left me to die."

"Your mother would never have abandoned you." He adds, almost accusingly, "She died that night."

"You knew her?"

He looks at me like that should have been obvious. "Of course. She was my—"

"*Sire.*"

Heborian gives the white-haired Drifter a sharp look. "Wulfstan, I will speak."

"Why?" I snarl, clinging hard to anger, terrified to let it go and find myself shattered by more things Belos did not tell me. Somehow, I know what Heborian is about to say, even though it makes no sense at all, even though I don't believe it and don't want to hear it. I have learned to deal with the ugliness of what I am. What will I be if his words remake me into something worse?

Heborian says gravely, "You need to know the truth."

"No, I don't."

He crosses his arms. "There are many things I knew you would become, but I never thought you'd be a coward."

My breath stops. My heart hammers. I am not a coward.

I harden my jaw, and he nods.

"Wulfstan, take Prince Rood out. I would speak with my daughter alone."

Even though I somehow expected this, the word makes me go deaf. The arguing voices grow distant, and I register only the blurs of Rood and Wulstan moving, the dragging of the unconscious guard. Heborian is a dark smudge in front of me.

When the doors slam shut, I jump, scrambling to my feet. "What do you want? How can I know you're not lying?"

"I'm not lying, Astarti. You are my daughter. Your mother was named Sibyl, and she was an Earthmaker. A Healer, cast out by her stubborn, foolish people."

I cover my ears and stalk to the window, where the rising sun blinds me. I catch myself against the window sill. Maybe I am a coward; I don't want to hear this after all.

"Astarti—"

"You *cannot* be my father."

He doesn't answer.

My heart is beating with panic, and I throw Bran's guess at him. "My father was an Earthmaker—"

"Your *mother* was an Earthmaker."

My mother. For so long that word has filled me with bitterness. I say, still wanting to hate her, needing to cling to what I know, "She abandoned me. I was nothing to her."

He says softly, "You were everything to her."

I whip around. Heborian's dark eyes are too bright, too shiny. His pain makes me furious. "I don't believe you! I never even met you before that night your son was taken."

"Your brother. Half-brother, anyway."

I grit my teeth. Without consciously willing it, my Drift-spear shapes in my hand. "Prove it." I curl my lip, triumphant, certain he can't.

Heborian eyes my spear, not with worry but with interest. "You bear the Griever's Mark. On the back of your neck. A blue mark like a Y, with a third line dividing the wings."

I stare, dumbfounded, then insist weakly, "Lucky guess."

"I marked you with it myself, when you were a baby."

"To protect me on my journey into death?"

"Like I said, I sold you to Belos." His mouth twists with disgust, but I don't know for whom. "Was that not a journey into death? The Mark was the one small thing I could give you that Belos could not take away."

I shake my head, troubled by his twisted logic. The Griever's Mark is something I've hidden in shame all my life; I don't want to talk about it, to think about it, to even try to see it as anything but an ugly stain. I can only take so much at once. I steer the conversation back to more pressing issues. "If this is true, what do you mean that you sold me?"

His mouth works on an answer.

My eyes narrow. "You made a deal with him."

Heborian turns away and walks to a table along the far wall. I hear the slide of a crystal stopper and the gurgling flow of liquid. He throws his head back and drinks. He stands at the table, head bowed.

By the gods—if they exist—he really means it. Some part of me had hoped all this was some trick, some trap, something for which I could later call myself stupid for even listening to. The earth seems to shift under me. I try to ground myself with facts. "What was the deal?"

Heborian comes back my way, a cup in his hand. He sits on a padded footstool by the fire. He nods to the footstool beside him.

I glare.

He sighs through his nose. "Have you ever been to Rune?"

I snap with impatience. "What does that matter?"

He fingers the rim of his silver cup. "It's a cold, brutal land. Very little grows, and when winter is harsh, which it usually is, the game is poor and starving, just as the people are. We have always raided, taking from the lands around us, from Heradyn and the eastern plains, but they are poor as well." He looks wistful when he adds, "The north is beautiful. Harsh and cruel—but beautiful." He shakes his head. "Twenty years ago, Rune suffered through one harsh winter too many."

"What does this have to do with me?"

"Everything, Astarti. It is the beginning. Listen."

He watches me until I lean back against the lead-paned window, then he turns his eyes to the fire and continues.

"Our people were dying. Mothers' milk dried in the breast, and the babies starved. Have you ever seen an infant that starved to death? Cheeks hollow, its tiny body shrunken to nothing. It doesn't even look human." He closes his eyes, remembering. "Something had to be done.

"Rune never had kings, only chieftains. I was a chieftain, as my father had been. After the Long Winter, I called together all chieftains who would swear fealty to me, all the warriors who would come, every Drifter I could find. I promised them a richer life in the south. They were desperate. They didn't take much convincing. We sailed. At first we did well, sacking the northern Keldan towns. Barreston sent troops after us, but they were nothing to my Runian warriors.

"We talked about returning to Rune with our bounty, but I knew the problems would only return with the next winter. We could not eat gold, after all. The move had to be permanent. Some of the men wanted to settle in northern Kelda, but I knew Barreston wouldn't stand for it. Eventually, he would send more troops than even we could handle. We had to take Tornelaine. We took horses from every town. Our force was large, strong, driven by need. We were heading south along the Kiss River when I met your mother."

My chest aches at the word, and I'm torn between my comfortable, familiar anger and a new, painful hope.

"Some of the men found her. She was weak with hunger; she'd been wandering for a long time. As is typical with men on the march, they thought to make sport of her, but she broke open the earth under their feet and set two of them on fire. She may have been an Earthmaker, but she had a Runish warrior's heart, your mother."

A smile tugs the corner of his mouth, and his eyes are far away. I am jealous, saddened. I wish I could see what he is seeing. Then he shakes his head, throwing the image away. He takes a deep drink. His mouth settles back into a grim line.

"We could have taken Tornelaine easily, you know, if the Earthmakers had stayed out of it. But they couldn't stand the thought of a Drifter king, and they joined Barreston. It went on for months." He frowns into the cup. "We had just suffered a major defeat when Belos first came to me."

I feel my lip curl. I can picture this all too well.

"I refused him. I told him I would never wear a Leash."

"Let me guess: you suggested a different kind of deal?"

Heborian's eyes snap to me. "It wasn't like that."

"Oh? And how was it then?"

Heborian's hand clenches on the cup. "Belos waited until I was truly desperate. Until my men lay half-frozen in their tents, and more abandoned our cause each night. He waited until Barreston had us surrounded, until I loved Sibyl far too much and knew she would die along with the rest of us. Then he came again. I told him I would let him Leash me if he would save my people, and Sibyl. He refused. I begged. It is the only time I have been on my knees before any man. But he didn't want me anymore."

Gooseflesh prickles along my arms and legs. "He wanted me."

"Sibyl and I weren't even married yet. We had never discussed children. The thought of my firstborn child was not very real to me."

Later, I'm sure that will hurt me, but right now there is a greater horror roiling through my belly. "Why did Belos want me?"

"You can probably answer that better than I can. You know him as I do not."

"Because I'm a Drifter?"

"Not only that. You're an Earthmaker also. Your mother was a Healer. Very powerful."

"Why did Belos never tell me about my mother? If I had known, maybe I could have learned earthmagic."

"What would you have done, had you known the truth?"

I shrug. "Come after you? I don't know."

"And how would that have served Belos's interests?"

I grunt acknowledgment. "Belos wanted me to believe I had nothing but him. But he was right. My mother was dead. You had thrown me away. His story wasn't that far off."

I want Heborian to look away in shame, but he doesn't. "Oh, but it was. Why do you think Belos has joined Martel? Why do you think he wants to destroy me?"

A few more things click into place, confirming earlier suspicions. "You stood against him."

"We took Tornelaine, with Belos's help. But, months later, after Sibyl and I were married and she told me she pregnant, I cannot describe to you how my blood ran cold. For the first time it was real to me, that it was not just my own child I had promised. It was Sibyl's."

My fingers clench on the cold stone windowsill. "And she knew nothing of your deal?"

When Heborian shakes his head, the joy I have been holding back surges through me. My mother did not abandon me. But the joy dims quickly, because I will never know her. I am hollow and aching with loss as I listen to Heborian.

"She didn't know until Belos came for you. You were six months old, a beautiful baby. I had tried to tell Sibyl so many times." Heborian raises his cup with a shaking hand and finds it empty. He rests it on his knee, his hand clamped over the top.

"When Belos came, I yelled for Sibyl to run, and she fled with you in her arms. I fought Belos in the Drift." His story comes now in a rush of words. "I held him off for a time, but it wasn't enough. Belos caught up with Sibyl on the beach. She had escaped through a secret passageway and was making for the trees. I don't know what she intended, but I suspect she meant to go to Avydos in the hope that they would take you in, even if they threw her out again. She had been Stricken, after all, and they take that seriously." His voice flattens. "But she didn't make it. Belos caught up with her. I arrived moments too late. I saw Belos vanish with you in his arms."

"Where was Sibyl?"

"Gone. I don't know. I'm sure he killed her. Or one of the Seven did." His voice is emotionless, dead.

I study Heborian's profile, seeing now my own dark hair, my own straight nose. What else comes from him? "I should kill you, you know."

"Yes." Heborian stands from the footstool and walks to the hearth. He plants one palm against the edge of the mantel, leaning his weight on it, staring into the fire.

"Just like that?"

"I've done you wrong. You have every right to hate me. You have every right to attempt revenge."

I don't fail to hear the word "attempt."

He smiles ruefully. "That's how we clean things up in Rune."

I frown. "But you won't apologize? For giving me to Belos?"

"And would that make it better? Undo anything that has happened?" He shakes his head. "What would it mean, really? I am sorry for what you've undoubtedly suffered, but I would make the same choice again. To save my people, to build this life for them here. I cannot pretend otherwise."

"But you said you tried to stop Belos."

"Yes. But I was motivated by feeling, not a sound way to make decisions. Faced with it again? Weighting the pros and cons with a cool mind? I'm afraid I know what I would do."

Anger, so distant before, rolls through me suddenly, like a floodgate has lifted. The emotion is easy, comfortable, familiar, and I let it wash away all other feeling. For the first time since Heborian began his story, I feel like myself again. This, I understand. This, I can be. I ease along my mooring.

As I shift, I feel the lick of fire. The flames tease and pull, responding to my fury with heat of their own. I slide myself deep into their wild, destructive energy. They whip through me with fierce need, and I revel in the turbulence, drawing myself deep into the burning heart.

Heborian stands mere feet from me. It would be easy to destroy him, to burn away his indifference, his callousness, to show him that it's unacceptable. I flare and lash around him, exulting when he stumbles back with a cry. For once, I am the one in power.

I snap and crackle, whip, burn. The fire lets me *be* what I feel.

Heborian stares into the flames. Why doesn't he run? Doesn't he know I could kill him? I whip out with a tendril of flame and encircle his wrist. He jerks away, frantically patting his sleeve to extinguish the flame. He keeps his distance, but he still doesn't run, doesn't flee into the Drift. He holds his wrist, pain scrunching around his eyes. It dampens me.

Am I really what Belos has made me? Someone who would take pleasure in killing, as the Seven do? Someone who would murder her own father? Logan believes I can remake myself. What would he think of me, to see my now?

With a straining, tearing effort, I wrench myself from the flames. I rise from the hearthstones as the fire settles behind me, a mindless force once more.

Heborian, still holding his wrist, blinks at me, mutters, "She always said it was possible."

It takes a moment to penetrate. "What are you talking about?"

He clears his throat, and his voice normalizes, "The blending. Of the Drift and the elements. She always called the Drift 'the fifth element.' That's why they cast her out."

The pieces click together. Sibyl was Stricken for her ideas. Hearing this, I can understand why. Nothing would horrify an Earthmaker more than to hear that the Drift is an element.

Heborian's eyebrows lower as he remembers something. "Sibyl was always curious about the Drift. She would have me take her into it, and she had less trouble entering than you would think. She was gathering evidence, she said. I think she meant to go back to her people, to tell them they were wrong. I begged her to let it go, to forget them, but she couldn't." Heborian shakes his head at this remembered frustration, but his mouth quirks when he adds, "She was so stubborn."

I look guiltily at the blackened edge of his left sleeve and the puffy red burn circling his wrist. He follows my eyes but says nothing.

I want to hate him. No, more than that: I want to be disgusted, to look down on him. I want him to be pathetic. I could hate him if he was pathetic. But he's proud, strong, unmoving. I am angry with him, yes, furious, but there is a grudging respect growing within me. I really don't know what to do with him.

"You look so much like her."

I start. "What?"

"Like your mother. You have her cheekbones, her pale eyes."

Wanting something to stay angry about, I accuse, "You moved on awfully quickly. Rood isn't much younger than I am."

Heborian grimaces. "That wasn't for love. It was political. My marriage to Margitte brought the LeVarre family into alliance with me. That's all."

"Does Rood know that?"

"He's a prince. He understands these things. And his mother has been dead for ten years. It's hardly relevant now."

"I wonder if it seems that way to Rood."

He eyes me, warning me. "I know my own son."

I shrug. Maybe he's right, maybe not.

Someone knocks on the door, and I jerk in surprise. Heborian's dark eyebrows lower dangerously.

"What is it?" he barks in a tone that makes even me flinch.

The white-haired Drifter, Wulfstan, ducks his head through the doorway. "Deepest apologies, Your Majesty," he says, though he doesn't look sorry. "But two young men, Earthmakers by their looks, have tried to enter the castle. They are looking for a woman"—Wulfstan's eyes slide to me—"and one of them put up quite a fight when we tried to turn them away. We've arrested them, of course, but given their interest"—his eyes slip to me again—"I thought you should know. Your orders?"

My heart races. Two Earthmakers. Logan, undoubtedly. Who else?

I step forward. "Bring them here."

Wulfstan ignores me, waiting for Heborian's answer.

Heborian jerks his chin. "Bring them."

CHAPTER 27

Booted feet tromp through the foyer. The double doors swing open, and eight guards shuffle inside with the prisoners. I see Bran first because he is upright, hands bound behind his back and a guard's gloved fingers clamping his shoulder. Then I notice Logan, hunched and stumbling, hands bound, being half-dragged by two of the guards. I can't see his face, but I hear his rasping breath.

"Let him go!"

The guards hesitate, looking to Heborian. He must nod because the guards take their hands away. Logan crumples to the stone floor. Bran tries to catch his brother, but a guard's hand stops him.

I run to Logan.

His face is pressed to the floor, and he's trying to get up. I grab his shoulder to help, and he grunts in pain. A knob of bone is out of place, and I snatch my hand back, not wanting to hurt him. More carefully, avoiding the injury, I work my hands under his chest to turn him over. An ugly bruise is already forming along his jaw. His eyes are confused, out of focus. I lift his head and feel the sticky warmth of blood.

I look across him to the guards. "What have you done to him?"

One of the men, a captain by his shoulder stripes, answers defensively, "He attacked my men. We had to stop him."

"I told him not to," mutters Bran, jerking away from the guard to crouch beside us.

I push Logan's messy gold hair back from his face, and he blinks me into focus. "Thank the eternal earth," he says, and I am relieved to hear that his voice is clear.

His eyes close, and I shake him a little, worried he will lose consciousness.

"Someone get a physician," I say firmly, but no one moves.

Logan's eyes open again, and they are a flat blue that I don't like. He struggles into a sitting position. I reach behind him to work loose the knotted rope, and he pulls his hands free. The injured shoulder, his right, sags as he moves it with careful slowness. His right hand lies limp on his thigh.

"I'm all right," he insists.

"You're swaying."

"I am not. You are. Just be still for a second."

I bite my lip in concern. "What were you thinking?"

With his left hand, he grabs my shoulder as though to steady me. "They wouldn't let us in."

I put a hand on the back of his neck and pull him down so I can see his head. His breath hisses when I probe the split flesh. The bones feel whole. "And why were you in such a hurry to get in?"

He jerks upright, nearly smacking my chin with his head, and surges to his feet. I scramble up beside him and steady him when he sways. I have one hand pressed to his back, the other to his belly. I feel the hard notches of muscle through his shirt.

Despite my worry, sweet warmth spreads through my body at the touch.

Logan twists away from me and grips my arm with his good hand. His eyes are a swirl of blue and green. Relief floods me; that's what he's supposed to look like. "You shouldn't have left Avydos. You have to let us take you back. Right now. If he senses your Leash—"

"You are *Leashed?*"

Heborian's voice is harsh with horror, and I wheel around to find him staring at me. "You have no business acting disgusted with me. It's *your* fault—"

Heborian's eyes soften. "That's not what I meant. I just—I didn't think Belos would do that. The Seven aren't Leashed."

"Well, I guess he trusts them more than he trusts me." I blink with sudden realization. "And I guess he was right. I have betrayed him."

"He'll come after you."

"I know that."

"Please, Astarti," Logan pleads, and his fingers find my arm again. He is shaking, and I turn back to him in concern.

I look over my shoulder at Heborian. "I want a physician to look at him right now."

"Just listen!" Logan's fingers tighten painfully. "You have to get out of here. If he finds you, he'll kill you."

"Oh, he won't kill her." Heborian comes to stand beside me. "She's far too valuable for that. He'll use her Leash to control her, to take her mind and enslave her to his will."

I shudder, closing my eyes.

"Please, Astarti," Logan begs, and there is such fear in his eyes, such concern for me, that my heart fills with sudden joy.

"Astarti, come with me." Heborian brushes past me, and the guards scatter out of his way. "Captain Inverre, you are dismissed."

The captain bows briskly, and Wulfstan strides uninvited after Heborian. I hesitate, clinging to Logan.

Heborian stops when I don't follow. His voice snaps at me, harsh and impatient, "Now, Astarti. Unless you want to remain tied to Belos?"

"But—"

Bran puts my question into words. "Are you saying you can destroy her Leash?"

"I won't leave Logan," I say stubbornly.

"This is more important," Heborian insists.

Logan pushes me forward. "I can make it. If he can help you, then I can make it anywhere."

Heborian looks at Logan critically. "He won't make it up the stairs. Leave him. I'll have my own physician sent if it makes you feel better."

Logan straightens. "I can make it."

Heborian looks at him skeptically but shrugs. He turns and strides through the foyer, not looking back this time. Wulstan is on his heels.

I hold Logan back when he moves to follow Heborian. I don't know how serious his head injury is, and he needs to lie down and wait for the physician. But I don't like the thought of leaving him alone in the belly of this castle with eight guards nearby who just beat the hell out of him. Eight guards sporting enough of their own cuts and bruises to tell me they might want a rematch.

"Bran, stay with him. Don't let him out of your sight."

Bran nods, but Logan says sharply, "If you leave me behind, I will start a fight."

His eyes are a swirl of green and blue, and a muscle jumps in his bruised jaw. Bran's closed eyes confirm my suspicion: it's not an empty threat.

"You are the most stubborn, unreasonable man I have ever known." He gives me a lopsided grin, and I force a scowl to cover my smile. "Fine. Come on. Let's see what this is about."

One of the guards hastily unties Bran's hands, and Bran and I walk beside Logan, ready to catch him. As we move through the foyer, where Heborian has finally deigned to wait for us, my heart lurches with fear and with absurd, wild hope. Can he really help me? No, I caution myself. A Leash cannot be destroyed.

Heborian leads us through hallway after hallway, up stairways and around corners. I would pay more attention to the route, but I have too much of my mind on Logan. He is keeping up amazingly well, but he's limping, his right shoulder sagging, his face scrunched with pain. Blood runs down the back of his neck. I know he's dizzy because every now and then, he closes his eyes and swallows hard. I wait for him to collapse, to give up, but he doesn't. Bran and I share looks, and I see that he's as worried as I am.

When Heborian leads us to another set of stairs, this one winding through a tower, I put a hand on Logan's chest.

"Please. Don't."

"This is the last climb," Heborian calls back from halfway up the stairs.

I sigh with resignation as Logan starts up the stairs ahead of me. Bran shakes his head.

At the top of the stairs, Heborian stops. I see the faint bluish glow of Drift-work. Despite all the other emotions coursing through me, I can't suppress a little curiosity. He is unraveling a barrier, one similar to that which encompasses the entire castle. How is that done? And what could be behind that door that's so important to protect?

We enter what looks to be a sparsely furnished apartment, with a divan stretched along one wall, a blanket crumpled on it, and a single chair sitting before an empty fireplace. Another door indicates a further room beyond.

Logan staggers through the doorway and catches himself against the chair. He is breathing hard, his head hanging.

"You are so stubborn," I tell him as I brush hair back from his sweaty face.

Heborian pauses at the second door. "The Earthmakers stay out here." He nods to Logan. "He needs to lie down. Wulstan, stay with the Earthmakers. Astarti." He beckons me forward, but I ignore him, helping Bran get Logan over to the divan.

Logan collapses onto it. "I'm right here, if you need me."

I suppress a smile. "Good to know."

Wulfstan, glowering at us from the corner, rolls his eyes.

"I've got him," Bran assures me.

I rise and move cautiously toward Heborian.

CHAPTER 28

I follow Heborian into a workroom, and he closes the door behind us. Unlit candles stand all around the room, on small tables and chests, even in an iron chandelier suspended over a heavy worktable, and hardened wax drippings cover every surface. Light filters through high windows to fall in broad stripes on the worktable. Strange metal tools lie scattered across it. I recognize clamps, a sharp awl for boring holes, files of varying coarseness, hammers, and knives, but the rest are a mystery. One, a wickedly pointed screw with a crank handle, looks like a torture device. At the end of the table lie drawings and plans, all sketched with precision. I pull one toward me. The picture looks like a modified crossbow with an arrow made of bone.

"Just ideas," Heborian says gruffly, tugging the sketch away. He turns it face down.

He goes to a large metal chest and crouches before it. He presses his hands to the top, and I catch the glow of Drift-work. The box opens with a faint click. He shifts uncomfortably when

I come to look over his shoulder, but he doesn't object. He flicks a cloth wrapping aside to reveal a knife made of bone. Next to it, lying curled like a snake, its cuffs open and waiting—

I stagger back. "Why do you have a Shackle?"

Heborian frowns as I bump into the table behind me. "They were once used to teach. This has been in my family for generations."

My heart beats hard in my throat.

Heborian lifts the Shackle from the box and brings it toward me. I skitter away, and he lays it on the table.

"Do you know what it's made of?" he asks.

"Bone."

"Do you know whose bones?"

"Does it matter?"

"Yes. Come look at it. It's a tool, child, nothing to be afraid of."

"Easy for you to say," I grumble, but I come to his side. I'm not a child.

The Shackle is smooth and white with age. It's so glossy, like Belos's, that it doesn't really look like bone at all. Heborian runs a finger over it, and I shudder. When I notice Heborian looking at my wrist, I realize I am rubbing it unconsciously. I stop and straighten myself. I glare at him. For the briefest moment, some deep sadness clouds his eyes, then it's gone.

"The Shackles were all made of the bones of the Lost Gods, as the Runians call them. The Earthmakers call the gods the Old Ones, though they rarely speak of them."

I nod impatiently. I know the stories of ancient beings who shaped the world. Children's tales.

"They were real," Heborian insists, his dark eyes burning on me. "Don't ever doubt that. You cannot make a Shackle out of ordinary bone."

"No one can make a Shackle at all," I say shortly, eager to dismiss all this. "The knowledge has been lost for hundreds of years."

Heborian smiles, and there is something disturbingly wolfish in it. King Heborian, the Wolf. He goes to the box and brings back the knife, carrying it like it's the most precious gem on earth.

"Can you guess what this is?"

"A knife?"

"Don't be flippant."

I sigh and take a better look. The knife is simple in shape, but it has the same glossy whiteness as the Shackle. "A bone knife?" I amend.

"Better. This"—his expression grows intense, hungry—"is something of my own creation."

I stare at him, my heart thumping. No. I will not dare to hope.

He nods. "Yes."

I continue to stare, refusing to believe it until he says it.

"I will cut your Leash, Astarti."

I whisper, "That's not possible."

A faint flicker of doubt passes through his dark eyes. If I weren't staring at him so hard, I wouldn't have noticed it. He says, too firmly, "It will work."

"But you're not sure, are you?"

"It will work."

"Have you ever cut a Leash before?"

"Step into the Drift with me."

He holds out his hand. I don't take it. I might want to throw myself into this dizzy hope like a fool, but I won't. Nothing would hurt more than to hope and be disappointed.

When I don't take his hand, Heborian lets it drop. He admonishes me, "Have courage."

I steady my breathing. I will ground myself with doubt, let it center me. "But you don't know, do you? Don't lie to me."

"I am ruthless, when I must be, cold, when it serves me. But I am never a liar. You're right, I don't know. But I am sure nonetheless."

Gooseflesh rises along my arm and legs. I duck my chin.

"We must be quick." The faintest glow of Drift-energy surrounds him, then he's gone.

I ease along my own mooring. The room falls away, and Heborian and I are sharply defined forms in the dimness. The knife glows bright white in his hand. He studies the whitish-blue Leash that runs from under my heart into the distance. He glances at me to see if I'm ready, and I nod. I keep my thoughts locked away. I will not allow myself to feel anything. He might not be a liar, but he could be mistaken. If I refuse to hope, I will not be disappointed.

Heborian swipes the knife through my Leash. I am seized by nausea and pain, and for a second I think he has taken control of my Leash, that he's pulling it as Belos does. He has tricked me!

But the sensation vanishes, and I stagger back.

I am light as I have never been. I could float away. I look down and stare numbly at my silvery form, whole, independent, unleashed.

Heborian shifts beside me, and despite the strain and distance of his voice, I don't mistake his urgency when he says, "We have to go."

But I need a moment to see this, to believe it's real. I look for my broken Leash in the distance, but there is nothing. Gone. Like it never existed. I am dizzy. Dumbfounded.

I am free.

Suddenly, wind rushes toward me. My energy pulses with fear as the Hounding skims around and through my energy form. I have a moment to consider fleeing before my thoughts scatter in the whipping wind, leaving my mind in hazy dullness. When the wind tugs at me, I feel myself submitting. A foreign thought invades me: I want to go into this wind. It calls me with its mystery, with its strange, otherworldly power. Yes, I will go.

A flashing Drift-sword whips through the wind. The wind screams in protest—pain?—swirling away from the weapon. My mind clears, and I stagger back. Heborian swipes through the wind again. It forms tendrils of mist, faint, nebulous fingers, which lash and grab at his sword. Heborian vanishes.

I dive into the safety of my mooring.

When the physical world resolves itself around me, I clutch the table for support. I did not know the Hounding could take my mind. I shudder. Heborian's face, I am glad to see, is as pale as my own must be.

"Is the Hounding drawn to the knife?"

His eyes appraise me. I think I see approval in him, and my chest warms with satisfaction, though it makes me annoyed with myself. I shouldn't care what he thinks.

He doesn't answer my question. "Well? How do you feel?"

I press fingers to my sternum and the edge of my ribs. Despite the Hounding, I want to return to the Drift, to see it again.

I say numbly, still disbelieving, "It worked."

Heborian studies the glossy white knife in his hand. His mouth sets with satisfaction.

My eyes prickle. "Thank you."

Heborian freezes, then turns away in discomfort, refusing to accept my thanks. I understand why: it was his deal with Belos that led to my Leash, and I should not feel grateful, but I do. He has done something that I did not believe possible. He is, I realize, a brilliant man.

He carefully lays the knife into the chest and lowers the lid. It seals with a click. He rises as the glow dies around it.

He says roughly, "We should check on your friend. He needs to rest. Will you stay until he's better? He should not travel today."

I nod and follow Heborian to the door. For a moment, I had forgotten about Logan.

When the door swings open, Logan jerks upright on the divan. "What's wrong? What happened?"

I realize there are tears on my face, and I brush them away. "Nothing is wrong."

He glares at Heborian then staggers over to me and grabs my arm with his strong left hand. His eyes search my face, and I wipe self-consciously at the new tears. I am happy. Why, then, am I crying? I never cry.

"I—my"—I gesture in frustration—"he cut it." I laugh a little. "It's gone."

Logan makes a sound like someone hit him in the stomach. He crushes me to his chest and holds me more tightly than I have ever been held in my life. He kisses the top of my head. I am so warmed by this that fresh tears slide down my cheeks.

I laugh again and push him back. I rub my face against my shoulder. "I'm such an idiot."

"None of my children are idiots," Heborian says gruffly.

Logan freezes. As he stares at Heborian, I realize that he doesn't know.

I put a hand on Logan's arm. "It's a long story, but I won't tell it to you until you've seen the physician. Bran? A little help?"

It takes some pushing and some sharp words to get Logan moving, but when we do, the fight goes out of him, and he leans on Bran heavily. I try to help by supporting his right side.

Even though I avoid his shoulder, just touching his arm brings a sound of pain from him.

"It's dislocated," Wulfstan says from behind me, and I drop my hands, hovering uselessly behind Logan as we start down the stairs and work our way through the castle.

Heborian leads us to a different wing, one where the carpets grow progressively richer and the sconces more ornate. He barks orders to a young pageboy, who scurries off to fetch the physician.

We reach a beautifully carved door and follow Heborian into a richly furnished sitting room. I have little time to register the stuffed chairs and yawning fireplace before we pass into a further room with a wide bed. A window looks out onto a garden.

Bran tries to make Logan lie down on the bed but succeeds only in making him sit. He does accept water, which he gulps down. At every moment I expect Heborian to leave, indifferent to us, but he stays, pacing along the wall before the bedroom's smaller fireplace.

We have only minutes to wait before the physician, a sharp-eyed little man with a fringe of short brown hair around his bald head, bustles into the room.

"Renald," Heborian greets him, and the physician bows with a quick, "Your Majesty."

Renald hurries to the bed and sets a black satchel on the bedside table. He takes Logan's head in his hands. Logan jerks in surprise, and Renald mutters impatiently, "Hold still." He peers at the back of Logan's head, probing.

When he looks into Logan's eyes, he draws back sharply. "What is wrong with your eyes?"

I wince, thinking how I asked Logan the same thing when I first met him.

Logan's jaw sets.

Renald blinks, shakes his head, and resumes his inspection. "What caused the blow to the head?"

"Sword pommel," answers Bran.

"Mm-hm. And he's not been moved, I trust, except straight to this room?"

We all squirm a little guiltily as Renald stares around at us. He knows we moved him. He lets us sweat for a moment before he assures us, "He should be fine with rest."

I sag with relief.

Renald motions Logan to take off his shirt but has to help when Logan can't use his right arm. I wince when I see the knob of bone where his shoulder is out of place. Renald nods at it but turns his attention to Logan's ribs. He takes no apparent notice of the arcing scar across Logan's chest, but he freezes when he looks at his back, and I know he is staring at the horrible lash scars. Logan tenses, but Renald doesn't comment and is soon back to work, probing Logan's bruised ribs along his back and front.

"Three cracked," he pronounces. "Now lie down, right arm at the edge of the bed."

Logan complies, and Renald takes hold of Logan's hand. He plants a foot in Logan's armpit and pulls. Logan's eyes close at the pain. His shoulder makes a sickening pop, and he bites back a cry. His breathing is harsh and fast, but he soon calms.

"Better?" asks Renald.

Logan's face is white, but his voice is strong and steady. "Thank you."

Renald helps Logan sit up, and I am antsy, fidgety, wanting to help. I twist my fingers together to keep myself still.

Renald takes a large square of white cloth from his satchel and forms a sling. He sets Logan's arm into it with a stern, "Keep this as still as possible."

Renald goes to the washstand and pours water into the bowl. "Once I clean his head wound, he needs to rest, but I don't want him to sleep deeply for the first two hours. Who will stay with him and wake him every quarter hour, then check on him hourly after that?"

"I will," both Bran and I say at once. We look at each other, and Bran says, "Let me do it. You should rest. You look exhausted."

I hesitate, wanting to be the one to stay with Logan, but I know Bran cares as much as I do. I nod acceptance, not because I'm tired but because my mind is such a whirl, and I could use a little time alone to sort through the mess.

I go to Logan, guilty at leaving him, but he takes my hand. His eyes search mine. "Are you all right?"

"You're the one I'm worried about."

"He's fine," says Renald as he comes back with a damp cloth.

"I'll check on you later," I say and turn away before he can stop me.

Leaving Logan with Renald and Bran, I follow Heborian to the door. Wulfstan is already gone.

Heborian leads me into the sitting room and to another door. This one opens onto a second suite of rooms.

"For you."

I nod but refuse to look at him. He has given me and Logan adjoining rooms as though we are lovers.

Heborian doesn't acknowledge my discomfort. He simply sweeps to the door, saying, "I have things to do. Rest. If you want me, just tell one of the pages or servants. I will let them know you are to be brought to me immediately at your request."

"Heborian," I call as he reaches the door.

He halts, but when he looks back I find I have nothing to say. He seems to understand because he nods to me then leaves.

&ent; &ent;

After glancing over the rich furnishings of the rooms—stuffed chairs and ornately carved tables, crystal chandeliers, stone fireplaces, a lush bed and huge armoire in the bedroom—I open the glass doors that lead out to the little garden shared by Logan's room and mine. This is indeed a suite for lovers. What on earth made Heborian think that Logan and I are together like that?

I trace the far, curving expanse of a high wall. Within its spacious confines lie the curling fingers of flower beds, fans of trellised vines, and the knobby shape of a tree. Sunlight sparks in my face as I follow a winding stone path.

I hear the trickling of water and follow it to a little pond with a bubbling fountain. On the far side of the pond stands an old crabapple, its pink blossoms beginning to emerge from gray-green buds. Below the tree rests a stone bench, flanked on either side by trumpet-faced daffodils. Green nubs protruding from the earth in farther beds promise more growth as summer approaches.

I wander to the bench and fall onto it with a sigh. I am not used to lounging in gardens, but I think I could enjoy this. A breeze wafts over me, stirring my hair.

All my thoughts, all the disturbing new facts I had planned to assimilate, float away. I am empty and glad to be so. For a few moments, I will not think.

I don't realize I've fallen asleep until someone nudges me. I sit up with a start, wincing at the crick in my neck. I blink Bran into focus.

I stifle a yawn. "How's Logan?"

Bran plops down beside me. "Sleeping. After the first two hours, he wouldn't settle, so the physician gave him a poppy tea. I'll check on him soon."

I nod, rubbing an impression of the carved bench from my cheek. Chilled by the spring air and the stone bench, I pull my knees up in front of me for warmth.

Bran picks at a loose thread on his sleeve and twists it between his fingers. "He cares for you very much."

I study Bran's face as he stares blindly at the pond, the thread still twisting in his fingers. "And what do you think of that?"

"That it means trouble."

My heart sinks. Of course he's right, and of course he thinks that, but it still hurts. Can't we ignore reality for one moment?

"But. I do like you, Astarti. And you are so good for him, even though it's against our customs. And laws." He shakes his head. "You have no idea how good you are for him."

My heart flutters with hope. "What do you mean?"

His brow wrinkles as he considers his answer. "He's more centered. He's moving forward instead of back. Things have been hard for him, since our father died." He grunts. "They were hard before that, but our father's death only made things worse."

I hesitate with my question, afraid he won't tell me, won't trust me. "Why were they hard? Why is he so…different?"

Bran draws up a knee, knits his fingers. I recognize uncertainty, but is he uncertain of his answer? Or just of sharing it with me?

"The truth is that no one knows, least of all Logan himself. My mother, perhaps, might know, but she has never said."

Bran gives me a moment to puzzle over that. Why would his mother know if no one else does? Comprehension dawns. "You think he's a—" I stop, refusing to say the word "bastard."

"Some say that. But even that doesn't account for everything."

I lean forward with a question, but Bran puts up a hand. "Trust me, there's nothing you could ask that I haven't, and I have no answers for you."

I sit back, frustrated. "But you still care for him."

He's offended. "Of course."

"Aron doesn't."

"Oh, Aron cares for him, don't doubt that. But Aron doesn't know how to handle him. To be fair, Aron's not alone in that. Logan is very difficult. He refuses to behave like the rest of us, to think like the rest of us. Maybe he can't? But Aron also has issues of his own. He feels he should have been able to save our father, that he should have been there. He and Logan have been fighting over who should feel the worst guilt for five years now." He shrugs. "A pointless argument."

"And what about you?"

Bran's eyes harden. "I know there's only one person to blame, and it's not Logan or Aron."

I draw back, stung. It will always come back to this. My Leash may be cut, but I will never really be free of it.

Bran puts a hand on my knee. "I mean Belos, Astarti. I do not hold you to blame."

I feel myself melt, and I am shocked by my own need to hear such words. Bran pulls me to him. Because I am weak, I give in and lean against his shoulder.

⁞  

When Bran leaves to check on Logan, I wander along the garden path and back to my rooms, where someone has left a gleaming silver tray. I peek under one of the round silver covers, which releases curls of steam and scents of beef and rosemary. I grab a blanket from a chair. The slippery silk won't stay on my shoulders, so I tie two corners in a knot and wear it like a cloak. I set to work on the food, slathering butter on a heel of fresh bread. I groan as I stuff the soft, delicious thing into my mouth. I cut into the beef and dab it in the thick gravy.

When my full belly is pressing uncomfortably against my waistband, I explore the further rooms, finding a bathing chamber with gray and white tiles and a huge porcelain tub. I go to the hallway door, planning to seek out some hot water. A young pageboy is sitting on a stool right outside my door, his swinging legs indicating boredom. He jumps up and nods when I tell him what I want. He takes off at a brisk walk, his short legs showing how he longs to break into a run.

When maids come bearing buckets of steaming water, I thank them for their trouble, and they stare at me. I guess most of the inhabitants here expect to be waited on. When they ask whether I want help, it's my turn to stare. I assure them I can take my own bath. As they leave, I shudder at the thought of anyone helping me bathe.

I strip off my clothes and slip into the steaming water. The heat soaks into me, driving out the chill of the garden. I have never been in a bathing tub so big. Leaning against the high back, my feet don't even reach the other end. I let one foot rise to break the water's surface and sigh at the luxury. I grab a bar of rose-scented soap from the tray beside the tub and work it in my hands until I have a bubbling lather.

When I've finished my bath and returned to the bedroom, I find a pile of folded clothes on the bed. I am disturbed that someone entered my rooms without my notice. I cannot let these little luxuries make me so careless; I will have to pay more attention.

I sort through the clothes, which are mostly dresses, until I find a pair of black riding breeches and a loose, pale blue silk blouse. The colors are dramatic with my dark hair, and the shirt drapes elegantly. I frown when I look at myself in the huge tilting mirror. Who do they think I am to wear such fine clothes? My eyebrows jump with sudden realization. For the first time it occurs to me that I am, apparently, the daughter of a king. I am, actually, his oldest child. I step away from the mirror guiltily. No, I won't think of myself that way.

I go to the door to Logan's rooms and ease it open. I tiptoe into the bedroom, where the curtains are drawn to keep the room dim. I look for Bran, but he's gone. Logan is sleeping, and I creep silently to his side. With his face relaxed in sleep, he looks so much younger. All the tension is gone. Seeing him like this I realize how troubled his face usually is.

Above the edge of the blanket, I can see the deep bruising developing across his right shoulder. His eyelids flutter open. He raises his hand, lifting the sling. I ease his hand down. His eyes close, and he's asleep again.

I sit in the chair by the bed, where Bran has clearly been sitting. I prop my feet on the edge of the mattress and lean back.

At some point, Bran ducks his head through the door. Seeing me, he nods and disappears again.

As I watch Logan sleep, I memorize his face. He is so beautiful that my chest aches with it. It occurs to me that I should stop staring, that it might be wrong of me, but I can't stop. I want to look at him, to take him in with my eyes. I don't ever want to let go of this moment, of the knowledge that buzzes so warmly within me: he came after me. He was worried about me and got into a stupid fight over it. He wouldn't let me go alone with Heborian, even when he must have known his injuries made him useless. It doesn't matter that he couldn't have helped me. It was that he wanted to, that it meant so much to him to stay with me. No one has ever cared about me like that before.

෨ ෬

It's evening when Logan wakes. The sun has slid away and the room is dark. My eyes are used to the dimness, so I see him stir. I can even make out the shape of his torso when he sits up. He starts when he notices me.

"Sorry," I say. I should have known a figure in the dark would startle him.

"Astarti."

I love the way my name sounds when he says it, like each syllable matters.

I get up and use flint and steel to strike flame into the lantern on the side table. Golden light blooms over the bed. Logan tosses the covers aside and swings his legs out.

"Easy," I chide when he has to catch himself against one of the bedposts. I make him sit. I check the sling, my fingers avoiding his skin. I am all too aware of the brush of fabric and the occasional brief touch of warm flesh.

He assures me, "I'm just groggy."

I look at him skeptically, but he does seem better. The bruise on his jaw is darkening, and his shoulder is an ugly mess of purple, but his eyes are a clear blue, edged with green.

It was easy to watch him sleep, to think about how beautiful he is, about how much he has come to mean to me, but now that he's awake I don't know what to say.

He takes my hand, stroking my fingers. Shivers of pleasure shoot up my arm and through my body.

He plays with one of my fingers. "I was terrified when you were gone. Please don't run off like that ever again. You should have come to get me."

"I didn't think about it," I say honestly.

"Well, think about it next time, all right?" His voice is surprisingly petulant.

"Promise me something in return."

He eyes me warily, not promising.

"Don't get into any more stupid fights where you could get hurt."

"There were eight of them," he says defensively.

"That's why I called it a stupid fight."

He grins, and I have to laugh because I love his grin—rare, fleeting, mischievous.

We look at each other for too long, and I know my expression must be intensifying as Logan's is, shifting from playful to serious. An ache forms in my chest as the full truth, which I have been working so hard to deny, hits me with sudden force. This one moment of letting my guard down, one moment of watching my feelings reflected in his eyes, and I know: I love him. It's wrong, it's a disaster, but it's true.

I reach out tentatively and touch his hair, which is soft even though it's messy. His eyes swirl blue and green at the touch. His gaze is so hot, so full of longing and need that my breath catches.

"Your eyes are beautiful," I say softly.

He looks away, but I turn his face back to me with gentle fingers. He is pained, worried, and I am suddenly furious that he's been made to feel ashamed of something so extraordinary.

I say again, "They are beautiful."

He lets out a shuddering breath and stands. He is tall, and I have to crane my neck to look up at him. Gold edges through the blue and green of his eyes. I stare in wonder, letting myself look at them directly, as I have not allowed myself to before. His left hand comes to rest on my hip, and I am intensely aware of the narrow space between us. I reach my hands up to his chest, and his muscles tighten at my touch. I draw a sharp breath at the shock of pleasure the touch sends through me. Logan goes still, breath held.

Cautiously, shakily, I draw my hand across the curved planes of his chest, under the sling to trace his arcing scar. His heart quickens, throbbing under my hand. He breathes again, shallowly, chest rising and falling as I work my hand across the planes of muscle. A buzz of energy, almost like the Drift, tingles through my fingers where they touch him and spikes along my arm into my body.

When I trail my hand down the notched muscles of his belly, he lets out a soft moan. My fingers brush the band of his pants, where the hard cut of muscle shows at his hip. He sucks in a sharp breath.

His right hand is immobilized by the sling, but his left skims from my back to my buttocks, and he pulls me against him. My pulse races as his hand brushes my side and hip and up my back again. Careful of his injured shoulder, I explore his back with my hands in turn, feeling the ridges of muscle, the flat plates of his shoulder blades, the lines of his scars. He flinches when I touch the scars, and I draw back a little to see his face. His eyes are filled almost entirely with gold now, something I have never seen before, but green edges back through them. I have never been with a man before and I realize suddenly how much trust it takes, on both our parts.

The tension leaves him, and he leans down and kisses me. His lips are soft but insistent, and I find myself opening to him. Yes, I want this. I want him.

But I stop. I push him back.

He gives in reluctantly.

"I don't want you to be Stricken because of me."

His eyes swirl with green, chasing away the gold. "I don't care."

"I do."

"I *don't*."

"But I *do*."

He groans and turns away, free hand planted on the bed. His body is shaking.

But then, so is mine.

I touch his back and he moans softly. "You are torturing me."

I take my hand back. His head hangs, and he takes three deep breaths. He's getting control of himself.

When he stands up and faces me again, his eyes are still a raging battle of color, but his body has gone still. I worry briefly that he's angry with me, but he traces a lock of hair down my face. His eyes are hungry, unsatisfied. He is full of such fierce need, and something deeply primal in me answers to him. My hand, with a mind of its own, reaches out and touches his belly. He flinches.

"Please...go," he says brokenly. "I can't—I can't look at you and not want you right now."

I swallow hard. I don't want to leave.

"Please."

I turn and flee.

CHAPTER 29

I pace my rooms. Part of me hopes Logan will come to the door, because I want to be foolish and selfish, because I want to not care about his people's stupid rules. But he doesn't.

When my feet are sore and aching, I strip off my clothes, drag on a loose nightgown, and climb into the spacious bed.

I toss and turn in a froth of blankets. I get up and pace again, the cool night air chilling my bare arms. I stop repeatedly at the door to Logan's room. Has he gone to bed? Is he sleeping? Or is he pacing like I am?

There is no light and no sound, so perhaps it's just me. I return to bed, frustrated.

I doze, shifting in and out of sleep.

At some point in the night, I am awake, staring at the dark canopy, my mind fuzzy with tiredness but unable to escape into sleep, when I hear the sound I've been longing for: the door clicks open.

His feet are silent, but I imagine their approach, his toes on the carpets, his arches flexing. By the time he reaches the side of my bed, I am sitting up, imagining the shape of his body in the dark. Just enough moonlight filters through my curtains to show his shoulder, the edge of his jaw, his flat belly.

He says sternly, almost challengingly, "We will have to figure this out."

"Yes."

"Can I stay?"

His calm, controlled tone tells me he has mastered himself, so I understand that he's asking only to be here. I check my disappointment. This is better really—he wants to be with me simply to be with me.

I toss the covers back and scoot over. He slides into the bed. I am on his uninjured side, but I still hesitate, unsure whether or not to keep some distance. But his hand works itself under my shoulder, and I slide to him, wedging myself under his arm, my cheek on his shoulder. My body is pressed to his, but this is different from our earlier touching. This is simply being together, and it feels so, so right.

His breathing evens out and so does mine. Soon we are in rhythm. Soon, we are asleep.

⥼ ⥽

I wake in the dim light of dawn. Logan's hand is idly tracing my shoulder. I am filled with a new wave of longing, so I push away from him. I sit up, leaning against the padded headboard. Logan works himself into a sitting position beside me. From the corner of my eye, I see his bare torso, and I look away.

These feelings are so unfamiliar and so strong. I don't know what to do with myself.

Logan says abruptly, startling me, "What did Heborian mean?"

I stare at him dumbly. What?

"Yesterday. He said something. About his children."

For some reason, this makes me blush. "Oh. Yes." I clear my throat, unsure where to begin.

Logan startles me again by beginning for me, cutting right to the heart of it. "He's your father, isn't he?"

My eyes snap to his. "How did you guess that?"

He shrugs, not answering. I did not realize he was so perceptive.

He gives me a tender look. "I assume you learned about your mother also?"

I am nodding, unable to work up any words, then I say simply, "Sibyl."

The name feels strange in my mouth. My mother. The thought of her has always filled me with anger and bitterness, but now I feel only loss. She did not abandon me. She tried to protect me. She…loved me. And I will never know her.

Logan stares at me, dumbfounded, then he shakes his head in wonder. Of course he knows the name. "How did that happen?"

Haltingly, with much backtracking and self-correction as I try to put it all together, I repeat Heborian's story. At first, Logan listens eagerly, particularly to the parts about Sibyl. His people may pretend indifference to those who are Stricken, but I don't believe it, especially of Logan. He is hearing the answers to many long-unanswered questions. When I get to the part about Heborian's deal with Belos, Logan's face darkens. I sum the rest up quickly, but even so, Logan looks furious. His nostrils are flared, his breathing harsh. His left hand is clenched into a fist.

When I finish rather lamely with, "And then Belos, apparently, you know, took me," he says, "I should kill him."

I know he means Heborian, and I say firmly, "No."

"Why not?"

"Because. I don't know. He's the only family I have? I never had that before."

His eyes are green and gold, and a muscle jumps in his jaw. "He *sold* you to Belos."

I say sharply, "I understand exactly what he did, and don't make the mistake of thinking I forgive him."

"And don't you make the mistake of thinking that I *ever* will."

We glare at each other, stubbornness setting in in both of us.

I remind him, "He did cut my Leash."

Logan throws the cover aside and shoves himself from the bed. "That makes up for nothing. Why are you defending him?"

"I'm not defending him. But he *did* cut my Leash." I am filled with lightness at the thought. I rub my chest, amazed. I am no longer Leashed.

Logan sits back down, his expression softening. His fingers find mine across the bed. "I am so, so happy for you."

I close my eyes, letting his words soak into me, letting the warm touch of his hand tell me it's real.

A thought occurs to me, and my eyes pop open. "We could cut Martel's Leash."

His eyes grow thoughtful. "We could."

I scramble into a kneeling position, losing track of Logan's hand in my excitement. "It would sever his tie to Belos."

"But he could still ally himself with Belos, even without a Leash."

I dismiss this. "I don't think he chose it. I think Belos must have forced him."

"How could you know that?"

"I don't. But I spoke with him, remember? He was horrified by the idea. Terrified."

Logan looks skeptical.

I snap, "Frankly, I don't care whether Martel chose it or not. I don't care about Martel at all. But I certainly don't want Belos to have him or anyone. He has too much power already."

As anger rolls through me, I realize that this is at the heart of what bothers me. Belos thinks he can take and take. And he can. When the rest of us let him.

Logan's forehead is crinkled in thought. "And if we just kill him, Belos will take his lifeforce?"

"Yes."

"So we cut his Leash, then kill him?"

"I'm not killing anyone." My words are sharp enough to sting, but Logan nods, not taking it personally.

"Then Heborian will."

I shake this away. "That's his decision. Martel is his enemy, not mine. I'm finished doing other people's dirty work."

Logan gives me a look of such understanding and compassion that I have to harden myself inside or I will be turned to water, and I could not bear to be so weak in front of him.

He gets up. "Then let's go get that knife."

୭ ଓ

When I try to convince Logan that he is in no fit state to travel or, potentially, fight, he gives me a look of such furious refusal that I know it's pointless to argue with him. Besides, I don't have time for it. Surely Heborian will stop him.

Logan goes back to his room to dress, and when I meet him in the hallway, he is wearing his leather pants and jacket and a green linen tunic that shows edges of Keldan embroidery. He has removed the sling but is holding his right arm carefully. When he sees me looking, his eyes warn me that he's ready to

266

argue if need be. I frown at him, just so he knows I don't approve.

I'm wearing the black breeches I wore yesterday and my Earthmaker boots that lace to the knee. Digging deep into the armoire, I uncovered a cream-colored shirt of sturdy linen, and I am relieved to not be wearing silk. The way silk slides over my skin, so smooth and fine, makes me self-conscious, like I'm trying to tell people that I'm something I'm not.

The same young pageboy has been swinging his legs on the stool outside my door, but he is on his feet now, ready for action. He nods hugely when I tell him to take us to Heborian. He strides ahead, his small chest puffed out with importance. He tells several other pageboys we meet that he is taking us to the king, and their young faces fill with awe and not a little envy. For some reason, their innocent reactions make my stomach flip. Heborian is, indeed, the king, the most important man here. My father.

Two hallways later, we are intercepted by a man who looks to be a high-level servant, judging by his velvet waistcoat, and he sends the boy to the kitchens. The boy's face falls with disappointment, but he is soon hurrying down another hallway, his steps light with excitement at the prospect of breakfast. It makes my own stomach rumble, and I wish we had stayed in our rooms until food came.

The serving-man leads us to Heborian's study, leaving us at the guarded double-doors and retreating back through the foyer. One of the guards, the one I flung through these doors yesterday, cracks the doors open to announce our arrival. He makes no acknowledgment of our fight. Good man.

After a brief exchange, the doors swing open. I catch a glimpse of several men gathered around the heavy table, which is littered with maps and reports. I recognize Wulfstan, who ignores me, but the others I have never seen. There are five of them, and I wonder if these are Heborian's other Drifters. At the far end of the table, Prince Rood stands and glares at me. Heborian, wearing a billowing cloak of maroon velvet, his hair braided back in Runish fashion, sweeps across the study. The guards bow him through the doors, pulling them shut behind him.

Heborian doesn't bother with pleasantries. "Well? Your plans?"

Logan is glaring at Heborian, and the tension of his body tells me how he itches for confrontation. Heborian gives him a measuring look, then turns back to me. I am astounded by how unshakable Heborian is.

I edge in front of Logan, not trusting him to be rational. "I want to take the knife and use it to cut Martel's Leash."

Heborian grabs my arm and tugs me along as he strides across the foyer, away from the guards. Logan follows so close behind me that his toes skim my heels. We stop at the fountain, where the splash of water will cover low voices. Heborian lets go of my arm.

He says, low and firm, "No."

The bluntness makes me blink. "Why not?"

"The knife will never leave this castle. And you will never tell anyone of its existence. Or speak of it. Do you understand?"

"But—"

"Do you understand?"

My jaw sets with stubbornness. He can't just order me around. "Tell me why."

"You have no idea what that knife could do in the wrong hands."

"You mean my hands?" I ask hotly.

"No, I don't mean your hands."

I cool a little. He means Belos's hands. "So tell me what it could do."

But here, apparently, his trust ends because he only looks at me steadily and says again, "That knife will never leave this castle."

My mind is blank. I don't know how to get past this outright refusal.

Logan shifts to my shoulder, unwilling to be kept back. "Then we will have to bring Martel to the knife."

Heborian frowns. "Better just to kill him."

I break in, "And let Belos have another source of power?"

"One more mere human?" Heborian shrugs. "It would make little difference."

His indifference makes my face hot. One more *mere* human is not acceptable. Nothing is acceptable.

I cross my arms. "Belos cannot have him. If necessary, I will bring him here. You can do what you like with him once his Leash is cut."

Logan's fingers find my sleeve. "You keep saying 'I.'"

I refuse to meet his eyes, focusing instead on Heborian, on the fierce tattoo that hooks around his right eye and stabs down his cheek. "Will you send any help with me?"

"I cannot risk my Drifters for something so dangerous and so unlikely to succeed. What if Belos or his minions are there? This is foolish, Astarti. There will be a siege here. A better chance will open up during the battle."

"But what if we can prevent that battle?"

Heborian dismisses this with a flick of his hand. "This won't work. Too risky."

Logan forcibly turns me toward him. "Maybe he's right, Astarti. This isn't even your fight."

I see the fear and worry in his eyes, and it almost makes me soften, but I can't afford softness right now. "This *is* my fight."

"Why?"

My heart pounds with all the things I cannot say, how I must do something to ease the guilt and shame eating at my heart, how I would die to undo even a little of what I have done in service to Belos.

Instead I say, "Think about how many people will die in this battle. People who also have nothing to do with this fight, except that they owe loyalty to one man or another." I give Heborian a hard look, trying to spark some guilt in him, but his expression reveals nothing. He is used to being king, used to having people die for his causes. I shudder inwardly. I could never rule.

I look from Heborian to Logan. "I will go. Neither of you can stop me. I will capture Martel and bring him here. With him Leashed, I can take him straight into the Drift and have him here in minutes."

"If no one stops you," Heborian points out.

I don't answer that. Of course that might happen.

Logan's bruised jaw clenches. "If you do this, you know I'm coming with you."

I look to Heborian for support. "You must see that he can't possibly."

Heborian shrugs, and I want to scream. I was counting on him to side with me.

"I'm not a child or an invalid, Astarti. I make my own decisions, just as you do. I don't try to infringe on your freedom. Don't do it to me."

My eyes drop to the tiles, and the blue and gray pattern blurs through my vision. There is nothing he could have said that would make it more impossible for me to argue with him. Still, I make one last attempt, though my voice is feeble, resigned to defeat, "But you're already hurt."

Neither he nor Heborian say anything. I glare at Heborian, wanting to blame him, but he is looking at Logan with surprised approval.

Logan says, "I'll take you through the Current so that Belos, if he's near, won't sense your approach."

I realize suddenly that Logan has begun using Belos's name instead of calling him the Unnamed. I'd like to ask him why, but it's not the time.

I point out, "Bran could take me instead."

Logan's eyebrows jump. He looks to Heborian. "Where is my brother?"

"He returned to Avydos last night. He said he would be back later today. I had the impression he meant to speak to your mother and brother." As usual, Heborian's expression reveals nothing, even though he must now know that Logan is the Arcon's brother.

"Fine," I say. "But, Logan, you will take me there and back. You will not fight."

Heborian fixes me with a hard eye. "You ask too much of him."

I wheel on Heborian. "You ask too much of me."

His answer is stern, filled with layers of meaning, "I ask nothing of you."

Both their jaws are set with male stubbornness, and I want to scream at them. I throw my hands in the air.

Logan's mouth quirks. "I knew you'd come around."

"Oh, shut up."

Chapter 30

Heborian leads me and Logan through a hidden tunnel that provides quick escape from the castle. We emerge from damp darkness onto a beach. I freeze. This must be the route my mother took when she fled with me. I try to picture an Earthmaker woman with long blonde hair, a dark-haired babe in her arms, but the image is vague, blurry. I do not know what she looked like. I stare up and down the sandy beach. Where was the exact spot? Where did she die?

Heborian stands beside me, and for a moment I see loss in his eyes, so much deeper and more painful than I would have guessed from him. But it's soon gone, and he beckons me onward.

When a stand of trees comes into view at the edge of the beach, where sand, castle, and green hills meet, Heborian jerks his chin in their direction. We can enter the Current from there.

"You know where to go?"

"Yes," Logan answers, his hand on the pommel of the sword Heborian lent him. He has belted it at his waist for a left-hand draw because his right arm is all but useless. I have never seen him wield a sword left-handed. I hope he doesn't have to today.

Before we left the castle, Heborian used a detailed map to show us Martel's last known location. The information is two days old, but we know their destination, and we've made a guess at two days of progress.

Heborian nods, seemingly out of words. He studies my face until I feel uncomfortable. He raises a hand and almost brushes my cheek, but I pull away instinctively. He drops his hand. Logan bristles beside me. Logan and I are in agreement on one thing: Heborian has no right to touch me.

Heborian says gruffly, "Be safe," and strides away.

I watch his retreat, his maroon cloak billowing in the ocean breeze. His shoulders are broad and squared. I hate it, because he betrayed me even before I was born, but I am a little bit proud to know that my father is such a strong man.

Logan shifts impatiently beside me, and I follow him. When we reach the trees, he takes my hand and pulls me in the raging gold of the Current.

We step from the Current into wooded hills. We can't see the Green Wall from the cover of these trees, but it lies north of us, to our backs. Martel's army should be within a few miles. It's fairly easy to guess the speed of an army: slow. Wagons, war machines, oxen. They're not moving fast.

Logan takes me back into the Current, and we travel a few miles south. I wish I knew how the Earthmakers navigate the Current because it all looks the same to me. Maybe Logan will explain it to me someday. At least I am beginning to find the entry and exit easier. It's not unlike the Drift, really. There is a moment of darkness and pressure, like passing through my mooring. Only, it's not myself I am passing through, but the trees. That, I still find a little foreign.

When we step from the Current again, I hear the distant creak of wagons, the occasional whinny of horses. Even in the early morning they are already on the march.

I take a deep breath to prepare myself, but Logan grabs my arm.

His fingers clench. "I changed my mind. I don't like this plan."

I gently pry his fingers away. "We agreed. This is the only way. I can only grab Martel easily if I reach him through the Drift. It will only be seconds. I'll grab him, bring him back here to you, and you can take us all through the Current to Tornelaine."

"What if—"

"We agreed."

He takes a shuddering breath. "Just be careful. And quick."

"You'll barely know I'm gone."

"I always know when you're gone."

My heart swells, and I turn fully to him, to really look at him. He reaches for my face, and I allow him what I denied Heborian. His hand slips across my cheek and behind my head. His fingers knot in my braid. Heat swells within me, and I answer his touch with my own, sliding my hands around his torso. He leans down and kisses me. It is deep, hungry, full of promises.

My hands skim upward to tangle in his hair, and he moans softly against my mouth. Our kiss deepens until I am dizzy with it. When we break away, he rests his cheek against my temple. His heart pounds, as mine does. I know this is forbidden and that we must stop, that we will have to give each other up. But for this one moment, he is mine and I will allow myself to love him.

His fingers stray to the back of my neck, and I tense when they brush my tattoo. His cheek is still pressed to my temple, so his fingers are moving blindly. Even so, they trace the Mark, gliding up and down each branch of it. I cringe. He knows it's there. He's seen it.

When I start to pull away, he grips me tighter, and his lips press against my hairline, just above my ear. At last, I understand. He is accepting me, every part of me. I melt.

When I lean back to look at him, his eyes are green and gold, his face so beautiful. I gather my strength and push away. If I look at him any longer, I will not be able to leave him, not even for a few seconds.

I ease along my mooring and into the Drift. Around me, the world darkens, lit only by the energies of living things. For the first time, I notice that the trees are indeed part of this glow. They are dim within the Drift but more present than I had realized before. I feel Logan's wild energy behind me, feel the fine thread connecting us by proximity, by feeling. He sensed me in the Drift once before. Does he sense me now? I don't let myself look at him for confirmation, to see if his attention is on me. We will have time for those questions later.

Just ahead, Martel's army is a faintly glowing serpent winding through the hills. Relief washes through me when I see they are only human. None of the Seven. No Belos. It doesn't surprise me, really. Belos will only come for the battle, for the end. He doesn't waste his time on mundane tasks like getting wagons and war machines through wooded hills.

I drift to the snaking army, finding Martel riding in the vanguard, near the front. I know him by the white Leash that flows from his sternum, fading into the distance. I take a moment to marvel at my own free form.

I position myself behind him and travel my mooring into the physical world.

Martel cries out in surprise when I wrap my arms around him. His men shout. A hastily-drawn sword flashes toward me, but I am already dragging Martel into the Drift. The lighted forms of the men mill about in confusion. Martel's horse has bolted.

Martel struggles with shocking strength, and I begin to worry. How much power has Belos given him? How much of Belos is *in* him? A human should not be able to fight me in the Drift. I wrestle him down, winding threads of my energy around and around him. I haul him along, but he wills himself away from me, and I have to grapple with him constantly. I did not expect this. It's taking too long.

When his Leash pulses brighter, fear rips through me, and I do something I've never done before, something horrible. I jab my hand into the center of Martel's energy, gripping him from inside. He goes limp with shock. I hope I haven't killed him, but there is no time to check. I drag him along.

Ahead, Logan's bright, gold and silver form appears. I fill with joy at the sight, even though I've only been away a few moments. His energy is knotted with fear. He is worried about me. I wonder if that will ever stop filling me with surprised delight.

I reach Logan and am about to ease along my mooring when Martel's Leash flares brilliant white. Panic surges through me. I know what that means. I follow the line into the distance, where a raging torrent of energy flies toward us.

I shove Martel aside and shape my spear, bracing myself for Belos's attack.

CHAPTER 31

I turn Belos's sword aside with my spear, but the blow reverberates through my energy, lacing me with pain. I scramble back to make space.

Belos's energy rages, a whirling madness of silver and gold and sickly orange. Within that chaos, one face or another will take brief shape. Hands appear and grapple with one another. Belos's form is in constant flux, all the conflicting energies seeming to tear him apart and reshape him at every moment, but he doesn't seem to notice. His face contorts with rage, turning him fully, deeply ugly. I'm afraid, terrified even, but I am exhilarated also. For the first time, he cannot force me into submission. For the first time, I can fight.

I whip my spear around to slash at his belly, hoping to cut right through his energy, to kill him. I will it with every fragment of my being. Death in the Drift is death.

He spins away and shapes a second sword. The weapons flash in his hands, reflecting his will. He charges. I leap, using the fluidity of the Drift to lift myself over his head. I stab downward to pierce his neck. He twists, and my spear slashes across his shoulder instead. He staggers back, and I stare in wonder at the small, dark tear in his energy. I have hurt him.

I am glowing with triumph, stupid with it, when his blast hits me. Fierce, angry energy slams into my chest. I am flung back, stunned, as the energies whip around me like vicious, scrabbling hands, tearing at me. My mind seems to fray, and I am lost in their prodding and grabbing.

Belos stalks near. He will kill me. No. He will Leash me again.

He will take my mind, make me a slave in truth. I will be nothing.

With the last shreds of my concentration, I will myself through my mooring and flee into the physical world.

ⅎ ℥

I stagger, tripping over deadfall. Green branches and pale blue sky spin overhead. Where am I? What happened?

"Astarti!"

Running steps snap twigs and scatter dry leaves.

Am I whole? Am I me?

"Astarti!"

Hands grab my arms. Someone spins me, and I sway with dizziness until Logan's face swims into focus. His eyes are a swirl of color, and his fear sharpens me.

"We have to go. Now!"

"What—"

The blast hits Logan from behind, and he crashes into me, knocking me down a muddy, deadfall-littered slope. As the world rolls around me, I catch flashes of Logan falling, flashes of a dark shape at the top of the slope. I plant my feet, grinding to a stop as I reach the stream at the bottom. Mud sucks at my boots, but I jerk free. I scramble up, shaping my spear.

Belos looks down from the top. I can't see his face clearly from this distance, but his stiff posture tells me that his anger is beyond fury. It is cold, hating.

I wait for him to attack, but his gaze shifts away from me. I follow it to Logan, who is staggering to his feet a little way up the slope, injured shoulder sagging. He jerks his sword from its sheath. Panic swells within me.

"Logan!"

Belos vanishes.

Logan looks to me, and so he doesn't see Belos appear behind him.

I scream again, something inarticulate. I try to find my mooring, to enter the Drift, but my mind is like a thousand pieces of shattered glass.

Belos's hands clamp onto Logan from behind.

Logan's eyes widen in surprise. Belos smiles at me.

They vanish.

ఴ ಞ

I only realize I have been screaming when my voice cuts off hoarsely, when I am gasping and choking on the dregs of that scream.

I get up, not remembering my fall into the water. My clothes cling wetly, but the chill of my body is distant, not quite real to me.

Only a Drifter can enter the Drift without preparation or Leashing. To drag a human or Earthmaker into it—

I clutch at my chest. I cannot breathe. I fall back into the water.

The cold grip of water returns some of my wits to me, and I still my mind and step into the Drift.

I am alone.

There is no sign of Belos. No sign of Logan.

Even Martel is gone.

ॐ ☙

I step from the Drift into a busy street. A mule lets out a screeching bray. Hooves scrabble on cobblestone. A man shouts. People shift around me. Some are yelling.

I stumble forward.

I bump into a cart stacked with baskets, sending a few of them rolling from the stack. I watch numbly as one rolls into the path of a wagon and is crushed into a mess of broken strips.

Beefy hands grab and shake me. A ruddy face slides in and out of focus before me, and the sharp smells of sweat and musty straw fill my nostrils. The man shakes me again.

"Hey!"

I dimly register the familiarity of the voice.

"Let her go!"

Another voice, also familiar.

I slump against the side of the cart as two sets of hands grab my attacker.

I stagger to my feet and stumble onward.

Someone calls my name.

I steady myself against a drainpipe.

My name again.

Someone grabs my arm and jerks me around. All I see is Logan's face, and the breath leaves my body. Then the jaw squares itself, and the hair shifts to red-gold. Blue Earthmaker eyes search my face.

My mouth works on his name, finding it, giving it to him hoarsely, "Bran."

"What happened?"

Another face, so similar but so much harsher, appears at Bran's shoulder.

Aron's eyes narrow. "Where is Logan?"

The words are slow to form as Aron and Bran stare at me. "Bel—" I swallow something horrible. "Belos. Took him. Into the Drift."

Bran cries out and staggers away from me, but Aron lunges forward and grabs my arms. My hands go numb under the pressure of his grip.

"What did you say?"

I can only stare at him.

"What did you do?" He shakes me. "What did you do?"

"Aronos," calls a deep voice from behind, and stocky Polemarc Clitus steps forward.

Aron shoves me away and I slam into the drainpipe. My head cracks against it. Bright light flashes, then wonderful, empty darkness takes me.

Chapter 32

LOGAN

The world has disappeared. I am lost in darkness.

But not really darkness, because there is one brilliant, horrifying light. I will myself away from it, every instinct screaming for me to flee, but it wrenches me back. The face of my enemy looms over me, lit with madness. His form bulges and twists.

In the distance, a wind rises.

Belos looks up, and his brow furrows. He steadies his grip on me. In the next moment, we are flying through darkness, fleeing the wind.

Lights flit here and there, gold, silver, blue, pink, green. At some point we pass over a great concentration of them. I struggle weakly, but I am powerless here, and my enemy tows me like a fish on a line.

Lights disappear and we are moving now through nothingness. The wind gains on us, and I feel its fingers brush me. They are hungry, voracious.

Suddenly, I am squeezed all around, like I am being pressed through some tunnel that is too small. The wind is gone. Everything is gone.

Light blinds me.

Heat engulfs me.

I stumble back and fall onto hard, parched earth. I gasp dry air into my lungs.

He crouches beside me, light gleaming on the silver studs lining his shoulders. One shoulder has an ugly black slash, like a burn. His face is so familiar, so similar to the faces of my own people. Its planes are clean, proud.

He frowns at me. "What are you?"

I collapse onto my back. Pain is returning to me. My head spins. My right arm feels like it's been torn away at the shoulder.

He nudges me roughly in the ribs. "Hmm? You can't be an Earthmaker. And yet, you are. What are you?"

His questions skim over me. I have no answers for him and none for myself. The Drift should have killed me. I should be dead. But I am not. Which means I am not one of my people.

Belos sighs impatiently, prods me again. "What do you want with Astarti?"

Her name snaps me back into reality. I scramble away from Belos and stagger to my feet. I reach for my sword, but I've lost it.

He laughs. "You can fight me just as well without a sword as with one. Which is to say: not at all."

"Where is Astarti?"

Blond eyebrows rise. "You should be much more worried about where you are."

I dart a look around. We are at the foot of a plateau. The rest of the land is flat and dry, featureless except for strange fingers of stone on the distant horizon.

Reality stuns me. "This is the Dry Land."

His mouth quirks in a smile. "It's not much, but it's home. For now."

He tries to circle me, but I spin to keep my eyes on him.

He frowns. "I know your face."

I try to hide my angry reaction, but his smile tells me I've failed.

"You look much like your mother." He adds snidely, "My dear Gaiana."

I freeze. Though it's whispered, unacknowledged, all my people know the story of the Unnamed and how he loved my mother. And how they laughed at him when he asked for her hand in marriage.

No one has laughed at him since.

I say, because I will not die meek and cowed, "How could you ever have thought she would choose you?"

Anger sparks in his blue Earthmaker eyes. "Because Arothos was such a prize?" With a flick of his hand, he slaps the thought of my father away like a pesky insect. "He was weak."

"My father wasn't—"

"Your *father*? Please. I had his head on a pike for an entire month, until the stink became too much to bear. I know every inch of his face, and I see none of it in you." He looks at me thoughtfully. "You are something else entirely."

At his words, something gives way inside me, like a dam bursting. No one else would say this. So often my people have thought it, perhaps whispered it among themselves, but no one would say it, not to my face. I am furious, ashamed, yet somehow exhilarated as I tear into the dead, barely pulsing heart of this land. Yes, I am something else.

The dry ground cracks and heaves, buckling around me, snapping, breaking, bursting, and I come alive with the power of it.

Everything else vanishes, everything but this wild, hungry need. Dimly, I realize I am losing myself again; dimly, I remember Belos and that I should fight him. But how can any of that matter compared to the infinite power of earth? What could matter but this wild, beautiful movement?

I rip and tear, bending and shaping the earth around me. I find idle, nearly lifeless currents of air and wrench them into sudden movement. Deep, deep, deep, I feel the slow trickle of water. High and far, blazing with ancient anger, burns the sun. I draw them all to me. I will make something new here, something beautiful.

Pain explodes across my back. I am spinning.

Falling.

I suck in ragged, pained breaths, and fine dust stirs at my mouth and nose. The earth rumbles in discontentment, unsatisfied, but it is quieting, returning to sleep.

A boot slams into my ribs, shocking me with pain. I try to get up from the torn and tumbled ground, but something heavy hits me from behind. A fist punches into my stomach. I swing wildly, but a heavy blow comes down on my arm. Another blow to the back of my knee brings me down. Now they are raining on me, and my world is flashes of pain.

"Enough!"

Several booted feet step away from me. I cannot raise my eyes, but I know who these newcomers are: the Seven.

"Koricus! The Shackle!"

Shackle. I know that word, and it drives panic through my pain. I try to get to my feet. I have to fight. I have to make them kill me. I cannot be Leashed.

Hands grab me. A smooth, warm cuff claps onto my wrist. I jerk away, but I'm already being sucked through that tight space and into the darkness of the Drift.

I will myself away, but Belos yanks the Shackle, and I fall before him. I scrape at the cuff, but it is insubstantial, only energy. A white thread snakes along it from Belos to me. I flail wildly, but the thread twists around my wrist and disappears within me. I feel it slide through me, violating the very core of my being. I am sickened.

The wind flares to life around us. It grabs me, and I beg it to take me, to kill me, but something yanks at my heart, sending sharp nausea through me. I am squeezed tight again and wrenched into the harsh, dry brightness.

I fall to my knees, retching, wracked by nausea. But though my stomach heaves, I can't throw up the Leash.

He crouches beside me, and I shove him. The punishment is immediate. Something jerks within me, and I am slammed face first to the torn ground. He turns me over roughly and plants a hand on my chest.

I scream at the pain and violation. I try to pull away, but I am trapped, helpless. I feel my mind break apart as a cruel, sick, foreign will spills into me. With the last fragment of my mind, I grab for something, anything, and it is Astarti's face. It hovers, pale and beautiful.

Then it's gone.

CHAPTER 33

I wake with sunlight in my eyes. I am tangled in slippery silk blankets. A cream-colored, embroidered canopy stretches above me. Tornelaine. Heborian's castle. I'm in the same bed where I awoke with Logan—

The brightness swims. Despair deadens me, weighs down my body. I am a corpse. I will never rise.

"I was worried you wouldn't wake."

Bran's voice startles the feeling of deadness from me. I hastily swipe tears from my eyes so he won't see. He is sitting in a deeply cushioned red chair, one leg draped over the other. He wears a pale gray tunic and loose linen pants. His reddish-gold hair is pulled back at the nape of his neck. Tidy, as usual. But, though his face reflects that Earthmaker calm, I see hints of pain scrunched around his eyes.

"Bran."

He rises fluidly from the chair and comes to the bed, resting one hipbone on the edge of the mattress. He knits his fingers in his lap. "What happened?"

I tear the covers aside and push myself from the bed. I am wearing the sleeveless nightgown. Who changed my clothes? I feel exposed, so I grab a finely woven wool blanket from the chair where Bran was sitting and snug it around my shoulders. It's still warm from Bran's body.

Head throbbing enough to nauseate me, I pace to the glass doors that open to the garden. The mild spring colors look out of place, surreal.

"Astarti, what happened?"

I close my eyes, willing everything to disappear, but only the Drift responds to will. Here, nothing is changed. I open my eyes to find the garden still childishly ignorant of reality. I want to tear the faces off those daffodils, whack the blossoms from the crabapple. Their fragility sickens me. I press one fingernail to the glass pane and make a long, slow downward scratch.

"Astarti."

Why is he making me say it? I already told him.

"Please leave." I whisper it. If I let my voice grow any louder, I might shout.

"Don't you think I have a right to know what happened to my brother?"

I bow my head, pressing it against the cool glass. Of course he has a right to know.

"Start from the beginning. Heborian said you and Logan went after Martel, that you were going to bring him here so his Leash could be cut. But that was all he could tell us. What happened with Martel?"

That, at least, I can tell him, though my voice comes out flat and foreign. "Martel was riding with his army. I grabbed him. I was going to meet up with—" My voice cuts out on Logan's name. I am stuck, my mind a blank.

"Yes?"

I clear my throat, find my voice again. "We were going to meet up. But Belos came. Belos and I fought in the Drift, but he was too strong. I couldn't—I wasn't strong enough. I couldn't stay there. I should have, but I couldn't. If I would have, Belos would've killed me, and it would be over, and Logan—" His name chokes me. "—wouldn't have—he'd still be—"

I don't hear Bran approach, but his arms slide around me. I grab onto him, clinging like it will save my life. I don't cry, but I am sick, sick, sick.

Bran finishes the story, "He took Logan into the Drift."

I close my eyes, but even there I cannot escape the vision of Belos. His hands clamp onto Logan. He smiles. Logan's eyes widen with surprise. They vanish.

I wrench away from Bran. "Why are you here? What do you want?"

"I wanted to know what happened."

I want to strike that Earthmaker calm from Bran's face, so I hold my fists against my belly. "Now you know. Leave me alone. I know how you must hate me. Stop pretending to be nice!"

"I'm not pretending anything."

Bran's hands are flat and calm, loose at his sides. I feel reckless and out of control next to him. I feel like a child, and that snaps the last of my restraint.

"I *know* you hate me. I am a vile, *filthy* Drifter, and I took your brother away, and now he's—"

"I've known Logan much longer than you have. I know better than to blame anyone else for his choices."

I want to scream that it's my fault, that I couldn't save him, but the words won't come out. They are lodged deep, their barbs hooked within me.

Bran says, "Get dressed. Then walk with me. I'll wait in the sitting room." He starts for the door but pauses when he hears no movement from me. "Unless you want to sit in here all day?"

After the door clicks shut, it takes me ten minutes of pacing to realize that Bran is right. I don't want to be in here. I stalk to the armoire.

Minutes later, not even sure what I'm wearing, I am following Bran through corridor after corridor. When we see people, I do not look at them. We could walk right by Heborian and I wouldn't know. I am determined not to know. I will not tell the story again.

Bran takes me up a narrow flight of stairs. I dimly note how well he already knows the castle. When my legs are burning from the climb, we reach a door, which opens onto the battlements. I suck in a surprised breath at the rush of cool spring air and wince at the crisp blue sky of afternoon. The fine weather is determined to mock me.

I follow Bran to the wall, where I lean against the square-toothed crenellations, pressing through one of the slots designed for an archer. The cool breeze slips through the loose weave of my shirt. I shiver, wrapping my arms tighter around myself. Our bodies don't care about our grief; they make all their usual demands.

Beyond the castle, hilly Tornelaine bustles. Soldiers line the city wall. More move through the streets, where people dart out of their way. I look to the neat rows of barracks within the castle grounds. What are Heborian's numbers? I shake my head. I don't care. None of this means anything to me.

The question seems to occur to Bran also, but he does, apparently, care. "Heborian has just over a thousand within Tornelaine. A sizable standing army, really. And he's been calling up the countryside. They'll organize to the west.

Heborian's council is hoping that this second force, some two thousand at the most optimistic estimate, will be able to attack Martel's troops from behind once they've set in to siege us. Another four hundred are already on their way to ambush Martel when his army passes through the river valley to the north. They're hoping to at least pick off some of his number." When I don't react, Bran asks, "What will you do?"

"What do you mean?"

"Will you join Heborian?"

I shrug.

"This fight still matters."

I say harshly, "Not to me."

"I don't believe you."

Bran looks down into the courtyard, ignoring my glare. I follow his eyes to the grouping of blond heads. Earthmakers. Hmm. And I know Aron is here. And Clitus. I remember them from—never mind.

I frown at the blond heads, realizing their significance. "Will *you* join Heborian?"

"Aron is trying to use it to make a deal"—I shudder at the word—"but Heborian is very...strong-minded. Every time Aron reminds him that *we* are helping *him*, Heborian says that Belos is *our* 'monster.' Aron isn't happy, but, yes, we will fight."

"So your Council finally woke up."

"Uncharitable, but yes, you could say that. They don't like to make hasty, irrational decisions, but they do, in the end, decide."

I sniff. "Almost too late."

"I hope *you* won't be too late."

I look at him, puzzled. "Why do you care what I do?"

Bran leans into the arrow slot next to mine so I can't see his face. "If Logan were here, and you had been taken, would you want him to give up? Mope around while other people stand up to Belos? How do you think that would make him feel years later, looking back on himself?"

I stare at the pitted surface of the stone. The answer is obvious. Bran, to his credit, doesn't make me say it.

A gull, winging in gray and white over the castle, screeches into our silence.

I say softly, "Logan is dead."

"Probably."

My head snaps up, and I am abruptly, unreasonably angry. "What do you mean 'probably'? Of course he is. Well?" I demand when Bran is silent. "What did you mean?"

Bran wedges himself more deeply into his arrow slot. "Nothing, Astarti. Just forget it."

ῴ ῳ

Whether I want to be involved in this or not, I am dragged in by questions. Heborian, his Drifters, Aron, and Clitus all want to weed information from me.

Even before the midday meal, I find myself once more in Heborian's study, barraged by questions.

"What are the capabilities of each of the Seven?"

"What are their weaknesses?"

"What are Belos's weaknesses?"

"Where will Belos position himself?"

"How strong is Martel?"

"What is the state of Martel's army?"

I have never been so much the center of attention in my life. When someone—I have completely lost track of who is speaking—asks about how Belos will use Martel's Leash, I grip my head in my hands and shout at them all to be silent for one second.

Everyone backs away like I might burst into flames.

I hear the sound of a stopper being pulled from a decanter. Heborian hands me a glass filled with two inches of amber liquid.

I set it on my knee. I won't drink the stuff, but it's nice to have something to wrap my hands around to keep them from shaking.

"I'm sorry," I tell them, and I am. I know their questions are important, and I am pleased, really, to be able to help, to betray Belos just a little more.

I begin to explain that power flows both directions along a Leash. Belos can use Martel's Leash to control him, but he can also imbue him with unnatural physical strength and speed, with greater intelligence, even with some control of the Drift.

"But Martel can still be killed?" someone asks.

"Of course. He's still mortal. But Leashed, his death will only give Belos more power." I flick my eyes to Heborian when I say this, wanting to blame him, but his dark eyes are as impassive as ever, giving me nothing.

When they have exhausted their list of questions and my head is throbbing enough to pop my eyes from my skull, I am free to go. I hurry for the door, desperate to get away. Someone is on my heels, so I pick up my pace.

Aron catches up with me halfway across the foyer. "Astarti."

I close my eyes. "What now?"

"I'm sorry," he says gruffly.

I spin around in surprise. "For what?"

He looks uncomfortable, shifting from one foot to the other. "For pushing you."

"Oh. That." I wave it away.

"It was inexcusable, losing my temper like that. I certainly didn't mean to hurt you."

"It doesn't matter."

I can see that he has something else to say, but I turn away. I don't want to hear him say anything about Logan.

⁞  

I try staying in my room because I don't want to talk to anyone, but I only find myself pacing and watching, in my memory, as Belos grabs Logan again and again. Here, being still, I cannot escape it.

I practice with my Drift-spear in the garden, slashing at the flowers that are so offensive to me right now. When I cut the heads off a clump of daffodils, I stare at the scattered yellow trumpets. Stupidly, it's this little thing that almost makes me cry. I am cruel, a monster. I gently sweep the severed heads off the stone path and into the soil.

I seek out the training yard, a grassy field near the barracks. Men practice archery at one end, expertly firing arrows into the concentric rings painted on canvas and stretched over straw bales. Other men train against one another with swords and spears. I am the only woman here. No one meets my eyes. No one wants to join me.

When I'm on the verge of leaving, someone calls out with a Runish accent, "I'm Horik."

I turn to see one of Heborian's Drifters, whom I recognize from the grueling question session, leaving a small group of young men to approach me. He looks to be one of the youngest Drifters here, probably in his late-thirties. His dark hair is braided away from his face in the Runish style, and his deep orange tunic shows Runish embroidery—wolves, bears, and serpents—along the edges. His big, muscular body moves with surprising grace. Though he must have been young when he left Rune with Heborian, he looks every inch a Northerner. He stops a few feet from me, but even at the distance he seems to loom.

"I did not get to introduce myself properly before. Horik." He presses a hand to his chest, then gestures to me. "You are Astarti."

I don't say anything. He knows who I am. I will wait, see what this is about before I react.

He adds, undaunted by my cold reception, "I remember you. I was a young man, but I remember the firstborn."

The way he says it, like it means something, sparks a flicker of pride within me. I am the firstborn of the king. But a cool breeze wending through the training field lifts stray hairs from the back of my neck, and I imagine the Griever's Mark exposed, flashing bright blue. Firstborn, yes, but still forsaken.

Horik bows to me, as though only the first part matters. "Spar with me? I would see what the king's daughter can do."

I search for a mocking smile, glance at his companions to see if they are laughing, but Horik is only waiting for me to meet his challenge. An involuntary smile tugs at my stiff mouth when I shape my Drift-spear.

Horik nods appreciatively at the notched blade. "A true Runish weapon. But then, so is this."

A heavy battle axe appears in his hand. The blade boasts a long, wicked beard, gleaming with the power of the Drift. He smiles, jerks his chin, and I follow him to an open space in the center of the field.

Horik faces me, hefts his axe, and raises his eyebrows to ask if I'm ready. I take a deep breath to still and focus my mind. Everything around us recedes. The world is filled only with me and my spear, Horik, and his axe. I nod.

His powerful lunge surprises me. He's not playing around. I dart back, whipping my spear over my head and spinning to slash the blade at his neck. He blocks with his axe, but his eyes pop in surprise. I am very fast.

His blows are powerful, his movements smooth and well-timed. I have never fought a man so big and strong, and I have to compensate for my weakness with greater speed and agility.

Crouch, leap, slash, roll, deflect. I am soon panting. I did not realize I was so out of shape. Horik, though, is just as tired, his blows heavier, his reactions slower. He is used to fighting men who fight as he does. I make him work harder, make him chase me, make him lunge again and again.

When Horik overreaches, a little too desperate to end this, I slide under his blow and slap him in the back of the knees with my spear shaft. His knees buckle, and I am on my feet before he reaches the ground, the point of my spear tight against the back of his neck.

Silence. I become aware that a crowd has gathered around us, and that crowd is holding its breath, stunned. Time seems to have stopped.

Then Horik laughs, and someone else laughs. A few start clapping, and then the whistling begins, and excited debate draws attention away from me.

Horik climbs to his feet. The knees of his linen pants are damp and dirty from his fall. "You did not disappoint me, firstborn. If I were less of a man, I might be ashamed to be beaten by a girl, especially when I am the king's champion."

His humility and arrogance are so interwoven that I don't know where one ends and the other begins, but I decide that I like him, and I clasp his forearm when he offers it to me.

I am elated, riding high on this first hint of acceptance, when I see Prince Rood stalking away, disgust apparent in the curl of his lip. We still have not spoken. Because I don't know him, it shouldn't hurt me. But he is my brother, even if only by half, and he, like my father, has rejected me.

I excuse myself from the field. I walk around the castle grounds for the rest of the day, past the field and the barracks, the armory, the smithy, the stables, the cooking houses. After my sixth or seventh lap, people begin to stare at me, but I ignore them.

When my feet ache from the uneven cobblestones and the evening grows dim and cool, I return to my rooms and fall, fully clothed, into bed.

႙ ႘

I dream of Logan. He is beautiful, grinning that mischievous grin of his, but his eyes widen in surprise when a spear bursts through his chest. He is yanked backward, away from me.

I wake with a cry, reaching for him. My hand closes on empty air.

CHAPTER 34

For the next two days, as Tornelaine teems with brisk, sometimes frantic preparations, I busy myself with any task I can find. I spar with Horik and with others, now that the men have seen I'm worth their time. I try to help in the stables, because I want to see the horses, but I know nothing about horses, never having had a need for one. Because I'm in the way, I leave. Instead, I help in the armory, handing out weapons and fixing armor.

On the third day, in the dark hours before dawn, a small group rides hard to the gates. I see them come in, a tight knot of horsemen, because I am up on the battlements, waiting for dawn, unable to sleep.

I make my way to Heborian's study, where a light shows at the bottom edge of the door. I guess I'm not the only one not sleeping. I wait in the dimly-lit foyer as a captain in torn, bloody armor limps to the door, flanked by guards. I don't try to follow because I don't want to be told to leave.

When the captain emerges again and limps away, I pace around the fountain. The door guards watch me but say nothing.

When Heborian and a surprisingly large group of people come out, Heborian stops in his track. He motions everyone onward and approaches me.

He says nothing of my lurking, only appraises me. "Are you ready?"

"That didn't look good."

Light from a sconce flickers across Heborian's stern face. "Of the four hundred sent to harry Martel, sixty have returned."

"Only sixty?"

Heborian's mouth sets in a grim line. "The Seven now travel with Martel."

He offers no more detail, but I don't need it. I know what the Seven are capable of.

"So." He looks fixedly at me. "What will you do?"

It irritates me. "What do you think? That I'll betray you?"

"No."

The simple answer deflates me. "I will fight."

One dark eyebrow lifts. "After you were brought back, I thought—"

I don't want to hear what he thought. I don't want to talk about that day, so I shut him up with a bit of honesty. "I would be ashamed to stand aside while others fight." Besides, this is what I have often wanted: to choose my own enemies. And I have chosen. I will kill Belos for what he did to Logan. Or I will die trying.

Heborian looks at me for too long, then the corner of his mouth quirks upward. "Then prepare. The enemy will be at our gates by dawn."

℘ ℭ

The bells are rung, and the deep brass warning booms through Tornelaine. Soldiers pour out to the city walls. The massive beams barring the gates are checked and double-checked. The people stay hidden in their homes, and when I follow Heborian and his Drifters along the hilly streets to the wall, the streets are gray and empty. It makes gooseflesh rise on my arms.

I am wearing leather breeches bound at the shin by light steel greaves. Armguards protect my forearms, curving plates cover my shoulders, and a light breastplate protects my torso. When I chose this, the armorer tried to get me to wear chainmail and heavier plate, but speed and agility are my best protections, not metal. Even this is cumbersome, and I wish I could strip it off and wear only my close-fitting tunic.

We climb the steps to the platform over the main gate. Heborian takes position in the center, and I move with Horik, Rood, and the other Drifters to the space left for us just beyond the gate. The wall is two paces deep and protected by a square-toothed crenellation, much like the one atop the emptied castle.

Already the east is paling, and the temperature has dropped with the predawn chill. The Drifters' expressions are grim and ready. Most wear heavier armor than I do: layered steel breastplates and heavy, grinding chainmail, gauntlets, sweeping neck guards. Horik towers above us all, and he grins at me from within his steel helmet. At least someone is excited about this.

Beyond our tight group Heborian stands with his personal guard and with Wulfstan, the only Drifter who is not part of our plan, because he will not leave the king's side. Next to Heborian's cluster of guards stand Aron, Clitus, and Bran, and beyond them a long string of Wardens.

For the last few days, the Wardens have walked the fields around Tornelaine, "studying the earth's lines," as Bran unhelpfully explained. Except for the various shades of blond hair and the presence of women among them, no one would guess they weren't Keldans. In their leather pants and stiff vests of boiled leather, they look like Heborian's archers. Only Aron and Clitus wear the broad-sleeved tunics typical of Earthmakers, each with a tighter tunic beneath. But even their armor is light, meant only to protect them here on the wall. They won't be going onto the field like the Drifters will. The swords belted at their waists are only backup protection, in case the wall is breached.

Down the line, I spot Korinna peering over the wall. Regret flashes within me. I did not even know she was here until last night, and I have not yet spoken with her, mostly because I didn't know what to say. She is, after all, my cousin, the daughter of Sibyl's sister. I worry it would appall her to learn of our relationship. Now, realizing that one of us might die today, I wish I had tried.

Archers fan out along the rest of the wall, interspersed with compact catapults, their round metal buckets secured at the end of their thick wooden arms. Heavy stones, glowing ever so faintly with Drift-energy, lie ready in the buckets and in piles.

Below and behind us, in the city, soldiers wait with swords and spears. Hopefully the fight will not come to them. If it does, if Martel's army breaks through the wall to reach this last line of defense, chances are that Tornelaine is already lost.

I glance at Rood, who stands on the other side of Horik. Rood wears a gleaming, unblemished silver breastplate. Even if that didn't mark him as new to battle, the nervous twitch of his fingers would, as would the barely-healed tattoo peeking from under the neck rim of his breastplate. So. A Runish tattoo. One, no doubt, of protection or strength. My own tattoo burns in shameful response on the back of my neck.

Rood meets my scrutiny with a look of cold disdain. His twitching fingers go still, and he looks resolutely forward.

From across the cluster of Drifters, I notice Heborian glancing our way, his worry betrayed only by the scrunch of his tattoo around his right eye. Heborian did not want Rood among the Drifters, not only because the boy is inexperienced, but also because we have the most dangerous assignment. We will try to draw the Seven off, away from the city so that Martel's troops will have to fight a more human battle.

We wait.

₭ ₨

Martel's army crests the hills with the dawn, the war machines like black fingers against the rising sun. Heborian's army will have the sun in its eyes. I wonder who timed this. Martel? Belos? Straton? I wish I knew what is going on in that strange alliance.

The army moves like a snake, coiled and tight. I can pick out the Seven, wearing the black of war, controlling the fringes of the army, forcing the serpent of men to coil more and more tightly. Where is Belos in that mass?

The front of the army halts on the broad field beyond the city wall, the serpent shape dissolving into sudden fluidity as the middle and rear sweep around like water, spreading wide and deep, reaching almost to the rolling west of the city orchard. They have stopped beyond the range of Heborian's archers. The red banners of House Deveral, Martel's house, wave at the edges, a challenge to the blue and black atop Tornelaine's gates.

I can't stop my gasp when Straton appears, hovering in the air not twenty feet from Heborian. I have never seen the Drift used this way. Neither, apparently, have Heborian's Drifters.

Some gasp like I do; some even step back. Straton smiles condescendingly, enjoying our surprise.

But it's Heborian's turn to smile when Straton bounces into a sparking net of energy and floats back with a hiss of pain. Of all Heborian's inventions, this one amazes me most. I cannot begin to explain it except to say it's like a barrier brought into the physical world. I always thought the Drift had certain rules and limitations, ones I understood, but Heborian, it seems, is more creative than I am.

Straton recovers quickly, giving no further acknowledgment of the net. His black robes are edged with the bright light of dawn, his silver shoulder guards gleaming. He looks down his nose at Heborian, forcing the king to crane his neck. Heborian, dark hair braided down the side, his golden armor flashing a reflection of the pink dawn, does not look intimidated. Pride spikes through me. Few would stand like that before Straton.

"Your terms?" Heborian demands.

Straton's answer is loud and imperious: "Complete surrender. You will yield yourself to Belos, and your people will be his. In exchange, we will not tear this city stone from stone." Straton smiles before he adds, "Or your son limb from limb."

Heborian, I'm sure, expected as much, so there is no hesitation when he answers, "No."

"I couldn't hear that," Straton lies. Everyone heard it.

"I won't parley with you. Be gone!"

The power in Heborian's voice makes my nape prickle. I begin to understand the will and resolve of a man who sailed from Rune to Kelda and took what he wanted.

Straton's lip curls. "Today, Heborian, you will pay for trying to renege on your deal, and you will lose *both* your children to Belos. And, you—"

My spine stiffens as Straton turns his gaze to me. "What do you think Belos does with traitors?"

I raise my chin, ignoring the spider of fear crawling over me. "I will find you, Straton. Mark me, I will."

He gives me a measuring look. "Why would you serve the man who sold you?"

Anger flares in my chest. Straton knows, has always known, my story. They have all lied to me. Before I can think of a retort, Straton vanishes with a rush of air. How like him to throw in the last word and disappear. I will find him. I will kill him. I will accomplish that much before I die today.

Martel's army buzzes with activity, and the distant clank of metal gears tells me they are cranking the catapults. Heborian shouts orders to the soldiers manning Tornelaine's own, smaller machines, and men recheck their levers.

The noise of orders and cranking machines dulls to a hum in my ears as the huge arms of Martel's catapults spring upright. The first massive stones that fly from the distant machines disappear into the blinding sunrise, reappearing just before impact. The crack of stone on stone and the vibration under my feet makes me duck instinctively. Others do the same around me.

On the field below, the men lash the oxen to drag their machines closer.

In the buckets of Heborian's own catapults, the Drift-charged stones glow faintly. At a shout, Heborian's men trigger the machines, slinging the charged stones into the army below. Several fall short, exploding into the ground in a spray of dirt, carving craters the oxen cannot cross. Two charged stones bounce into the teeming mass, their explosions sending men flying like sticks in a children's game.

It doesn't take long for the earth to start rumbling. I trace the tremors to the blotch of black that marks the Seven. My legs vibrating with the shudders of earthmagic, I dart a look at Heborian. When will he give the order? He ignores us. He's stalling. He doesn't want to risk us. Or perhaps he doesn't want to risk his son.

Around Heborian, the Wardens' faces are still with concentration. Even Bran, Aron, and Clitus have that distant look of working earthmagic.

A wind rises over the city with a whistle and swirl of dust and debris. As the wind whips over us, a Drifter behind me slams into my back, crushing me against the wall. I brace myself with straining arms as he squirms heavily behind me. I work an eye to the arrow slot to see the wind sweep over the army, bowing them like grass.

With an abrupt shriek, the wind reverses, screaming toward the wall. It reverses again, sweeping toward the army. The fighting currents whip dirt into the air until even the sun is diffused in the dusty haze. I bury my nose and mouth in the crook of my arm, breathing through the fabric of my shirt to keep the dust from my lungs. My eyes water from the grit.

Bursts of energy fizzle against Heborian's net. The blows shift away from Heborian, searching for weak points. I seethe with impatience. The net may cover the whole of Tornelaine, but how long can it hold up to this barrage? And how long before the Seven find the hidden gap? When they break through, we will lose our advantage.

I lose track of time as the dizzying winds and the rumbling, splitting earth force me to huddle among the other Drifters. The catapults clank into firing position again and again. Men bark orders. Steel boots scrape and thump along the stone wall. Close around me, metal breastplates and chainmail scratch against stone as the Drifters shift.

Then the fires start.

Heborian's catapults go first, their wooden arms igniting. The wind tugs the flames back and forth, spreading the fire to Heborian's blue and black banners, licking over the men as they dive away, yelling. The flames vanish abruptly, leaving smoking, blackened timbers and the drifting ash of ruined banners.

I can feel nothing of the inner currents of earthmagic, of what the Seven are doing, or the Wardens, but seeing the scale of this power, Drift-work looks small and petty.

Next come the flaming arrows, each of them shot cold then exploding with fire as they sail over the wall. Men scream in the courtyard below. I hear the long cry and sudden silence of a man falling from the wall to the stones below. I chance a look through the arrow slot. Martel's army is inching closer. Then I see Martel himself.

He lumbers to the front of his force, body unnaturally large, his shoulders disproportioned. What has Belos done to him? Martel grabs a spear from a nearby soldier, who recoils from him, as all his men do. Martel rears back and hurls the spear. It flies with incredible speed and precision, winging to the top of the wall, straight for Heborian.

Heborian ducks, and the spear flies over him to clatter against the roof tiles of a nearby house. That throw was impossible.

Martel rages at the front of his army, clawing at his chest. No, his mind is not his own.

"Heborian!" I yell, but my voice is lost in the wind and the chaos of screaming men. I promised to wait for his command, we all did, but he is pushing that promise too far. Will he wait until Belos's men are scaling the wall? All this risk to protect his son one moment longer?

To the west, beyond the dust, metal glints in the sun.

My breath catches as the reinforcements charge over the hills to slam into the rear of Martel's army. Chaos is instantaneous. The field swarms and shifts, breaking here and there into isolated fights. I search for the black spot of the Seven and find them at the fringe, edging away from the fighting. *Is Belos among them?*

With the distraction of the new conflict, now is the time to surprise them.

"We must move!" I shout over the twang of bows as Heborian's archers fire against Martel's troops. The black splotch of the Seven shifts away, gathered tight. A perfect target.

"We have to wait for our order!" shouts Rood, his voice high with fear.

"He's right!" adds one of the Drifters, a man with Runish tattoos on his face and hands. "The king said—"

I glare at the man. "Will you hide behind that? Now is the time!"

"She's right!" shouts Horik. "Prepare!"

I see Rood's jaw harden, but then I forget him. He can cower here if he wants. There won't be a better chance.

Easing along my mooring, I let the world around me dissolve into the chaotic, swirling energies of the Drift. With so much earthmagic surrounding me, with the elements so strong, I feel myself tugged and pummeled by them. The wild breath of wind. The deep, angry rumble of earth. The madness of fire as it seeks something, anything to burn. I have never felt this within the Drift. I close myself to all of it. This is no time for curiosity.

I drift through the hidden gap in Heborian's net, rushing over the surging battlefield toward the seething energies of the Seven. I spot Theron and feel a mixture of regret and anger. Of all of them, he is the only one I cared for. But even he lied to me. He could have told me, at any time, where I came from. I turn away. He doesn't matter.

I find Straton by his tightly coiled energy, his position far from the arrows and swords. I ease along my mooring to appear behind him, my Drift-spear light and ready in my hand.

I should just stab him in the back, but I can't quite bring myself that low. Because that's what *he* would do.

I whip my spear to get his attention. Straton spins with a shout, and I sweep my spear toward his neck. He throws a blast of energy at me, and I dive away from it, rolling and rising with my spear. I lunge. He vanishes. I tense for his reappearance. When I feel him behind me, I grab his arm and wrench him into the Drift with me.

His energy strains against mine, ripping away bit by bit until he breaks free. His energy form flares bright, dangerous, and I dive into the safety of my mooring.

I roll and skid under a lacy canopy of branches and white blossoms. How far did I go? Understanding clicks—the orchard—a second before Straton's boot catches me in the jaw. Pain explodes; my teeth snap together. The white blossoms of the apple trees jerk and sway above me. A blow to my chest drives the air from my lungs and knocks me to my back. I whip my spear blindly through the air. Straton leaps away, his dark robes tangling around the blade with a sound of ripping cloth. I scramble up.

A sudden, deep rumble of the earth nearly shakes me to the ground again. The sound of cracking stone stabs into my ears. I look to Straton in shock, not expecting such power from him, but he's lost his balance as well.

He laughs, catching himself against a tree. "Did you know he was so strong?"

I stare at him dumbly.

Straton's blond eyebrows twitch together. "You don't know, do you? I wondered why you hadn't come for him. I never thought you a coward. Stupid, maybe, but not a coward."

His words dance and flick around me. I cannot make sense of them, and I am dizzy with disbelief, with denial, and with faint, wild hope. "What—"

Straton's chin sets with that condescending look of his. "You really don't know."

The high, awful sound of splitting rock echoes from beyond the orchard.

Straton shakes his head, taunting me. "Stupid child, your lover is no Earthmaker, at least not fully. Belos brought him through the Drift, into the Dry Land."

I am frozen, my skin tight with gooseflesh. When I find my voice, I can only manage, "He's—alive?"

Straton shrugs. "More or less."

Numb, stupid with shock, I pull myself into the Drift and fly back to the battle. I am dizzy, frantic.

The seething mass of energies almost hides him, but I find him near the front, because I will always find him.

A swirl of energy, power wilder and more primal than any I have ever seen. I fill to bursting with mad joy.

He is alive.

But both my joy and my energy drain away like water when I see the Leash, not the usual white, but black and thick, sick and oily, anchored deep within him.

CHAPTER 35

I ease along my mooring to appear behind him where he stalks the battlefield, his movements a sensuous blend of grace and power. His shirt hangs in tattered, bloody strips, and I glimpse lashes and deep bruises along his exposed skin.

The earth rips and buckles before him. I watch in horror as the ground splits open between him and the city. The low tearing sound rises to a high snapping as a crack snakes up the wall.

I reenter the Drift and position myself to one side of the narrow cleft. I pass through my mooring again. He freezes when I appear. His face is bruised and coated in dust, his golden hair dulled to the color of the battlefield. Half his shirt is gone, exposing a stretch of bruised and bloody torso. A black stain makes his eyes horribly cruel, and they show me no recognition.

"Stop."

He stares ahead to the city, his expression dead.

"Logan."

A muscle bunches in his jaw. The black stain shifts like oil over water. Horror closes my throat.

"*Logan.*"

Green swirls through the black, flickering—there and gone, there and gone.

"Please." I take a step toward him, agonized to be so close yet unable to reach him. He is deep, deep within himself, if he's there at all. But I must believe he is. I must believe he can hear me. "*Fight* him."

He makes a sound of pain and turns away. Cautiously, heart pounding, I approach. I touch his shaking back, closing my eyes at the mess of blood and flesh and torn fabric.

"Please, Logan." My fingers tremble up to his shoulder. "Come back to me."

He hunches, head bowing low. Hope teases me. I reach for his hair and stroke the dirt-caked ends of it. He falls to his knees, and I crouch beside him.

His voice shivers out from somewhere deep, breaking on each syllable of my name, "A-star-ti."

I throw my arms around him. He is here. He is mine.

"Please," he begs, shaking. "Please." He twists his neck to look at me, and there, for a moment, is the gorgeous swirl of color that is his eyes. But the shape of those eyes is pain. And terror. "Please. Kill me."

I recoil.

His fingers find mine and tighten painfully. "You must. Before it's too late. *Please.*"

I shake my head. I can't!

He says the horrible words again, whispering, "Kill me."

When I don't respond, he rises, shouting something inarticulate, and in that moment, I lose him again. Black floods back into his eyes. His face contorts as he tries to fight it. For the briefest moment, color returns, then it's gone. His face deadens.

Cruel, horrible, mindless. Not Logan at all.

I take a step back, but it's not enough. His punch to my gut lifts me from the ground.

I collapse around his fist. The moment seems to go on forever: the shock of pain, the dizzy spin of the battlefield, the black of Logan's eyes.

He flings me away. I tumble and roll. I claw my way to my knees, choking for air.

Logan stalks near. He looms above me.

Fear squeezes my chest as I stare into the torn and trampled grass. He will kill me. I close my eyes, waiting.

Wind lifts the fines hairs that have escaped from my braid. The wind builds, tugging at me. I brace against its pull and look up.

Logan's face has gone completely still, but his eyes boil blackly, and his whole body is primed. The wind whips around him, swirling dirt and stones and someone's lost gauntlet.

Logan vanishes into the mad wind.

§Ω CR

I watch numbly as the wind tears across the field, spraying dirt. Debris slams into the wall, some sweeping over the top to make the men there duck and yell. The crack widens, splitting from the top. He will break through. And it will be over for Tornelaine and everyone within it. All those men on the wall. Bran. Korinna. Aron. If he kills his brothers, it will be my fault, because I could not kill him.

No.

This is not my doing. Or Logan's.

This is Belos.

Always it comes back to him. What would this world be, without Belos? What would I be?

I lurch to my feet. Behind me, the battle rages, the living surging and stumbling over the heaped bodies of the dead. At one edge, the Seven drive their men toward the brutal attack of Heborian's troops. I catch flashes of Drift-work among them and hope that means Heborian's Drifters are still alive and fighting.

I turn away from the Seven. They don't matter right now. There is one cause of all this. One man's greed. One man's will. And I will make him pay for what he's done to Logan.

I surge along my mooring into the Drift. I find the black Leash and follow it. I streak over the surging mass of energies. On a hilltop, far behind the jagged line of men, stands a solitary figure, arms crossed. A dozen white Leashes flow from him, some into the distance, one to Martel, another, black and oozing, to Logan. Within Belos, energies rage against one another, fighting for control.

With a shriek of rage that echoes even in the Drift, I dive along my mooring, willing my spear into my hand.

Belos looks up in surprise as I dive toward him. I slash at his face, thrilling at the tear of soft flesh. Belos twists away with a yell.

I tumble, skidding to a stop. I scramble up as Belos stalks my way. A ragged flap of cheek spills blood down his face. I almost got his eye.

"I wondered when I would see you."

I take a step back, spear pulsing in my hand. "Hiding behind the lines, are you? Coward."

His mouth turns at the word, teasing another line of blood from the slash. "You know I always let little people do the grunt work. Don't worry, the Seven know not to kill Heborian, or the prince, or Gaiana's sons. Those pleasures will be mine."

My blood chills. When Logan breaks through that wall, Belos will get his chance. All of them will die. I fall back on the word he hates, "Coward."

He snarls. His sword flares to life in his hand, the blade's silvery length almost white with power. He swings.

With a ring of metal, I catch the blow in one of my spearhead's notches, but the notch breaks, and Belos's sword slides down the length of my shaft.

I twist away to free my spear and make space to slash at his belly. He jumps back heavily. I press the advantage, whipping quick blows as he retreats. My world narrows to this one purpose: lunge, advance, sweep, advance.

My foot catches a stone.

The stumble drops my spear only a fraction, but it's enough. Belos slashes at my right shoulder. White pain flares as he cuts through my shoulder guard, and my arm sags. I scuttle back, bracing for his attack.

He shrugs his shoulders, and a second blade flashes into his other hand.

Memories tumble. This is just like every other time I tried to defy him. He will punish me. He will break me. I am powerless. I cannot win.

Belos sees it in my face, and he sneers. His face seems to grow, to fill my whole world.

But curiosity overcomes him, and he asks, "How did you destroy the Leash?"

His question, the fact that I know of some power he does not, clears my mind. "You don't know?"

His lip curls. He likes to think he is smarter than everyone. "You will tell me, once I have Leashed you again. And like your lover, you will serve me, you will *be* me."

I say, as though my heart is not pounding in my throat, "I will never serve you again."

He smiles cruelly. "But that is the very thing you were born to do, the very purpose of your existence."

I scream, forcing rage into myself, as his words dig at the fears lodged so deep in my gut. I scream until the rage takes root, and then, for a moment, I forget pain, forget fear and weariness. I forget that I will lose.

I charge.

The power of my first two blows surprise Belos into hurried blocks, then he snaps one sword at me, almost slicing my face, and thrusts the other at my thigh. I duck and spin. Belos drives me aside with a flurry of blows, the two swords weaving and slashing. I block and evade. My injured arm is too slow, and each slash is closer, closer.

I cry out as pain slices my thigh.

Belos closes the distance and kicks my feet out from under me. I fall with a grunt.

Belos looms over me, his eyes dark with anger, his slashed cheek dripping blood. He holds both swords above my chest.

"You *are* mine, Astarti. In the deepest corners of your little heart, you know you always will be. I shaped you, I *made* you. You will remember that before the end. With your last breath, you will give yourself back to me."

I grit my teeth. I cannot let it come to that. If I die, I will die free of him. With a speed born of desperation, I roll from under the pointed swords.

As Belos lunges, the blades a blur of metal and energy, I dive into my mooring, hovering at the edge of the Drift, not quite within it. I watch the blur of confused, turbulent energy that is Belos stumble to a halt.

I should escape. This is my chance.

But then I feel the angry rumble of earthmagic. I *feel* it, dark, dense. A deep and sleeping power. Elemental. Impossibly strong. So much stronger than I am. I slide into it.

஀ ଔ

I pulse through the veins of the earth, pass through the cold trickle of an underground stream. I ease through the hairline cracks between dense, crowded masses of stone.

I sense Belos's roiling energy somewhere above. I wedge myself into one of the cracks below him. I wrench the crack wide, barreling upward to explode in a shower of earth.

Belos staggers back with a cry of surprise as I, half myself, half stone, lunge toward him with my spear, its glow dimmed in stone. I stab him through the chest. He screams, and warm blood splatters my face.

Belos falls back, his swords gone, clutching at the spurting wound.

I step from the earth, dragging myself free of stone. I feel suddenly light, weightless in my human form. My mind soars with victory.

"Your death," I tell him, "is the only one I will permit myself to enjoy."

Belos sags to his knees. His head jerks back. He gulps for air.

Then he laughs, a wet bubbling sound filled with blood.

He climbs to his feet, all black leather and flashing silver studs, all blond hair and gaunt beauty and blood.

He should be dead. His face is white and his eyes twitch with pain, but he laughs.

"Did you really think you could kill me? This?" His hand drops from the wound. "Nothing." It pulses blood, glistening wetly on his leather vest, but already the drain is slowing. "Do you understand yet the enemy you've made?"

"Better your enemy than your slave."

His eyes turn unexpectedly gentle. "You loved me once."

I recoil, stepping instinctively away from him.

"You did. I remember you, five years old, grabbing my hand and saying, 'Look!' You were so proud of that first glow of Drift-light, no bigger than a firefly. And it was *me* you wanted to show."

"Do you think that means I loved you? You *stole* me from my mother!"

He shrugs, cold again, and I realize that the gentleness of a moment ago was just another lie. He says, "I paid for you. I didn't steal you."

"And that's okay?"

"You have no one else. Who cares for you but me? The Earthmakers? Heborian? Don't fool yourself."

"Logan—" In my desperation, I am making myself weak—I know this. I am exposing myself, and Belos doesn't miss the opportunity to exploit it.

He laughs. "The Warden? Broken, weak. And besides, he belongs to me now. *My* creature. He will never escape. I will torment him until he begs for death, but I will not let him die. And I will remind him always of how you betrayed him." He smiles at my horror. "Yes, I know he begged you to kill him. And I know you refused. I will not let him forget that. In the brief spaces between madness and pain, I will remind him."

I scream at Belos, all the rage and hate breaking my voice into a shriek. I wrench myself into the Drift.

ⅎ ⅍

I search the energies of the battlefield and feel the whirling pull of wind. Logan. So much power, it disturbs even the Drift. The oily black Leash trails from the vortex.

The Leash.

Within the Drift, I freeze.

A Leash, Heborian has shown me, can be cut.

I streak to the net, dashing through the hidden gap and over the city, unable to slow myself before I collide with Heborian's twisting barrier. It snaps and sizzles, lashing at me as I tear away. I squeeze through my mooring, falling to the cobblestones of the bridge. I run for the gates.

The guards shout, but I don't have time for them. I draw heavily through my mooring, shaping energy into a ram. I hurl this at the gate, which explodes in a booming shower of timbers.

Crossbow bolts whiz past me from the stone arch over the gaping, debris-littered gateway. I ignore them until one grazes my hip. I cry out, stumbling. More bolts fly at me, and I escape into the Drift.

There is a secondary barrier around the castle itself, but I drift to it, planning to drop onto a roof, as I did before.

I am still hovering dangerously high when the first lash takes me across the chest. My energy form sizzles with pain, and I dart back. The barrier crouches over the dark form of the castle, shifting with what looks like a will of its own. Another invention of Heborian's?

When I snuck into the castle last time, I traveled within the wind, not through the Drift. I grope for currents of air to replicate this but find nothing. I approach again, but whips of lights snap at me from the barrier.

My scream of frustration rings into the dead silence of the Drift.

I shoot back to the city wall, marking Heborian by his blaze of energy. I flood through my mooring.

Guards shout in surprise when I appear, and I have to duck and dodge several swords before Heborian commands, "Stop!"

I scramble to my feet and dart toward him. Wulfstan strikes me in the throat and I fall, choking. Boots scuffle around me, voices shout, then everything quiets and Heborian crouches beside me.

"The knife," I choke out. "I need it."

"No."

I grab the armhole of Heborian's breastplate. "You don't understand—"

"I see him. I know why you want it. The answer is no. It's too dangerous."

"Listen to me!"

"Stay here, Astarti. You've done enough."

I lunge upwards, grabbing for his throat. "Give it to me!"

Pain explodes in my chest as I fly back to slam into the wall.

I am still gasping for air when Heborian stalks near. He looms over me, his dark eyes furious. "I gave you my answer. Calm yourself, or I will restrain you."

"Sire—"

Heborian raises a hand to cut Wulfstan off, but his eyes never leave me. "I'm sorry, Astarti, but no. I will not risk the knife."

I am gathering myself to lunge for him again when the howling wind batters the wall, sending men and weapons tumbling away. I hear Heborian's surprised cry as he skids across stone.

The wall cracks, begins to tear apart behind me.

I dive for the Drift, but here, so near the raging currents of air, I flow into them instead. I touch the strength and madness at their heart. I grapple, grabbing at the swirl, trying to wrestle it to stillness. It whips away from me. I gather all my strength and shape a net of energy. I do not know how I am doing it, but the net is Drift-work and wind, the two blended beyond separation.

I cast my net around the wind's heart. Logan strains furiously, but I drag him and fling him from the wind.

I tumble to the torn earth of the battlefield. The mass of soldiers spins through my vision. The sky swings and slides. I smack painfully against stone then roll to a stop on something soft. I feel a curled hand beneath my back and scramble away in horror. A dead soldier.

Sections of the battle rage behind me, but the bulk of the action is hidden beyond mounded stones covered with fresh earth and the stringy roots of grass. Soldiers shout and grunt somewhere beyond, and metal rings on metal. I rise shakily and claw my way to the top of the soil-covered stones. Elbows sinking in the loose, moist earth, I lie flat on my belly.

Fifteen feet away, Logan staggers to his feet. Soldiers push and shove to get away from him.

I glance at the city wall, crumbling, almost broken. One more battering, and it will fall. Tornelaine will fall.

I think despairingly of the knife, but now there's no time for it. There's no time.

I deaden myself. I cannot afford to feel anything. I tell myself: this what he wants. This is what I would want him to do for me, to stop me. I will give him this gift of death because I love him.

I draw out a thread of Drift-energy and shape it into a bow and arrow.

I nock the faintly glowing arrow and take aim.

Logan shakes his head. He sways and falls to his knees. He lays a hand over his ribs, hunching around the pain. His shirt hangs in dirty, bloody strips. He flops onto his back, his chest heaving. I know that chest; I have touched its warmth and solidity, kissed its smooth planes and the ridged arc of scar. But I must put an arrow through it. I must.

Now.

Now.

Now.

I shudder, and the bow shakes in my hands. I swallow the surge of denial, the refusal, and fix my aim, seeking Logan again. One shot. He will hardly feel anything.

The bow blurs.

Logan blurs.

With the dead weight of defeat in my chest, the pain of my weakness and cowardice, the bow hisses from my hands. My head falls against my arms. My fingers dig into the loose earth, scratching deep to the stone below. My eyes burn. I cannot. I hate myself for it, but I cannot.

Logan's grunt as he rolls and staggers to his feet makes me look up. He shakes his head, looks my way. For one beautiful, torturous second, he seems to see me, to know me, then he is gone, his expression dead as Belos's power closes over him once more.

I shove to my feet with a surge of rage. I snarl as I withdraw into my mooring, hovering at the edge of the Drift, at the edge of everything. Aching, mad with pain, I reach instinctively into the deep, sleeping energy of the earth, down into the deeper, angry turbulence far below its surface. I want it, need it. Nothing else can express my fury.

I plunge.

I tear through the earth, splitting wide every crack and crevice, bursting to the surface to slash and lunge at the massed army. I fling stone, stab, and smash. Shields splinter. Swords snap. Men flee. I am an ocean of earth, ruthless with power.

I sweep to the fringes where I know the Seven will be. I rip myself from the earth to grab and tear, to haul them into the crushing embrace of stone, but they vanish into the Drift. Cowards!

Furious, I grab the nearest body, to bury it in stone, and hear the scream of a young voice. I pause, half myself, half stone. I feel the air on my skin as my human face emerges. Rood, in his silver breastplate, now dented and dirty, smeared with blood, struggles in my stony grasp. I drop him with a gasp. He scrambles away, the horror in his face showing that he recognizes me.

"I'm sorry." My voice comes out an earthy rumble. I almost killed my own brother. What am I doing?

With a scream of horror, I plunge into myself and through the earth again, rippling through the ground to where I left Belos. This is no one's fault but his. I might not be able to kill him, but maybe I can bind him, trap him in the earth.

I burst from the ground on the hilltop, twisting around with a crunch of stone, searching wildly.

Gone.

CHAPTER 36

LOGAN

I am rage.

I howl with it.

I rip the ground around me.

Men scream.

Some other force has been raging around me, wild and powerful, familiar somehow.

I search for it, but it's gone now.

I begin to dive into the wind, to lose myself, but something yanks at the core of my being, wracking me with nausea.

I am wrenched into another place, where lights shift and vanish. The Other yanks me toward him, and I think I will be ripped in half. His energies rage within him, tearing, clawing for release. I know this because he is the other part of me, or I am of him. Even so, I don't like him. I try to wrench away, but he rears above me, and I am sucked into his madness.

We are one.

We race along, seven others beside us. It goes on forever as we skim toward that place of deadness.

I am squeezed through some narrow tunnel, then I fall to dry earth, blinded by light, swallowed by heat.

Around me, men argue. They are angry, frightened.

I gasp with relief. I am myself. The Other has withdrawn. I see in my mind how I tore through the battlefield. I see Bran's face as I whipped at the wall. I see his horror, his sadness, his resignation. I almost killed him.

I stagger to my feet.

I find him—the Other—not three feet from me, arguing with his men, blood soaking his chest, his cheek ragged and torn.

I lunge for his throat.

He spins my way, teeth gritted.

He clenches his fist, and pain sears through me. I scream as the very root of my being is twisted, torn, beaten.

"Down," he commands.

"You are not—"

"Your will is *mine*! Down!"

I howl with rage, but it fades as my mind dims.

I hear his voice as though from a distance: "I can't have him fighting all the time. Break him."

I feel my body dragged across hot, dry ground, stone scraping against my torn flesh, but I cannot fight. My mind shrinks to a pinpoint, letting through nothing but light and pain.

CHAPTER 37

From the hilltop, I watch the remainder of the army flee, Martel himself a lumbering, oversized figure taking down his own men as they abandon him. But even he turns to run when the gates of Tornelaine swing open and Heborian's men ride out with swords and lances. They will give no quarter. Anyone captured will be executed. Heborian promised as much before the battle. Funny how rebellion looks different from one side or the other. Who really is the rightful king? Does anyone have that right at all?

I shake my head. I don't care. Not right now. Belos is gone. The Seven are gone. Logan—

I take a shuddering breath and trudge down the hill.

Bodies litter the field before the city wall. I weave among them, grateful for the sharp pains in my leg, my hip, my shoulder. Without pain to focus on, I would throw up from the horror. One man slumps around the spear in his belly. Another's half severed neck is caked with blood and dirt. I smell the sharp odor of blood and the stink of spilled entrails. Some of the bodies shift, men not quite dead.

I round a crevice where it looks like someone dug a plow ten feet into the earth, past the soil and into the rocky bones of the hill. Two men lie crushed in stone. Did Logan do that? Or did I? My stomach heaves suddenly, and I fall to my knees, retching into the torn grass. I wipe shakily at my mouth with the back of a sleeve.

I hear someone sobbing.

I raise my head to see a man dragging himself across the rubble-strewn ground. One leg is twisted at the wrong angle and blood seeps from a stomach wound. He is headed nowhere, just moving. I go to him.

The man cringes when he sees me, but I kneel down anyway. Just as I lay a hand on his shoulder to calm him, a voice snaps at me from behind.

"That's one of Martel's men."

I twist to see Rood, his silver breastplate dull with dirt, his face smeared with blood, picking his way around the bodies.

"He's just a soldier. He does what he's told, as Heborian's men do."

Rood's dark eyebrows twitch. "What do you care about him? After the way you tore through everyone."

I flinch. Will there be no end to my mistakes?

Rood crouches beside me with a crunch of chainmail. "You—" He cuts himself off, shakes his head. He starts again, "Without you, Tornelaine would have fallen. Our victory is yours." He finishes stiffly, "Thank you."

"I almost killed you," I whisper.

"But you didn't."

"But—"

"If you hadn't done what you did, the wall would have fallen. Belos would have taken the city. I would be dead by now. And so would everyone else. Enjoy your victory." He rises abruptly. "I have to find my father." His face reddens, and the unspoken correction—*our* father—hangs in the air.

I say nothing.

He hangs there a moment, then the rushing air of his disappearance stirs my hair. I turn back to the wounded man. He's gone still. I nudge him, roll him over. His eyes stare, wide and sightless, into the sky.

₧ ₧

I stand in one of the yellow and white striped physicians' tents at the edge of the field, the afternoon sun blazing through the canvas. I wring out a clean, wet cloth. Carts lumbered from the city once the victory was certain, and the tents were soon buzzing with activity as men bearing litters brought the wounded inside. The new stitches in my thigh and shoulder throb, but I refused to return to the city. I'm not ready to face anyone there.

I bend over the man on the table, gently scrubbing the deep gash that runs from his wrist to elbow. One of the physicians, a portly man in a white apron streaked with blood, peers over my shoulder.

"Do you need someone to stitch it for you?"

"I can do it."

I catch the physician's nod out of the corner of my eye as he hurries off to tend the more seriously wounded.

The man on the table grits his teeth when I take the needle and thread to his arm. My stitches are clean, even, necessary, but it still feels like I am only hurting him. If only I knew something of Healing.

When the stitching is done and the man has joined the other lightly wounded in preparing bandages, I walk to the opening in the tent. I duck into the fresh air, glad to leave behind the stink of death and injury. I move away, and the moans from inside fade. Men with litters continue to scour the field.

"Astarti!"

I look up in surprise to see Bran hurrying my way. Dirt streaks his face and his red-gold hair clings in sweaty clumps to his forehead.

I acknowledge him with a lift of my chin. "You're all right?"

Bran stops before me, his worn face anxious. "Are you? Rood said—"

"I'm fine," I say woodenly.

"What are you doing here?"

I draw away. "Helping clean up the mess I made."

"None of this is your fault."

"Then why does it feel like it?"

He doesn't answer me, but he jerks his chin, indicating for me to follow. Reluctantly, I do. It is easier than arguing. We walk between two of the striped tents, stepping over the stakes and angled ropes, to emerge into the open space behind. The city wall looms over us.

I ask, suddenly worried, "Is Aron all right? And Korinna?"

"Aron is fine. Korinna took at arrow to the arm, but she'll be all right. She and the other injured Wardens are already on their way to Avydos for Healing."

This drives us to awkward silence as the injured Keldans groan within the striped tents. There will be no Healing for them, only the slow, natural reknitting of flesh. Or death.

When we reach the end of the line of tents, Bran takes a deep breath that I know will be followed by words I do not want to hear.

"So. Belos has him."

My heart deadens.

"He is Leashed?"

I let my eyes tell him. I can't bear to say the word. Bran deflates as his last hope leaves him.

I accuse, "You knew he would not be dead. You didn't tell me."

Bran looks at me steadily. "I thought it possible. I didn't want to give you false hope."

"How did you know?" My voice is angry, like this is somehow Bran's fault, but he doesn't seem offended.

"I'm a scholar, Astarti."

I grit my teeth at this non-answer.

"Only my mother knows for sure. It is her secret to tell or keep."

I flash with anger. "It's not hers. Logan has a right to know where he came from."

Bran looks at me sympathetically, and I tear my eyes away. He changes the subject. "I saw you tear him from the wind. You're blending Drift-work and earthmagic."

I shrug. "I guess."

His silence makes me prickle with dread. What is he thinking?

I admit, "I understand now why it's forbidden. You saw what I did with it."

Bran hesitates before he says carefully, "Yes."

I wish he would tell me it wasn't my fault, but he doesn't, and I won't ask him to. Instead I ask, making things worse, "Did I kill any of our own?"

Bran says quietly, "I don't know."

My eyes prickle, threating to embarrass me with tears. I widen them until they go dry.

"It was a battle, Astarti. Your blood was up. War is different. All of us were fighting and killing. I can't know whether my earthmagic killed any of our own either. It's not precise like Drift-work."

Even though that is sort of what I wanted him to say, it doesn't make me feel better. It doesn't change anything. I am still filthy with guilt.

He adds, "I also saw what happened just before."

I stiffen, staring into the trampled grass. I try to hold the image away, but I see Logan: confused, hurt. I feel my failure as my bow vanishes.

I know I should have done it, should have killed him, if for no other reason than to spare him what he must be enduring now. He is in the Dry Land; I feel it in my gut as a certainty. Will they chain him? Beat him? How much will he hate me for leaving him to that fate?

Bran says gently, "I wouldn't have been able to do it either."

"I have to get back to the tents."

I spin away from Bran. He lays a hand on my shoulder. I want to acknowledge the gesture, to comfort him because this hurts him also, but I am too weak. I pull away.

₲ ℛ

Night drapes itself over Tornelaine. I slide from the back of the physician's cart as it bumps and rolls through the city gates. I hear it clatter away as I climb the shallow steps to the top of the wall. The guards on the platform over the gate ignore me as I walk past them.

The moon, rising in the east, flashes through the arrow slots as I walk. Just ahead, its light lies heavily over the crumbled section of wall that almost brought disaster to Tornelaine.

The deadness that got me through the afternoon fades, exposing pain in its wake. My chest begins to constrict. I gasp for air, bending over my knees as panic and horror course through my body. I lost him.

I *lost him*.

I slide down, my shoulder scraping against the rough stone, sparking with pain as my stitches snag. I crouch in the shadow of the wall, slowing my breathing, fighting down the panic.

As the moon edges higher, creeping over my shoulder through the arrow slot, the horror dulls, and a slow anger starts to burn in its place. This is not the end. I will not allow it to be.

I see the dim glow of Drift-energy on the distant guards' platform, but I ignore it. I refuse to look up even when the steady thump of footsteps draws near. They stop a few paces away.

Heborian says, "What are you doing? I've been looking for you."

Anger licks through me at the sound of his voice. I stare at the dark humps of my knees, not trusting myself to look at him. "Why?"

He doesn't answer.

When I do look up, moonlight limns his cheek, gleaming along the blue tattoo, clinging around the tired lines framing his eyes.

He says roughly, "I'm sorry. About Logan."

Anger flares. "I will *never* forgive you."

"I couldn't let you take the knife out there."

"Why?" I grind out the question, making it an accusation.

Heborian leans into one of the arrow slots. "The knife is *very* dangerous. If it ever got into Belos's hands—"

"What do you care if Belos can cut Leashes? He's the only one who *makes* them."

Heborian is too silent, too still.

I push to my feet, hover behind him, suspicions nagging. "What else does the knife do?"

Heborian says nothing.

"You still don't trust me," I accuse.

"It's nothing personal. Rood doesn't know either."

"This doesn't concern Rood. But it does concern me."

Heborian takes a deep breath. "The knife can cut through barriers. Do you understand how dangerous that makes it?"

He doesn't look at me. He is ever so slightly hunched, protecting something. The signs are subtle, but I have been trained to read such things. It's not a complete lie, but it's not the whole truth either. All the same, it's enough truth to tell me he's right about one thing: the knife is dangerous. If Belos had that in his hands, he could drift straight into the castle.

I say weakly, "But I needed it."

"I know."

We both fall silent on this impasse.

Heborian shifts, and I feel him looking at me. He says softly, gently, "I'm sorry, Astarti."

He's not talking about Logan now. Instinctively, I know what he means, and I refuse to meet his eyes, refuse to hear the apology. He was right when he said that it wouldn't change anything. I ask, partly because I want to know, partly because I want to rub in the guilt, "Why didn't you come after me?"

"I did. I tried."

I look up in surprise.

"Where do you think I got the bone for the knife? In the Dry Land, in the broken city. The Old Ones built that place."

That sparks some curiosity in me, but I store it away for another time. "I never saw you."

Heborian answers gruffly, "I couldn't get to you. The Seven almost captured me. I gave up." He pauses, and his next words are heavy with admission. "Sometimes I think I should have fought harder, that I should have tried again."

His words prick at me like needles. I don't want to hear his regret; I don't want to care about his pain. But I can't stop myself from asking, "Why didn't you?"

He takes a deep breath, and when he speaks, his voice is his own again: firm, certain, unapologetic. "Sibyl was gone, I was sure of that. You were firmly in Belos's clutches. I still had a kingdom to run."

I prefer him this way, so hard and unyielding. I don't want to hear any more apologies, ever again. That is over and done, in the past, irrelevant. The prickling across the back of my neck, through the Mark, calls me a liar, but I ignore it, shut it out. I have more important things to think about right now. Like how I will steal that knife.

I turn from Heborian, staring beyond the moon-drenched field to the dark horizon. "I will fight harder than you did."

Heborian doesn't answer, but I feel his eyes on me, weighing me, judging.

I swear, more to myself than to him, "I *will* get Logan back."

He says, "You are so much like your mother."

಄ ಃ

I don't know when Heborian leaves me. As the moon climbs higher and the night turns cold, I stay at the wall, gripping the stones in silent promise: I'm coming.

ABOUT THE AUTHOR

Katherine Buel grew up in Kansas with two passions: stories and horses. She's taken both of those with her through much of the upper Midwest, then out to Maine and back again.

She also loves mountain biking and kayaking—and too many other things that there's never enough time for.

Printed in Great Britain
by Amazon

67002098R00203